F MAC

SI MAY 2016
KR AUG 2018

FINDING JACOB

FINDING JACOB

ERIN MacADAMS

FINDING JACOB

©2014 Erin MacAdams. All rights reserved.

No portion of this book may be reproduced or transmitted in any form or by any means, electronic or mechanical, including fax, photocopying, recording or any information storage or retrieval system without permission in writing from Author or Publisher (except by a reviewer, who may quote brief passages and/or show brief video or audio clips in a review, or by the purchaser for his or her own use).

FINDING JACOB is a work of fiction set in a background of history. All characters appearing in this work are fictitious. Any resemblance to real persons, living or dead, is purely coincidental. Neither the Publisher nor the Author shall be liable for damages arising herefrom. The fact that an organization is referred to in this work as a citation and/or a potential source of further information does not mean that the Author or Publisher endorses the information the organization may provide or recommendations it may make.

This publication is a creative work fully protected by all applicable rights.

All rights reserved.

ISBN-13: 978-1495977695
ISBN-10: 1495977692

Printed in the United States of America
First printing: October 2014

First Edition

Editor:	Erin MacAdams
Book and Cover Design:	Erin MacAdams
Cover Photos:	© Can Stock Photo Inc./rolffimages
	© Can Stock Photo Inc./myper
Contact:	ErinMacAdams@gmail.com

For Dad.
You showed me the way.

1

New York City
Thursday, 14 August 2003

Le An MacDonald stared out her office window, searching for a sliver of sky in the forest of Manhattan high-rises, unsure why she was feeling as if her day were about to cause a domino-effect of major changes. She couldn't quite clarify the jittery feeling and lock it down, but it was the kind of nagging anticipation of events about to unfold which hinted at extremes—with the potential to turn out either hit-the-lottery great or lose-your-life-going-over-a-cliff disaster.

Nothing in between.

That was what her life was about: extremes depicting both ends of life's spectrum, swinging like a pendulum from wealthy and fabulously famous stars-of-the-moment to wrongfully convicted prisoners and war-weary refugees.

Television viewers wanted extreme news and that's what she and her associates gave them. Which was fine with Le An because she'd always been an adrenaline junky, but lately her heavy travel schedule and long work hours were starting to wear on her.

As a senior producer at USN's three-nights-a-week news-magazine *AmeriView*, she was always jetting off somewhere to cover a story. Many times, especially if it was breaking news, she'd leave for the airport as soon as the travel department booked her flight. That's why she always kept one of her two passports in her purse and a packed bag in her office closet, ready to go at a moment's notice.

She conducted many of the interviews used in her segments, but viewers never saw her or even heard her voice. That was the news industry's little 'secret'—that producers in major cities and at network were the real workhorses, the more highly-paid, easy-on-the-eyes correspondents or anchors merely showing up at the end to do some on-camera interviews and voice the producer-written scripts.

That was why she'd decided to become a producer: because she wanted to be the power player behind the cameras, in total control of the story—as much as a breaking news story could be controlled.

She was the ultimate control freak—and everyone knew it.

Picking up her mug of hot tea, Le An stared for a moment at the navy-blue-and-gold USN News logo on the side, then cupped it between her hands and swiveled around to look out at the city again, inhaling deeply as she enjoyed the brief calm.

She knew within the hour, her office phone, cellphone and BlackBerry would start ringing incessantly, signaling the start of another day. She'd fight to find time to finish writing her scripts, make it to the edit suites and plan the interviews and video shoots for her next assignments, before she'd finally stagger home exhausted late that night to grab a few hours sleep.

Just then her phone started ringing.

She swiveled back toward her desk and glared at the phone, trying to will it to stop, then sighed in resignation and reached for the receiver.

2

Tel Dan, Northern Israel
Thursday, 14 August 2003

Doctor Jacob Jeremy Winston Spencer-Hilson wandered through the Tel Dan Nature Reserve in northern Galilee, listening to the rushing, icy springs, the idyllic setting belying the dangers a few miles away.

Israel's northern border collided uneasily with Lebanon and Syria, making it easy for the Shi'a Islamic military group *Hizb'allah*—'the party of God'—to frequently lob Katyusha rockets into the area. Hizb'allah didn't believe Israel had a right to exist—but then neither did most of the Arab world.

Peace never lasted long in the Middle East.

On top of that, tensions in the area had moved up a notch after the Americans and their coalition armies had invaded Iraq five months before.

Jeremy Hilson was mindful of the dangers, but didn't dwell on them. Sticking a finger under the rim of his khaki hat, he pushed it back from his well-tanned face, barely noticing the familiar sight of young Israeli soldiers walking past him, American-made M-16s slung over their shoulders.

Israel was always in a state of readiness for war. Countless times the country had been forced to fight off attacks from terrorists and surrounding Arab nations, including the day after its formation in 1948.

When Jeremy's rented mobile phone started ringing, he patted his pockets, trying to remember where he'd put it. The ringing stopped, but only for a few seconds, then insistently started again.

"Yes? Hello?" he said, fumbling with the phone when he finally found it.

"Doctor Spencer-Hilson? Is this Doctor Jacob Spencer-

Hilson?" a breathless female voice asked in a distinctive New York accent.

"Yes, this is Jeremy Hilson."

"Oh, thank goodness! I've been calling all over Israel trying to find you. It took forever to get your cellphone number. My name's April Greenlaw and I'm an associate producer with USN News in New York."

3

New York City
Thursday, 14 August 2003

Le An reluctantly answered her phone on the fourth ring, just before it went into voice mail.

"Why are you at work so early?" asked her mother. "It's only 7:30."

"Why are you calling my office so early?" Le An teased.

"Because I called your house and your cellphone and you didn't answer, brat," said Kate Grandison in her softly musical Southern accent. "I've emailed you, left messages for you on your office phone, your cellphone and your home phone three days in a row and you still haven't called me back or even answered my emails. You've either been avoiding me or you're dead."

"I'm not dead, though I feel like it most days," said Le An. "And I'm not avoiding you. You said it wasn't an emergency and I've been swamped with work."

"Does it have to be an emergency for you to call your mother and let her know you're alive?"

"Only if I'm swamped with work."

"You're always swamped with work," said Kate. "Are you traveling this week?"

"I don't think so," said Le An. "But you know how quickly that can change. Week after next I'm going to Ireland."

"Well, at least you won't be in that awful Iraq," said Kate. "Dahlin', promise me you won't ask to go back there."

Le An and her crew had recently returned from covering the US-involved war to overthrow Saddam Hussein. Together with correspondent Luke Conte, videographer Barry Spirelli and Khaled al Zayed, a secular Sunni from Baghdad who worked as their fixer, translator and soundman, they'd broken the story about Saddam's sons Uday and Qusay being killed in a firefight at a villa in Mosul.

Luck had been with them that July day. They'd been the only non-military journalists embedded with the 'Screaming Eagles' of the 101st Airborne when 200 troops—along with the elite, super-secret Task Force 20—had ended the Hussein brothers' reign of terror.

"Don't worry, Amma. I've had my fill of Iraqi heat. Ireland will be a nice change," said Le An as she started attacking the previous day's stack of unopened mail and FedEx boxes on her desk.

"Oh, dahlin', I'm so glad to hear you say that. I'm always a nervous wreck when you're in Iraq," said Kate. "Just because you've been safe so far, doesn't mean you should keep pushing your luck. Are you coming home for Thanksgiving?"

"I'll try, but I can't make any promises," she said as she looked at a chipped nail which badly needed filing.

If she didn't have so much to do, she would have indulged in a manicure and a trip to the hair salon. Flipping up the ends of her chestnut-ebony-colored hair, her pale-green eyes squinted in disgust at the split ends. It had been months since her last trim and her hair now flowed halfway down her back—about four inches longer than she normally preferred. The last few days every mirror she stared into had given her the good news she was long overdue for a dye job to conceal her ever-increasing gray roots.

"Why won't they let you take a vacation?" asked Kate. "How's your love life?"

"So many questions. You should have been a field producer, Ma."

"What's that noise?"

"The weather segment," said Le An, grabbing her TV's remote and muting the volume. "The morning show producers love to get the crowds screaming hysterically because that helps people forget they've been standing in the heat for hours."

"I hate that. Tell them to stop," said Kate.

"My word carries no weight with the morning show," she said as she grabbed a nail file from her drawer. "Besides, if everyone stopped screaming, a cold front would turn into a hot back and the producers would get fired. I think it's in their contract.

Viewers panic when they don't hear rock-concert hysteria with their weather."

A bouquet of red roses appeared in the doorway, a pair of tanned fingers clutching the stripped-of-thorns base. Skylar Coltrane, a correspondent with *AmeriView*, oiled his way into her office, sliding his tall, perfect, Armani-suited body into the chair across from her desk.

Le An hated red roses.

She wasn't too fond of Skylar either.

"Amma, can I call you back?" she asked, not willing to have Skylar eavesdrop on her private conversation.

"But I haven't talked to you in days," said Kate.

Skylar pushed the roses into her nose and as she pulled her head back from the crush of petals, he started fiddling with the pictures on her desk, her pen holder and her business card holder, then tried to grab her day-planner. She smacked his hand hard enough that he dropped the corner of the book and uttered a soft, "Ow!"

"Mom, gotta go. I'll call you later," said Le An.

"Last night was great," Skylar winked as she hung up the phone.

"Yeah, you really know how to order a mean carryout. And that time in the edit room... so *special*," she said sarcastically.

She glanced at at his impish face, pure bad-boy to the core, a strand of blond hair edging its way toward his cobalt eyes. On air, he never would have allowed that stray hair. Instead, his perfectly-trimmed hair would have been sprayed to withstand category-five-hurricane winds.

"You haven't invited me over to your place," he said with a sly smile.

"And I don't intend to," she said, going back to her stack of mail.

"I'm offended."

"You'll get over it."

"Why do you call your mom 'Amma'?"

"It's a morph of 'aunt' and 'mama.' She's my aunt, but she and my uncle adopted and raised me."

"So much I don't know about you," he said. "But we can get to that tonight at your apartment."

"That would be no."

"Why won't you go out with me?" he asked.

"I don't like to date co-workers."

"Not true, according to the grapevine," he said, shifting his eyebrows up and down in a sinister fashion.

She looked up and flushed slightly. "Grapevine's wrong. I said I don't *like* to date co-workers. That doesn't mean I don't occasionally slip."

"I hear Luke Conte's moved on," he said and smirked a little. "Guy's a jerk to ditch you. I'd treat you better."

"Excuse me?" she said indignantly. "We are not having this conversation."

"You're afraid you might lose control with me, right?" smirked Skylar.

"True. I'd lose control and choke you," she said. "Then we'd have to do a crime segment on it. But on the plus side, they'd arrest me and I could finally get some sleep in jail. Don't tempt me, Coltrane."

"We could go back to my place. It's decorator ready."

"You hired a decorator?" she asked, looking up at him.

"Doesn't everybody? Who has time to do it themselves?" he said. "I have an image to maintain and a disgusting apartment isn't it. Can't have bigwigs over to a pit, now can I? What time should I stop by? Do you like red or white?"

"Roses? I prefer pink or peach," she said.

"I meant wine. What's wrong with red roses?" he sounded hurt.

Le An looked down at her day-planner and flipped a page.

"I won't be home. I have to finish editing your package tonight for tomorrow's show. Don't leave today without tracking the ending," she said, referring to an audio-track-only recording of the script.

"Who's editing it?" he asked.

"Tony. Linda started it, but got pulled off to finish Todd's piece on the Dems' latest catfight and that leaked memo."

"Next year'll be worse. Gotta love an election year. Hopefully, it won't be as bad as 2000," he said. "I was sick of pregnant chads and Tallahassee. There's no place to park in that city."

He crossed a jiggling Italian-shoed foot over a perfectly-creased pants leg, then turned more photos on her desk to face him, bumping a carefully balanced stack of papers, magazines, tapes and DVDs. The pile slid just enough to threaten toppling the pile of unopened FedEx boxes next to it. Le An grabbed both piles to steady them and threw him a dirty look.

"Who's this guy? The love of your life?" Skylar asked as he picked up a photo of a blond man.

"My brother Judson," she said. "He beats up people who bother his sister."

"You don't really look like him."

"That's because I'm biologically his first cousin. You know that whole adoption thing we were just talking about? Do you listen this badly when you're conducting interviews? No wonder your producers have to work so hard. Hey, Coltrane, cut it out! What, are you two?"

She grabbed her day-planner as he whipped it off her desk.

"Who's in that book you don't want me to know about?" Skylar teased. "Is it my competition?"

"Stop waving those roses at me. No vase? I have to supply my own?"

"Who says they're for you? You said you don't like red roses. Maybe they're for the new intern. She's hot."

"So go give them to her," Le An answered in a bored tone. "Knock yourself out. Maybe she's into cliches."

"Maybe she'll appreciate me more," he said.

"Safe bet when you get them that young. 'Ooooh, Skylar,'" she mimicked in a baby voice, "'Like, could you, like, help me with my resume tape so I can, like, get hired as a full-time anchor-babe?'"

"She'll go far." He adjusted his blue silk tie, which was perfectly coordinated with his eyes. "Are you playing hard to get?"

"I *am* hard to get," she drawled in a soft, Carolina accent, a sharp contrast to her AmerAsian features.

"Do I scare you?" Skylar smirked.

"No, I know Krav Maga."

Just then her phone buzzed and *AmeriView*'s executive producer Paul Silverblatt boomed over the intercom, "Le An! In my office! Now!" followed by a loud click as he hung up.

"Glad he's in his usual good mood," she mumbled.

"Oh, please, everybody knows you're Paul's favorite princess," he said. "A true JAP."

"I'm not Jewish or Japanese," she said, giving him a disgusted look.

"You're not?"

"I'm a VASP," she said.

"A what?"

"Vietnamese-American Southern Princess. We're a very rare breed. And if Paul appreciates me, it's only because I work about a zillion hours a week and never take a vacation. You, too, could be his favorite if you killed yourself."

"That may happen," he said and made no motion to leave, just kept waving the roses as he held her gaze. "Paul's sending me back to Iraq. I've been asking to go for weeks. It's good for my image."

Skylar had embedded with a Marine unit during Operation Iraqi Freedom in March and had stayed for eight weeks. Le An and her crew had crossed paths with him a few times, but fortunately, hadn't been forced to spend much time together. She found his arrogance annoying and it bothered her he wasn't a solid journalist.

"Good for you," she said, relieved he wouldn't be around to bug her.

She stood up and grabbed her day-planner, a pen and a lavender-colored notepad.

He stood up, too, and closed the door before she could reach it, dropping the roses on top of her bookcase. Standing uncomfortably close in her personal space, he leaned in, put his lips near her ear and whispered, "Will you miss me?"

She leaned away almost in a back bend, trying to put distance between them, then pushed him, accidentally jabbing him with her pen as she smacked him in the head with her day-planner.

"Ow!" He rubbed the side of head.

"I think you bent my pen," she said indignantly. "Out of my office, Coltrane. I've got a meeting."

"I know. I requested you as my producer in Iraq."

"What?" She pulled back, smacked him on his arm and pushed against his chest to get away from him. "I don't want to go to Iraq with you. It's bad enough it's 120 degrees in the shade this time of year without having to put up with you, too. Is this why Paul wants to talk to me? Because you volunteered me?"

"Probably. I couldn't stand to be away from you. I get lonely."

She knew his type and wasn't buying his obvious advances.

He'd find a female to occupy him in Baghdad—either another journalist, or an Iraqi interpreter, or both, probably juggle two or three at the same time. Fidelity wasn't his strong suit.

"Out of my office, Coltrane," she repeated. "And don't leave this building until you track that script."

Her intercom buzzed again.

"MacDonald! You'd better have left that office and be on your way down here!" boomed Paul. "And that'd better not be you I hear talking. You think I have all day to wait for you?"

"Sorry, I was dealing with a pest control problem. I'm on my way," she called out.

Giving Skylar a slight shove to move him out of her way, she opened the door quickly, forcing him to suddenly duck backward and throw up a hand to protect his head.

"You're going to have to do better than flowers, Coltrane."

4

New York City
Thursday, 14 August 2003

Le An pushed a pile of manila folders out of the way and sat down on the couch in her executive producer's office. As she straightened her pink silk blazer and crossed her blue-jean-clad legs, one of her tennis shoes accidentally kicked four DVD cases off a stack on the floor.

"These resume tapes of people crazy enough to want to work here?" she asked as she restacked them.

"Every flipping day those things come in," said Paul Silverblatt as he took a swig of coffee. "I have nightmares I'm being chased by stacks of reels. No telling how many thousands HR weeds out first. Have you seen Skylar this morning? Wait a minute."

He cut her off before she could answer and pressed the intercom to his assistant. "Shelly! Where's my Danish? If I keep drinking coffee on an empty stomach, I'm going to make my ulcer bleed again. Get me some food!"

He switched off the intercom without waiting for her to answer, then took a swig from a bottle of Maalox on his desk, grimaced and made a sound like a cat with a hairball. "Have you talked to Skylar?"

"I saw him briefly," she said, a look of disgust on her face over his morning culinary concoction.

"You get to go back to Iraq," he said, leaning back in his chair and propping his legs on the corner of his desk. "No need to thank me. Network's doing a two-hour special on that hell hole, so I was sure you'd want to be part of that plum assignment. Brad's anchoring it from here in New York," he said referring to USN network's main anchor Bradford Norrish.

"We're covering the war every day in our newscasts and in a lot of our *AmeriView* segments," she said, not thrilled she had to go back, but not wanting to miss out on producing a network special. "I hope we're doing something different."

"We are. For one, we're going more in depth with Iraq's history and archaeology, which is where you come in," he said. "During the initial invasion, as I'm sure you remember, we and every other network mapped out for viewers the ancient cities mentioned in the Bible. Cradle of civilization and all that. We're going more in depth now. For years, Saddam hasn't let most archaeologists into the country, so now we can get a closer look at some of these places. And since almost eighty percent of Americans claim to be Christians or Jews and the Bible's their book, we're hoping for big ratings with these segments."

"I hate religion segments," she groaned. "I can't even remember the last time I was in a church."

"You've done segments on rapists and murderers and I'm pretty sure you're not one. That's what we do, sweetheart." He slowly enunciated each syllable for her, as if talking to a child, "We're jour-na-lists."

She gave him an irritated look.

He kept child-talking to her, "We report on things we don't know. And what do we do when we don't know something? We research so we can better inform our miserable viewers who think we're *swell*. Religion's the new hot topic."

"Since when?"

"I know you've been knee deep in a war zone for weeks, but there's religious buzz lately," he said. "There's all that controversy about that new movie coming out next year about Jesus' passion or something. Plus all the hype with that new book that came out a few months ago about Da Vinci's code. And, may I remind you, the other networks do religion stories. Look at our competition: their main anchor was searching for Jesus three years ago and did a two-hour special on it."

"I bet their switchboard lit up after it aired," she said. "Probably to tell them the Jews aren't saved and all journalists are going to hell."

"Yeah, my uncle the rabbi always gets a kick out of that. People are digging religion. Now with us, they can dig archaeology." He started snort-laughing at his own joke. "Get it? Dig archaeology."

She gave him a concerned look. "Have you been getting enough sleep?"

"Who can sleep with this ulcer and this much money flying out the door? Do you know how much covering this war is costing us? Do you know how many millions a year we're spending on insurance for you guys and your equipment? Never become an EP. It's a nightmare. This war's killing my budget. No wonder we had to close so many of our foreign bureaus. Nothing going on in the rest of the world anyway, right?" he said sarcastically.

"Even if there were, Americans wouldn't care," she said. "I still say we should profile the EU. It's trying to get rid of individual countries' rights. The Germans want control of Europe, but what else is new?"

"The only aspect of Europe Americans care about is whether they can afford to go there on their vacation, that thing you don't know how to take." He took another swig of Maalox and hit the intercom again. "Shelly! Get me my Danish!"

His frantic executive assistant came running in. "Sorry, Paul. Hi, Le An. They were backed up at the coffee shop and then they got your order wrong, but I didn't..."

"Edited version, Shelly. I'm in a meeting," he snapped.

She dumped a white bag on his desk and ran out.

"You are so mean when you're hungry," said Le An.

"It's this stupid ulcer. I'm miserable."

"Shouldn't you be drinking milk instead of coffee?" she asked.

"Give up coffee? Are you crazy?" He dug into the bag and retrieved his breakfast, biting off a piece of the pastry. "Good, blueberry. The EU can take over Europe and nobody in America would give a tiny rat's ass. Won't draw the ratings."

"They have legislative, executive and judicial branches now. A united Europe outnumbers the US by 200 million people. That's almost twice our population."

"Bah! Executive branch," scoffed Paul. "Their president holds office for what? About a nano-second? They're powerless. Nobody cares. Is the EU starting a war? If it starts a war, we might be interested. If Europeans start killing Americans, we'll be interested."

"Are we only reactionaries to world events?" she asked.

"Yes, we're reactionaries. Broadcast news reacts *when* events happen, not *before*, because that's what viewers want to see. Just because Europeans are uniting to get better commerce deals doesn't mean they're starting World War Three. Americans don't care about the EU. And if no one cares and we take the time and money to produce a segment on it, no one will watch. And if no one watches, we've spent a lot of money, wasted time, lost ratings and lost money." He leaned forward and sneered, "Now *that* makes me cranky. But more importantly, it makes network suits cranky and they start looking for my replacement."

"What if Europe passes a constitution which creates a United States of Europe with laws superceding all the individual countries' rights?" she asked. "What if they decide not to be friendly with the US anymore?"

"Hell, they're not too friendly to us now. The Brits are supposed to be our friends, but they were so nasty to our former ambassador right after 9/11, they almost made him cry on live TV."

"Yeah, that was pretty brutal."

"Anything they do gets bogged down in the muck of all their languages and cultures anyway. Find me a story Americans actually care about. Start a war in Europe and you can cover it."

"I'll get right on it," she said.

"I'm letting you do that piece on Ireland. Isn't that enough?"

"It's a start. Don't forget I'm shooting over there in eleven days. I talked to a financial expert in Dublin this morning and he said Ireland's growth is all smoke, mirrors and loan money. He says within a few years the country's economy is going to tank and the same thing's going to happen in Europe and the US. Apparently, we'll be kissing our real estate and 401(k)s buh-bye."

"There's a great way to start my day. Any other financial experts saying the same thing?"

"Not that I know of," she said. "This guy should be a good counter to the happy talk about Ireland's growth I'm getting from the other experts."

"We're going to tack Iraq onto the back end of your Ireland trip. Plan accordingly."

"Which correspondent are you assigning to front the Ireland story?" she asked.

"I don't have anyone to spare. Iraq's screwed up our assignments for months and this special isn't helping. I can't give you anyone from our London bureau because almost everyone there is sick. Britain's a first-world socialist country with tax-funded, free healthcare and they can't cure the flu? Only two people are holding down the entire bureau. We're not talkin' twenty-four hour bug either: most people have been sick for a week. John Lockhart was the only reporter who could barely stay upright yesterday and he kept throwing up off-camera after each live stand-up. It's a miracle he didn't throw up on air."

Le An made a face. "I thought his face looked a little green."

"Do the Ireland interviews yourself and we'll send you back later with a correspondent to reinterview the ones you think need an on-camera presence," he said.

"That's what I figured. There's another story I've been investigating dealing with ethanol gas," she said, looking at her notepad. "People in Chicago say they were guinea pigs and it ruined their older cars. They wouldn't start, cost thousands in repairs and most had to buy new cars. I've talked to a guy who tests fuel quality and he says it's not so much a problem with newer cars, but it can really mess up older ones, particularly smaller engines."

"I like it. People will have a fit if they think green technology gas is damaging their cars and forcing them to buy new ones. Remind me in the morning meeting so we can put you on the schedule for it. OK, Iraq," he said as he took another bite of his pastry. "We're working on a tight schedule, so don't plan on coming back to New York to write and edit. Do as much as you can over there and finish up at the London bureau. You're probably going to want to shoot at the British Museum for some of the archaeology anyway. Besides, we're going to have all our editors and edit suites tied up here working all three shifts, so it's better if you do most of your editing in London. And while you're in Iraq, see if you can find Saddam. I'd love to be the network that breaks that story. Knocking off the Hussein boys a few weeks ago was sweet, though, wasn't it? Ha! You're a rock star. Great for ratings."

"Thanks for the special."

"Brad asked for you specifically," said Paul.

"He did not."

It was a big deal to have main anchor Bradford Norrish notice anyone's existence.

"He did, Le. I'm not lying. He'd probably snatch you to produce more segments on *Night News* if he had his way. Just make sure your Iraq segments get the attention of eighty percent of US viewers."

"No pressure there."

"This is a two-hour special. Your segments should be twenty minutes total or less, but I know you—you'll find something interesting and beg for more time."

She started to protest and he waved her off.

"Save your breath. You're talking to someone who knows you," he said. "We'll get the Muslim interest with Iraq, the Jews and Christians with the segment focus and the atheists with the archaeology. It's a slam dunk. You'll only be in Iraq for two weeks max. I'll even make you take vacation time. Just don't do it during November sweeps or the last two weeks of October. I might consider giving you Thanksgiving this year. By the way HR is asking why you never take a vacation. They think I'm threatening you. Please tell them I'm not."

"You don't threaten me, Paul. You just whine and never let me take one. Hard to believe, but I do want Thanksgiving off this year. It's been years since I've been able to get together with my family for a holiday."

"Just don't tell HR I won't let you take vacations. By the way, they said if you don't take this year's vacation time by the end of December, you'll lose it for the year." He leaned back and smiled at her. "So you'll go?"

"On vacation? Love to," she said. "I thought y'all'd never ask."

He made a growling noise. "Two weeks max in Iraq with comp time and hazard pay."

"You owe me Thanksgiving," she said. "Do you know how much vacation time I haven't taken in the years I've been here?"

He started laughing. "Who are you kidding? You wouldn't know how to take a vacation if it was forced on you. Skylar's going to be in Iraq for two or three months. I'm plugging you in and out. It's a fast trip. Talk to Mary in travel. She's made all your arrangements."

"Who's my photog and editor?" she asked.

"Barry. Take a little sat setup as backup. We've got two sat trucks there now. I live in dread someone's going to carjack or blow up one of those things. Do you know how much they cost? We've got a few big dishes set up at the house in Baghdad. They're feeding video twenty-four hours a day now. One sat's for a direct phone line back here to New York. If you get in a time crunch or the locals damage something, you may need the mini sat. You know, we moved out of the hotel right after you left. We're in a house near CPA. Walled compound. Ritzy. Marble floors and chandeliers. Pool. Nice new generators so you don't have to suffer those nasty blackouts the rest of the country's going through. Air conditioning. You'll practically forget you're in a war zone. I hear the parties in Baghdad are pretty good, too. See, it'll be just like a vacation. You won't need to take one when you get back. Ha!"

"Ha! Is this ulcer humor?" she said. "The manse is a nice touch and the sat dishes will make life easier. Glad we're out of that death-trap hotel."

"We're renting the villa from some Ba'athist bigwig who's hiding in Jordan or Syria now. We've got people from a French newspaper and a Danish one renting a room or two each, a South African TV group doing their own stuff and working with a correspondent from our Brit sister-network BTN. I think the *Herald* and *Post Chronicle* are renting some rooms, too. They come and go. Rest of the house is ours. Thing's costing us a fortune, but at least it's cheaper than the hotel and we're making money renting out rooms. Take two extra cameras. Don't lose anything and bring back everything in one piece."

"If I can."

"We're pulling Tim out of Baghdad right after he finishes his segments for the special. He's burned out covering the war—or whatever the Pentagon's calling it these days. I've gotta get the guy out of there for a little R-and-R and bring him back stateside. I'm rotating in a producer from our London bureau—Emily Westingham—but she's sick."

Paul bit off more of the Danish and let out a deep, long sigh, then said, "Khaled's working as your audio guy and translator again. Plus, we've got Dark Knight Security for you and the house."

Le An groaned. "All those guys are so obvious with their Marine-inspired buzz cuts, mirrored sunglasses and clean-cut, no-beard, little faces. They're all ex-military and look like CIA. We might as well stick a sign on our car that says, 'Hey, terrorists! Hit this car! Important foreigners on board!'"

"We're paying for them and you *will* use them, understand?" he growled. "No ditching them like last time. If it makes you feel better, tell them to lose their razors and grow out their hair. Drive in from Kuwait. We're trying to set it up so you can fly out of Baghdad on a military transport. You're going to be traveling with a British archaeologist we hired as a consultant."

"Good to hear," she said. "How old is he?"

"Late fifties, I think. April's your AP. She made the initial contact with him. He's one of the foremost authorities on Iraqi archaeology and a Greek, Aramaic and Hebrew scholar. I think he speaks Arabic, too. Please don't get him killed."

"Tell that to Dark Knight Security. Where am I meeting him?" she asked.

"Jerusalem. Cross over to Amman and fly into Kuwait."

"Who's the archaeologist?" she asked.

Paul picked up a piece of paper and read, "The Honorable Doctor Jacob Jeremy Winston Spencer-Hilson. The Spencer-Hilson is one of those British hyphenated last names."

"What?" she started laughing. "Is he titled gentry? Great. Say that again."

"See for yourself. Here's your copy," he said as he shoved the paper toward her with such force it flew off the corner of his desk and floated through the air, landing at her feet.

"Nice shot. The Honorable Doctor Jacob Jeremy Winston Spencer-Hilson," she read out loud. "Winston Spencer-Hilson. You know, most people don't know Winston Churchill's name was actually Winston Spencer-Churchill. There must be some family connection. If so, that's pretty cool. The Honorable Doctor Jacob Jeremy Winston Spencer-Hilson. If he's referred to as 'Honorable,' that probably means the family's titled, but he's not the oldest son who's next in line to inherit the title and the estate. If so, he'd be Viscount Doctor Jacob Spencer-Hilson."

Paul raised an eyebrow at her. "Bit of an Anglophile, are we?"

"A bit. British landed gentry fascinate me. Don't know why."

"Well, as you can see from his dossier, the honorable doctor's been teaching at an American college. He did a summer dig in Israel, but just started a year sabbatical, so he has no time constraints," he said. "The controversy the last couple of months is how some renowned archaeologists overreacted to the looting of artifacts at museums in Iraq and now it turns out not as many items are missing as they first thought. A few news organizations are backtracking and saying they were misled. They're pointing fingers at museum curators, former museum employees, other archaeologists. I think there's a story there. Is this bashing the military and America because it's the thing to do or was the looting that bad? Find out."

"Why don't you send Luke Conte instead of Skylar? He's done a great job in Iraq."

"Conte's good, but no, I'm sending Coltrane. Viewers know him from the initial invasion. He's replacing Margaret Kirkwood. I'm rotating her out for some R-and-R."

"Luke went in during the invasion, too. He's knows his way around, the troops respect him, the locals like him."

"I know why you want Conte. Yes, he's one of the best," he said, looking at her mischievously. "But I've heard the rumors: that you and Conte were a bit of an item in Iraq."

She looked up startled and blushed.

"Come on," he said. "We're a news department. We're all big gossips. Everybody knows everybody else's business—sometimes even before it happens. You didn't really think I wouldn't find out, did you? And much as I'd like to accommodate budding love..."

She rolled her eyes, embarrassed they were discussing her personal life.

"...I need him stateside to recharge before I send him back," Paul continued. "Conte was over there five months. The guy needed a break. He asked for assignments on the West coast so he could spend time with his family and that's what I'm giving him."

"You're a sweetheart," she said.

"Got that right, but don't let it get around. I'm sending Coltrane to Baghdad a week ahead of you and Barry. Now get outta here. And tell Shelly I need another Danish."

5

New York City
Thursday, 14 August 2003

Le An finished writing Skylar's script scheduled to air the next night, filed a copy to the folder for *AmeriView*'s next show on the network server, then emailed a copy to Skylar, one to Tony—her editor on the story—one to the legal department and another to Paul.

She hit the intercom and buzzed edit room eight.

"Tony?"

"MacDonald! Where's the rest of my script?" he yelled. She could hear the audio from her package playing in the background. "You promised me I'd have it before lunch and it's after three."

"I haven't had lunch yet, so, technically, I kept my word. The script's in the bin for tomorrow night's show and I emailed you a copy. I'll be down in a few minutes."

"It looks good, but tell Coltrane to track the rest of it. I don't plan on being here all night. My wife's gonna divorce me if I don't go home sometime."

"I'll call Sky. See you in a few," she said.

She looked over at the vase of red roses on her desk and shook her head. They'd appeared a few hours before when she'd been out. When she buzzed Skylar's office, she could hear a female's voice in the background, but all talking stopped when they heard the intercom.

"Skylar?" Le An asked.

He picked up the phone so whoever was in the office couldn't hear her side of the conversation.

"I just finished your script. I need you to track the ending," she said. "Make sure Tony gets it. He's in edit eight."

"I know. I was down there an hour ago. The piece looks good. Listen, I'm in a meeting. Can I call you back?" he asked.

"Don't bother. Just telling you about the script. I'm going down to editing."

"Notice anything in your office?" he asked.

"You mean the intern's roses you left here? I'll make sure she gets them," she said.

"They're for you," he said.

She hung up and made a face. "Blech."

She had bigger problems. She hadn't told her mother she was going back to Iraq. Biting the bullet, she picked up the phone and punched in her number.

"What's wrong?" Kate asked.

"Wrong?" Le An tried to mask her voice and sound chipper.

"Tell me," Kate demanded.

"I'm going back to Iraq. How are Neil and Jud?" Le An quickly changed the subject to her brothers.

"What?! No!" Kate exploded. "I thought you didn't want to go back. Why are they sending you?"

"I guess since I was over there recently, it's easy to drop me back in," she said. "But I'm not covering the war. I'm doing some history and archaeology segments. Sounds interesting."

There was silence on the other end of the phone. Le An picked up a pen and started banging one end of it across the open pages of her day-planner, then doodled geometric patterns around the date.

"Momma? Say something."

Kate audibly sighed, "Why should I bother? You never listen to me anyway."

"Amma, don't start," she groaned. "It's my job. Besides, I'm good in wars. I was born in one. Wars-R-Us. The good news is I'm coming home for Thanksgiving."

She silently added, *I think.*

Nothing was certain in the news business. Le An flipped ahead in her day-planner and circled Thanksgiving five times to remember to book the flight before she left for Iraq.

"If you're still alive," said Kate.

"You're in my will. You get it all."

"Listen, little missy, that is not funny," Kate snapped. "It's no wonder I'm gray. You kids worry me to death."

"I'm coming home for Thanksgiving," repeated Le An, hoping to appease her.

"Finally. Your brothers are going to be here, too. It'll be the first time we've all been together in a long time. The Rottweiler always has her tacky hill-william family invade poor Jud for the holidays. Of course, she'd never dream of including us. Not that we'd want to spend time with those alcoholics, chucking back cheap beer and yee-hawing all over the backyard."

Kate refused to even speak the name of her arch nemesis. To say she and Judson's wife Renee—aka 'The Rottweiler'—didn't get along was putting it mildly.

"You're so bad," Le An smiled.

"Oh, pooh. That woman is the bane of my existence."

Kate MacDonald Grandison was the quintessential Southern lady: dignified, proper, hospitable, mannered, gracious—and feisty to the core, everything Renee wasn't.

Renee was whiney, tactless and conniving, always trying to find ways to overspend Judson's money. A gold-digger and social-climber from Gator Junction, Louisiana, she'd been relentless pursuing Judson. After she'd convinced him to marry her, she'd worked overtime to keep him away from his family. The MacDonald-Grandison clan despised her.

Le An and Judson had been close from the time she'd arrived from Vietnam to join the Grandison family. Five years older than she, he'd taken the scared little girl under his wing, catering to her every need. They'd been inseparable. A gifted athlete, Jud had coached Le An in sports, encouraging her to excel. She'd acquired her fiercely competitive nature from him.

Le An's other brother Neil, seven years her senior, and his wife Keri were lawyers in Charlotte, North Carolina.

"I bet Renee finds some way to back out of Thanksgiving," said Le An. "She hasn't braved our family for years. She's too afraid you'll bite her head off."

"Oh, pooh. It's no secret I only want Judson and the kids to come. Maybe she'll run off with the garbage man and high-tail it back to Louisiana to be with her mangy family. Or get run over by a bus. Either way, I'd be happy," said Kate.

"You're terrible."

"Neil and Keri are going to Atlanta to spend Christmas with her family. I guess I'll be all alone unless you decide to come."

There was no mistaking the pitiful manipulation in her voice.

"I don't know where I'll be, Amma, but I'll be home for Thanksgiving."

"You're not going to be in Iraq for Christmas, are you? Please tell me you're not going to be over there."

The Christmas manipulation was still on.

"I don't think so," said Le An. "I'm only going for a few weeks to produce these segments for the special."

"Will I get to see you before you go?"

"Probably not. I've got a ton of work."

"So, unless I fly up to New York, I may never see you again? I still haven't seen your new apartment. You've been there eight months and you have yet to invite me."

That was the last thing Le An wanted.

"I'll come to Charlotte before I go overseas," she said quickly before she'd thought it through.

"Now I'm happy." said Kate.

Bullet dodged.

"I've been working on the MacDonald genealogy a bit," said Kate. "There's so much information online now. We're descended from Charlemagne, some French and Italian kings and Robert the Bruce."

"Charlemagne? My great-granddaddy was an emperor who ruled a reincarnation of the Roman Empire?"

"Um hum. And from what I can tell of your mother's ancestry, you're descended from Charlemagne on her French father's side, too."

"Wow, a double dose of Charlemagne. Isn't that what breeds insanity? When cousins marry?"

"Only if they're first cousins. I'm quite sure your insanity was acquired, not inherited."

"Oh, Mom, everybody knows Southerners are inherently crazy. Who was that other guy you mentioned?"

"Robert the Bruce," said Kate.

"Who was that? Some mass murderer?" Le An wrote down his name as a reminder to research him in her spare time—which would be never.

"He was king of Scotland," said Kate.

"Another royal. Do we get to dust off our crowns now? Did he leave us a drafty castle? Is Neil going to be laird like *Laird of the Highlands*?"

Le An and Kate were both fans of the BBC show and felt a familial kinship with the comedic drama about a Scottish family named MacDonald.

"No, we don't inherit anything, not even Edinburgh Castle," said Kate. "The tourists have that now."

After Le An hung up, she realized she wouldn't have time to fly to Charlotte before flying overseas.

"Great," she moaned, putting her head in hands.

"What's wrong? Who gave you the roses?" said her close friend and fellow producer Elena Fernandez as she plopped into the chair across from the desk.

"I can't go to Charlotte before I go to Iraq. Amma's going to hit the roof. By the way, I'm going back to Iraq."

"Yeah, I already know." Elena lifted the lid to the jar of Ghirardelli chocolate pieces on the desk and shook out a handful. "You single-handedly have caused me to gain ten pounds. Why do you leave these things here?"

"It's a Southern hospitality thing. We have to be feeding you at all times otherwise we turn into dreaded Yankees. Here, try these." She unlocked her middle drawer and pulled out a brown box. "Jud just sent me these from Savannah. Ever had divinity?"

Elena bit into the white, creamy candy. "Ooh, this is sinful. How many pounds will it slap on my thighs? You know, for someone who's into nutrition, you push *mucho* processed sugar. Is it a conspiracy to make us all sick so you end up producing the best stories? Are you working tonight?"

"Yeah, I'm going to be here late," she said as she sorted through a stack of papers.

"Ahh... *chica*." Elena tapped the side of the vase. "Are they from Luke? Something to tell me?"

"They're from Skylar. I don't know why he gave them to me. Probably guilt for harassing me. Aren't they awful? Red roses are so cliche. Want 'em?"

Elena stuck her nose in the petals. "Wouldn't Sky be hurt if he found them on my desk? Give the guy a break. It's romantic. Aren't you even a little smitten? He's quite the eye candy and you two look good together."

Le An gave her a drop-dead look.

"*Chica*," Elena said and reached across the desk to pat her arm. "Are you waiting for Luke? Because, ah, word is he's moved on. Sorry, but if I don't tell you, someone else will."

"I already heard. It's a newsroom. Gossip travels fast."

"Then use Sky to get even. You said yourself Luke wasn't a serious thing."

"It was serious," she protested.

Elena gave her a dubious look.

"OK, it wasn't really serious. It was a brief dalliance, but maybe I was hoping it would lead to serious. We were in Iraq, surrounded by blood, gore and war and, well, you know. It was just a silly flirtation, I guess. We'd been eyeing each other for a while. Maybe if we could've stayed in the same city for more than a few weeks, it might have been more. Most men bore me, but Luke's intelligent and amusing."

"Have you tried calling him or emailing?" asked Elena.

Le An looked disgusted. "No."

"*Chica*, it's the twenty-first century. Please move into it," said Elena.

"He's moved on and you want me to call him? That's pathetic and I don't do pathetic."

"Maybe he thinks you're not interested," said Elena.

"Men aren't that deep. They don't think about relationships," said Le An. "They have short attention spans. They see what they want, go get it, then move on to their next compartmentalized obsession."

"Like Sky with you?" said Elena as she pointed to the roses.

Le An gave her another disgusted look. "If Luke's not interested enough to stay in touch, why would I want him? Why would I want someone not interested in me?"

"You're so analytical about everything," sighed Elena. "Face it, you're thirty-four. We're in that dreaded twenty-eight-to-thirty-five zone where our bodies keep telling our minds we're desperate for a man. I can't figure out how you're always so in control. Are AmerAsian women immune or something?"

"Obviously not. Exhibit A: Luke. War and death do strange things to people. It doesn't matter. I don't have time for a social life. And no more pretty-boy, alleged 'talents,'" she said mocking the industry term for anchors and reporters. "Most of them, married or single, are juggling six to ten women. Why would I want that?"

"You want someone ugly? Are you *loca?* The ugly ones get crazy jealous and shoot you," said Elena. "Eye-candy men go a long way. If you don't want Skylar, toss him to me."

"He's a total *play-ah*. Haven't you heard the stories about him? Escapades in stairwells? Stealing society wives? It's a wonder he doesn't pop up on in the gossip columns more often. Take him. With my blessing."

"He's got wicked blue eyes," sighed Elena. "How long are you going to be in Iraq?"

"Not long. Just to produce segments for the special."

"Why don't they use someone already over there?" asked Elena.

"My shots are up to date, someone's burned out, someone's throwing up, Paul's trying to drive me crazy, Skylar's harassing me—take your pick."

Just then, everything went black.

6

New York City
Thursday, 14 August 2003

Le An spun around in her dark office toward the two large windows, noticing there were no working traffic lights as far as she could see.

"What happened? Another terrorist attack?" Elena jumped up and jerked open the door.

The inner offices were dark and chaotic.

"Why hasn't the generator kicked in?" Le An asked, then yelled, "It's more than our building! No power for as far as I can see!"

"Why don't we have dial tones?" barked Paul as he slammed down a phone. "Why hasn't our generator kicked in? Where are my engineers? Someone find an engineer and go down to the generator to see what's wrong. That thing should have kicked in by now. Shelly!"

Le An pulled a large flashlight from her drawer, shined it toward a cabinet in the main room and called out, "If you don't have a flashlight, grab one from the cabinet. Does anyone still have internet?"

Le An and Elena kept trying to get dial tones with their cellphones and Le An's landline.

"Welcome to Iraq," Skylar joked as he stumbled into Le An's office. "Electricity is so overrated. Al-Qaeda again? Le, I'm taking a crew out with a sat truck. I want you as my producer. Paul said yes." He smirked at the way he'd trumped her. "Nice roses. Who gave you those?"

Elena shot her a look and said, "Le's kinda busy. Why don't I produce for you?"

Le An turned to face the windows to keep from laughing.

"Great idea," she said.

When she turned around, Skylar leveled a cold gaze at her.

She moved past him to the door of her office and yelled down the hall toward the main room, "Everyone check your cellphones and landlines. First person with a dial tone, call the Newark or Hartford bureaus and see if they've got power. If they don't, try Philly and DC."

"Elevators!" screamed Shelly. "We've got people stuck in the elevators! Can anyone help get them out?"

"What's *Night News* doing?" asked Elena as she and Le An kept trying to get dial tones.

They heard Paul ordering someone down to network's assignment desk in the newsroom two floors below.

"Brad's EP'll get him out to a sat truck," said Le An.

"Is this another Osama calling card?" asked Barry Spirelli, the photographer and editor who'd been part of Le An's crew in Iraq. He pushed past her and Elena as he barged into the office and dropped his backpack behind the desk. "Le, watch that while I find out how these little jokers destroyed the generator. Did they learn nothing from 9/11 about emergency preps?"

He propped his flashlight on the desk and pulled a roll of duct tape from his backpack.

"I don't see smoke or flames," he said looking out the window.

He pressed his nose up to the glass, trying to see as far in either direction as he could. Le An, Skylar and Elena crowded around the windows, too, looking in all directions for any sign of power.

"No planes sticking out of buildings," said Barry.

"God forbid," muttered Elena, crossing herself and kissing her hand, more from the habit and superstition of warding off evil than from being a devout Catholic.

"I bet a ten spot it's Muslim terrorists at Niagara Falls' power station, Canadian side," said Barry.

"I bet it's local—tree down on power lines in New York," said Skylar.

"Ten on fried rodents trying to gnaw through wires at a power substation, American side. Le?" said Elena.

"Ten on cascading summer blackout," she said. "It's a scorcher out there. Millions of people overloading the grid, running their ACs, combined with operator error, like engineers sleeping at their consoles or playing solitaire."

Barry left to fix the generator as Elena shook another handful of chocolates into her hand.

"You ready, Sky?" she asked.

"Yeah," he muttered and looked at Le An again, then held out his hand for chocolates before heading for the door, Elena right behind him, to let Paul know about the producer switch.

Le An, relieved she didn't have to endure hours of his overt advances that night, winked at Elena and mouthed a silent 'thank you' as both fought back smiles. Her wall clock read 4:15. Already she could feel the building starting to heat up, the sun cooking Manhattan to a steamy ninety-three degrees. The windows in the USN building didn't open and, without air conditioning, it was going to be a sweatbox. She hoped she could snag another crew and cover the story in an air-conditioned satellite truck—any place but a skyscraper with no power. It was going to be a long, hot evening.

She locked her office door and opened her closet, pulling out a suitcase which was always packed and ready for last-minute assignments out of town. After changing into a khaki cotton skirt, a short-sleeved pullover and white sneakers, she opened her office door just as Paul was screaming for her.

"Where's Le An?" he yelled. "Shelly! Get her in my office for a meeting. I want her coordinating coverage."

"Coming!" Le An called back, then murmured, "Great. Sweatbox skyscraper it is."

By giving Elena her slot as Skylar's producer, she'd passed up any hope of air-conditioning.

Before the night was over, they learned terrorists hadn't caused the blackout. Sagging power lines in Ohio had hit trees and knocked systems off-line. Computer errors and non-functioning alarms had caused one power grid after another to surge and cascade onto other grids. Eight northern states, including New York, were left in the dark, along with one third of eastern Canada—more than 50-million people without power.

Terrorists were, however, causing havoc half a world away in Iraq, blowing up oil pipelines, water mains and a building which housed both the International Monetary Fund and the UN.

7

New York City
Monday, 25 August 2003

Barry steered the USN-owned black SUV through Manhattan's taxi-honking streets toward the Upper East Side. Le An had forgotten her luggage that morning and the trip was a detour before they drove to the airport.

In the backseat was April Greenlaw, an associate producer at *AmeriView* who frequently was assigned to do research and planning for Le An and her crew. April was not only riding with them in order to return the SUV to the office garage, but was also using the opportunity to brief Le An and Barry on the locations where they'd be shooting in Ireland and Iraq.

Le An looked out the window, feeling exhausted. She really wasn't up to making this grueling trip to... she ticked off the countries in her head, trying to remember where she was going: Ireland, England, Israel, Jordan, Kuwait, Iraq and back again. Propping her arm on the handle of the SUV's door, she leaned her head against it and closed her eyes. She'd been so busy at work, she hadn't had a chance to discuss the research with April before now, which meant she was going to have to cram on the plane.

Skylar had left for the Middle East the week before and Le An was glad to see him go. She grimaced at the thought of meeting up with him in Iraq and producing his segments there. Hopefully, he'd have moved on to fresh pasture by the time she got there. Le An figured his next conquest would be poor Emily Westingham from the London bureau, slated to be his producer in Iraq after Le An left—well, as soon as Emily could stand up without throwing up.

"Le An, I can't believe you forgot your luggage," said Barry.

"You never forget anything. Where do I turn? I forget."

"Here. Slow down. It's the beige one on the left," she said. "I was thinking about the package I had to finish, not luggage."

"A driveway. I'm impressed," said April as Barry pulled in at the painted-brick townhouse. "Do you own this? I'm looking for an apartment."

"I own it with my brother Jud. I live on the first floor and rent out the second and third together. If you can hang on, I can let you rent the ground floor studio. It's a mess now, but it opens onto the backyard, which maybe one day I'll get around to landscaping."

"That would be great," said April wistfully. "Remember you promised it to me first. I hope I can afford it."

That was the only real way to find decent apartments in Manhattan—word of mouth.

"How big is your apartment?" asked April.

"Two bedrooms, one bath," she said.

"I need to use that one bath," said Barry.

"Me, too," said April.

Le An gave them a horrified look. The last thing she wanted was visitors.

"Didn't y'all go at the office?" she asked.

"No!" they said in unison.

"Can't y'all hold it in?" she asked. "I'm only going to be a minute."

Barry and April both started loudly protesting and opened their car doors.

"Le An, I'm not sitting in a traffic jam out to JFK, in agony because you're too selfish to let us come in and use your precious john," said Barry. "Besides, you've never let me past the front door. What's up with that?"

By now, they were all out of the SUV. Barry hit the button on the remote activating the alarm as he and April stood there looking at Le An.

"Fine!" she snapped. "But if either of y'all breathes a word of this, I'll know where it came from. Elena's the only one who's been here and she knows I'll kill her if she talks."

Barry and April exchanged concerned looks.

"You hiding a dead body in there?" asked Barry.

Le An unlocked the wide front door which led into the entry

hall, then opened three locks on an inner door immediately to the left and disarmed her alarm.

She spun around and glared at them. "I'm warning y'all: not one word to anyone."

Scores of moving boxes, chest high, filled the room with only a narrow path for the three to squeeze through.

"Whoa! What a mess!" Barry gasped.

"You want to hold that in all the way to JFK?" Le An threatened.

"Not a chance," he said. "You haven't unpacked in a year?"

"Eight months. I don't have a wife like you. Y'all don't understand. I don't have time to unpack. I never have time for anything. I'm either traveling or working late. I don't have time to sleep. I grab food at the office because I don't have time to shop for groceries and my schedule's too crazy to book deliveries."

She squeezed through the box maze in the combined living and dining room, past the kitchen to the bathroom where she stopped and pointed, "I do take time to buy toilet paper."

"Good to hear," mumbled April.

In her bedroom, Le An transferred her passport, wallet and tickets from her purse to her leather backpack, then put her laptop in there, too, sliding it between foam padding. After buckling together the two suitcases she'd packed the night before, she popped up the handle on the larger one and rolled it behind her into the living room.

"Find someone to unpack for you, Le," said Barry.

"Do they have professional unpackers?" she asked.

"This from the brilliant producer," said April. "Yes, people will unpack for you, even paint and color-coordinate things. They're called interior designers. Why don't I see if someone at work can recommend one? Is this why you haven't rented out the basement studio?"

"Yeah, it's full of boxes, too," she said. "You know, I would love it if I could get everything unpacked. Get someone who's bonded. I don't want them stealing my jewelry."

"I don't think decorators steal," said April.

"This is New York. Everybody steals," she said.

"You're not afraid of someone stealing," said Barry as he wagged a finger at her. "You haven't hired anyone because you want to do it yourself. I know you, MacDonald. You're too much of a control freak to let anyone arrange your things."

"True," she admitted.

"Can we get my apartment ready at the same time?" asked April. "I dream about a neighborhood like this. That studio's mine, Le An. You rent it to anyone else and I promise to personally sabotage every one of your projects."

"Where are you living now?" she asked.

"Brooklyn...with my parents...and they're driving me crazy. Plus, the commute's killing me."

"Sure, we can fix up the basement," she said. "I wouldn't mind the extra income."

"What does this overlook?" asked Barry as he made his way to a railing near the front windows and peered below. "It's your car!"

Six feet down, on a black marble floor, sat her black Mazda Miata.

"The car kinda becomes art, like a sculpture, don't you think?" joked Le An.

"Sweet. I bet a single guy owned this," he said.

"Nope. Married couple with a Porsche who went through a nasty divorce."

"Who got the Porsche?" asked Barry.

"That's such a guy question," said April. "Who cares? The important thing is Le An ended up with a garage and my future apartment."

8

Ireland
Tuesday, 26 August 2003

Le An slept through most of the Aer Lingus flight, waking up only twice—to eat dinner and to disembark when the plane landed at Dublin Airport. After going through customs, she and Barry crammed into a taxi—Le An in the back, Barry up front with the driver—along with their luggage and black equipment trunks.

Barry was usually part of Le An's crew and this assignment was no exception. Besides being one of her closest friends at USN, he was also one of the network's best videographers and editors. To fill out their crew for this shoot, they'd hired an Irish freelance sound technician named Sean O'Flannery who was joining them later that day.

"Ireland beats Iraq, that's for sure," said Barry. "Thanks for landing us this sweet assignment."

As the taxi slowly inched south from the airport toward Dublin on the rain-soaked M1 motorway, their driver Daniel apologized for the morning traffic jam.

"Construction on the Dublin Port Tunnel," he grumbled, adding the digging had kept traffic snarled for two years and was expected to last another two, then asked, "Have you e'er been to Ireland? Any Irish family?"

"I'm *Italiano*," grinned Barry. "Both sides of the family. Never really been here. I've only flown through Dublin's and Shannon's airports. Never got off the plane."

"I don't think I have any Irish roots," said Le An. "I was here in Ireland once... over in Galway, when I was doing a story on an author from Limmerick."

"You're journalists?" asked Daniel.

"Yup, we're here to blow the lid off Viagra," Barry smirked.

"One of our stories is about the pharmaceutical plant in Ringaskiddy and its effect on the town," Le An clarified.

Love—or possibly lust—was in the air in Ringaskiddy where the active ingredient in Viagra was manufactured. Residents claimed the dust from the plant was wafting through the air and 'inspiring' them.

"Gas mask for you, pal," Le An said to Barry.

Daniel laughed out loud.

"We hear Ringaskiddy is *very* popular," said Barry.

"The men are happy," grinned the driver.

"I bet," said Le An. "Wonder what the women think. We hear there's a baby boom, the hospital nursery's at capacity and even the rabbits are having twice as many bunnies."

"Aye," chuckled Daniel.

"We're also covering Ireland's economic growth the last few years," she said.

"Aye, we're growing," he said proudly. "*An Tíogar Ceilteach*...the Celtic Tiger."

That growth was obviously clogging Dublin's roadways. Construction cranes, signs of the booming housing industry, were visible everywhere.

"'Tis true, Erin's growing," Daniel repeated. "They're even wantin' to run a carriageway through the Hill of Tara."

"What's that?" asked Le An, thinking that might be a good addition to her story.

"'Tis the heart and soul of the Irish," he said, "where our high kings once ruled."

Le An jotted down the name and looked at the gridlock all around them. Tara may have been the heart and soul of Ireland, but if a new highway could ease this congestion, she was all for it. It took an hour in rush-hour traffic to travel only six miles south from the airport into the center of the nation's capital.

Though more than a million people occupied Dublin, its cityscape wasn't choked with high-rises. Most buildings were only a few stories high and parts of the city, like the Georgian district, even had a quaint feel, with cobblestone streets and eighteenth-century brick mansions sporting colorful front doors and delicate, fan-shaped windows.

"We have an interview with the prime minister this afternoon," said Le An, giving Barry their schedule for the day.

"The *Taoiseach*," said Daniel.

"It's pronounced *Tee-shack*?" she said, looking at her paper. "I never would have guessed that. It means the 'chief,' right?"

"Aye," said Daniel.

"And his deputy is the..." she stopped, afraid she'd butcher the word.

"*Tánaiste*," said Daniel.

"*Taw-nish-ta*," said Le An, writing out both names phonetically. "That means 'heir to the chief.'"

Barry started humming *Hail to the Chief*, then said, "Sounds like some girl in the 'hood I used to know."

"Did you make out with her behind your school?" Le An smirked.

"You choose now to get back an obscure part of your memory?" he asked. "Lately you've been forgetting half the stuff stored in your head, but you have to remember that?"

"Of course," she said. "You Catholic boys are quite randy."

Daniel started laughing.

"Are you Catholic, Daniel?" she asked.

"Aye," he said.

"I'd always go to Mass Saturday afternoons before drinking Saturday nights," said Barry. "A few *Hail Marys* and *Our Fathers*, confess a few bad thoughts, apologize in advance and I was good to go for the weekend."

Daniel laughed out loud and slapped his steering wheel, nodding his head in agreement.

"Ahh, that's how it's done," said Le An. "Religion 101. That way you could sleep off Saturday night's hangover and not have to get up for church Sunday morning."

"Boo, got that right," said Barry. "Many a time, young MacDonald, I wouldn't even beat the paper in the house Sunday morning. Like I was really going to turn around and go to church an hour later when I hadn't been to bed yet."

"Of course not. Sensible and religious," she said. "I hate jet-lag. We should have taken a day to adjust before we started shooting, but I think today's the only time the *Taoiseach*'s available for a meeting. Daniel, we're also doing a story about how next March Ireland's going to ban smoking in all enclosed public places. No cigs while enjoying a pint at the pub. How do you feel about that?"

"'Tis craziness," he said and shook his head.

"We need to hit some pubs and restaurants to get bites from customers and owners to see what they think about this," she said. "We have an interview with a local doctor to get the medical side of second-hand smoke."

"Hitting pubs, huh? There's a tough gig," grinned Barry.

As Daniel pulled up in front of the Westin Dublin, a stately 140-year-old Georgian-style hotel, he pointed across the street. "Trinity College and the Book of Kells."

"Kells?" Le An said, trying to remember why it sounded familiar.

"'Tis the four gospels in Latin from the ninth century," said Daniel. "The most beautiful you're ever to see."

His answer didn't help. She had no clue what the four gospels were, though they sounded religious.

"I still speak a little Latin from years of Mass," Barry said, as he unloaded their luggage and gear. He motioned to a bellhop, then held up two fingers, indicating one cart wouldn't be enough. "I used to be an altar boy."

"Yes, I know, as you frequently remind me," she said.

After they'd checked in and were heading for the elevator, Barry asked, "Do I have time for a micro-nap? That kid behind me kept waking me up kicking my seat through the whole flight. I was ready to stuff the little brat in an overhead and throw his parents out the back of the plane. With some kids, you know you don't want the parents to live and spawn again, ya know what I'm sayin'?"

"Unfortunately, I do know. Yeah, you can catch a quick nap," she said. "I don't think Sean's picking us up until eleven. I didn't feel the kid kicking. Didn't hear anything either. I was too exhausted, I guess."

"I thought you were dead. Even stuck a mirror under your nose once. If you hadn't fogged it, you were gonna get slapped. About ten guys lined up in the aisle offering to give you mouth-to-mouth. When was the last time you slept?"

"Only ten? Were they cute?" she asked.

"Dogs. I beat 'em back."

"My hero. I don't think I've had more than three hours sleep a night for at least three weeks. I've been too busy. What did Kristin say about you going back to Iraq?"

"She started beating the ground with a hoe," he said. "Might have been picturing my face there—until she realized my hazard pay's funding her shopping sprees."

"I only have to deal with my mother getting hysterical," she said.

"I've got that, too, plus my kids freaking out. I told them to quit watching the news."

Once in her room, Le An called the financial expert who'd given her a dire economic forecast for Ireland and the world, reconfirming their interview for the next day.

Le An found April had emailed the names of five interior designers, along with their estimates for unpacking and decorating. The figures were heart-attack inducing. Much as she wanted her apartment to not look like the inside of a moving van, she couldn't see spending that much.

"Don't think so," she mumbled as she hit reply and typed: *Find a young, hungry designer who doesn't want my firstborn as payment. Just need to unpack, not make the cover of Southern Accents.*

Suddenly she got a familiar sharp pain in her chest which left her gasping for air. Quickly she grabbed her left arm and pulled it in tightly to her chest as she leaned back against the headboard.

9

Dublin, Ireland
Wednesday, 27 August 2003

Sean O'Flannery was not only an ace audio technician, but also one of the most colorful Irish tour guides network's money could buy. The thirty-two-year-old was wiry and thin, only five-nine, almost nose-to-nose with Le An, and his emerald-isle eyes were always scrunched up and prankster gleaming, his mouth in a perpetual smirk, as he traded humorous stories and news anecdotes. His chaos-cut, reddish-brown hair fell into his face with every laugh and, as he drew deeply on his never-ending cigarettes, Le An knew he'd be hit hard by Ireland's upcoming commercial-space smoking ban. If she didn't think it was total journalistic incest, she'd have turned the camera on him as one of her man-on-the-street interviews.

On Wednesday the three got an early start, choosing a hearty breakfast at Bewley's Cafe on nearby Grafton Street. As the sun filtered through the tall stained-glass windows, Le An sipped her tea and flipped through the morning's *Irish Times*. A headline announced plans to build a motorway near the Hill of Tara.

"Hill of Tara. Our taxi driver was talking about that place yesterday. Sean, is '*Tara*' Irish for 'land?'" she asked. "I forget, is Ireland's language called Irish, Celtic or Gaelic?"

"You forget? Again? Le, have you suffered a concussion or something?" Barry asked, now starting to get concerned.

He knew she had an almost photographic memory and rarely forgot anything. To even hear her say the words 'I forget' was memorable.

"Don't start," she grumbled. "I'm not caffeinated."

"The official national language 'tis Irish," said Sean, "but not many speak it. The government's trying to keep it alive, making it mandatory far poor defenseless children, but 'tis dyin'."

"Sounds like what Israel did when they reintroduced Hebrew, but that caught on," she said.

"English 'tis the second official language," Sean continued. "Irish, Scottish and Welsh Gaelic are Celtic dialects. Do ye know what 'Dublin' means?"

They shook they heads.

Sean pulled out a pen and wrote on a napkin DUBH LINN. "'Black pool.' 'Tis the name the Vikings gave this area."

"Where's the black pool?" asked Barry.

"We don't let tourists or nattering Yanks see it," he said fighting back a smile as he waited for a reaction from them. "The Vikings used to sail up the Liffey to the River Poddle and into a deep, black pool of water where they'd moor their ships. You can see a wee bit of the Poddle where it flows into the Liffey at Wellington Quay. We only let tourists at the Clarence Hotel see."

"So half your stories are blarney?" asked Le An.

"Well, you don't have to stay at the hotel to see the Poddle," grinned Sean, "but, on my grandmother's grave, may she rest in peace, the rest 'tis true. The black pool's underground, under the gardens at Dublin Castle. Only the rats see it now."

"So Dublin really means 'black pool?'" she asked.

"Would these eyes lie to you?" he asked as he leaned closer to her face, his eyes scrunched up in mock indignation. "Those black waters inspired Arthur Guinness to brew his dark ale, something near and dear to my over-intoxicated little Irish heart. I would never lie about the inspiration far Dublin's most famous ale."

"I could go for some of that ale," said Barry.

"Did you know when the new Republic of Ireland 'twas looking far a coat of arms and emblem in 1922, they wanted to use the Guinness harp?" asked Sean.

"Guinness has a harp?" she asked.

"On the label, the logo," said Sean. "'Tis a right-facing harp. But Guinness wouldn't let Ireland use their emblem. So the government flipped it and used it anyway."

"Flipped it?" she asked.

"To a left-facing harp," he said.

"Because y'all wanted to be known as a nation of ale drinkers?" she asked, baffled.

"Don't be daft," said Sean.

"Is it because y'all are musically gifted?" she asked.

"Aye, but nae. Some say 'tis the harp of Ireland's high king Brian Boru, but others say 'tis David's."

"David?" she asked.

"King David."

"Sorry, I'm not familiar with Irish kings," she said.

"Not the Irish king," said Sean. "The first King David."

Barry and Le An looked at each other and shrugged, then looked back at Sean.

"What King David?" she asked.

"*The* King David. From the Bible," said Sean. "He played the harp."

"Ooh," she said, still not sure why Ireland and Guinness Ale would claim that as their logo. "Why is David's harp so special?"

"Because 'tis ours," said Sean.

The conversation seemed to be going in circles and Le An suspected much of it was blarney.

"Back to the article," she said, tapping her newspaper. "Is '*Tara*' Irish for 'land? You know, *Gone with the Wind* kind of Tara?" she asked, swinging out in a deep Southern accent, "Where shall I go? I'll go to Tara.'"

Sean, fighting back a smile, said, "I'll need many pints far this shoot."

"You never saw *Gone with the Wind*?" she asked.

Her right foot bumped against Barry's camera case under the table. Easing the side of her shoe against it as a security measure to guarantee no stranger walked off with it, she looked down and saw the case's strap safely secured under one leg of Barry's chair. If someone tried for the camera, they'd first have to tip over 210 pounds of irate New Yorker.

"Katie Le Scarlett, it's only in the South *Gone with the Wind* is required viewing," said Barry.

"Of course, it's required," she said, "as I'm sure *The Godfather* is in your Italian, Yankee family."

Barry slammed down his fist-held fork in mock anger. "Yes, it is! Uncle Guido made us watch it."

"Many pints needed," muttered Sean. "No, Le An, Tara's not Irish far land. Why are ye askin'?"

"This article," she said. "'*An Bord Pleanala*...'"

Sean corrected her pronunciation.

"Is that some kind of planning board?" she asked.

"You'd be bang on," he said.

She continued reading out loud. The article said the planning board had given permission to run a 50-kilometer motorway through an archaeologically important area in County Meath near Tara.

"Where is that?" She unfolded her map of Ireland. "Is that Tara Street we passed yesterday? They're running an expressway through the center of Dublin?"

"Worse. They're wanting to run the M3 through the Hill of Tara, narth and west of Dublin. Here," he pointed to her map. "'Twas the seat of Erin's high kings, the spiritual heart of Ireland. 'Tis our history they're wantin' to be burying under a carriageway."

"Are there castles there?" she asked.

"Nae more," said Sean. "And if they build the M3, we'll never know what history's buried there."

"That's a shame," she said. "You don't think of Ireland and Scotland having kings because they've been without them so long, only Britain. But I guess British royalty's a sore subject over here, huh?"

"The Irish and the English...'tis a complicated relationship," said Sean. "We live in each other's countries, we marry each other. We fought England for independence, but then half the Irish army deserted to fight with them against the Germans in World War Two, though the Irish government punished those who did."

"Ireland punished Irish soldiers for fighting in World War Two? Why? Because Ireland was neutral in the war?" she asked.

"Officially we we're neutral, but more than half the country 'twas hoping the Nazis would win because they hated the English so much. The government didn't like Irish soldiers fightin' alongside them. 'Tis complicated."

"How did they punish the soldiers?" she asked, a story idea brewing in her head. She jotted it in her notebook before she forgot.

"They court-marshalled them, even dead ones and those who'd won medals. They published their names so they couldn't get jobs. But they didn't punish soldiers who deserted just to be thieving and causing mischief—only those who'd fought with

England. 'Twasn't right. Me uncle was part of D-Day and liberated a concentration camp, but he couldn't find work because the government blacklisted him. He and others on the list moved to England so they wouldn't starve. Me uncle came back to Ireland, but he's lived his whole life fearing they'd come arrest him."

"It's been sixty years since the war," said Le An. "They'd arrest an old man for fighting bravely in World War Two?"

"Aye," said Sean.

"That's messed up," said Barry.

"World War Two 'twas twenty years on from our own war breakin' free of the English," said Sean. "A lot of Irish would have started another civil war if we'd officially helped them."

"Did any non-military Irish fight with England?" she said.

"Aye. Tens of thousands 'twere punished and blacklisted, too."

"So I guess the Irish don't like British royalty," she said.

"'Tis complicated," Sean repeated. "A lot of Irish don't like England's government, but they secretly like English royals—Wills and Harry are a bit popular—and feel terrible they killed Philip's uncle. He was friendly to Ireland. 'Tis a shame."

"Yeah, that was awful," said Le An, remembering how the Irish Republican Army had assassinated Lord Louis Mountbatten, blowing up his fishing boat with him on it.

The blast had also claimed the lives of Lord Louie's fourteen-year-old grandson, an eighty-three-year-old woman and an Irish teenager crewing for them.

Barry waved his fork at Le An's plate, then stabbed one of her sausages and swiped her bacon. The two had a comfort level which came from years of working together as a team. They'd had to rely on each other, often in dangerous situations, logging thousands of hours of air travel and suffering through third-world-country conditions.

Sean raised his eyebrows, startled at Barry's bold advance on her plate.

"She doesn't eat pork," Barry said in defense of his actions. "She always lets me have it."

"No dead swine," she said. "Stopped eating it when I was fifteen after my grandmother dropped dead from a heart attack and pork-clogged arteries. Giving it up was no small task for a Southern girl. Y'all'd think I'd announced I was a Yankee the way my mother carried on. That's why I like Muslim countries: I don't have to worry about somebody slipping me a porkchop."

"Nothing wrong with Yankees or pigs," Barry said as he stabbed at her plate again to retrieve the last of the meat and stuff it in his mouth.

"I can hear your arteries slamming shut," she said.

"'See it, eat it' is my motto. Never met a pig I didn't like. We all have to die of something," he said as he gave her a closed smile bulging over a mouth full of food.

She shook her head and went back to the paper. "How's crime over here, Sean?"

He shrugged and said it had a dropped after the murder of a local journalist.

"The one gunned down in Dublin?" she asked.

"You knew her?" asked Sean.

"Not personally, but I'd heard she went after drug lords here," said Le An.

"Aye. The drug dealers hunted her down and killed her sitting in her car at a red light. All far what she'd found and reported on them. No one thought they'd actually shoot her, not here in Ireland. Most Gardai don't even carry guns," he said referring to the *An Garda Síochána na hÉireann*—Guardian of the Peace of Ireland—the mainly unarmed police force. Only certain detective and emergency response units carried firearms.

"Criminals kill to protect their interests. Journalists' occupational hazard," mumbled Le An, as she went back to reading the paper, uncomfortable with dwelling too long on the risks they all took.

"Did they get the people who murdered her?" asked Barry.

"Some are in prison, others went underground," said Sean.

"Speaking of dying, terrorists are using suicide bombers again in Jerusalem," said Le An, trying to change the subject. "They hit a bus last week and killed almost twenty people coming back from the Wailing Wall. Hot dog, we get two war zones—Israel and Iraq."

"Do you call them terrorists?" asked Sean.

She looked up. "Yeah, I call suicide bombers 'terrorists' when they hit buses full of unarmed civilians and tourists."

"Some people would argue the Palestinians should be called freedom fighters," he said.

"I call anyone who targets innocent civilians a terrorist," said

Barry. "Armed troops fighting armed troops is one thing, but deliberately bombing unarmed, innocent civilians is another."

"Some would call that war's collateral damage. I'm just saying..." Sean said, but Barry forcefully cut him off, his deep voice rising in volume.

"Collateral damage? Look, man, you're talking to two people who were near the Twin Towers on 9/11, who lost friends and family that day. We don't like terrorists, yes *terrorists*, bombing innocent, unarmed civilians. Case closed. I know you Europeans think somehow we're to blame and we deserved it, but..."

"I never said that..." interrupted Sean.

"We've heard that one, too," said Barry, his voice rising. "We know some people cheered when 3,000 innocent people died. New Yorkers didn't deserve it and Americans didn't deserve it."

Le An ducked behind her newspaper. It was too early to do battle with Irish sound guys and grumpy New York cameramen.

"OK, lad, ease off. Nae more fightin'," said Sean. "'Twas just having a chat. I don't side with bombers. I'm only saying some think we need to find another word far 'terrorist.'"

"They'd be wrong," snarled Barry as he aggressively stabbed at a piece of food.

"Don't make me put y'all in time out," said Le An and changed the subject, carefully avoiding the word 'terrorist.' "I imagine Baghdad's going to be jittery after the suicide bombing at the UN compound. Uptick in IED attacks on convoys, too. That'll make it fun to travel with the military. Nothing like having a big red bullseye on your back for... insurgents," she said, carefully choosing her last word.

"Why would they bomb the UN?" asked Barry. "They were there to help."

"Revenge," she mumbled from behind her paper.

"Yeah, the Irish know that game," agreed Sean.

He draped an arm over the back of his chair, nervously jittering as he tapped the heel of one shoe up and down, a side effect of nicotine craving and over-caffeination.

Le An peeked out from behind her paper. "Oh, yeah. Didn't think about that."

"Revenge for what?" asked Barry.

"For years of sanctions which ruined Iraq," she said. "The Iraqis hate the UN. Don't you remember that guy Ahmed we interviewed a few months ago? The guy was practically foaming at the mouth at the mention of the UN."

"I just thought he was purging thirty years of suppressed whining," said Barry. "They probably bombed the UN to drive out other countries and isolate America so we have to cough up all the aid money."

Sean and Le An looked at each other and shook their heads.

"Nah, I'm sticking with revenge," she said.

"Revenge," agreed Sean, "though you make a good point, laddie."

"You're saying even though it was Saddam's fault UN sanctions were imposed in the first place," said Barry, "he somehow convinced Iraqis the UN was persecuting them, causing them to get revenge on the very people trying to help them?"

"Brilliant propaganda, isn't it?" said Le An. "That's what happens when there's no free press and the dictator of a country controls the media."

"You been in Iraq, Sean?" asked Barry.

"Got back a fortnight ago," he said. "Doing audio and some camera far BTN out of London."

"That's our sister network," said Le An. "Does your family live in Dublin?"

"Dublin and all Erin, Europe and America—Boston and New York. But with more jobs now in Ireland, they're moving back."

Her eyes lit up. "Any of them want to be interviewed?"

10

*Dublin, Ireland
Friday, 29 August 2003*

After three days of interviews and pub crawls, Le An and Barry piled into Sean's SUV for a ride back to the airport. As they pulled away from the hotel, Sean handed Le An a CD of local musical groups they'd heard at some pubs.

"Ooh, thank you! Gotta have my *trad*," she said, using the slang for Ireland's traditional music.

She always traveled with music. When things became too stressful, it calmed her and helped her refocus—no matter how gruesome the world was around her.

They drove west along the Quays on the south side of the River Liffey, then crossed the bridge onto Church Street.

"Sean, what's that green-domed building?" she asked.

"'Tis Far Courts," he said. "Ireland's Supreme Court and High Court."

"Far like far away or far like one-two-three-four?" she asked.

"Three-far," he said. "The Irish Civil War started there. Mick Collins... have ye heard of him? Do you know Irish history?"

"No, sorry," she said.

"You never saw the movie *Michael Collins*?" asked Barry.

"Oh, that Mick Collins," she said. "Nope, didn't see the movie."

"Mick 'twas leadin' the IRA to free Ireland from the English, but the English, they're bein' stubborn," said Sean. "Mick finally signs a treaty with them agreeing far them to take the narth and giving the rest of Ireland more independence, but with some ties to the English. Most in the IRA, they're supportin' Mick—anything far some freedom—and they become the Irish Army. But the rest of the IRA, they didn't like Mick not consultin' 'em about the treaty and they're wantin' all of Ireland to be free, not just the south. Sinn Fein didn't agree with Mick and one of their boys 'twas prime minister. When they voted, the ones supportin' Mick's plan won and they gave the boot to the Sinn Fein PM."

He slammed on the brakes to avoid hitting a car which had pulled in front of him, then continued with his story. "Sinn Fein members against Mick's plan seize Far Courts and other buildings, so Mick and the Irish government, they try talkin' some sense into wee, stubborn heads. Finally, Mick loses patience and orders the Irish Army supportin' him to shell Far Courts. Sinn Fein rebels, they know they've got to be leavin', but they leave a little gift of their own. They booby trap the Public Records Office and the archives of census records with 1,000 years of Irish history and *boom*!"

Le An and Barry vibrated a little.

"Aye, 'tis a scary thing they did blowing up Far Courts," said Sean, delighted he'd scared them.

"That's sad about Ireland's records being lost," said Le An, thinking about her mother's genealogy interest.

"Aye, 'tis."

"What happened to Mick Collins?" she asked.

"Assassinated a few months on from the fightin'," he said. "Too many enemies."

"Four Courts is beautiful," she said.

"Aye, 'tis. They restored it, but the original dome and carvings were destroyed."

"Carvings of what?" she asked.

"Great lawgivers... Moses, King Alfred..." Sean said, then paused. Le An saw a slight smile as she caught his reflection in the rearview mirror. "... and Ollamh Fodhla."

Barry and Le An looked at each other and shrugged.

"Who?" she asked.

"Ollamh Fodhla," Sean said slowly. "The greatest lawgiver Ireland's ever known."

"Ola Fola," she repeated.

"Ollamh Fodhla," said Sean.

"Moses is on our Supreme Court, too," said Barry.

"One of the nine justices, is he?" asked Le An. "Conservative or liberal?"

"Conservative," he said.

"How do you know it's Moses? Seen pics of him lately?" she asked.

"He has a beard and he's carrying two tablets of commandments," he said.

"Ah, the tablets," she said. "Always a dead giveaway and, in this case, obviously giving away the dead. But the more important question would be: how do *you* know Moses is on the Supreme Court building?"

"Got some b-roll of it when I was shooting for that profile on the justices we did last fall. Moses is on that carved thingy above the back entrance, right in the middle under where the roof peaks, the one sitting down with a bunch of other people."

"Guess Moses is the lawgiver of choice for everyone's courthouse architecture," she said.

At the airport, as they watched Sean drive away, Barry shouted, "Ollamh Fodhla!"

"Ollamh Fodhla!" said Le An. "Like we're supposed to know who that is?"

11

Israel
Sunday, 31 August 2003

On Sunday, Le An and Barry flew from England into Israel's Ben-Gurion International Airport outside Tel Aviv. After clearing customs, they hired a car to drive them the thirty miles from the traffic-clogged Mediterranean coast up Highway One to the mountains of Jerusalem.

By the time they reached the King David Hotel, it was bathed in soft, golden, late-afternoon sun. Though somewhat plain on the outside, the hotel was anything but on the inside. The lobby evoked an Egyptian-palace motif, with oriental rugs resting on marble floors, golden drapes flanking tall windows and white-carved pillars rising two stories to the coffered ceiling. Fresh flowers were everywhere.

"Another four- or five-star hotel?" Barry whispered as they checked in. "Did travel find discount coupons?"

As employees of network news, they usually stayed in nice hotels, but USN's travel department had made their accommodations especially nice this trip.

"They probably want to impress our archaeologist before we send him to his possible death in a war zone," she said. "Enjoy it while you can."

"Too bad travel didn't upgrade our flights to first class," he grumbled.

"Has Jacob Spencer-Hilson checked in?" Le An asked the desk clerk. "His room gets billed to our account."

"Jacob Spencer-Hilson? No," he said as he checked the computer and frowned. "We do have a Doctor Jeremy Hilson whose expenses are being billed to you, Miss MacDonald. Could that be the same person?"

"Yes, I believe so," she said, trying to remember all of his names. She dug around in her backpack and pulled out her reference sheet. "Jacob Jeremy Winston Spencer-Hilson. He must go by one of his middle names."

"You're kidding me," said Barry, looking over her shoulder to read the paper. "How many names does this guy have?"

"Doctor Jeremy Hilson checked in a few hours ago," said the desk clerk.

"Has he been through hostile environment training?" Barry asked Le An.

"I hope so," she said. "I can't see USN letting him go to Iraq without it."

Most media outlets sent their employees covering Iraq or other war zones through US or UK training programs which former soldiers ran. Journalists learned how to recognize land mines and deal with gun-toting locals forming their own roadblocks. They also learned how to avoid being kidnapped and, in the unfortunate event that they were, how to react.

"I'm ordering room service and calling Kristin instead of having dinner with you and Doctor-Twenty-Names," Barry said as Le An tipped the bellhop outside their rooms.

"OK, we'll talk tomorrow," she said.

"Ollamh Fodhla!"

"Ollamh Fodhla, dude!"

After settling into her room, Le An called her mother. Much as she hated to have her see her box-filled disaster of an apartment, Kate Grandison was the key to finally getting a livable home. April had found a young, hungry designer who charged a fourth of what the others did. Le An had gone online to view her small, but stylish portfolio, but what she liked most was her website provided in-progress photos for her clients. That meant Le An, control freak that she was, could monitor her job and give input from half-a-world away. But she still wanted someone she trusted monitoring the designer on site.

"Mom, did you get my email with your ticket?"

"Yes, dahlin'. Where are you?"

"King David Hotel in Jerusalem. It's on the itinerary I emailed you," she said. "You sure you don't mind going to New York? I feel guilty asking you to handle all this."

"Oh, pooh. You know I love decorating and organizing. Your

apartment can't be any worse than your bedroom all through high school."

"It's about ninety times worse, but thanks for giving me a horror flashback of you cleaning my room by throwing out everything not nailed down. If you get that urge, lie down until the feeling goes away. Don't throw away any of my papers, magazines, books or anything. I mean it, Mom. I know you. Don't throw away anything. You're just organizing, not purging."

"Yes, Miss Bossy."

"Did Jud FedEx you copies of my keys?" she asked. "You have my alarm's security code and you're clear how to deactivate it and set it? I don't want the police throwing you in jail for breaking and entering."

"I have it all. I have an alarm here, remember? I'm not a total moron."

"I never said you were. I just don't want you thrown in jail."

"I can't believe you haven't unpacked in eight months. And I can't believe you hid this from me. What else aren't you telling me?"

Le An sighed audibly. "I didn't tell you because I knew you'd have a fit my schedule was that busy."

"It's only because I love you and don't want you working all the time," said Kate. "You need to relax and enjoy your life."

"I know, Mom," she said softly. "The good news is you're going to be working with a young designer who, fortunately, charges a lot less than the others. The bad news is you're going to be working with a young designer, which is why I want you there keeping an eye on things."

"You mean if I didn't go you're afraid you'd get what you pay for?"

"Something like that. I don't want her suddenly going way over on costs because she, oops, forgot to add something. Just rein her in if she gets dollar signs in her eyes. She's going to post progress photos on her website so I can keep an eye on how things are going. Please check with me about everything. I don't want any design surprises. You have Elena's, April's and my upstairs tenants' numbers if you need them? I told my tenants to be on the lookout for you."

"Yes, dear," she said in a bored tone.

"Remember the photos from when Jud and I first bought the

place? The living room overlooks the garage area. Make sure when she unpacks she doesn't drop boxes on my car. And don't give her a key. Make sure you keep my jewelry with you all the time. Stay in my bedroom and tell her to make it the last room she does. You can make that your base of operations since that's the most unpacked room at the moment. Or you could have her start with the basement studio and then you move down there. That might be best. Have her clear out the boxes and fix it up, then she can do my bedroom, then you move back up there. And don't let her look at any papers in my office."

"Any more orders?" Kate asked.

"No, ma'am," she said, then, putting on her perkiest attitude, cooed in a sing-song voice, "I love you."

"I'm sure you do."

"Listen, I don't know how often I can call you once I get to Iraq, since we're going to be on a really tight schedule and there's an eight-hour time difference. But I'll email. You don't mind doing this?"

"I don't mind. Stay safe, peanut. I love you."

"Love you, too, Mom. Thank you."

Le An sat on the side of the bed for a moment, missing her mother horribly, but quickly shook it off and walked over to the floor-to-ceiling windows which overlooked the Old City. There was something about Jerusalem which enticed. She couldn't quite identify it, but she knew she'd never felt it anywhere else in the world. No wonder Jews, Muslims and Christians fought over control of this tiny strip of real estate. Jerusalem was special.

After calling Doctor Hilson's room and arranging to meet him for dinner, Le An took a quick shower and changed into black pants, an ice-green cotton sweater and a black blazer, then slipped into black flats. Just as she was walking out the door, Barry phoned.

"One of our cameras is acting up," he said. "Probably because a bunch of baggage handlers drop-kicked it around the tarmac. I have to go to the bureau tomorrow and see if they have a camera I can take to Iraq."

"Go early," she said. "We leave for Jordan late morning. Wonder how the latest bombing here has affected the bureau."

USN's Jerusalem bureau, like most networks in Israel, employed Christians, Jews and Muslims and most producer-reporter-videographer teams were a mix of faiths. With travel frequently passing between Jewish and Arab-controlled areas, it helped to have one person who could act as intermediary with locals should trouble arise.

"Israel's always in war mode," said Barry. "Ollamh Fodhla, dudette."

"Ollamh Fodhla, dude. We're eating on the terrace if you need me."

Doctor Jacob Jeremy Winston Spencer-Hilson was already seated at the King's Garden Restaurant when Le An arrived. He stood when she and the maitre d' came to the white-clothed table and, with impeccable manners, helped her with her chair. The outdoor restaurant's ambiance was relaxing, the flickering candlelight and views of the old city mesmerizing.

"Do you prefer being called 'doctor' or 'professor'?" she asked, knowing some Ph.D.s were downright militant about being addressed as 'doctor.'

"I answer to either," he said in a proper British accent, then smiled.

"Doctor Jacob Jeremy Winston Spencer-Hilson. Do you go by Hilson or Spencer-Hilson?"

"Hilson. I rarely use Spencer," he said.

"I noticed you signed in at the front desk as 'Jeremy,' not 'Jacob.' You go by your middle name?"

"I prefer it, but I answer to either," he said.

"Are you related to Winston Churchill?" she asked.

"Distant cousin," he said and smiled.

"I've always admired him. Would you like us to reference you as Doctor Jeremy Hilson in our segments?"

"Yes, if you would."

"An archaeologist. That's an exciting profession. What made you choose it?" she asked.

"It's in the blood. My ancestors had been digging up artifacts around the world and collecting them for hundreds of years. It was a bit natural for me to follow in their footsteps. My grandfather always told me stories associated with some of the antiquities he, his father and his grandfather had collected."

"Is your family home like Castle Howard or Chatsworth?" she asked.

"Not quite on that scale," he said and shyly smiled as he

looked down at the table. "But somewhat similar. I take it you've visited those estates?"

"Years ago. I just remember their fabulous art collections: Gainsboroughs, Rubens, Rembrandts, da Vincis, Van Dycks, Italian sculptures, Egyptian artifacts. It amazes me to think one family could collect so many priceless works of art. How old is your family's estate?"

"Construction of the main house began in the 1600s, but various generations added wings."

"It sounds fabulous."

"The estate's smaller now," he said. "After both world wars my grandfather sold some of our land, art and artifacts in order to maintain what was left, as did my father after we'd moved into the house. Once, a rather large piece of stonework cracked off a balcony and crashed near my mum as we were leaving the house. It could have killed us. The cost is enormous to maintain that drafty old building. That's not even considering the taxes. By selling off some, my family's been able to keep our estate, but it's taken its toll. I don't envy my father or my brother. I consider it a blessing I was the third son and not the first. Many families find it's easier to sell everything and escape the financial burden."

"I guess with two older brothers you won't inherit your father's title and estate," she said.

"Quite sure not to inherit either. Both elder brothers have sons."

"Has your family opened your house for tours like some of the other estates?" she asked.

"Yes, which is good," he said. "The paintings and artifacts should be shared with others. We also have it for hire for weddings and such to bring in necessary funds to repair the ancient plumbing—which is practically an archaeological relic of its own."

Le An smiled, then asked, "How was your summer dig? Where were you?"

"Tel Hazor."

She picked up her napkin and placed it across her lap, nodding as if she knew where that was. Even though she was familiar with some of the country, she hadn't the slightest idea where Tel Hazor was located. Israel had hundreds, if not thousands, of active dig sites. Only archaeologists could keep them straight.

"Tel Hazor is the largest archeological site in Israel," he said, as if reading her thoughts.

"Oh. Do you only participate in the digs during the summer?"

He nodded. "Six to eight weeks during June and July. Normally in the fall I return to teaching, but I'm on sabbatical until next year."

"Do any of your students participate in the digs?" she asked.

"They do."

"They must be very dedicated," she said. "I imagine it's very hot, back-breaking work."

"It is. Much as I try to warn them, most have no idea how physically demanding it is," he said. "Some are dedicated and others merely picture themselves in a movie discovering golden arks or silver grails."

Le An smiled. "I bet you've found some really interesting things over the years."

He nodded. "Jewelry, pottery, tools, coins, idols, as well as written historical records carved into stone. One of our most exciting discoveries was in northern Israel during the summers of 1993 and 1994. We unearthed three stone fragments of the Tel Dan Stele dating from approximately the eighth or ninth century BCE. It bears the inscription 'House of David'—Israel's most famous king and his dynasty." He looked at her for recognition and when he didn't find any, he said, "The King David whose name this hotel borrowed."

"Oh, yes, of course," she said. "Archaeology sounds like very hard work."

"We're a hearty lot," he smiled. "I dare say much like journalists who brave war zones."

"We're a hearty lot," she smiled.

"It's a privilege to be able to unearth the remains and secrets of civilizations defeated in war—lest they be forgotten," he said. "Journalists report the wars as they're happening. Archaeologists dig up what's left hundreds or thousands of years on from those battles and report to later generations what happened. We all have our part in history."

"I never thought of it that way," she said.

After the waiter had taken their order, Jeremy said, "Tell me about yourself."

Le An took a quick sip of her wine. "I was raised in Charlotte,

North Carolina, but I was born in Vietnam."

"During the war?"

"Yes, my mother was Vietnamese—actually half-French, half-Vietnamese. My father was an American Air Force pilot. They married secretly in a Catholic ceremony, but US military and immigration wouldn't recognize the marriage unless it was performed on a US base in Vietnam and they wouldn't allow that until I was born. My father had to bribe every official in sight to smuggle me out. Getting me into America wasn't hard. It was getting me out of Vietnam that was tricky."

"So your father returned safely?"

"The first time, not the second. The Viet Cong shot him down and held him in the Hanoi Hilton," she said, referring to *Maison Centrale,* the notorious Hoa Lo prison in Hanoi. "We know that much from other pilots who were held with him. I don't know how much you know about it..."

"Not much, I'm afraid."

"Prisoners never really saw each other, but they used a tap code to communicate with each other. Some who got out confirmed my father had been there. We know he was moved to 'The Zoo,' another POW camp in Hanoi that was a film studio before the war and went back to that after."

"Did he die there?"

"We don't know. He wasn't released when other POWs came home at the end of the war. I went to Hanoi to search for information about him a few years ago. USN sent a crew with me and we did a segment on my story and two other Americans doing 'vision quests' to find some answers."

"And did you find answers?" he asked softly, his kind, blue eyes staring into hers.

Jeremy emitted a friendly, warm aura, but there was a distance about him as if he were engulfed in his own serenity bubble, above the chaos, cool and all-knowing.

"I kept hoping I'd turn a corner and he'd be there waiting for me," she said as she fingered her wine glass. "Isn't that crazy? The trip gave me a better idea where my mother lived her life and where my father had been. I wanted to know what he'd been through and what had happened to him. I believe he was alive at the end of the war. Personally, I think there were hundreds of POWs the North Vietnamese wouldn't release because they wanted to use them as leverage to get money out of America for rebuilding after the war. They probably kept them as slave labor when our government wouldn't negotiate. My family would have paid to get my father back. I know America's official line is everyone alive at the end came home, but there are a lot of us who don't believe that. There were too many sightings of Americans there years after the war ended."

"How tragic for your family," he said softly.

"A few years ago, the Vietnamese released the remains of some Americans and DNA confirmed my father was one of them. There was evidence of broken bones. We don't really know what happened. Maybe they killed him during interrogations, maybe he got sick, maybe he tried to escape and was killed. Maybe he lived there for years doing slave labor and had a whole other life. I don't know. No one knows. Or if they know, they won't talk."

"I'm dreadfully sorry."

"We were luckier than most," she said. "At least we had his remains to confirm it was him. There are still about 1,800 Americans unaccounted for in Vietnam. It's hard not knowing what happened to your loved one."

"Did your mum survive the war?" he asked, as the waiter put two plates in front of them and their appetizer in the center of the table—a platter of hummus, techina, stuffed vine leaves, vegetables, roasted eggplant, kubeh and falafel.

"When my father brought me back to America at the end of his first tour, my mother stayed in Vietnam to try and get her family out. She and my father thought it was temporary and they wouldn't be separated for long," she said as she motioned for him to dish up his plate first, but he nodded for her to proceed first.

As a producer, Le An was quick to question people she met and could usually get their life stories out of them within five minutes. It came naturally to her. People and their lives fascinated her and she was always on the lookout for *AmeriView* segments, but most people were never curious enough to question her. She was surprised to find Jeremy showed the same interest in people she did.

"Was your mother able to get her family out?" he asked.

"No, she and most of her family were killed in a mortar attack. The rest were conscripted into South Vietnam's army. My father took me to America at the end of his first tour and left me with his sister and her husband in Charlotte. He gave them legal guardianship in case anything happened to him and, eventually, they adopted me. He went back for a second tour because there was no word from my mother and he didn't know what had happened to her. When he got back to Vietnam, he found out she was dead."

"He was captured after that?"

"Yes," she said.

"It was fortunate you escaped the war and put down roots in a new country," he said. "As many have throughout history."

"I ended up with a great life. If I'd stayed there, I would have been killed or become an orphan, considered a 'child of the dirt' for not being full Vietnamese. Apparently, my mother had suffered a lot being mixed herself. She was illegitimate. Her French father—my grandfather—was a soldier there when Vietnam was France's colony. He abandoned my mother and my Vietnamese grandmother, never married her. The Vietnamese don't like half-breeds. You have to be full-blooded to be worth anything, to get an education, a job, or have a place to live. I probably would've ended up living on the street."

"Do you remember your father?"

"No, but my adoptive mom is his older sister and she always kept his memory alive. I did get his dog tags back, though. A man visiting Vietnam found a kid selling old tags, including my father's, so he bought all of them, brought them home, cleaned them up and tracked down the vets or their families. Such a wonderful person. Sent them to me and didn't ask for a dime. I thought what he was doing was so great, I produced a segment on him and a few other people doing the same thing. It was powerful to hold those tags and know they'd once been around my father's neck."

"Were you able to discover anything about your mother?" he asked.

"Not much. She looks beautiful in photos my father had. And I have his letters to his family describing her. They were very much in love, I know that much."

"Is MacDonald your father's or uncle's surname?" he asked.

"My father's. My uncle Bennett Grandison and my aunt Kate legally adopted me, but Kate wanted me to keep my father's last name for sentimental reasons. They're the only parents I've ever really known. The day before my fifteenth birthday, Bennett died in a plane crash. He was out flying with a buddy and the plane had mechanical problems. He was a wonderful dad, but I suppose I was destined to lose fathers as a result of plane crashes."

"I'm dreadfully sorry, my dear. Do you have any other family?"

"I have two older brothers—who are technically my first cousins. Neil and his wife are lawyers in Charlotte and Judson's a contractor in Charleston, South Carolina. His wife hates me, so that complicates things a bit."

"Why does she hate you?" he asked.

"Because I hate her and tried to keep him from marrying her," she said matter-of-factly, eliciting a chuckle from him. "She's a bad influence on him. It's changed our relationship a lot."

"The spelling of 'Le An'—is it Vietnamese?" he said.

"It is. Everyone pronounces it 'Lee Ann,' which I prefer, but technically, it should be pronounced 'Lye Awn.' '*Le*' was my grandmother's family name and means 'tears.' The family name always comes first. '*An*' is my given name and means 'peace.' I like to think of it as 'peace comes after tears.'"

"Quite profound," he said gently. "Your father was of Scottish descent?"

"Yes. My mother's discovered we're even descended from a Scottish king."

"A displaced princess, are you?" he smiled.

"I'm not going to start shopping for crowns, since I'm sure Amma will soon find mass-murderers, horse thieves and pirates hanging from the family tree."

"Which king?"

"I forget," she said. "It was two men's names and a 'the,' which was weird."

"Robert the Bruce?"

"That's it. You've heard of him?"

Jeremy fought back a smile. "I have. He's quite well known."

"Not to me. What's a 'Bruce'? Why is he called Robert *the Bruce*?" she asked.

"It's from '*de Bruis*'...'of Bruis' or Brix, a location in Normandy near Cherbourg. The family landed in Scotland the beginning of the twelfth century."

"They were French? I'm more French than I thought."

"Anglo-Norman descent," he said. "The Belgae, Celts and

Gauls were in Normandy as early as the fourth century BCE. The Normans were a mix of Saxons, Franks, Scandinavians, Norse, Danes and Gauls. They conquered England, Wales and Ireland."

"Wait a minute... all that memorizing I did for history exams is coming back," she said. "William of Norman and the Battle of Hastings in 1066, right?"

"Precisely. Excellent," he smiled.

"Ready to go over our schedule?" she asked as she pulled out two copies of their travel itinerary and handed one to him. "This is more or less how we plan to proceed. Since it's a war zone, I'm sure we'll have to make changes. By the way, have you had hostile environment training?"

"Not in many years," he said as he put on a pair of reading glasses. "Though I often work in hostile areas of the world. I've dealt with mad gunmen and talked myself out of many a dodgy situation, so you needn't worry about me."

"Oh," she said, a bit troubled by the revelation. "And USN knows you haven't been through recent training? They were OK with that?"

"They appeared to be."

"Well, OK, then," she said hesitantly, then returned to their itinerary. "We're planning to enter Iraq from the south and first travel to the southern marshes where the Garden of Eden was and..."

"It wasn't," he interrupted her.

"It's... I'm sorry... what?"

"There's no evidence the Garden of Eden was in southern Iraq," he said.

She was momentarily stunned. "But, I thought... I mean all the news organizations have been reporting that's the location."

"Yes, I know."

"They're all wrong? Every single international news agency is wrong?" she asked.

Great, she thought. *April's found a nut for an expert. Didn't she vet this guy?*

"Yes, they're all wrong," he said emphatically. "And they obviously didn't do their research. Did any of them bother to ask a biblical archaeologist?"

"Well... I... guess..." she stammered.

"I doubt it," he said. "The fact is... and we do want to go with facts, I assume... we have no way of knowing precisely where the Garden of Eden was located."

"We don't?"

"It was antediluvian."

"It was what?" she asked.

"Antediluvian. Pre-flood, to use layman's terms. The flood would have erased all evidence of the Garden of Eden and its landmarks."

"So you believe there was a flood? Jonah and the ark?"

He fought back a smile. "You mean Noah and the ark. Jonah was paired with the rather large fish."

"Oh, yeah, the whale..."

"Large fish," he corrected her.

"That's... that's what I meant," she mumbled and looked down at the itinerary.

"There's ample evidence of a catastrophic world flood," he said. "Did you know in the center of Australia, on the mountain the Aborigines call *Uluru*—Ayres Rock—there are fossils of sea creatures, including jellyfish, high above sea level? There are countless other examples, but, suffice it to say, continents, rivers, mountains, seas either disappeared, shifted or, in some cases, appeared where none had been prior. The earth broke open in spots and released a torrent of underground water. There's no way of knowing precisely where geographical landmarks were located prior to that."

She stared at the itinerary, wondering whether they should drop Eden and skip the marshes.

"You'll find writings from many ancient civilizations describe a worldwide flood," he continued, "such as Mesopotamia's Epic of Gilgamesh and the records in scripture your network has indicated it wants to use for this program. History is preserved when eyewitnesses write about an event. Or, in more modern times, when they're filmed, as you're doing."

"Taping. We're taping, not filming," she corrected him.

"Many ancient civilizations recorded their history in written records. In the case of Mesopotamia, hundreds of thousands of those records still exist. Following generations re-recorded that information in new historical records, sometimes citing the original author. That's how history is preserved. It's passed down from generation to generation."

She glanced at the research notes April had prepared for her. "But don't those written records say the Tigris and Euphrates rivers are associated with Eden? They come together outside Basra near the mouth of the Persian Gulf, so why wouldn't Iraq's southern marshes be the location?"

Jeremy motioned for her to hand him her notebook and pen. "The scriptural account says a river flowed through Eden, then split and became the headwaters of four rivers—headwaters being the key word. It's where a river originates. The Tigris and Euphrates, called the Dijla and Furat in Arabic, don't originate in Iraq's southern marshes. Their headwaters are in the mountains of Turkey. They're flowing the wrong way for your theory to work."

He began sketching a rough outline of the countries of the Middle East.

"Because water flows down to a lower elevation, not up," she said, beginning to feel April hadn't done adequate enough research.

"Precisely. The scriptural account of Eden, which is from Moses' records dated approximately 1443 BCE, names the four rivers: the Pishon, the Hiddekel, the Gihon and the Euphrates, which is the only one with the same name today," he said, still sketching.

"What happened to the Tigris?" she asked, looking at her research material.

"It may have been the Hiddekel. We can only guess where the four rivers were located because, no doubt, the flood erased them or changed their course, but there are some clues. Written information after the flood said the Pishon encompassed the land of Havilah, where gold and onyx were located, possibly near today's Saudi Arabia, though we can't know for sure. The Hiddekel flowed east toward Assyria—today's northern Iraq. And the Gihon was said to encompass the land of Cush, which is Africa. Gihon provides the clue Eden might have been farther west than Iraq. Here..."

He turned the notebook toward her and she could see four lines representing rivers radiating outward from the ancient city like spokes on a wheel.

"Jerusalem?" she gasped. "You think Eden was here?"

"Do you know which stream runs beneath this city?"

She shook her head 'no.'

"The Gihon," he said.

"Gihon, as in one of the four rivers out of Eden?" she asked, wide-eyed. "You think it flowed from Jerusalem to Africa?"

He shrugged. "Who knows? It's quite possible. It's also possible Eden was in the northern mountains of today's Turkey. Some believe a place called Gobekli Tepe in eastern Turkey was Eden. Nine years ago, a Kurdish shepherd discovered the area. The German Archaeological Institute in Istanbul headed the excavation, uncovering scores of large stones with carvings of lions, serpents, reptiles, boars and ducks."

Le An sighed and stared at the itinerary in front of her, thinking out loud how they could make changes. "All right, we'll cross off Eden. We still need to go to some sites south of Baghdad like Ur and Babylon, but it's gotten pretty dangerous on parts of the highway north of Umm Qasr. Robbers wait for convoys crossing the border from Kuwait. Maybe we should drive into Iraq from Jordan. It's a ten-hour drive through the desert, but doable. Or we could go to Camp Doha—that's Central Command's forward operating base outside Kuwait City—and hitch a ride on a military flight into Baghdad. Terrifying landing, but maybe the best."

"Whatever you wish."

As the waiter started clearing their appetizer dishes, Barry approached their table and extended a hand to Jeremy.

"Professor? I'm Barry Spirelli. Do you go by Jacob, Jake or Jeremy?"

"I prefer Jeremy. Pleasure to meet you," he said.

"Jeremy it is," said Barry.

"The Garden of Eden wasn't in Iraq," said Le An.

"What? How much wine have you chucked back? Jeremy, you may need to straighten her out."

"Eden may have been in Turkey or right here in Jerusalem," she said, holding up Jeremy's sketch. "Apparently all the networks have been wrong locating it in Iraq's southern marshes."

"That's insane," he snorted and laughed. "Oh, I get it. You're jerking my chain."

"Nope, not kidding," she said.

"We're not 'jerking your chain,'" Jeremy smiled, enunciating as though the words were foreign to his lips.

"We'll be the network with a different take on Eden," she said, then quickly added, "Are you joining us for dinner?"

"No, I already ate," said Barry. "Just came to tell you April needs to talk to you, so call her as soon as you can."

"I'll call when I get back to my room," she said. "Since the southern marshes are out, we'll change our itinerary."

"If we can avoid that southern highway, it might be safer," said Barry. "Road banditos have been attacking cars coming out of Umm Qasr up Highway 8. We could book passage on a military flight out of Doha and fly into Baghdad."

"That's what I was thinking," she said. "I'll get April to make the arrangements. We'll have to let Skylar know to stay in Baghdad."

"Or not," grinned Barry. "The threat reports show trouble between Baghdad and Babil. Much as you hate it, we might need to travel with military convoys. Security reports were recommending Highway 8, but now they say all roads including Highway 1 between Al Hillah and Baghdad are 'no go' zones. Not that it ever stops us, but just thought you should know."

"I'll see what the Baghdad bureau recommends," she said. "Al Hillah's near Babylon, right?"

"Ten kilometers south of Babylon," said Jeremy.

"That's what? A little more than half a mile?" she asked. "And before I forget, could you remember when you're on camera to use miles instead of kilometers?"

"Certainly. I do for my American students."

"Jeremy, I'm sure we'll be spending a lot of time together the next few weeks," said Barry. "Goodnight you two, or as Le An would say, 'Goodnight, *y'all*.'" He laughed as he mocked her accent, then winked, patted her on her back and said, "Ollamh Fodhla!"

"Ollamh Fodhla!" she laughed as he walked away.

"Sorry?" Jeremy asked and cocked his head slightly.

"Ollamh Fodhla. It's a running joke Barry and I have had since Ireland."

At the mention of Ireland, he raised his eyebrows.

"It was something our sound guy said to us. It's nothing. It's... it's stupid," she said, waving her hand and almost knocking over her glass of wine, prompting him to reach out and steady it. "We were passing Four Courts in Dublin and Sean said before the building burned during Ireland's civil war, the dome had carvings of famous lawmakers like Moses..."

"Law*givers*," he said.

"Lawgivers. Do you know the building?" she asked.

"I know it well."

"Really? Sean said one of the lawgivers on the dome was Ollamh Fodhla…"

"Yes. He had a great influence on Ireland and is quite revered there," he said as the waiter placed their dinner plates in front of them. "There are wildly varying dates for when he lived, but the most accurate appears to be the sixth century BCE."

"I've never heard of him," she said.

Jeremy picked up his fork with his left hand, flipped it over and stabbed a piece of sea bream with the sweet potato under it, then used his knife to load the back of the fork with vegetables, mashing them down slightly so they wouldn't fall off. Le An watched him, thinking the Brits, for all their sophistication, could look so uncouth when they ate.

"I brought something I thought you'd like to see," she said, pulling out the *Irish Times* article she'd saved from Dublin. "The Irish are planning to build a highway through a place called the Hill of Tara."

Jeremy's head jerked up, an alarmed look on his face. "Tara? They're building a motorway through the Hill of Tara? Impossible."

He took the newspaper, shaking his head in disbelief as he read the article by the flickering candlelight.

"Only archaeologists should be digging at Tara," he whispered. "This is utterly horrendous."

12

Jerusalem
Sunday, 31 August 2003

Jeremy stared at the article about the proposed construction near the Hill of Tara, continuing to shake his head in disbelief.

"I understand Tara was the ancient seat of Ireland's high kings," Le An said after a few minutes, finally breaking the silence.

"Yes. It's so sacred, they haven't allowed archaeologists to dig in some areas, yet they're going to have lorries roll through, destroy it, then cover it with tar. I can't tell you how utterly shocking this is. If we weren't going to Iraq, I'd be on a flight to the UK to see if someone is organizing a protest." He shook his head again and sighed deeply, then took off his glasses and set aside the article. "Well, we'll have to scuttle that for a fortnight. Your network hired me to discuss locations in Iraq which correspond to scripture. I've seen the research Miss Greenlaw provided, but as diligent as your associates are, I don't entirely trust the accuracy of those unfamiliar with my profession. If you'll allow me..."

"Absolutely. Our research can't compare to your years of experience," she said, knowing she would still fact-check everything he told her.

"More than once, Jerusalem's been conquered, destroyed and burned," he said as he stretched out his right hand toward the Mount of Olives. "Do you know what a 'tell' is?"

"It's a hill, right? Do they spell it with one 'l' or two?" she asked as she wrote it down.

"Both ways. In Israel, it's one. For the sake of conformity, let's use two," he said. "Yes, it's an artificial hill comprised of ruins from older settlements—cities built atop older conquered or destroyed cities. Jerusalem fell more than 2,500 years ago—in 586 BCE—to Babylon and King Nebuchadnezzar."

"BCE's the same as BC, right?" she asked.

"Most archaeologists don't use BC and AD anymore. BCE and CE have come into use in the last decade: BCE for 'Before Common Era' has replaced BC for 'Before Christ;' and CE for 'Common Era' has replaced AD, the Latin *Anno Domini* which translates 'in the year of the Lord.' Some Christians say the change is too secular. Personally, I find it cumbersome adding the third letter to BCE."

"Let's stick with BC and AD," she said. "BCE and CE will confuse our viewers. They sound too much alike. You said Jerusalem fell to Nebuchadnezzar. The same Nebuchadnezzar Saddam Hussein's been trying to channel for years?"

"The same. Though I suspect Saddam doesn't want the same thing to happen to him which happened to Nebuchadnezzar."

"What's that?" she asked.

"Nebuchadnezzar went rather daft for seven years, crawled on all fours, ate grass, quite out of his mind. During that time, his top government official, a Jew named Daniel—or Belteshazzar, as Nebuchadnezzar called him—ran the kingdom for him, kept it intact for those seven years, then returned control to him when he came to his senses. That's Daniel in the lion's den, if you know your scriptures."

"I don't know them, but I do vaguely remember that story from Sunday school," she said. "I think Saddam would have a fit if he thought a Jew was running his country for seven minutes, let alone seven years. Have you seen his statue near the Iraq border honoring his scud attacks on Israel during the '91 Gulf War?"

"I have," he said. "What's your religious background, if I may ask?"

"I don't really do religion, but when I was a kid we were Episcopalians," she said. "How did a Jew end up controlling Iraq?"

"Babylon, not Iraq," he corrected her, "Daniel was a member of the Jewish royal family, probably a teenager, taken captive in Nebuchadnezzar's first invasion of Jerusalem—approximately 605 BC. He and his three friends were amongst those trained in Babylonian ways and language, a three-year course instructing them how to serve Nebuchadnezzar. Daniel eventually rose to prominence in the government."

"Get them young and flip them to your side? So Iraq and Israel have a shared history?"

"They do. Allow me to share information about Israel which might help you understand the historical context of some places we'll be visiting. What happened millennia ago set the stage for current world events, particularly here in the Middle East, so I consider it vitally important."

"Absolutely," she said.

"To begin with: King David and his descendants ruled from Jerusalem in an unbroken dynasty for nineteen generations—more than 400 of the nation's 800-year existence. A generation didn't pass without a descendant of King David's ruling."

"I never think of Israel existing 800 years," she said. "The US has only existed for a little more than 200 years. I can't imagine George Washington's descendants—even though he didn't have any—being the only presidents ever, though I guess your British royal family's existed for that many generations."

"Quite a bit more. Are you interested in a sweet?" he asked.

They'd both finished their meal, their knives and forks perfectly parallel across the centers of both their plates, a signal to the waiter to remove them. Le An had been raised to out-British the British when it came to proper table etiquette.

"I'd love coffee and something chocolate," she said, as a busboy removed their dinner plates. "Care to split a dessert?"

He lifted his left hand slightly and caught the waiter's eye. After placing their order, he continued, "Some in the House of David were good rulers, some brutal and evil."

"Everything from George Washington to Idi Amin?"

"Precisely. King Josiah was Judah's last good king, but he was killed in battle against the Egyptians. Four more kings ruled after him—his three sons and a grandson, all of them utterly horrendous. A few were popular with the people, but popularity doesn't indicate a good ruler."

"Popularity wins elections," she said.

"I imagine people would be better served if their rulers served them rather than being slaves of popularity."

"That's an interesting way to put it," she said.

"Ultimately, a ruler's moral character and wise advisors determine how well he or she reigns. It's not popularity or strategizing politically."

Their waiter brought their coffee, dessert bowls and a chocolate, pyramid-shaped treat, drenched in rum and filled with raisins, along with a pitcher of thick cream—Jeremy's specific request. Le An was always amused at how her British friends loved to drench every dessert in cream—even cake, fruit and pie.

"This is wonderful," said Le An as she downed a spoonful.

Jeremy smiled and nodded. "Delighted we're dining at the hotel's dairy restaurant. I'd hate to have to endure a sweet without cream."

The King David Hotel had separate meat and dairy restaurants: a necessity since those who ate kosher diets were forbidden from mixing the two.

"Of the last four kings who ruled here in Jerusalem," Jeremy continued, "one died in an Egyptian prison and Nebuchadnezzar conquered the last three. He killed one and locked another in a Babylonian prison. The utterly un-wise advisors to the last king, Zedekiah, convinced him to rebel against Babylon and start a war. In return, Nebuchadnezzar surrounded Jerusalem for eighteen months. Food ran out and some Jews resorted to cannibalism."

"Where we're eating, they were eating each other?" asked Le An, grimacing.

"Yes. A rather ghastly subject to discuss while dining," he said. "The Babylonians captured Zedekiah as he tried to escape, then blinded him and locked him in prison. The Babylonians stole anything of value, burned Jerusalem and pulled down the walls."

"Imagine if enemy troops burned Washington to the ground. Oh, wait, you Brits did try that in the summer of 1814, didn't you?" she teased.

"Sorry, so sorry," he smiled.

"Now I understand why Nebuchadnezzar is Saddam's role model," she said. "He conquered Jerusalem and enslaved the Jews. Saddam would love to replicate that."

"Indeed. There was one wise man who kept telling Zedekiah and his counselors to surrender to Nebuchadnezzar. He said they'd be taken captive, but would eventually make a life for themselves in Babylon, as had the Jews taken captive years before."

"Like Daniel?"

"Precisely. Daniel and his three friends proved their loyalty to Nebuchadnezzar and were given high positions of authority." He poured more cream on his dessert. "Decades on, after the Medes and Persians conquered Babylon, they permitted Jewish exiles to return to Jerusalem and rebuild the temple, but, by then, many were unwilling to return. They were leading such prosperous lives in Babylon and their families had grown so much, exactly as promised, that they were quite unwilling to leave."

"You called the man who told them to surrender wise. Are you saying rulers should always surrender?"

"By no means. I remember my parents discussing Hitler's bombing blitz on Britain during World War Two. Hitler wanted us to surrender and I'm rather glad we didn't. Different times call for different actions. There were Jewish kings who refused to surrender and their nation was miraculously saved. Wisdom comes in knowing when to surrender and when to fight. At times, fighting is the better choice; at others, surrender should be considered."

"We covered the assault last month on the Mosul house where Uday and Qusay Hussein were hiding," she said. "They were ordered to surrender, but they were probably wise to fight to the death. There are too many Iraqis who wanted to execute them. But if someone told our country to surrender to a foreign power, I don't think that would go over too well."

"Nor in the UK. For a while, Nebuchadnezzar was willing to spare those who surrendered. However, the longer the siege wore on, the less generous he felt."

"Who was this wise surrender-advocate?" she asked.

"His name was Jeremiah."

"What happened to him?" she asked.

"The Babylonians took him captive, along with 800 other Jews still alive in Jerusalem," he said. "Jeremiah was a lone voice of reason, but King Zedekiah chose instead to listen to evil advisors and the religious leaders. The priests told him he'd be victorious, even as the Babylonians were breaching Jerusalem's walls, but then they'd also told him Nebuchadnezzar would never attack Judah."

"Sounds like the Iraqi Information Minister we nicknamed

Baghdad Bob," she said. "US troops controlled the airport and were inside Baghdad and he kept telling the press the Americans weren't there."

"I remember. He was quite amusing," said Jeremy and smiled, then continued. "Judah's priests had strayed far from the religious beliefs of King David. Instead, they practiced a mix of traditional and pagan rituals, including human sacrifice."

"How horrible."

"Utterly."

Le An looked out over the old city, trying to imagine what it had been like in the last days before Babylonian troops conquered it.

"Jerusalem wasn't a poor village," continued Jeremy. "It was one of the wealthiest cities on earth. During King Solomon's reign, gold was abundant and silver was as common as stones."

"That's pretty wealthy," she said.

"Jerusalem had been the perfection of beauty, but no one could save her. She paid for her peoples' unfaithful ways and her enemies rejoiced as they watched her die."

13

Camp Doha, Kuwait
Wednesday, 3 September 2003

Le An, Barry and Jeremy had to wait almost a day at Camp Doha in Kuwait before a US Air Force C-130 Hercules finally had enough space to fly them into Baghdad.

After climbing up a large rear ramp at the back of the Herk and settling in, crews loaded large pallets of heavy equipment and supplies behind them, blocking their exit. Some light cargo and baggage were packed along both sides behind red-strapped mesh curtains. The only seats were long benches running lengthwise, the mesh-curtains forming a back rest for passengers who faced each other across the narrow center aisle. Anyone crossing their legs had to be careful not to kick the shins or groins of people across from them.

Le An adjusted her bullet-proof vest and took a sip from her water bottle, the heat inside the fuselage almost unbearable. She decided if the plane didn't take off soon and cool off in the higher elevations, she'd take her chances and chuck the vest until they landed.

"You going to be OK with the landing, Jeremy?" she asked. "It can get a little rough going into Baghdad. The pilots come in hot and go into a steep drop to avoid surface-to-air missiles. Your ears pop, the G's kill you, then you hit the tarmac. It's kind of a rush, but some people freak out."

"I'll be quite all right," he smiled.

She felt pretty secure in the Herk, probably because she'd flown this route into Baghdad's airport twice the last few months and knew what to expect. The pilots were some of the best in the world. She'd fly with a military pilot any day. But the more she flew and the older she got, the less she liked air travel. It wasn't just the complications of customs and security checks. There'd been too many flights where she'd experienced close calls, usually on sketchy airlines from third-world countries with equally sketchy pilots flying ancient planes which never received proper maintenance.

As she stuffed a pair of Air-Force-issued, green-and-orange earplugs into her ears, she glanced across at Barry, his eyes closed trying to endure the heat.

After more than an hour, the Herk suddenly plunged downward, then quickly leveled out as it slammed into the tarmac at Baghdad International, formerly Saddam Hussein Airport.

The US Army had established a large complex of bases on the grounds, using Saddam's former 450,000-square-foot Al-Faw Palace as their headquarters and command center. The sixty-two-room palace, with its ornate French-provincial gold furniture and twenty-nine bathrooms, was Saddam's poor attempt to recreate France's Versailles Palace.

Before the war, the complex had been a resort for Saddam's elite, a place where leaders from around the Arab world had hunted imported exotic animals or fished in large man-made lakes, created by diverting irrigation water from farmers. Water meant power to Iraqis and Saddam wanted everyone to see he was the one who held that power.

Nine palaces at the resort had borne names such as 'Victory over Kuwait' and 'Victory over Iran,' where helmets from dead Iranians were embedded in an arc above the double front doors. The 'Victory over America' palace had been under construction when US troops bombed it.

The largest American base at the complex was Camp Victory, a tent city built to accommodate about 12,000 troops. Soldiers were teaming up with Iraqi contractors to construct a forty-foot-wide road to relieve traffic jams there. Three other bases—Camp Striker, Camp Slayer and Camp Liberty, which had originally been Camp Victory North—occupied the rest of the complex, along with American fast-food restaurants—an alternative to MREs and mess halls.

Six members of Dark Knight Security, part of the team guarding USN's Baghdad villa, and three heavily up-armored SUVs were waiting for Le An and her team. After leaving the airport grounds, they made an adrenaline-pumping, seven-and-a-half-mile, high-speed dash into Baghdad along the Qadisiyah Expressway—"Route Irish." Nicknamed after the Fighting Irish of Notre Dame, the road was one of the deadliest in the world, a magnet for snipers and suicide bombers who averaged at least one attack a day.

Le An was glad to see USN's Baghdad bureau was now a large, gated, mud-colored villa in one of Baghdad's wealthy residential neighborhoods—a welcome improvement from the seedy hotel they'd been in right after the invasion, but still hideous according to her tastes. Growing up in an upper-middle-class neighborhood of Charlotte, North Carolina, she was used to exquisite, tasteful architecture, with interiors straight out of *Southern Accents* magazine—and this wasn't even close.

Her green eyes squinted in disgust at the ugly ceramic tiles glued to the exterior.

Probably filled with tacky gold furniture, she thought.

Wealthy Middle Easterners seemed to have a fondness for gold everything.

"Hootie hoo!" Le An called out to bureau chief Mike Carmichael as they entered the front door.

"Look what the cat dragged in," Mike said as he gave her a hug, then pointed at Barry. "You had to bring this guy? Didn't I tell you not to bring home strays?"

Barry flicked his hand under his chin mafia-style.

"Did you bring the groceries I asked for?" Mike asked.

"I did," she said, "including your macadamias."

He pulled her bags from her hands.

"Gimme. Which one's it in? We just started cocktail hour. What can I get *y'all?*" He swung out on the word in a fake Southern accent mocking her, then extended a hand to Jeremy. "Hi there. Mike Carmichael. I'll be your bureau chief cruise director this trip."

"Jeremy Hilson. Pleasure."

"Ah, the archaeologist, right? What can I pour you, Jeremy?"

"I'd fancy a good whiskey."

"We've got the best Scotch in Baghdad, courtesy of that guy," said Mike, pointing to the end of the enormous entry hallway where a tall figure with his back to them was deep in conversation on his cellphone.

Le An glanced at the benevolent whiskey provider, but couldn't see his face. "Room assignments, Mikey. I'm sure Jeremy would like to get settled after our relaxing trip."

Mike snorted a laugh and pulled out a clipboard. "Roller coaster drop into Saddam Air, huh? You know the CPA wonks have been quietly opting lately to chopper from the airport instead of taking Route Irish."

"Leave the real world to the little people," she said. "Though I'm not sure which is scarier: riding in a low-flying RPG target or taking Route Irish."

Choppers terrified Le An, both the commercial ones she and her videographers used to get aerial shots for stories and the military ones flying through war zones. Either way, she was always convinced they were about to crash and burn. In Iraq, her fear was well founded since insurgents frequently aimed surface-to-air missiles at them.

"Numbers are taped to the doors upstairs," said Mike. "Barry's in with Skylar in room six and we'll give Jeremy his own room in four so he has a quiet, sane place to recover. Top of the stairs is your room, princess—room one. You're bunking with Kerin Karlsen from that Danish newspaper I can never pronounce."

"Is Margaret Kirkwood still here?"

"Yeah, she's unhappily bunking with Michelle Melois, some French-wire-service chick no one can understand. Woman's got a foul temper. Use your pathetic French and see if you can figure out what her problem is," he grumbled as he ducked back into his office. "Welcome home, honey. We missed you. Hope you like the new digs."

"Definitely a step up from that death-trap hotel we were in before," she said.

Barry and Jeremy grabbed their bags and headed up the opulent, curving staircase to settle into their rooms, but Le An stayed downstairs and called after them, "Hurry back for happy hour."

"Count on it," Barry yelled.

Their noise caused the mysterious whiskey benefactor to plug his free ear with his finger so he could finish his conversation.

"Oops, sorry," she whispered, then asked Mike, "Who is that?"

"Hugh."

"Who?"

"Hugh."

"Hugh who?"

Before Mike could explain, one of the phones rang and when he'd hung up, Le An started peppering him with questions to bring her up to speed on what was going on.

"Is Khaled here? Is he doing sound and translating for us?" she asked as she dug into one of her bags and produced the cans of macadamia nuts she'd brought him.

"I love ya, ya hear me. It's love. Total love." He grabbed her head, his big beefy hands mashing both her ears as he planted a big kiss on her forehead, his day-old stubble raking across her skin. Popping open one of the cans, he offered her first dibs. "Yeah, Khaled's your sound man. He was pretty psyched to hear you and Barry were coming back. You must have brainwashed the poor, crazy thing. He's out with Sky and Margaret right now. They're traveling with the military working on a story over in Fallujah. They'll be back later."

"Fallujah? Aren't they still having problems with IED and RPG attacks there? Fedayeen's all over that area."

"That's the story they're working on," he said. "Fedayeen, or whoever, is popping more than a dozen attacks a day in the Sunni Triangle."

The triangle-shaped Sunni Muslim stronghold of Saddam's Ba'athist and tribal supporters stretched 100 miles north from Baghdad to Tikrit and southwest to Ramadi.

"Is the ambassador slash proconsul in country?" she asked, referring to the American administrator of Iraq.

"He's around. Just got back from the States a few days ago. Came back as soon as he heard about Friday's car bombings in Najaf. Why? Do you need SOTs from him for something?"

"I might. That and it's always amusing to hear the government's glossed-over version of events."

"The other day in a presser some newbie reporter asked if CPA knew there were gas shortages and some government wonk looks at his clipboard and says, 'But it says there's plenty.' Do these people ever get out of their fairy-tale Green Zone?"

"The proconsul does, but apparently the others don't," she said. "That's why I prefer dealing with the military. At least they know what's going on."

"I got news for you, Mac, nobody knows what's going on," he snorted. "How can you fact check anything? The khaki-wearing wonks at CPA say one thing, the military says something else,

Sunnis something else, Shiites something completely different and Kurds just want their own country. People are ratting out neighbors they hate, saying they're terrorists, and most aren't. Just warmed-over vendettas. The military can't fact check and neither can we."

"Fact checking's pretty much out the door here," she said.

"We shoot it and feed it," said Mike. "There're so many freakin' stories every day we can't get to them all. Carjackings and kidnappings are up among the locals. Crime's off the charts and there are no police. We're feeding stuff to New York twenty-four-seven and we're just scratching the surface. I've got a story I want to assign, but I can't find anyone with enough free time to do it."

"What is it?" she asked.

"Saddam closed down all the banks after the first Gulf War, so Iraqis started keeping their money at home. Then when the banks reopened, the exchange rate was pathetic, so they still kept their life savings at home. Since they don't want it ripped off, they're all armed like Texans. US military comes calling in the middle of the night, Iraqis open the door toting their guns because they think they're being robbed and *bang*! American soldiers shoot them. And, P.S., the soldiers come stomping into their houses wearing boots, an insult because you're supposed to take your shoes off when you go in an Iraqi house. Now Iraqis who supported us hate us."

"Didn't anyone in the State Department bother to examine Iraqi customs before this mess?" she sighed.

"Shoo, baby, Pentagon and White House don't do no State Department."

"Don't get me started," she said. "They expect the military to do nation building when they never had a plan."

"Government wonks claim there were secret plans for nation building."

"So secret no one knew," she said. "Marines and Army folks break things. They kick in doors, shoot to kill and blow up stuff. That's what they're trained to do. What do they know about nation building when the White House doesn't even know? They're asking these guys to do stuff they're not trained to do. Unless they deliberately wanted to create chaos and never intended to do nation building. Maybe they wanted Muslims to turn on each other so they'd leave the West alone."

"Then why not get out now and leave Iraq a chaotic mess?" he asked. "Let it go into sectarian infighting and have one big civil war while the Coalition skips off into the sunset singing *Kumbaya*. Problem solved and we save money. Big mess, but no more soldiers dying."

"Because the world would skewer America more than it already does. You break it, you fix it."

"Leave it to Republicans to start a war," he said.

"Oh, Dems have done the same, my friend. Remember a little war called Vietnam?" she asked. "My father died there as a POW, so I'm not big on military dying in a useless war. I started off thinking this one could have a positive outcome, get rid of a horrible dictator and we could help the Iraqis, but now I think the whole thing's ridiculous."

"Snarky from the plane ride?" he asked.

"No, probably from the heat, Route Irish and the fact I've finally decided I want to take a vacation," she said. "So what's the proconsul up to?"

"He's banging his head on his desk on a daily basis trying to get the Iraqi Governing Council to shape up. Uphill battle. Man's gotta be working on a major ulcer. Wouldn't want his job. Wouldn't want to be him. A lot of mortar rounds and rockets have been hitting in and around the Green Zone the last few weeks. They think they're coming from the southwest across the Tigris. So far they haven't hit near us."

They both superstitiously knocked on the Louis XV seafoam-and-gold-painted dining room table now serving as the base for feed decks.

"Was this the dining room?" asked Le An, looking around the room and up at the opulent chandelier.

"One of three... well, four if you count the breakfast room. You should see the main one down the hall. Three living rooms, including one with cushions all over it; two kitchens: one for real, one for show, which is weird, but all these mini-palaces are like that. The house has ten bedrooms and fourteen bathrooms, a pool and two guest houses out back DK guards are using for their personal quarters. Liquor store owned by Christians down the street. All the Westerners are giving them great business. I'm sure the Shi'a are in an uproar over that."

"Do wealthy Middle Easterners have the worst taste ever or what?" she asked as she looked around the room. "Gold doors? Do they have to slap gold on everything?"

"Better than that flea-ridden hotel we were in before."

"Oh, I definitely prefer this to the el-ranko-rancid hotel, but it's so *nouveau riche gauche*," she said. "Those Najaf bombings on Friday were nasty. That'll start a holy war between the Shi'ites and Sunnis, sure as shootin'. You got a casualty count?"

"Rough figures are 124 dead and 142 injured. Before I forget, Paul wants you to call him to let him know you got here in one piece."

"Sweet, but I suspect he's more worried about Jeremy's safe arrival than ours, other than checking to see if he should cash in our insurance policies," she said.

"You mean he doesn't give a 'tiny rat's ass'?" Mike smirked. "We've got a satellite on the roof which gives us direct phone lines to network in New York. Phones in every room along with two-way radios linked directly to DK security. We've got internet and we're feeding to New York twenty-four hours a day."

"You said that already."

"I'm losing my mind," he said. "I'd love an actual eight hours of sleep."

"Wouldn't we all."

"Still having nightmares?" he asked.

"Isn't everyone? I think this place will be with all of us for a long time," she said. "What else you got?"

"Word is members of Iraq's new Council are being sworn in," he said. "We'll get a crew over to CPA. Americans are turning over authority to Polish troops in some places in country today and the Brits are doing a 'pip pip' splendid job in the south."

"Yes, the Brits are doing a 'pip pip' splendid job, aren't they?" said someone with a Scottish brogue honed to reflect a more refined English tone. "So we meet again."

Le An turned to see the tall, mysterious 'whiskey benefactor' who'd been on his cellphone as they'd come in. His face was familiar. She didn't remember his name, but did remember he'd been a reporter for their sister news organization based in London. And she vividly remembered the details of that awful day when they'd first met.

"Well, hi. I know you," she said. "From New York... 9/11, right?"

"That's right. Hugh Rose, BTN News," he said, shaking hands with her. "Your network allowed us to edit in your facilities after our bureau in the World Trade Center was destroyed on 9/11. You were particularly brilliant in accommodating us."

"Y'all would have done the same for us, I'm sure. Le An MacDonald."

Hugh and his three-person crew—the entire BTN news bureau in Manhattan—had been in front of One World Trade Center waiting to tape the arrival of the Duchess of York. She'd scheduled an 8:45 meeting on the 101st floor in the offices of her charity, but was running late after interviews on the morning news shows. Hugh, his crew and the charity's staff were waiting in the lobby of the north tower for her when the first plane—American Airlines flight 11 out of Boston—hit the building at 8:46.

Immediately the BTN crew had shifted their story from duchess to disaster. They'd wisely decided not to return to their offices, choosing instead to shoot the mayhem on the streets around them. They'd barely escaped with their lives when both towers collapsed and, shortly after, had run out of tape. That's when they'd shown up at Le An's network, covered in dust and begging for editing machines, access to phones, satellite feeds—and more tape. Fortunately for BTN, that morning Hugh and his crew had decided to shoot with their American-format camera instead of the British-format most UK news crews used, so their camera was compatible with the tapes they borrowed from USN.

Le An had helped them as much as she could, even allowing them to crowd into her own small office until they finally were able to rent space in another building.

"You were an enormous help," said Hugh.

"Glad we could help."

"MacDonald? A wee bit of Scot in ye?" he asked, a slight smile crossing his lips.

"A wee bit," she smiled. "Half Scottish-American. My father was of Scottish descent."

She suddenly realized the days after 9/11 had left them all so frantic, overworked and stressed out, they'd never done proper introductions or learned much about each other. She wasn't sure she'd ever even known his last name.

"Your accent sounds a wee bit Scottish," she said.

"A wee bit you say?" he smiled. "I fancy I've been with those vile English too long. Aye, I'm a Scot. And I'm not the one toting the accent here. You ought to be ashamed, calling yourself Clan MacDonald and having that Yank accent."

"I'm a Southerner, not a Yankee," she corrected him. "Wouldn't be caught dead with a Yankee accent."

"Sorry?"

"Not a Yank. Sou-thern-er," she said slowly, enunciating each syllable. "Not a Yankee."

"Yeah, *y'all*," said Mike. "Don't ever call Boone a Yankee. She'll smack you silly."

Hugh's lips parted in a smile. "Sorry, 'Boone' did he say?"

"One of Mikey's many nicknames for me," she said.

"For Daniel Boone," Mike said in a fake hillbilly-Southern accent, "because she's from North Carolina."

"Sorry?" Hugh looked puzzled.

"Daniel Boone was an explorer in America," she said. "Blazed trails from North Carolina through the Cumberland Gap into Tennessee, Kentucky and farther west."

"Do you blaze trails?" Hugh asked.

"I try. As Boone famously said, 'I've never been lost, but I will admit to being confused for several weeks.'"

Hugh threw back his head and let out a loud laugh. "Brilliant. I must remember that. Boone it is then."

"I didn't say I actually liked that nickname," she said.

"Or you can call her Princess," Mike said as he threw an arm around her.

"Are you a princess?" Hugh asked amused.

"We call her that because she's picky and opinionated," said Mike. "But we love her anyway."

"It's because I'm a stickler for facts, not because I'm difficult," she said.

"Oh, she's difficult," said Mike. "But we love her anyway."

She rolled her eyes. "Are you still based in New York?"

"No, I went into Afghanistan with UK troops during the initial invasion," said Hugh. "I'm out of London now, but usually abroad. And yourself?"

"Still based in New York, but I've been in and out of here since

'Iraqi Freedom.' I'm in country for a short time producing a special about Iraq. We're traveling with a British archaeologist."

"Who? I might know him."

"Doctor Jeremy Hilson."

"Hilson... Oxford professor, yeah?" he asked.

"Not at the moment. He's been teaching in the States for a few years. Did you attend Oxford?"

"I did," said Hugh.

Shortly after Barry and Jeremy had rejoined them for drinks, Skylar, Margaret and Khaled came in from their day's assignment. Khaled enthusiastically greeted Le An and Barry, grabbing and holding Barry's hand, an Iraqi custom between close men friends which Barry found humiliating and uncomfortable—an affront to the heterosexual, macho image he always projected.

Skylar pinned Le An to the wall, enveloping her in a bear hug.

"You're here!" he beamed, then added in a low tone only she could hear, "I've missed you horribly."

She shot Barry a disgusted look, pushed away Skylar, then caught Hugh's amused look.

"Yes, you are horrible," she said as she patted the middle of Skylar's chest to give him one more shove away from her. "Don't grope the producer, Sky."

"Party tonight down the street," he said, then whispered near her ear, "But we can stay here if you'd like."

"Party down the street tonight sounds great, doesn't it, Barr?" she said and moved out of Skylar's reach.

"Great," grinned Barry as he intercepted Skylar.

The other journalists staying in the house filtered in and finished writing their assignments: the print reporters filing their stories with their newspapers or magazines; the broadcasters tracking and editing their packages before feeding them via satellite to their networks.

The Iraqi cook USN had hired served a delicious meal before leaving with her husband and his brother.

Most decided to attend the party at a villa other journalists were renting. Jeremy begged off and stayed behind, saying he was tired. Le An wanted to do the same, but knew she needed to reconnect with journalists at the party to get the latest threat report from those daily fanning out across the country.

The villa was walking distance from USN's—on the same

street and down the block—so Leo and Ryan, two gun-toting Dark Knight guards, accompanied them.

The party was packed, a stereo blasting *American Badass*. It was the same song the crew of the USS Cole had loudly broadcast from their deck as their wounded ship was hauled away from the Yemeni port of Aden three years before. Suicide bombers had blasted a huge hole in the side of the ship, killing seventeen and injuring dozens more. Nineteen days later, the crew had defiantly made a parting statement, standing at attention on deck, their battle flag flying, as first the national anthem, then *American Badass* blared.

After making the rounds and getting a fix on the areas they'd be traveling, Le An wandered into one of the mansion's ornate marble-floored rooms. Her gaze traveled up the carved, gold-paneled walls to the elaborate mural on the ceiling and the room's enormous chandelier, somewhat damaged from the Americans' 'shock and awe' bombing just prior to the invasion.

A large mahogany-and-marble bar, with the requisite touches of gold, took up most of one wall. She didn't know if the villa's former occupants had been religious, but figured they were either Christians or secular Sunnis who indulged heavily in alcohol, unlike their more devout Shi'a counterparts. Soldiers had found Saddam's own cellars fully stocked with Johnnie Walker Black Label Scotch, champagne and his personal favorite Mateus Rosé—a sweet Portuguese wine.

Whatever the previous occupants' religious practices, the bar was now overflowing with enough alcohol to give a devout Muslim heart failure.

Hugh was seated in front of the bar talking to Piet van Gruen and Kent Barkley, two African journalists also renting space at USN's villa. Piet, a tall, blonde Afrikaner from Johannesburg, South Africa, worked as a TV reporter, producer and sometime videographer. Kent, his short, stocky, black-haired physical opposite, was a videographer and editor, originally from Zimbabwe. He'd fled to South Africa when Zimbabwe's President Robert Mugabe and his followers had started their rampage of terror confiscating property and murdering white farmers. Kent's father had been axed to death, his mother severely beaten. Kent had managed to get her to South Africa, but the beating had left her unstable mentally and physically. She was wasting away in a Durban nursing home.

After chatting with the three for a few minutes, Le An suddenly realized how tired she was and decided to go back to the USN villa to review her research material for the next day's shoot. But, as she was about to leave, a fast-paced song came on and she reconsidered.

Relieved to see Skylar wouldn't bother her because he and his octopus arms were draped over two women, she turned to Hugh, Piet and Kent and asked, "Anybody want to dance?"

She figured it was a safe bet one of the three wouldn't leave her hanging, but they all glumly shook their heads 'no' and went back to their drinks and conversation.

"Fine," she mumbled, feeling slightly rejected.

As she turned to leave, Wentworth 'Wen' Darlington the Third, a freelance cameraman from Mountain Brook, Alabama, sporting torn jeans and a 'Who's Your Bagdaddy?' T-shirt, spun her around, rescuing her from total humiliation. They'd bonded over their common Southern roots years before covering other news stories and seeing him always made her feel she was coming home to a comfortable easy chair. Wen loved to brag he was a major disappointment to his father and grandfather because he'd refused to join their law firm, opting instead for a globetrotting, unstable financial future covering war zones and breaking news.

"Oh my stars, it's 'Bama Boy," she laughed as Wen gave her a big bear hug.

"I'll be your Dixie chicken, if you'll be my Carolina lamb," he grinned, his familiar greeting for her a take-off on a song by his favorite musical group. Grabbing her hand, he pulled her onto the dance floor. "Let's do it, Charlotte."

Wen's voice made her realize how homesick she was for Southern men and their charming ways. A very tipsy Barry danced over to them, trying to sing the song's lyrics.

Baghdad was hot and rocking, and the journalists had the best parties in town. Within months, as kidnappings and suicide bombings escalated, that would all change. But for now, in this packed-to-the-brim villa, stressed-out journalists took a break and enjoyed themselves.

When the music switched to a Latin salsa, Le An and Wen ducked into a quieter room to catch up with each other, but after a half hour she hugged him goodbye, saying they had to get an early start the next day. It took her another fifteen minutes to find Barry and Skylar, but neither was ready to leave. After reminding them they had to be back at the villa before Baghdad's curfew began at 11:00, she tried to find Leo and Ryan to give her a security escort back to the villa, but finally gave up. There were too many people and rooms. USN's house was at the end of the street and US tanks frequently rolled by on patrol, so she felt safe enough to walk the short distance alone.

She exited the villa with a group of people and their security guards, past the private guards on duty in the courtyard. She was half hoping they'd walk the same direction, but the group crossed the street, piled into a convoy of three SUVs and roared away.

Le An hesitated for a moment and thought about going back in to find Leo and Ryan, but brushed away doubt and started walking toward USN's villa. Baghdad was in the middle of another blackout, a common occurrence.

Saddam had left the country's electrical infrastructure a mess. Parts for the country's generating units had been hard to come by after the UN had imposed sanctions on Iraq after the 1991 Gulf War. Saddam was selective about doling out what electricity there was, rewarding his minority Sunnis with power, but leaving the rest of the majority Shi'ites in darkness.

Now everyone was in the dark.

Repairing the aging electrical grid was a nightmare American engineers had been struggling to repair for months. Bombings and thefts constantly erased any progress. At best, Iraq's twenty-nine power plants could only produce 3,500 megawatts of power, well below the 6,500 megawatts the country needed to function. But the main reason the power wasn't at full capacity was because the Coalition Provisional Authority had insisted on hiring woefully inadequate and unreliable Iraqi engineers to do the majority of work.

The White House administration had initially asked Congress for $230 million for emergency repairs to the grid, but, realizing that wasn't enough, was now pressing for $5.7 billion.

The villa where the party was held had its own powerful generator, as did USN's, so blackouts went virtually unnoticed, but some of the other villas on the street weren't as fortunate.

The eerily dark road in front of Le An unnerved her slightly. She'd been in worse predicaments, but the hairs on the back of her neck were suddenly standing up. Somehow her subconscious was trying to alert her danger was nearby. Her independent walk had been a foolish decision.

Stupid, stupid, stupid. I am so stupid, she thought.

Suddenly six men appeared out of the darkness from between the parked cars—directly in front of her.

14

Baghdad, Iraq
Wednesday, 3 September 2003

Quickly Le An ducked sideways between two parked cars as she headed for the street, hoping the men hadn't seen her. They were speaking Arabic, most likely *Ali Babas*—thieves up to no good, casing an upper-class neighborhood in hopes of scoring something from either wealthy Iraqis or even wealthier foreigners. Kidnappings were on the rise, so it was possible they were looking for a ransom victim. She knew many of the roaming bands of Iraqis were packing knives and some pretty heavy firepower, probably Kalashnakovs or Uzzis.

Whatever they were up to, Le An didn't want to make contact with them, even though she was trained in Krav Maga. Only the Bionic Woman could take on six men and win and she had less of a chance of surviving if one or more were armed. She'd already violated the first rule of her training which was to be aware of her surroundings. Too late, she'd realized she shouldn't have attempted even a short walk at night in an active war zone. The next rule in her training was to avoid confrontation, if at all possible, and that's what she planned to do.

By ducking between the cars, she figured if the men had seen her, she would force them into a straight line, as they, one at a time, also squeezed between the cars. Single file, she could take on the first one and disarm him, maybe push him back against the others and domino some of them onto the ground. But those still standing, especially with guns, would definitely be a problem.

She decided against letting out a bladder-loosening scream in case no one heard her. It might have the undesired effect of alerting the men to where she was.

She briefly considered returning to the party, but decided it was better to go forward the shorter distance toward USN's villa. Staying low and using the parked cars as cover, she moved quickly toward the USN villa. When she heard footsteps running behind her, she pushed her speed instead of turning to fight. A few feet from the villa, she started yelling, knowing guards were just inside the courtyard.

"Open the gates! It's Le An MacDonald of USN!" she screamed and gave the day's password, hoping they heard her.

The villa gates swung open just as she reached them and, as she ran through, she shouted, "Six men, possibly armed!"

Immediately she heard the *ping* of bullets ricocheting off cars nearby. The guards said something into their headsets, then pulled down their night vision goggles and suddenly opened fire.

The Iraqis' bullets bounced off the villa's walls just as the guards squeezed off their own rounds. The six men started to run back the way they'd come, but suddenly darted across the street, escaping into the darkness as shots, courtesy of Ryan and Leo, rang out from the direction of the party.

"Any casualties?" Ryan called out.

"I'm OK," said Le An, the drop in her adrenaline suddenly causing her legs to shake.

"Why didn't you tell us you were leaving the party?" he snapped. "You shouldn't have been walking alone. Don't you know this is a war zone, Le An? If anything had happened to you, we'd have hell to pay with USN and our bosses. Will you please just let us do our jobs? They warned us you'd be trouble."

"I'm sorry," she said, mortified she'd caused an uproar. "I was tired and I couldn't find you. Are you two OK?"

"Yeah, we're all right, but they aren't. I'm sure we hit one or two of them," said Ryan.

"How did you know I'd left?" she asked.

"This guy," he said pointing to Hugh who was behind them.

"I'm sorry," she repeated. "It was really stupid of me. Thank you."

Just then a US Army convoy, accompanied by a tank, rumbled by. She realized how foolish she'd been to count on the patrol guaranteeing her safety. Crime was the main occupation these days for many in the city and she'd almost been a victim. In the distance, they could hear the *thump, thump* of enemy mortars landing near the Green Zone.

"We've gotta go get the others," said Ryan.

He and Leo asked four more Dark Knight guards to accompany them in case the six men were still around, waiting in ambush. They called up more guards from the rest of the complex to guard the front gate while they were gone.

"I'm such an idiot," said Le An as she and Hugh walked to the front door. "How did you know I was leaving the party?"

"I was leaving, too," he said.

"I thought you'd stay longer."

He shook his head. "I'm sick of these parties. They're all starting to look alike. Been in Baghdad too long. I'm returning to London in a few days."

"How long have you been here?"

"Came in during the invasion," he said.

"Burned out?" she asked.

"Quite," he said, then added, "I knew you were going to walk back alone."

She wasn't sure how to take that. Either he was very attuned to people's body language or her independence was showing.

A concerned Jeremy was waiting for them in the front hall.

"What happened? I heard shouting and gunshots quite close," he said.

"We're OK. Six Iraqis chased me," she said as she smiled weakly at Hugh.

"What?!" Mike shouted as he came out of the satellite feed room. "Boone! Do *not* tell me you were blazing trails walking back here alone. Do not! Were you?!"

She looked down sheepishly. "I'm fine. I had this," she said as she jokingly pulled a small flashlight out of her pocket. "I think Leo and Ryan shot some of them."

"I oughta smack you myself," Mike said, shaking his head. "Are you all right?"

"I'm fine. Can we please just forget this?" she asked.

"Come to Papa, baby," said Mike as he held out his arms.

She gratefully accepted the hug and buried her head in his shoulder. The evening was making her feel very incompetent and she wasn't comfortable with that.

"Khaled's spending the night again," he said, motioning down the hall. "He's in the library."

"Good. That means we can leave right after curfew tomorrow

morning and won't have to wait for him to get here," she said.

In the large main living room, she kicked off her shoes and curled up on one of three large couches upholstered in a blue-and-gold patterned silk. Jeremy followed and sat opposite her on one of the many gold-leaf chairs in the room. Practically everything in the villa was gold—the lamps, the tables, the chests—even the drapes. The Oriental rugs thrown over the white marble floor and the silk upholstery were all a vibrant royal blue, but the overabundance of gold made the room look ostentatious.

The transient journalists had added their own tacky touch. Haphazardly scattered throughout the room were cheap, stackable, white plastic chairs, the kind found on most patios worldwide which seemed to mysteriously reproduce at rabbit rates. Over-the-top ostentatious with a touch of yahoo hillbilly.

Le An sighed and tried to calm herself. "Early day tomorrow, Jeremy. We're heading north to Mosul."

Hugh briefly appeared in the doorway. "Don't mean to be anti-social, but I'm going to sleep straightaway."

"You OK?" she asked.

"I'm intact," he said. "No doubt they would have tried to attack even if we'd all left together. You were good bait to draw them out. It's all for the best."

"Yes, always peachy to be the bait used to draw out criminals in a war zone," she said dryly.

"Next time wait for your security detail," he said as he left the room.

15

Baghdad, Iraq
Thursday, 4 September 2003

USN's three-car convoy began their trip north toward Mosul at 4:30 a.m. right after Baghdad's night curfew ended. Dark Knight security guards occupied the lead and rear SUVs, in addition to one guard and a Dark Knight driver in the front seat of the middle car which carried Le An, Jeremy, Skylar, Barry and Khaled.

Each wore a bright blue $2,000 Kevlar vest, with bullet-deflecting ceramic plates inserted in the large front and back pockets. The ceramic plates were more expensive than steel plates, but they weighed less and didn't bounce bullets and other projectiles up into faces and heads the way steel did.

Hanging on bands around their necks were Wiley-X blast-proof sunglasses to protect their eyes from speeding, possibly blindness-inducing shrapnel in an explosion. Inside the pockets of each person's vest, Le An had tucked a baggie of earplugs and two casualty bandages—just in case. All wore their Kevlar combat helmets, except Barry who'd tossed his at his feet.

Le An was wedged between Skylar and Jeremy in the second row of seats, Barry and Khaled behind them. Skylar and Barry, both still hung over and sleep-deprived from the party down the street the night before, fell asleep immediately and started softly snoring. Khaled, who hadn't been able to sleep through the night since the war began, soon drifted off as well.

As they moved onto Highway One heading north, Le An reviewed her background material with a small flashlight.

"I'd like to provide some information about Iraq which may not be in your notes," said Jeremy.

"OK," she said as she pulled out a small notepad and pen, not willing to fire up her computer on such pothole-filled roads.

"The descendants of the two nations of Israel and Judah have impacted the Middle East and the world for millennia," he began.

"I thought you said Iraq," she said.

"I'm getting to that, but it's important you understand where Israel and Judah were taken into captivity and where they migrated once they regained their freedom. First, you need to know all Jews are Israelites, but not all Israelites are Jews."

"I'm sorry, what?" she asked as the car hit a bone-jarring pothole. "All Jews are Israelis…"

She took off her helmet so she could hear better.

"You're familiar with Abraham?" he asked.

"Ahhh, the name sounds familiar," she said. "Don't both Muslims and Jews claim him as their ancestor?"

"Precisely, Arabs through his illegitimate son Ishmael, the Jews through his legal son Isaac," he said.

"Which is why they say all the trouble in the Middle East today is just one big family feud?"

"Something of that sort," he said. "Isaac's son Jacob was known as Israel. His twelve sons became Israelites, as did their descendants who became the twelve tribes of Israel. Israelites, not Israelis. Citizens of the modern state of Israel are Israelis. Descendants of the twelve tribes are Israelites."

"Israelites," she repeated, underlining the 'ite' ending. "All Jews are Israel-ITES. Not all Israelites are Jews."

"You've got it," he smiled.

"I don't get it," she said.

"I spoke too soon."

"Isn't the word 'Jew' just another name for an 'Israelite'?" she asked.

"No. May I?" he asked as he took her notepad and started writing. "The descendants of the twelve sons of Jacob, also known as Israel, became the twelve tribes of Israel. Reuben, Simeon, Levi, JUDAH, Dan, Napthali, Gad, Asher, Issachar, Zebulun, Joseph and Benjamin. That's their birth order."

He returned her notepad and pointed to one of the words. "The word 'Jew' is merely a shortened form of 'Judah.' Judah's children and his children's children, who became his tribe, were all called Jews. They're of the tribe of Judah and they're Israelites. However, those descended from Reuben or Simeon are Israelites, but not Jews."

"They're Reubs and Sims?" she asked.

He fought back a smile. "They're not often referenced in the same shortened form as the Jews, but you have the general idea. Another way to remember it, illegal immigrants not withstanding: all Virginians are Americans, but not all Americans are Virginians. All Jews are Israelites, but not all Israelites are Jews."

"All Jews are Israelites. Not all Israelites are Jews. Got it," she said.

"Good. You need to distinguish the proper Israel when you're writing your script. There's Israel, also known as Jacob, who was the man with twelve sons; there's Israel, the ancient nation which was comprised of millions of Jacob's descendants, also known as the twelve tribes which Moses led out of Egypt. Then there's Israel, a break-away nation comprised of ten of those twelve tribes which rebelled against the rulership of King David's grandson Rehoboam. That Israel became a totally separate nation from the remaining tribes comprising the nation of Judah. And lastly, there's the modern nation of Israel, which is comprised basically of only one tribe of Israel—the Jews. It's vitally important you understand these distinctions if you're going to fully grasp the history we're about to examine in Iraq. And because it's your task to simplify this for your viewers, you need to understand it."

"I've never heard an expert or minister say this," she said.

"Most experts aren't experts at all," he said. "Even ministers get it wrong, misidentifying Joseph, Moses, King Saul, Abraham, Isaac and Jacob as Jews. Not one was a Jew. Many ministers don't know scripture."

"Ministers don't know the Bible?" she asked, her eyes growing wide. "Did you just say Moses wasn't a Jew?"

"The experts are instructing others when they're the ones who need instruction. It's quite simple once people unlearn wrong information they've been taught."

"What?" mumbled Barry sleepily from the seat behind them. "Jeremy, did you just say Moses wasn't a Jew?"

"Welcome to the party," said Le An. "Did you just wake up?"

"Had to sleep off that party last night," he said. "Where's my thermos of coffee?"

"Where you can't get it," she said. "No liquids until we get past the Sunni Triangle. We're not stopping for pee breaks. I don't feel like having y'all picked off by a Fedayeen or Republican Guard sniper today. That's why I made y'all go before we left the house."

Barry sighed heavily to show his disapproval.

"Sigh all you want, you're not getting any liquids until later," she said.

"Bossy," he said.

"Cranky," she said. "Go on, Jeremy, you were saying Moses wasn't a Jew."

"Moses was a Levite, of the tribe of Levi, not Judah," said Jeremy. "After leaving Egypt, the Levites, not the Jews, became the priesthood for the nation of Israel."

"You said Joseph wasn't a Jew?" she asked as she wrote. "Is that Joseph from Andrew Lloyd Webber's *Joseph and the Amazing Technicolor Dreamcoat*?"

Jeremy fought back a smile. "Yes, Joseph was Judah's younger brother. He was an Israelite and a Hebrew, descended from his ancestor Eber, but he was never a Jew. His brothers sold him into slavery in Egypt."

"I would've beaten my brothers senseless if they'd sold me into slavery," said Barry.

"Joseph became prime minister of Egypt, the most powerful man after Pharaoh, and eventually his eleven brothers and his father Israel moved to Egypt to be with him," Jeremy continued. "Perhaps at this point you'd like to reference Cecil B. DeMille's *The Ten Commandments* with Charlton Heston?"

"You're a funny guy, aren't you?" she asked.

"We English are a clever lot," he said. "Merely trying to put it in a modern vernacular you understand. If you recall, Moses—or Mister Heston—led millions of Israelites out of Egypt approximately 1443 BC. Forty years on, they entered the land now named Israel. But to understand the twelve tribes, you need to stop thinking of ancient Israel in terms of modern Israel. Modern Israel is mainly populated by Jews, those descended from only one tribe—Judah."

"Where are the other eleven?" she asked.

"We'll get to that. After the twelve tribes of Israel came out of Egypt and wandered round the desert for forty years..."

"Didn't God know how to get out of the desert?" asked Barry sarcastically.

Le An looked over her shoulder at him.

"What?" he grinned. "I'm just asking. I get cranky without caffeine."

"You had two cups this morning at breakfast," she said.

"I need more for this hangover."

"You're not getting it," she said. "Look out the window and distract yourself."

"It's depressing looking at bombed out Mercedes and roadside graves," said Barry. "Makes me feel like I'm in a war zone. I'd rather bother you people."

She gave him her best 'zip it' look. "Go on, Jeremy."

"Israel wandered round the desert for a variety of reasons," he said, half-turning to address Barry. "That's another story. The twelve tribes settled in the land we now refer to as Israel and called themselves Israel."

"Finally, something makes sense," she said.

"Approximately 500 years on, as King David's grandson Rehoboam was beginning his reign, the ten northern tribes rebelled and broke away. They retained the name Israel for their nation. The remaining tribes of Judah and Benjamin became the nation of Judah. Most, but not all, of the Levites also chose to remain in Judah."

"So nine tribes broke away and three were left?" she asked.

"Ten broke away and two remained, with a remnant of the Levitical priests."

"There were thirteen tribes? When did you slip in another tribe?" she asked, flipping back through the pages in her notepad. "This is so confusing."

"I'll say," mumbled Barry.

"Remember your musical about Joseph?" asked Jeremy. "To compensate for his years of slavery and imprisonment in Egypt, his father Israel gave him a double inheritance by legally adopting his two sons Ephraim and Manasseh. Each of them received the same portion as Joseph's eleven brothers. That made it thirteen tribes. Joseph, through his two sons, received a double portion."

"You mean Joseph didn't get any inheritance?" she asked.

"He was prime minister of Egypt, already quite wealthy," said Jeremy.

"Oh, yeah. Forgot about that," she said. "Joseph's sons sure made out. They inherited their father's estate, plus with their eleven uncles an equal share of their grandfather's estate. But if it's thirteen tribes, why do you keep calling them the twelve tribes of Israel?"

"Twelve tribes with Joseph getting a double portion or you could say twelve tribes plus the separate Levitical priesthood. The tribe of Levi received no land allocations when Israel became a nation. Levites received a few cities throughout Israel and the other twelve tribes gave them tithes—ten percent of all their increase."

"OK, thirteen tribes—also known as twelve tribes and a priesthood," she said.

"Is that like *Four Weddings and a Funeral?*" asked Barry. "Eight maids a leapin' and a partridge in a pear tree?"

"You're on a tear today, Barr, aren't you?" she said, half turning to look at him. "See, you're zippy without the caffeine."

"I want coffee. And I'm hungry. Where are the sandwiches?" he asked.

"There are pitas in the cooler in the back," she pointed behind him.

Barry leaned forward and sniffed her. "You smell like a good Italian girl."

"What?!" she glared at him.

"Quit giving me the eye, Le An," he said. "It's a compliment. You smell like garlic and onions. Reminds me of Mom's Sunday dinners, the whole family around the dining room table, digging into lasagna and ziti, the house smelling like garlic, onions and tomato sauce. Oh, man, I'd love some good lasagna right now."

"Shut up, Barry," mumbled Skylar, half-awake now. "You're making me hungry."

"Le An's garlicky-onion perfume is making me hungry. Where are we?" asked Barry.

"Tikrit," Khaled said, now awake because of Barry's constant chattering.

"Saddam's hometown," said Barry. "He's gotta be around here somewhere. Maybe driving in that car... or that one..."

"Jeremy, when the ten northern tribes broke away, was that a civil war?" asked Le An.

"Yes, the result of high taxes courtesy of King David's son Solomon and his son Rehoboam, who raised them even higher."

"Must have been Democrats," said Barry.

"Taxes," she said with a twinkle in her eye. "Same reason that little American colony broke away from you Brits."

"Ah, yes, if we'd merely cut the tax on tea, you'd still be part of the empire," smiled Jeremy.

Barry snorted from the back seat.

Jeremy continued, "About 200 years on from the civil war, Assyria, which occupied today's northern Iraq, took the northern ten tribes of Israel into captivity in a series of raids. The final defeat was 721 BC. And 135 years on from that, in 586 BC, Nebuchadnezzar took the nation of Judah into captivity in Babylon."

"The northern ten tribes went into captivity in the northern part of Iraq in Assyria and the southern two tribes and part of the priesthood went into captivity in the southern part of Iraq in Babylon," she repeated to make sure she understood it. "Israel in the north to Assyria, Judah in the south to Babylon."

"You've got it," said Jeremy.

Just then, a BMW pulled alongside their convoy. A man wearing a red-and-white-checkered *khafit* wrapped around his head and face, with only his eyes uncovered, stood up through the BMW's sunroof and opened fire on the USN convoy.

16

Tikrit, Iraq
Thursday, 4 September 2003

As the gunman stood up through the sunroof, Le An spotted his automatic weapon and screamed, "Gun!" then instinctively reached out both hands, one on Jeremy's neck, the other on Skylar's, to force their heads down.

"Put your glasses on!" she screamed, concerned flying glass or metal could blind them.

The gunman sprayed bullets at all three SUVs, then concentrated on the middle one Le An and her crew were in. Everyone but Barry bent forward, trying to keep their faces and bodies low, with only their backs exposed just below the bottom edges of the windows.

Barry had kept his camera next to him, occasionally lowering the automatic window in order to videotape the passing scenery. He now instinctively hoisted his camera onto his shoulder and turned it toward the BMW.

"Barry, don't even think about lowering that window to get a better shot!" screamed Le An, knowing, without looking at him, what he was about to do. "You'll get us all killed."

The three Chevy Suburban SUVs were outfitted with ballistic steel reinforcement, armored exterior and 'run flat' tire inserts—airless, hard rings around the wheel rims which acted as backup spares within the tires. The run flats were supposed to provide at least an hour at sixty miles-per-hour if the tires were deflated. That wasn't always true, but they did usually allow enough time to drive out of a 'kill zone.'

The SUVs were also outfitted with thick, bullet-proof glass which stopped most calibers. The side and back windows of each vehicle were tinted to block outsiders from being able to see inside the passenger compartment.

The three SUVs pushed their speeds trying to outrun the BMW. The crew could hear Leo coordinating with the lead and rear convoy vehicles through his headset. Le An wasn't sure which was scarier, the terrorists with weapons or the high speeds they were now traveling. If any of the vehicles in the convoy hit anything, the rollover might kill them all. She grabbed her helmet off the floor and fastened the strap under her chin.

The bullets *pinged* against the sides of the SUVs, at times puncturing the exterior metal, but were blocked from entering the passenger compartments. They also embedded in the outside layer of the glass, leaving white, opaque, circular blots and a spider-web of cracked glass difficult to see through.

Ryan, riding shotgun in the rear vehicle, fired at the insurgents' car and tires as his driver moved behind the BMW and rammed it, almost knocking the gunman from the sunroof. A Dark Knight guard in the lead vehicle fired also, the combined action causing the BMW's rear window and front windshield to blow out. In a coordinated move between the DK drivers, the USN crew's SUV dropped behind the action as the lead SUV slowed enough to come alongside the BMW, suddenly swerving into it and bumping it sideways. At the same time, the rear SUV bumped the BMW from behind. The car careened off the road and rolled over three times as its tires hit the edge of the highway, ejecting the gunman through the BMW's open sunroof. Ryan's SUV quickly pulled back behind the USN crew car.

They could hear cars crashing behind them and hoped no one besides the insurgents had been killed or injured, but they didn't dare stop until they were in a safer area. Anyone bold enough to fire on a three-vehicle, official-looking convoy probably wasn't your basic car thief—and may have had accomplices. The BMW, more than likely, was filled with Sunni insurgents or some of Saddam's elite forces. Leo noted the GPS location and radioed the DK command center, which in turn notified American troops of the incident.

As the cars slowed to forty miles-per-hour, Leo turned to Le An and said, "We've got two blown tires. We're down to run flats."

17

Tikrit, Iraq
Thursday, 4 September 2003

The roads were already hot from the 120-degree, searing, summer temperatures and the Dark Knight drivers didn't want to add more heat from high speeds to the run flats. Leo suggested since they were close to Camp Speicher, they go there to change tires or have replacement vehicles meet them. They were still at least 150 miles from Mosul and, much as Le An hated losing time to divert to the base, she knew it wasn't safe to change tires in the open in the Sunni Triangle. Fortunately, no bullets had penetrated the glass or passenger cabs, and everyone was fine, if a bit shaken.

Camp Speicher was one of the larger Army bases in Iraq and had become the headquarters of the Multinational Division North. It had originally been Al Sahra Airfield, Iraq's main air force academy base under Saddam Hussein. During the invasion, the Coalition had purposely avoided major bombing there, leaving most of the runways and larger buildings intact in order to use them later. But before US forces could take possession of it, looters carted off anything not nailed down—and then some.

The base had been renamed Camp Speicher after Michael 'Scott' Speicher, a US Navy pilot missing in action since the first Gulf War. Speicher's F/A-18 Hornet had been shot down over Anbar Province in January 1991, but since neither his remains nor his plane had been found, his status had shifted over the years from 'missing in action' to 'killed in action/body not recovered.'

In 1993, a military official from Qatar had finally discovered what was left of Speicher's plane in the Iraq desert. Eight years later, the US Secretary of the Navy had changed his status back to 'missing in action.' American soldiers were still searching for information about what had happened to him—whether he'd died trying to eject from his plane or been taken prisoner.

"We need to let Camp Speicher know we're coming," said Le An, reaching for her sat phone.

"Already done," said Leo. "Base command notified them."

Dark Knight could easily open doors at most bases in the country. The company had friends in high places: DK guards—ex-military from America, Britain, New Zealand, Australia and South Africa—were on the Pentagon's payroll, providing private security for some of the top military and administrative people in Iraq.

"Roger that," said Leo into his headset. "Le An, DK base command just told me it'll be hours before they can get us replacements. They've got vehicles up north and can meet us with three new ones in Mosul at the 101 late this afternoon."

"Can you guys see OK to drive? I don't like having part of our vision blocked with bullet dings," she asked as she peered at the white opaque blobs.

"It's not ideal," mumbled their driver Stan.

"Is there other damage? Anything mechanical?" she asked. "I don't want us to get stranded somewhere. Triple A would never find us."

"Ha!" said Barry.

"No one's reporting any problems," said Leo. "These SUVs are pretty tough."

"All right, let's get to the base and maybe they'll let us borrow one of their mechanics to check them out," she said. "Worst case scenario, we consolidate into two vehicles and leave the one with the worst windshield. Or consolidate into one and leave some guards behind."

With their camera equipment, five USN people, a driver and a guard, they already had a full car. She figured they could squeeze in one more guard, which meant the other three would have to be left behind with the damaged SUVs.

"Not an option, Le," said Leo. "Two car minimum and you have to keep all your guards."

Everyone remained quiet for a few minutes, the gravity of what had happened beginning to sink in. Le An kept looking out the windows on either side, wondering if another car was going to open fire on them. She noticed everyone else doing the same thing. Between roadside IEDs and assassins shooting from cars, most people in Iraq had become nervous drivers and passengers.

As much as she hated traveling with security guards, she was thankful for the up-armoring of their vehicles. It was possible they never would've been targeted if they hadn't been in the high profile black SUVs, but then again, they might have. And if they were going to get hit, they might as well be heavily protected with metal and guns. Better that than dead.

"I got some good footage," said Barry, as he reviewed video of the attack.

"Good. Use the baby sat and feed it to New York when we get to Camp Speicher," she said.

Once through the base's gates, the three SUVs were ordered off to the side to wait for a US Army public affairs officer to clear them. The USN crew was slightly unnerved to see so many bullet holes in their vehicles, but fortunately the SUVs' armored protection hadn't allowed any of the shots to reach the interior cabs.

Still, Le An wasn't thrilled about making the trip to Mosul in SUVs which might have mechanical damage and hard-to-see-through windshields. The rear SUV had taken the most shots to the windshield as it had approached the BMW to ram it. The middle vehicle the USN crew had been in had moderate damage, the lead vehicle the least amount.

Just as the DK guards started changing tires, the base's PAO, a tall, fortyish-and-graying, bespectacled major named Walt Smith, showed up. Le An was relieved he was non-hostile, even borderline friendly, but when she requested a few mechanics to assist them, he balked.

"The sooner we change tires and check the engines, the sooner we're out of here," she smiled sweetly.

"I'll see what I can do," said Major Walt, then walked off.

Nearby, helicopters were taking off and landing. Just the sight of them gave Le An a queasy feeling, but knowing it would help their schedule, when Major Walt came back she asked him if a large-capacity Chinook was available to transport the eleven-member USN crew to Mosul. She didn't know if she was relieved or annoyed when he told her space for that many wouldn't be available for a day or two.

"How about five people?" she asked as she pulled Walt aside where the DK guards couldn't hear her. She was willing to break the rules and dump all their guards. After all, she and her crew would be flying with military, landing at a military base and going on patrol with the Army. They'd be surrounded with heavy fire-power and didn't need guards that day. "Can you find room for five people on a chopper to Mosul today?"

"Day or two," said Major Walt.

"Please," she smiled sweetly. "We need to get up to the 101 in Mosul today."

"Day or two," repeated Walt as he walked away.

Fortunately, the SUVs were built to take punishment and none had suffered mechanical damage. Leo made the decision to leave behind the one with the most windshield damage and shifted the USN crew to the lead SUV with the ding-free windshield.

"Probably safer. Insurgents always shoot at the middle car," said Barry, pointing to their old SUV.

"But lead cars hit the IEDs first," Le An reminded him.

"Not always. Sometimes insurgents target the second car," he said.

18

Iraq
Thursday, 4 September 2003

The highway to Mosul was in fairly good shape, allowing the USN convoy to make up time—when the traffic wasn't crawling or gridlocked.

"USN hires armed bodyguards for us, has armed guards protecting our house in Baghdad, but they won't let us carry guns," said Barry. "I want a gun."

"Oh, good grief," said Le An, as everyone snickered or dubiously raised their eyebrows. "With your hot temper, the last thing I want is for you to have a gun."

"Afraid I'll shoot you," he sneered.

"You'd wipe out the whole bureau for not making fresh coffee," she said.

"Lots of journalists over here carry guns," he said and started ticking off names.

"And a lot don't," she said. "We're observing and reporting on the story, not shooting people."

"What're you talking about, woman? Our guards just shot at people who're the story," he said. "And caused a rollover and probably killed them, along with innocent people in other cars."

"DK guards are well trained," she said. "They wouldn't shoot someone trying to take off the safety like you would. If you'd had a gun today, you would have killed us before you hit the insurgents."

"Thank you," said Leo.

"An armed journalist is better than a dead journalist," said Barry.

"Not if the armed journalist misses the insurgents and shoots the coworkers," she said.

"What if the armed guards shoot innocent Iraqis or cause accidents which kill innocent Iraqis?" he asked, prompting Leo to turn around and glare at him.

"What if you shoot at insurgents and instead kill innocent Iraqis?" she asked. "Who stands a better chance of hitting insurgents instead of innocent bystanders, you or professionals who are ex-military? Or should we let the insurgents kill innocent journalists?"

"I want a gun," he repeated.

Changing the subject, she said, "I'd like to remind y'all, we may run into hospitable Iraqis toting tea. If you can find a way to actually not drink it—put it to your lips and dribble it down your chin or stealthily pour it on the ground—fine. But you have to take the tea offered to you."

Barry and Skylar groaned, Khaled and Jeremy laughed, and Leo gave her a dirty look.

"DK guards are exempt," she said. "But the rest of y'all can keep your groans to yourself. We're not insulting any Iraqis. They boil the water... sort of. But you'll be happy to know I have Imodium and InterStop to deal with the aftereffects if you get sick. May I suggest you also eat garlic, onions and yogurt."

"Where's a gun when you need one?" muttered Barry. "We survive an assassination attempt and you want to kill us with cholera from dirty water in unwashed cups?"

"You just insulted Khaled's country," she said.

"He knows I'm only insulting Tigris River water in dirty cups," he said.

"I drink tea and do not feel ill," said Khaled.

"I bet New York water would make you as sick as Iraq water makes us," said Barry. "It's what bacteria your system's used to."

"I would drink New York water," said Khaled.

"What if someone made you eat pork, Le An?" asked Barry.

"I'd fake it," she said. "Act like I'm chewing, but spit it in my napkin. Or hide it under my spinach."

Khaled made a face. "I do not eat pork. To serve pork would be insult."

"You would insult your host?" asked Barry.

"He insult me with pork," said Khaled. "If he insult me, I insult him and do not eat."

"OK, that's my excuse," said Barry. "It's an insult for people to serve me dirty tea in unwashed glasses. I will not be insulted. Besides, I'm a coffee man."

"The lovely Iraqis who offer tea are showing hospitality and graciousness and we will not insult them," said Le An.

"So are people who serve pork," he said.

"I didn't say you have to drink it, just accept it and use evasion tactics, same as I would with pork," she said. "Accept it, don't drink it, fake it."

Jeremy chuckled at their bickering.

"Tell her why our health is more important than hospitality," Skylar said to him.

"Oh, I quite agree with Le An and Khaled," said Jeremy. "You must not insult the kind Iraqis who offer tea."

Barry let a low bear-like growl roll around his throat.

"Dude, I'm with you. Last time I was here I got sick from tea someone gave me," Skylar said to him. "Let's not get up close and personal with people who offer tea."

"Jeremy, I've scheduled our trip south to Babylon on Saturday," said Le An.

"Remember, I won't be able to assist you on Saturdays because of Sabbath," he said.

"I'm sorry, I did forget," she said. "We'll bump it to Sunday. Shouldn't be a problem. Does it make you nervous being in a Muslim country because you're Jewish?"

"You are a Jew?" asked Khaled.

19

Iraq
Thursday, 4 September 2003

Khaled's voice was low, but the anti-Semitic tone was unmistakable, sending a chill shooting through Le An's body. It landed with a thud in the pit of her stomach, giving her a queasy feeling.

In Israel, Jewish and Arab journalists frequently worked together as crews, an uneasy, but necessary, truce. But this was Iraq and Muslim journalists here weren't used to playing nice with Jews. She'd hadn't considered how everyone's religious beliefs would affect her crew or this assignment. Khaled didn't seem to have a problem with Christians or Americans, but she'd failed to consider how opposed he'd be to the professor's beliefs, not that she even really knew what they were.

"I'm not a Jew," said Jeremy. "I'm a Christian."

Khaled narrowed his eyes and clinched his jaw.

"What?" asked Barry and leaned forward, resting his hand on Le An's hair.

"Ow! Barry, quit pulling my hair!" she said. "Jeremy, you're Christian, but you observe Saturday instead of Sunday?"

"That's correct," he said.

"Are you Seventh Day..." she tried to remember the denomination.

"Adventist? No."

"A Christian who keeps the Jewish Sabbath?" she asked.

"That's weird," said Barry.

"Haven't you done the same thing, Barr?" she asked. "You told me you'd go to Saturday Mass so you could stay out all night binge drinking and not have to get up for Sunday services. Weren't you keeping a Saturday Sabbath?"

Barry was too hung over to come up with a snappy reply and,

leaning back in his seat grumbled, "You've been forgetting everything else lately, but you remember that?"

"Jeremy, do you observe Jewish days like Rosh Hashanah? Or Christmas and Easter?" she asked.

He smiled as if somewhat amused. "They're not 'Jewish' days, but, yes, I observe those and not Christmas or Easter."

"You are a Jew," repeated Khaled.

"No, Christian," Jeremy repeated.

"You don't keep Christmas and Easter and you're Christian? Why?" asked Le An, hoping Khaled wouldn't do anything stupid.

"Because those days predate Christianity by thousands of years. They originated as pagan rituals to idols, as you'll soon see in our travels through Iraq," he said. "The early church didn't observe them either."

"Wait a minute!" Barry said, agitated, as he again leaned on the back of Le An's seat.

"Stop pulling my hair!" she said, reaching over her shoulder to slap his arm.

"You should cut it," he snapped. "Jeremy, tell me you did not just call Christmas and Easter pagan."

"Don't cut your hair, Le. I love it long," said Skylar, as he reached up to twirl a strand of it and gave her a half-smile.

She ignored his come-on and quickly tilted her head sideways toward Jeremy as she reached up to remove her hair from his roaming fingers.

"Calm down, Barry," she said, annoyed at the religious battle which was brewing. "I know you think Catholicism is the only religion, but First Amendment, baby. People can worship however they want. What do you care what someone believes? You're not even that religious."

Barry sat back in his seat and, huffing his displeasure, crossed his arms over his chest.

"He is a Jew," Khaled said to him.

"Barry, I do admire your passion for your beliefs," said Jeremy. "We merely believe different things. I'm dreadfully sorry if it offends you."

"I grew up with Christmas, Santa Claus and all the presents, but I don't really keep it now," said Le An, trying to fill the strained silence. "I'm usually on assignment somewhere and the other journalists I'm with are maudlin, morose or drunk, usually homesick. But even when I am home with family, Christmas never lives up to its expectations. Everybody thinks it'll be great, but mostly it's disappointing. It's all over in an hour, there's wrapping paper all over the floor and I feel depressed and dissatisfied with stuff I didn't want. Christmas lifts you way up, then drops you off a cliff. It's empty."

"That's because you're single," said Barry. "If you had kids, you wouldn't feel that way. Christmas is for children. I like seeing my kids get excited about what I get them. Maybe you need to get married and have kids to appreciate it."

"Oh, please. It doesn't have to be Christmas for kids to get excited about new toys. That's anytime," she said.

"I like Christmas," said Skylar.

"I think it's more about family," said Le An. "People don't need gifts so much as they need to be with someone who loves them so they don't feel alone. I think Christmas is a tradition that makes people feel safe in a crazy world."

"Quite profound," said Jeremy. "And utterly true. However, families could accomplish that on other days, wouldn't you say?"

"Well, yes, because different religions observe different days and they enjoy the same thing—being together with their families," she said. "Right, Khaled? Don't you enjoy being with your family on Muslim holidays?"

"Yes," he said.

She thought back over her own Christmases as a child. She loved being with her family, but her mother was always stressed and exhausted, her brothers indifferent to anything but motorized or electronic gifts, her father grumbling about the bills.

"I bet you don't even shop for your kids' Christmas presents, Barry," she said. "I bet it's Kristin. When do you have time to shop?"

He grumbled and admitted his wife bought the gifts, but added defiantly, "But I pay for them and I like watching my kids tear into their presents."

"Presents don't mean that much to me," she said. "I don't like the materialism and I hate shopping. I shopped in Ireland because I found some great things I knew my family and friends would love, but I don't like feeling I *have* to get people gifts because someone else decided I should."

"You don't like getting presents?" asked Barry.

"I really don't," she said. "I'm picky and no one ever gets me what I want. Besides, I don't need anything. And I never have time to return things I don't want, so I have a lot of useless gifts I end up re-gifting."

"You palm off your unwanted gifts on someone else?" laughed Skylar.

"Doesn't everybody?" she asked.

"So that's what's in all those boxes in your apartment?" snorted Barry. "You should see Le An's apartment. Boxes to the ceiling. You have to turn sideways to get in the place."

She turned and gave him a dirty look, not pleased he'd broken her confidence. "See if I ever let you in to use my bathroom. You can pee in the street from now on."

"So that's why you wouldn't let me come over," Skylar whispered to her and gave her a wicked smile.

She tried to ignore him.

"Le An moved a year ago and she still hasn't unpacked," Barry continued.

"Eight months," she corrected him. "And everything's currently being unpacked as we speak, courtesy of my mother and a decorator."

"I never would have unpacked if I hadn't hired a decorator," said Skylar. "What journalist at network has time? You've got a wife, Barry. Single people don't have someone hanging around the house all day, unpacking boxes and moving furniture. Admit it: when you moved into your house, how much unpacking did you do?"

"I was on assignment," he said, which was greeted with a chorus of told-you-so laughter. "No, now, laugh all you want, but Kristin beat me to it. Besides, she and her sisters love doing all that girly stuff."

"Barry, you have to admit Christmas isn't really religious anymore," she said. "Look at USN and every other news organization. We cover how it impacts merchants and the American economy. It's a shopping event, not a religious event."

"It's religious," he said, irritated.

"Santa Claus isn't religious. He isn't in the Bible," she said, then turned to Jeremy and whispered, "Is he?"

He shook his head 'no.'

"I didn't think so," she said. "I never wanted to sit on that fat guy's lap. His suit was tacky. Who wears a red leisure suit? And his clones are everywhere. It's creepy."

"My kids love Santa," said Barry.

"Do they think he's real?" she asked.

"Of course," he said.

"See, now that's disturbing. Why do parents lie to kids about that?" she said and suddenly started pointing her finger in a moment of understanding. "That's it! These holidays are geared to kids, so when they become adults, it's a big nostalgia play for their emotions, trying to recapture the innocence and family time from when they were young. My mom endlessly talks about her memories of Christmas when she was a child, how wonderful it was, and she's miserable now because it can't ever be like that again. Her parents are never going to be alive to celebrate Christmas with her, no matter how much she tries to recreate everything. Christmas is a big old play for your emotions, when your parents were alive and your world was carefree. That's why people cling to it. They're trying to turn back the years to when they were kids."

"What an utterly brilliant insight," said Jeremy. "Beware of nostalgia."

"Life in the rearview mirror," she muttered, more to herself than anyone else. "Not being able to let go of your past. It keeps pulling you backward so you can't go forward."

"That's ridiculous," said Barry in disgust.

"What religion are you, Le?" asked Skylar.

"I'm not anything. I guess I believe there's a God, but it gets confusing after that," she said.

"So you admit you don't know anything about religion," smirked Barry.

"So presents are your only defense for observing Christmas?" she shot back.

"We're supposed to give gifts because the three wise men gave gifts to baby Jesus," said Barry. "We give gifts on birthdays and it's his birthday."

"But they gave gifts to him, not each other," said Jeremy. "And there's quite a bit of evidence December twenty-fifth wasn't his birthday."

20

Iraq
Thursday, 4 September 2003

The professor's information bombs kept exploding inside the car—and Le An's head.

"It wasn't?" she and Skylar asked in unison.

"What?!" exploded Barry. "Of course, it's his birthday!"

"I beg to differ," said Jeremy. "Scripture records his birth took place during an empire-wide Roman census which required everyone to register in the city of their ancestry. The Romans were far from stupid."

"Got that right," huffed Barry. "Italians are freaking brilliant."

"The last thing the Romans would have required is for everyone to be on the roads traveling for a census in the middle of winter," he said. "Their empire extended north into areas which would have snow in late December and travel would have been difficult."

"I never thought of that," said Le An.

"Scripture records shepherds and their flocks were in the fields outside Bethlehem at the time of the birth," Jeremy continued. "However, they aren't in the fields in December because Israel's too cold at that time."

"That's true," she said. "I've been there in December."

"Many in the Roman Empire were farmers or tended flocks," he continued. "The Romans no doubt figured the optimum time for a census would be when everyone was available to travel, such as in the fall, after they'd harvested their crops. The weather was good, they had money from selling their crops and their time was free."

"Makes sense," she said. "So you think he was born in the fall?"

"There's no way of knowing, but clues indicate the date

would've been in September or October," he said.

"Clues?" asked Skylar.

"Records indicate he was born six months on from his cousin John the baptizer. John's father was a Levitical priest of the eighth division whose service in the temple was completed round about June. His wife Elizabeth conceived John straightaway after that."

"Eighth division? What's that?" asked Le An.

"King David divided the priests into twenty-four divisions for service in the temple. They were assigned to serve in rotation for one week, as well as during the three festival seasons."

"So if he completed his service in June, that means John would've been born around March or April," she said. "And if Jesus was born six months after John, that would be September or October. Wow. Facts can really get in the way of a good tradition, can't they? Why don't ministers tell you this stuff?"

"Because they wouldn't be employed. Most are utterly locked into the Christmas tradition," he said. "To challenge that means going contrary to most professing Christians. They, quite frankly, don't care they're observing a tradition born in paganism."

"There!" exploded Barry. "You see, he's calling it pagan!"

"Calm down. He's giving facts for not observing the traditional date, Barry," she said. "Khaled doesn't keep Christmas. Are you going to bite his head off, too?"

"I do not keep Christmas," said Khaled.

"Khaled's Muslim," said Barry. "He's allowed to not keep Christmas. Christians aren't."

The car erupted in a chorus of guffaws.

"Barry, do you hear yourself?" asked Le An.

"I like Christmas. I like the tree, the way it smells, the decorations, the music, the presents, the parties, more parties—especially the office parties," said Skylar, eliciting a snicker from the others.

"I am happy I do not keep Christmas. It is war what makes me depressed," interjected Khaled.

His comment temporarily silenced them.

"Thanks for putting it in perspective, Khaled," said Le An. "Jeremy, do members of your family have the same religious beliefs you do?"

"My father did, my mother was Anglican. Most of my brothers and sisters consider themselves Anglican, but some are agnostic or atheist and one became Buddhist."

"My family is Muslim," said Khaled.

"But you aren't that religious, are you?" she asked.

"No, but I am Muslim," he said.

"But within Islam you have Sunnis, Shi'as and other divisions, so even Muslims can't agree on what's true. And they observe different holidays," she said.

"How do you know if a religious belief is true?" asked Skylar.

"I want facts," said Le An.

"It doesn't matter if something's true if it makes you feel good," said Barry.

"You're saying lies are OK if they make you feel good?" she laughed. "I'm a journalist. I want to at least try and find out what's true."

"Most people remain with their religion because of family tradition," said Jeremy. "If it comforts them, they have no desire for truth. Truth is immaterial if all they need is emotional warmth."

"I don't care if Christmas is true. I'm keeping it," said Barry defiantly. "Why wouldn't you want to fit in with your family and friends. Isn't that what Khaled's doing?"

"I like being a Muslim," he said.

"Because you were raised that way and practically everyone in your country is Muslim," said Barry. "Which is my point."

"What point?" asked Le An. "That no one's supposed to think for themselves when it comes to religion? Khaled, if you were living in a Catholic neighborhood, would you still be Muslim?"

"I would never become Catholic," said Khaled, causing Barry to huff his disapproval. "It would dishonor my family."

"So your family dictates what you believe?" she asked. "Your family's more important than your neighbors?"

"I am Muslim," he said.

"Barry, do you have a problem with Khaled being Muslim?" she asked. "He's not Catholic."

"He can be whatever he wants," he snapped.

"But Jeremy can't be Christian because he doesn't keep Christmas?" she asked.

"Good one, Le," laughed Skylar.

"He is a Jew," Khaled mumbled.

"He can say he's Christian, but the only true Christians are Catholics," said Barry.

"Whoa!" Skylar and Le An erupted in laughter.

Barry quickly changed the subject. "Man, I'm going to miss this AC. Nothing like riding around all day in 120-degree heat in an un-air-conditioned Humvee."

"The troops are doing it," said Skylar. "And they don't get paid as well as we do."

"We don't get paid as well as you do," mumbled Barry.

"Iraqis do not have electricity or air conditioning to be cool in their houses," said Khaled.

"The ones without generators. But then Saddam never supplied electricity to most of Iraq, certainly not the Shi'a," said Le An, the truth silencing Khaled as he remembered his former privileged status.

The USN convoy made good time, arriving late morning at Post Freedom, the 101st Airborne's main command post and division headquarters in northwestern Mosul. The US military had taken over one of Saddam Hussein's former presidential complexes, complete with palaces, man-made waterfalls and three lakes on 540 acres overlooking the Tigris River.

Mosul, not far from the Turkish border, was Iraq's second largest city, a trade center whose main exports were cotton, marble and muslin. The city's 1.5 million people were a volatile mix of cultures and religions. The majority were Sunni Arabs, a fair number of them supporters of Saddam Hussein and his regime, but more than a third were Kurds and they had no love for Saddam. Even though both groups shared a religion, they despised each other and fought continuously for control of the city. Thrown into the mix were Turkomans and a large concentration of Aramaic-speaking Christians. The Kurds and Christians traditionally had always gotten along well and, in general, favored the Coalition forces, but the Sunni Arabs wanted to expel both groups, along with the Coalition. They'd benefited from Saddam and wanted him back.

The commander of the 101st Airborne, had come into northern Iraq with a show of force, immediately ending any looting or crime. With a thinking man's plan worthy of his Ivy-League Ph.D. in international relations, he'd opted to win over the locals. Some had accused him of being a politician—buying off as many people as he could. However he'd done it, he'd convinced Iraqis themselves to turn against the insurgents. While other commanders were using cordon-and-sweep operations to arrest all military-aged men, he'd utilized cordon-and-knock to surround targeted suspects, allowing them to quietly surrender in dignity.

His division commanders kept the peace through open lines of communication, conducting more than twenty meetings a day with local leaders, resulting in some of the lowest number of insurgent attacks in Iraq.

"Can't believe we were here just a month ago," said Barry. "Brings back good memories taking down Saddam's baby boys."

The trip reunited the USN crew with some of the soldiers they'd been embedded with during the Hussein brothers' raid, including Frank, the military public affairs officer accompanying them for the day.

"Glutton for punishment, aren't you?" asked Frank.

"We must be to spend the day with you," said Le An.

"We missed you, man," said Barry. "When the yelling stops, we don't feel the love."

"What happened to you?" Frank asked, pointing to their shot-up SUVs. "You in the Army now, MacDee? Where'd it happen?"

"Sunni Triangle," she said.

"If you'd been in a Humvee, you might not have lived to tell about it," he said.

"Don't we know it," she said.

After a bathroom break, Barry started unloading their gear and snarled, "Hey, people! Grab something! You think I'm carrying all this myself?"

Le An picked up her backpack, an equipment pack and two tripods. "OK, chop, chop, Frank. Enough chit-chat. Can you walk and talk?"

"You're the ones who're late," he growled. "My archaeology patrol was ready an hour ago. Say 'thank you, Frank' for not leaving your sorry butts behind."

"Thank you, Frank, for not leaving our sorry butts behind," she and Barry said in sing-song unison.

"Get in the Humvees, clowns," he grumbled. "Exactly how many DK guards do you have? I'm going to have to put on extra wheels just for you?"

"No DK guards are coming with us," she said.

"So the Army has to protect your sorry butts?" joked Frank. "All right. Let's go."

Leo started protesting about leaving him and the other guards behind, but Le An cut him off.

"It's a long drive back to Baghdad, part of it in the dark," she said. "I don't want anyone falling asleep at the wheel and killing us. You all stay here, sleep, stay cool and take delivery of the replacement vehicles. We're surrounded by guns and soldiers. We don't need guards today."

Leo didn't look happy, but reluctantly agreed.

Frank put on his best irritated look and snapped, "MacDee, can you get your entourage moving or is that asking too much? You think because you go through a little sniper storm, we're going to treat you like royalty?"

"Quit whining like a little girl," she said. "You had any embeds lately?"

"Naw, nobody's interested," he said. "We got a few people after we took down the Hussein boys, but most news orgs think we're too boring. There's not much action up here in the north because we do our jobs so well."

"You might be right," she said.

The USN group split up into different vehicles, with Le An pairing up with Jeremy and two soldiers in their Humvee.

Mosul spread across both sides of the Tigris: the main city on the western bank; the remains of ancient Assyria's capital Nineveh, along with some suburbs and various sized mounds, on the opposite bank. American military guarded the archaeological sites during the day.

As they drove over the Tigris bridge, Jeremy explained two of the largest mounds had been within Nineveh's walls, the larger one containing the remains of palaces once belonging to kings Sennacherib and Ashurbanipal. The smaller mound, for thousands of years, had been known as the location of the prophet Jonah's shrine and burial site, but archaeological excavation was limited because a mosque had been built over it.

"They can dig to build a mosque, but archaeologists can't dig because of the mosque?" asked Le An.

Jeremy smiled and nodded.

Paved highways kissed the edges of the partially reconstructed Nineveh city walls, the old civilization colliding uneasily with the new. Clusters of houses, Mosul's outlying suburbs, sprawled around the base of the mosque, right through the center third of where Nineveh had once been. The remains of the Assyrian empire lay buried under them, lost until the buildings could be razed. Even then, the site had been so compromised, much of the historical finds were lost forever.

"When was the last time you were here, Jeremy?" asked Le An.

"Thirteen years ago, prior to the first Gulf War."

The patrol first headed to the smaller of the two tells and the mosque atop it, its tall, limestone, cylindrical minaret rising high above the surrounding area. A grand staircase and six stone, landscaped tiers provided a stunning entrance from the modern, divided highway below. The mosque had been built around a Nestorian-Assyrian Christian church, which in turn had been built around the supposed burial site of the prophet Jonah. Nearby was a large, half-finished mosque—another of Saddam's many construction projects.

"The museum in Mosul was ransacked early in the invasion, priceless artifacts disappearing within hours," said Jeremy.

"That's because Turkey wouldn't give the US access for the invasion here in north," said Frank. "There weren't enough troops to secure the museum and prevent looting. Only a few special forces parachuted in when the war started."

Khaled attached wireless mics to Jeremy and Skylar, listening through his headphones to guarantee the sound was clear. After having Skylar hold up his piece of white paper in order to white-balance the camera for proper color, Barry started shooting, getting b-roll before Skylar started his interview.

"Doctor Hilson, tell us about this place," said Skylar.

"This site is known as *Tell Nebi Yunus*, which translates as 'the remains of the Prophet Jonah.' The western wall of ancient Nineveh came through here." Jeremy motioned with his arm, pointing in the direction of the larger mound a mile away. "The city extended beyond that second tell—*Tell Kouyunjik*. Nineveh's inner city wall, which you see reconstructed in some spots, was approximately three miles long. There hasn't been much archaeological excavation here since the mosque was built, though thirteen years ago some artifacts were unearthed. Archaeologists had to stop digging because it was affecting the mosque's foundation."

"What did they find?" asked Skylar.

"The head of a large *lamassu*, a mythical creature which appears throughout Mesopotamian art. Lamassu usually had the body of a lion or a bull, the face of a man and wings of an eagle."

He explained how earlier archaeological excavations had uncovered Assyrian writings which indicated the site had seen different usages, including an arsenal, a stable for horses and a small palace.

Le An was relieved to find Jeremy was a natural on camera, animated and engaging, not deadly dull like some professors.

"A synagogue was believed to have been here, a monastery and even, at one point, a temple to a fire god. Iraqis opened a shrine to Jonah in one of the rooms of the mosque approximately twenty years ago. A religious man was said to be buried here in an ebony coffin in the seventh century. When they opened the coffin in the thirteenth century, they found the body perfectly preserved, as if he were sleeping. In the nineteenth century, a man wrote the body was still in good condition. That's either extraordinary embalming or something miraculous going on because he's buried near Jonah."

"Who was Jonah?" asked Skylar.

"He was an Israelite who lived approximately 760 BC. He wrote God sent him to Nineveh to warn the Assyrians—who were utterly brutal—that they'd be destroyed if they didn't change their violent and evil ways."

"Did the Assyrians kill him or welcome him?" asked Sky.

"They didn't kill him, but as to whether they welcomed him, the Jewish and Christian writings differ from the Muslim account. In the Bible, Jonah flees, gets on a ship going to Tarshish—what we call Spain—is swallowed by a large fish and, three days on, is expelled and thrown onto land. He comes to Nineveh and is apparently received graciously. In the Qur'an, Jonah, called Yunus, goes straightaway to Nineveh, but the people reject him. He then flees, is swallowed by a fish, thrown out of the fish and returns to find the Ninevites have repented."

"A man surviving three days inside a whale is pretty hard to believe," said Skylar as he fought back a smile.

"A whale bone hangs inside this building, but we don't know that Jonah's fish was a whale. It could have been another large fish. The Hebrew translates as 'great fish,' the Greek as 'sea monster.'"

Skylar laughed. "Either way, it's hard to believe."

Jeremy smiled. "Not as hard as you'd imagine."

21

Nineveh, Iraq
Thursday, 4 September 2003

"You think someone could survive inside a whale?" laughed Skylar.

"There have been reports of sailors who lived for days after being washed overboard and swallowed by either sperm whales or rhinodon sharks," said Jeremy. "One incident took place in the English Channel, another near the Falkland Islands. In both cases, the men went into shock and became unconscious inside the fish when they realized where they were. Both men's shipmates located the fish, harpooned and cut them open to free the sailors. The men were successfully revived, though in one case the whale's gastric juices had bleached the man's skin and he became quite mad for a few weeks 'til he came round to a sound mind."

"That's quite a story," said Skylar.

"But true. Jonah wrote a small, obscure book in the Bible which might never have received much attention, except for two things: one is this shrine to him you see preserved in a Muslim country more than 2,700 years on from his death. The other is Jesus—or Yehoshua—mentioned this obscure prophet nine times. He said the only sign he'd give he was the Messiah was he'd be in his tomb the exact amount of time Jonah was in the belly of the fish—three days and three nights. Jonah even used the Hebrew term *sheol*, which means 'grave,' to refer to his time in the fish."

Skylar looked at the mosque and frowned. "Why would Muslims honor Jonah?"

"If Islam recognizes a prophet, such as Jonah, Muslims will give great honor, even when that prophet's also shared by a reviled religion. Muslims will tell you they revere and honor all their prophets, while Hebrews and Christians murder theirs. And, sadly, history shows that's true."

"Were Muslims the first to honor Jonah here?" asked Skylar.

"No, Muhammad established Islam more than 1,000 years on from Jonah. No doubt Israelites in captivity in Nineveh first honored Jonah and probably built the original shrine to him. Or the pagan Ninevites could have built it. They may have revered him because he'd warned them decades before. Then Christians honored him and, lastly, Muslims."

Le An glanced over at Khaled, who didn't look happy.

"Is this where Jonah's buried?" asked Skylar.

"There's no way of knowing for sure and the area's been compromised. Artifacts have likely been stolen or destroyed. For centuries written accounts stated he was buried here, but we have no solid archaeological proof and the book of Jonah tells nothing of what happened to him, other than a record of him advising a king of Israel on territory to take in battle some years on from his assignment to Nineveh. Assyria captured Israel in a series of invasions, so it's quite possible Jonah was amongst those brought here in captivity."

"The people he warned ended up conquering his own country and he became their captive?" said Skylar.

"Perhaps one reason he didn't want the assignment and tried to run. If Jonah suspected the Ninevites would be conquering Israel a few years on from his assignment, he may not have wanted them to repent or be spared."

"Why would the people of Nineveh listen to a Jewish prophet?" asked Skylar.

Le An sighed. She finally understood the difference between Jews and Israelites, but Skylar obviously hadn't been paying attention when she and the professor had prepped him.

"Jonah wasn't Jewish," Jeremy corrected him. "He was an Israelite, from the tribe of Zebulun."

Skylar stared at him blankly.

"Keep rolling. Sky, keep going," said Le An, knowing she could fix it in editing.

"Why would the people of Nineveh listen to an Israeli prophet?" asked Skylar.

"Israelite, not Israeli!" said Le An. "Keep rolling. Move on, Sky."

But instead of moving on, he became fixated with asking the

question correctly.

"Why would Ninevites listen to an Israelite prophet?" he asked again.

Frank and some of the soldiers started snickering.

"Excellent question," said Jeremy, seeking to soothe his interviewer's ego. "At the time Jonah came here, the Assyrians had recently suffered poverty, famines, plagues, internal revolt and external attacks. There'd even been an earthquake and a solar eclipse, which they may have taken as bad omens. They worshiped many pagan gods, but the gods weren't helping them. They recognized there was a main god which had more power than the others and, because they were suffering quite a lot, they were willing to shift their allegiance to a more powerful being. Jonah may well have said that was the one who sent him with the message. With the Ninevites, he uses the word *Elohim*, which carries a connotation of 'Supreme Being and Creator.'"

"And they listened," said Skylar.

"They did. Scripture says the Ninevites, even their king, fasted and repented of their violent ways. Jonah told them the one Supreme Being noticed their change in behavior and was willing to spare their city. That's a remarkable quality of Assyrians: once they realize they're wrong, they're quick to change. It's an extraordinary character trait."

"But wasn't it only because they thought one of their own gods was telling them what to do?" asked Skylar. "Wasn't it because they were superstitious about natural occurrences like earthquakes and floods?"

"They were superstitious, probably because they were quite polytheistic," said Jeremy.

Le An sighed, knowing her correspondent had no idea what the word meant.

Skylar out of ignorance said, "Polytheistic?"

"Yes, quite," said Jeremy. "They worshiped many gods, including Nebo and Merodach, though from the Akkadian period on, Nineveh's primary idol was Ishtar, the pagan goddess of fertility. Two temples dedicated to her were found here."

"That sounded like Easter," said Skylar.

"Yes, it's similar. Professing Christians adapted Ishtar's name and the pagan holiday celebrating her and fertility as a name for their own spring holiday. Hence the rabbits and colored eggs."

'Ask the question, ask the question, Skylar!' Le An was screaming in her head. *'Do a follow up on that!'*

He didn't ask the question. She was about to prompt Sky, when she glanced over and noticed the light on Barry's camera wasn't illuminated. Was his camera broken or had he accidentally turned it off? Not possible. If it was off, as experienced a videographer as he was, Barry would have known.

"Stop!" she screamed. "Ah, Barr, your camera's not on. Is there something wrong with it?"

He handed the camera to Khaled, grabbed her arm and pulled her over to the side.

"What are you doing?" she whispered. "What's wrong with you?"

"This guy's a nut," said Barry. "He attacks Christmas and Easter? Who found him anyway? Why bother to shoot this? Just let him ramble without wasting tape. It'll save us time when we edit. We won't have to go through all this garbage."

"I'm sorry, what?" she sputtered. "Are you having an aneurysm or has Iraqi heat fried what's left of your brain? Are you honestly telling your producer what sound bites will and will not be used in her script?"

"I always decide what to shoot. You don't tell me," he snapped.

"I do tell you what to shoot at times, as I do all my photogs. And I trust you to be professional enough to actually *be* shooting, not standing around watching and passing judgment. What are you objecting to?"

"He said Easter is a pagan holiday."

"So what? Maybe it is," she said, growing more frustrated and angry. "He said that goddess was this area's main pagan idol. They have archaeological proof of that. And he said Christianity adopted her name and traditions of worship, which obviously they did. What does that have to do with whether you're shooting this interview or not?"

"Easter isn't pagan."

"OK, Mister Mega-Catholic who never goes to Mass," she snapped. "Let's just let your beliefs totally screw up this shoot, 'K? Because, of course, you're totally correct with the only right religion in the world."

"Actually I am and it is," he shot back.

She took off her helmet and frantically ran her fingers through her hair. "I do not believe this. I do not believe you of all people are having a religious meltdown right now. I want you to shoot this interview. If you're not going to, tell me and I'll get Khaled to shoot it. Or I'll shoot the stupid thing myself. How long have you *not* been rolling tape? How much of his interview do we *not* have?"

They stood angrily glaring at each other until she took a deep breath and softened her approach.

"Barry, please, you know we're on a tight deadline. We have to shoot this interview. Can we argue about what's going in the script later when I'm writing it? Please? I need all the sound bites and b-roll I can get. Don't leave me without tape. My job's hard enough. I'm hot. I'm tired. I'm stressed out. I'm dealing with Skylar. I'm cramming in so much history my brain feels like it's going to explode. Do you want me to get another photog to finish the assignment? I'll send you home and get someone else when we get back to Baghdad. Maybe you're burned out and need a break from this place. We all do. I understand. Tim's burned out, you are, I'm a heartbeat away from it."

Even as she said it, her stomach was churning, upset at his sudden meltdown. She ran through her mind who she could get to replace him if he decided to bail on her and return to New York. It wasn't going to be easy. Barry was the best and if she had to use someone else, the quality wasn't going to be as good. Even in a war zone, Barry was the master artist when it came to camera angles, lighting and editing. He was as good as they got. That's why she always enjoyed working with him—up until now.

22

Nineveh, Iraq
Thursday, 4 September 2003

Barry glared at Le An, then said, "I'm finishing this assignment," and stomped back over to a stunned Khaled, grabbed the camera from him and hoisted it onto his shoulder. He turned to give her a disgusted look.

She walked over to him and whispered, "Can I trust you to do a good job on this or do I need to go back to Baghdad and get another shooter? Do you want me to hire Wen Darlington?"

Khaled looked confused, upset the two of them were fighting.

"I'm finishing this assignment," Barry repeated.

"Do you want to go back to New York tomorrow?"

"I'm finishing this assignment, Le An," he said through a clenched jaw. "And it will be Emmy worthy."

"That's all I need to know," she said, but now the doubt had been planted in her mind. Was he really going to be rolling tape every time she needed him to be shooting?

Through the camera, she watched what had been shot, then prepped Skylar and Jeremy on what they had to repeat and what follow-up questions they should do. When she glanced over at Barry's camera, this time it was on.

"The name Easter comes from a pagan goddess?" Skylar asked Jeremy. "Comes from a *woman*?"

"Yes. Those who worshiped Ishtar believed she had many lovers whom she treated cruelly. Her reputation as a fertility goddess eventually worked its way into the modern day Easter symbols of rabbits and eggs. Ancient Chaldeans even colored their eggs to worship her. Ishtar was an important idol in both Assyria and Babylon. In Babylon, she was even honored on one of the city's main gates."

Le An knew Barry was probably seething and didn't dare look at him. Instead, she jotted down a reminder to bring up the goddess Ishtar when they were shooting at Babylon.

"Are Assyrians still in this area?" asked Skylar.

"Some, but the majority migrated away from here 2,600 years ago when the Medes and Babylonians defeated them. In any war, people flee to get away from fighting, as a lot of Iraqis have fled this war and moved to Syria or Jordan."

Frank motioned the Army patrol was moving on toward the other tell. As they walked back to their vehicles for the short drive over, a young soldier walking next to Le An motioned to Jeremy.

"He's pretty interesting," he said.

"Yes, he is," she said and suddenly stopped.

The soldier gave her a puzzled look, fingering his gun as he anxiously scanned the area for anything suspicious.

"What?" he asked.

"Oh, sorry. I was just thinking about something the professor had said." She frowned as she started counting from the Friday crucifixion three full days on her fingers, "Friday to Saturday, Saturday to Sunday, Sunday to Monday? Monday?"

"What's happening Monday?" asked Skylar.

"No, if you count three full days and nights from a Friday afternoon crucifixion, like Jeremy said, you come to Monday afternoon, not Sunday morning. Jesus left the tomb Monday afternoon?"

"They're not supposed to be full days, I guess," said Skylar.

"They were full twenty-four-hour days," said Jeremy as he came up behind them. "And it's three days and three nights from the time he was placed in the tomb, not from his death. Scripture indicates he rose Saturday near sunset."

"But that's only one day and one night," she said.

"It's Sunday morning," Barry said emphatically, an annoyed tone creeping into his voice. "Sunday morning. Quit messing with established traditions."

"Whether it was Sunday morning or Saturday afternoon, that's still a day or a day-and-a-half, not three days," said Le An.

Barry held up three fingers as he counted out, "Friday one, Saturday two, Sunday three. Three days."

"That's not three twenty-four-hour days," she said, doing the math in her head. "Three days plus three nights equals seventy-two hours. Your way only comes to only thirty-six hours. That's half the time."

"Sunday morning," Barry repeated.

As they loaded the equipment into the vehicles, Le An asked Jeremy, "Could it be three twelve-hour segments of days?"

"No, the Hebrew says Jonah was in the belly of the fish three days and three nights. When 'day' is used with 'night,' it signifies a full twenty-four hours," he said.

"Sunday. Morning," repeated Barry.

"Jeremy, why does it say three days and three nights if it was only one day and one night or one day and two nights? Something's wrong," she said.

"Then it's consistently wrong approximately a dozen times in scripture," he said. "Or it could mean the crucifixion wasn't on Friday."

"Oh, for crying out loud," said Barry loudly in disgust.

But Le An was curious and kept pressing the point. "If not Friday, then when?"

"Wednesday," said Jeremy.

Barry loudly voiced his disapproval and stomped off.

"Wednesday?" Le An and Skylar asked in unison.

"There were two Sabbaths that week—a weekly Sabbath and an annual high holy day Sabbath after Passover. The annual holy days could fall on any day of the week, not just the weekly Sabbath," he said. "The mistake some make is assuming the two Sabbaths were on the same day. They weren't. Hebrews count days sunset to sunset, not midnight to midnight as the Romans did. Scripture says he was put to death and placed in the tomb near sunset at the start of the annual high Sabbath, which that year began at sunset Wednesday and continued to sunset Thursday. Three days and three nights from Wednesday bring you to the weekly Sabbath Saturday near sunset. Two Sabbaths, three days, three nights."

Everyone stared at him as they tried to count days and process what he'd said.

"Well, blow me away," said Skylar and everyone erupted in laughter—everyone except Barry.

He was still seething.

23

*Nineveh, Iraq
Thursday, 4 September 2003*

A mile from Jonah's shrine, rising more than sixty feet above the Tigris River plain, stood *Tell Kouyunjik*. Archaeologists had excavated the upper layers of the mound, revealing several temples and palaces, including the entry court and a few rooms of Sennacherib's palace. Originally, the walls had been covered with bas-reliefs, but Jeremy noted most now resided in the British Museum in London. What had been left had either been looted and sold on the black market, or was crumbling in decay.

"Greater Nineveh was rather large," he said. "Jonah wrote 120,000 people lived here and it took him three days to do a walkabout."

He explained Nineveh's mud-brick inner and outer walls had been high and thick—wide enough to allow three chariots to drive side by side on top of them. More than 1,000 watch towers and moats had encircled the city for additional protection. An opening on the eastern wall had allowed the Khosr River—now known as Khawsar Wadi—to flow into Nineveh, exit out the western wall, then empty into the Tigris a mile away.

Barry had been deftly moving from shooting two-shots, which included both Skylar and Jeremy, to close ups on each one as they spoke at length. That was fine part of the time, but Le An didn't want it all to be such shaky, on-the-move video.

A one-camera shoot was never optimal. The camera would be focused on the person being interviewed while the producer jotted down the correspondent's questions. After the interview was completed, the photographer would get 'cutaway' shots of the correspondent. While the producer read back the questions, the reporter would repeat them on camera, trying to act as if he were doing it real-time during the interview. It was not only time consuming, but also unnatural. For additional cutaways, before and after the interview, the photographer would get additional two-shots of the correspondent and the interviewee together.

That extra video was to provide shots for covering the edit points where two sound bites from a person were butted together. Without different video covering that section, the head of the person being videotaped would appear to bounce at the edit point, what journalists referred to as a 'jump cut.'

With more important interviews, USN sent two videographers, two cameras, a sound tech and a producer. If there were two cameras, but no second shooter available, the videographer would lock down one camera on a tripod focused on the correspondent, then position the second camera to focus on the person being interviewed, allowing the videographer to zoom in or pull back on the subject for a range of shots.

Le An quickly glanced around and noticed the soldiers were still either patrolling or talking to local residents who'd gathered near them.

"Barry, let's add a second camera on Skylar instead of doing cutaways," she said. "It's too time-consuming and we need to do this as quickly as possible. This is a war zone, even if it isn't as bad as other areas."

She unzipped the padded case holding the other camera and waited for him to pull it out, knowing how picky he was about people touching his equipment. He threw her a dirty look and grumbled under his breath.

"What's wrong?" she asked him in a low voice. "We always do this. As a matter of fact, I'm kinda surprised you didn't suggest it. Why are you mad?"

"Khaled can't do off-the-shoulder cam. He's not good enough," he said.

"Then put him on sticks," she said referring to a tripod. "Put him on Skylar so he doesn't have to move the camera or do a lot of zooms and pans."

Barry gave her an annoyed look, then pushed her aside.

"Move," he barked as he reached for the second camera and picked up a tripod, jerking the legs down into position before tightening them.

Le An pulled Skylar aside to review some questions she thought he should ask and tried to suppress a smirk as she noticed Barry opening a second tripod for himself.

He positioned Skylar and Jeremy in a secluded spot away from the highway in back of the reconstructed Mashki Gate, also known as the Gate of the Watering Places. Original stones formed the base of the wall, with new stones atop that. Barry took out his light meter to check readings, then pushed the men by their shoulders to move them into the best light. He took the sound equipment from Khaled and, putting the headphones on himself, motioned for him to keep an eye on the second camera positioned on Skylar. Khaled dutifully complied and trotted over to assume his new job as the second videographer.

Le An waited for Barry to give them the OK, but he kept zooming in and out, then panning slowly from one side to the other, adjusting his tripod and camera for the best view of Jeremy.

"You ready, Barry?" she asked.

"No!" he snapped, then moments later said, "Speed."

"Rolling," said Khaled.

"Are Assyria and Nineveh mentioned in the Bible?" Skylar asked Jeremy.

"Many times. Scripture's not only spiritual, but a historical record of Middle Eastern kingdoms, political uprisings, wars, deportations and migrations. The first time Nineveh's mentioned is in Genesis, its builder Nimrod, the great-grandson of Noah," he said, adding, "Noah who built the ark, the animal transport used in the flood—not to be confused with the lost ark of the covenant Hollywood was seeking."

Skylar started snort laughing and couldn't stop. "Sorry, Le."

"Still rolling," said Barry in an annoyed tone.

When Skylar composed himself, Jeremy continued, "Three Assyrian kings conquered the ten tribes of Israel and deported them to northern Mesopotamia—today's Turkey, Syria, Iran and northern Iraq, between the Black and Caspian seas. Some experts estimate from census numbers that six-million Israelites were deported."

Le An made a note USN's computer graphic artists would have to create an animated map, arrows sweeping north and east from Israel into Mesopotamia.

"This is northern Iraq," said Skylar. "Israel was deported here?"

"Yes. Assyria's policy toward rebellious nations was, to use your American baseball terms, 'three strikes and you're out.' With the first defeat, they'd turn a nation into a vassal state, require payments and place a puppet ruler on the throne. If the nation rebelled after that, strike two. Assyria would deport large numbers of the conquered peoples into areas where the land, language and culture were foreign—leaving the conquered so disheartened, they'd lose all will to fight. They'd also become buffers against Assyria's enemies. If yet another rebellion occurred, strike three: Assyria would deport the remaining population from their homeland and the nation would cease to exist. The Assyrians then deported other conquered peoples into that land. Babylon later somewhat followed this same policy."

"The Israelites rebelled three times?" asked Skylar.

"They did—and they ceased to exist as a nation, but not as a people. That's where many err when it comes to the ten tribes—incorrectly believing the entire population was either killed off in military offenses or scattered as individuals. Modern historians have a difficult time comprehending the ancient practice of mass deportations, though Hitler certainly seemed to grasp the concept. When Israel's ten tribes were deported, for the most part, they were still residing within the tribal boundaries Joshua had assigned them when they'd conquered the land beginning approximately 1403 BC."

"For hundreds of years people didn't move?" asked Skylar.

"Your American states are still within their boundaries hundreds of years on from your nation's creation. Most ancient peoples, unless they were an army or were forced to flee war or drought, remained within a few miles of their homes their entire lives. They didn't travel as extensively as we do today. And most Israelites married within their tribes because, by law, land couldn't transfer to another tribe. They'd lose their land and land was everything. It was an agrarian society. Israelites, for all their faults, were still a nation of civil laws, which had been in effect 700 years on from them settling the land until the time of their deportation to Assyria. Marrying within the same tribe is still the tradition in the Middle East. Throughout the world, most people marry someone from their own nation. Intermarriage isn't as frequent as you'd think and it certainly wasn't when the Israelite tribes were deported."

"Did the Assyrians have written records they conquered Israel?" asked Skylar.

"They did. Tiglath-Pileser, also called Pul, conquered Israel the first two times and inscribed on a victory stela—a stone pillar—that he'd deported all the house of Omri. Archaeologists found the phrase 'House of Omri' on Assyrian and Moabite stelae, such as the Mesha Stela, discovered in Jordan, and the Black Obelisk, found south of here at Kalhu."

"Omri? Who was that?" asked Skylar.

"A powerful military commander who became king of Israel. He was famous for hundreds of years on, even in foreign countries. 'Land of the House of Omri'—*Mat Bit-Khumri*—is the name the Assyrians gave Israel."

"They didn't call Israel 'Israel'?" asked Skylar.

"Not always. What a nation calls itself may not be how other countries refer to it, which is rather important to know when tracking a people's migrations. Omri's name became the name of Israel for the Assyrians. You Americans name your cities, roads and states after your popular presidents. It's the same concept."

Le An glanced around again, both for their safety and to make sure they still had time to complete all the interview they needed to do at that site before Frank told them they were moving on.

Some soldiers roamed the area checking on a few suspicious people at the site. Others talked to locals who had gathered around them with questions, problems, suggestions and complaints. A few soldiers were clustered nearby, listening to Skylar's interview as their eyes constantly shifted, on alert for any trouble.

"As powerful and wealthy as Nineveh had been, once it was conquered and destroyed in 612 BC, the city disappeared from view under layers of sand and dirt," said Jeremy. "Two hundred years on, when the Greek historian Xenophon marched past here with 10,000 troops, he could only find small traces of Nineveh. It was as if the city had never existed. For thousands of years, a record of Nineveh's existence only remained in the pages of scripture."

"Did archaeologists find the city?" asked Skylar.

"Yes, in the 1800s. Local tribes had a tradition Nineveh had been here, but there was no proof until the British archaeologist and historian Sir Austen Henry Layard began to dig here in 1847. Two years on he discovered Sennacherib's seventy-room palace over there and later Ashurbanipal's palace and library over there," he said as he pointed, "where they found 22,000 cuneiform-inscribed clay tablets. Archaeologists have found in excess of 300,000 Assyrian inscriptions and clay tablets—a wealth of information, but meaningless until Sir Henry Rawlinson and others managed to decipher them."

"How did they do that?" asked Skylar.

"The Persian Darius the Great had commissioned his history be carved in three different cuneiform languages on a cliff in Western Iran—what we refer to as the Behistun Inscription. A translator deciphered one of them and, because all three were identical accounts, Sir Rawlinson and others used that to decipher the other two languages. That allowed them to finally translate the writings found here in Nineveh and throughout Mesopotamia."

Le An made a note to find video or stills of the Behistun Inscription and a picture or illustration of Rawlinson.

"Archaeologists from Britain and France conducted digs in Iraq?" asked Skylar.

"Yes, as well as those from Germany, the US, Italy and other countries," said Jeremy. "The University of California Berkeley was doing brilliant work here in 1989 and 1990. That was the last time I was here. I see there's been quite a bit of damage to Sennacherib's palace."

"Is that war damage?" asked Skylar.

"Much is general decay from the environment. In the 1960s, the Iraqi government put a roof over Sennacherib's palace, but in thirteen years there've been two wars, UN sanctions, locals vandalizing and stealing bas-reliefs, selling them on the black market to private collectors. People are illegally digging all over archaeological sites like Nineveh, looking for artifacts or gold, jewelry and ivory to steal and sell. Saddam spent nearly $2 billion building palaces for himself, but he didn't protect his own country's heritage and the Iraqis aren't doing it themselves. Saddam possessed a personal fortune of $30 billion, but he wouldn't spend money to preserve his country's history. How many palaces did he have? Seventy? Eighty?"

"A lot," said Skylar, who wasn't sure of the official count. He pointed to the nearby suburban community. "Are those houses built over Nineveh?"

"Yes, isn't that utterly preposterous? They installed water and sewage lines through an archaeological site. Why aren't people in Mosul protecting their heritage?"

Le An glanced over at Khaled and he didn't look pleased at Jeremy's comments.

The group walked over to take a closer look at the remains of Sennacherib's palace as Jeremy explained how elaborate bas-relief panels on the walls had been been filled with accounts of the king's victories.

"Victories over nations such as Egypt, Israel and Judah," he said. "The Assyrians conquered Israel, but Sennacherib couldn't defeat Judah's King Hezekiah, though he twisted it into a victory of sorts."

"What do you mean?" asked Skylar.

Jeremy smiled. "Sennacherib's bas reliefs said he shut up Hezekiah in Jerusalem 'like a caged bird.' That was the phrase he used. He'd never have recorded the rest of the account because it would've been too humiliating. Scripture fills in the rest. One night 185,000 Assyrian soldiers camped round Jerusalem suddenly and mysteriously died."

24

Nineveh, Iraq
Thursday, 4 September 2003

"You said 185,000 Assyrian soldiers died? At once?" Skylar asked incredulously. "That's more than all the US forces in Iraq right now."

"Indeed. Imagine for a moment if that many of your Americans inexplicably died during the night," said Jeremy.

"It would be disastrous," said Skylar. "How did they die? What could kill that many people that fast?"

"Three books of scripture—Kings, Chronicles and Isaiah—say one night an angel killed them as they camped round Jerusalem."

"An angel?" Skylar laughed.

"How would you describe 185,000 soldiers dying suddenly at the same time?"

"A major plague?" said Skylar, shrugging his shoulders. "What did Sennacherib do?"

"He was with the rest of his army fighting Egypt, but, ever arrogant, he returned here to Nineveh and on carved wall panels all round one room, he boasted of defeating the Jewish city Lachish. The fact he devoted an entire room to the defeat demonstrates another interesting point: the room was where he greeted foreign dignitaries. He wanted other nations to know he had the military might to defeat Lachish because Judah was a powerful nation at that time. If he'd defeated a weak, ineffective nation, what would be the point of bragging? But to tell foreign nations you'd defeated a great city in a powerful nation like Judah... well, that was worth bragging about."

"How did he describe losing 185,000 soldiers?" asked Skylar.

"He didn't record that. His version was he'd caged King Hezekiah in Jerusalem."

Skylar laughed, "What happened to him?"

"Two of his sons murdered him as he worshiped in the temple of his pagan god Nisroch."

"Not a very heroic end."

"No, but did you catch what I said about Lachish?"

Skylar looked confused. "It was a powerful Jewish city Sennacherib defeated?"

"Yes, but what's truly extraordinary is the defeat's mentioned in scripture. Assyrian leaders never recorded their defeats, only their victories. They even turned a devastating loss of 185,000 soldiers into a victory. Scripture, on the other hand, records humiliating defeats of both Israel and Judah. That in itself speaks to its authenticity. What other ancient peoples recorded their own defeats? None."

"What happened to the Assyrians?"

"They were a brutal, warring people who conquered many nations, but eventually, their empire ended. They were weakened by civil war and finally invaded. Ninevites had boasted they could withstand a twenty-year siege, but, in the end, the Medes and Babylonians, with help from the Scythians and Cimmerians, conquered them in only two years."

Le An made a note to ask Jeremy who the Scythians and Cimmerians were.

"The Babylonians gained access to Nineveh where the Assyrians least suspected it. Flooding from the Tigris destroyed a section of the western wall over there," he said as he pointed, "providing a way for foreign troops to enter the city in 612 BC—ten or twenty years on from the writings of a minor Israelite prophet named Nahum, who predicted a flood would destroy Nineveh."

"Nineveh was destroyed exactly the way he said?" asked Skylar.

"Precisely. We'll see a shrine to Nahum this afternoon."

After the soldiers finished their patrol, they skirted Nineveh's perimeter, with Barry getting b-roll of the gates' and city walls' reconstruction, then drove nine miles northeast to what had been Khorsabad, Sargon the Second's capital.

Jeremy explained that for 2,500 years, Sargon had only existed in the pages of Judeo-Christian scripture, but in 1842, French diplomat and antiquities' hunter Paul-Emile Botta uncovered Sargon's palace and its wall inscriptions—archaeological proof the once-powerful Assyrian ruler had existed.

"Are some people in Mosul Israelites?" Skylar asked Jeremy as they packed up their gear.

"Perhaps a few remnants remain, but the majority migrated away when the Medes and Persians conquered the Assyrians."

"Did the Israelites become the Babylonians' slaves?" asked Skylar.

"No, some Israelites turned on their long-time captors and joined forces with the Medes and Babylonians to defeat Assyria. Others of the ten tribes took advantage of the war and began migrating north, west and east."

"Did many Israelites survive their captivity?" asked Le An.

"Oh my, yes," said Jeremy. "By the time the Assyrian Empire fell, the Israelites had grown to enormous numbers. Six hundred years on from that, near the end of the first century, the Jewish historian Josephus wrote the Israelites were an immense multitude."

"He knew where they were 800 years after they went into captivity?" she asked. "How is that possible?"

"Josephus and most of the Jews knew where their brother tribes were, though if you look for them in historical accounts of other nations, you won't find them referenced as 'Israel.' To the Jews, they were still identifiable as Israel and they most certainly weren't dead," he said. "Josephus lived in the Roman Empire and wrote there were only two of the twelve tribes in Europe and Asia subject to the Romans. That would've been the majority of people in the tribes of Judah and Benjamin, as well as some of the Levitical priesthood. He wrote the other ten tribes were outside the boundaries of the Roman Empire, beyond the Euphrates, and were so large they couldn't be estimated by numbers."

"That definitely doesn't sound as if they were dead," she said. "You said other nations referred to them by different names? Like what? The 'Land of the House of Omri' you talked about before?"

"*Mat Bit-Khumri*—yes. Peoples of different languages, even today, refer to countries by various names. For instance, English speakers say Germany, but Germans refer to their country as *Deutschland*."

"I never thought of that," said Skylar.

"Me neither," said Le An.

"And what do the French call Germany?" asked Jeremy, as if quizzing a classroom of his students.

"*Allemagne*," she said, her first language French easily coming back to her. "So if you only knew English and were looking for Germany in German or French records, you'd never find it."

"Precisely. You call the site of next year's summer Olympic games 'Greece,'" continued Jeremy. "However, the Greeks refer to their country as *Hellas*, which is pronounced with an 'H' sound, but the first letter *epsilon* visually resembles an 'E' in the English alphabet."

"Sigma Zeta Epsilon! Yeah!" said Skylar, as he fist-pumped the air in support of his old college fraternity, a move which prompted eye-rolls from most in the group.

Jeremy, ever the encouraging teacher, smiled softly, patting him on the back to graciously acknowledge his eager response. "A man with a knowledge of Greek. How do Spanish speakers refer to the United States?"

Skylar, who spoke fluent Spanish from his years covering news in Miami, again jumped in with an answer, in unison with one of the Hispanic-American soldiers, "*Los Estados Unidos*."

"Precisely. Germans refer to the United States as *die Vereinigten Staaten*. The Swedes call it *Förenta Staterna*. And the French?" Jeremy asked, turning to Le An.

"*Les Etats-Unis*," she said.

He nodded. "Different names for the same country. If you're going to look for a people, you have to know their many names or you'll never find them. The ten tribes were called different names and nicknames by foreign nations down through history, sometimes even identified in connection to their powerful leaders, such as 'House of Omri,' and sometimes as derivations of their individual tribal names. Find those names and you find where they migrated. Then add other historical information, such as where and when they were taken captive. It's rather like a puzzle. You put all the pieces together, here a little, there a little. It's not a simple process when you're digging into history, but the clues are there. And each year archaeological dig sites reveal more clues. We've only unearthed a small fraction of the past."

"You said the Scythians and Cimmerians joined the Medes and Babylonians to defeat Nineveh and the Assyrians," said Le An, looking down at her notes. "Who were they?"

"Israelites," Jeremy smiled.

25

Khorsabad, Iraq
Thursday, 4 September 2003

"Good on the Israelites for finally attacking their captors," said Skylar.

"They were called Scythians and Cimmerians, too?" asked Le An. "How'd they get those names? And how do you spell that?"

Jeremy wrote the names on her notepad.

"The 'C' in Cimmerians is like 'K,' a hard sound?" she asked. "It sounds a little guttural too, like a 'G.' Why would they call Israelites 'Cimmerians'?"

"The name's derived from *Khumri*, the way the Assyrians pronounced the name of the Israelite leader Omri," said Jeremy.

"He must have been really powerful for enemy nations to keep referring to the Israelites by his name," she said.

"Omri was rather well known to surrounding nations at that time and the name remained as an identifier of the tribes," said Jeremy. "The Cimmerians appeared quite suddenly approximately 714 BC, during the first two Assyrian invasions of Israel, where some of the ten tribes had been deported."

"Sounds like more than a coincidence," she said. "Where was that?"

"Today's Iran—south of Armenia," he said. "Approximately 150 miles northeast of here."

"That's pretty close," she said.

"Remember what I said: the Assyrians would resettle enemy nations as buffers against their other enemies," said Jeremy.

"But what if the resettled nations decided to join forces with Assyria's enemies?" asked Le An.

"That's precisely what happened," he said. "Some of the resettled Israelite tribes eventually joined forces with the Babylonians and the Medes, soundly defeating the Assyrians and ending their empire."

Skylar started laughing. "That's great."

"You said the Scythians were Israelites, too?" asked Le An.

"The Scythians appeared quite suddenly approximately 700 BC, northwest of here near the Black Sea," he said.

"So the Cimmerians and Scythians both suddenly appeared in areas where the Assyrians had resettled the ten tribes—and at the same time?"

"Precisely."

"Interesting. How'd they end up with the name Scythians?" she asked.

"From the Greeks who traded with them," he said. "Scythian comes from the word *Saka*, a form of Isaac—Abraham's son and Israel's father. Remember? Abraham, Isaac and Jacob? The Scythians dominated the Eurasian Steppes for hundreds of years until climate changes forced them to move on."

"Eurasian Steppes?" asked Skylar.

"Grasslands in southern Russia which stretch from Europe's Carpathian Mountains more than 4,000 miles east to Mongolia," said Jeremy.

Le An jotted down notes for another map.

"The Scythians were described as fair-haired, fierce warriors with large herds who moved freely across the Steppes and through the passes of the Caucasus Mountains," continued Jeremy. "Severe climate changes after 200 BC caused the Steppes to become quite arid, like a desert, and forced the Scythians to move north and west to find grazing land for their herds."

"Scythian gold," said Le An. "I remember that exhibit in New York about three years ago. They were really skilled at working with gold and designing jewelry."

"Yes, they were quite skilled in metal work," said Jeremy. "While the Scythians had a nomadic life roaming the Steppes, they also had a high level of sophistication which indicated a more stable, urban life in their past."

"You said Josephus wrote the ten tribes were beyond the Euphrates and outside the Roman Empire. Was he talking about the Eurasian Steppes?" she asked.

"Partially," he said, as Frank motioned for them to get going.

From Khorsabad, the military convoy headed fifteen miles

northwest to Al-Kosh, near Iraq's border with Turkey and Syria on the eastern bank of the Tigris River. The village of almost 5,000 people consisted of ancient stone houses which climbed the base of a mountain next to a fertile agricultural plain.

As they drove through the steep, narrow streets, Jeremy said, "Elkoshites claim both Assyrian and Babylonian ancestry. They're Assyrian Christians, yet also refer to themselves as Chaldean Catholics. Many speak at least three languages: Arabic, Kurdish and their dialect Syriac—a form of Aramaic we believe Jesus spoke. They're friendly to Americans, because of the shared Christian beliefs and because many of their family members have immigrated to America—primarily Detroit and San Diego."

As soon as the convoy parked, Barry jumped out and pulled out his camera. He started shooting the neighborhood as a few chickens scampered to get out of his way, then moved to get ahead of Skylar and Jeremy, walking backward to shoot their approach. Le An positioned herself behind him, fingers looped through his belt hoops, guiding him around potential pitfalls since he couldn't see what he was about to back into.

As they moved behind Saint Gurgis Church and down a small alleyway, the sidewalk became too treacherous for Barry to walk backward—rising up in some areas, sunken in others, grass and weeds growing in between enormous cracks and along the sides. Le An made Skylar and Jeremy stop until Barry could walk to the end and shoot their approach from the front of the crumbling ancient synagogue—the shrine and alleged tomb of Nahum the prophet.

Most of the roof was gone and the tops of the stone walls had fallen in. Concertina wire was strung across openings closest to the walkway. The building's fading green wooden door was locked and some of the soldiers who'd been there before went off in search of the caretaker who lived nearby. Others began walking and talking with members of the village who'd started grouping around them.

Walking past the front door of the building, the USN group rounded the corner and climbed up a grassy embankment which ran halfway up a caved-in wall. Peering down into the interior's ruins, they could see crumbling stone pillars barely supporting pointed arches. On one wall was a small plaque with what appeared to be Hebrew lettering, the mortar used to attach it slapped on in a not-so-neat manner.

The back of the structure was the only part with a remaining roof and that's where Nahum's supposed tomb stood, a large sarcophagus draped in green cloth with a metal fence completely surrounding it. In the grates of the fence were small tufts of paper, as if someone had started filling out a parade float. Jeremy explained they were prayers people had left behind.

An inner, grassy courtyard was punctuated with low stone foundations where walls had once stood. Along the perimeter, arched openings led to what had once been apartments for those from out of town who wished to stay overnight. Jeremy said a small building near the back of the property was believed to be the tomb of Nahum's sister Sarah.

"The Jews used to tell of miraculous physical and mental healings when people stayed and prayed through the night at the tomb," he said. "Jews would travel here during the year, especially on holy days. In early summer, on Shavuot—also known as Feast of Weeks or Pentecost—thousands would come to celebrate the Nahum festival, camping out in the open fields or staying here in the rooms of the synagogue. They would reenact Moses receiving the ten commandments, then stage an elaborate mock battle against the forces of evil."

The soldiers returned with the elderly caretaker and a smile came over his face in recognition as he pointed to Jeremy. They grasped hands, pulling each other close.

"Hello, my friend," Jeremy gave a warm smile.

He repeated it in Syriac and they continued their lively conversation for a few minutes, before the man ran to unlock the shrine's front door. Grinning, he motioned for the USN crew and soldiers to enter, then ran back to his home. He reappeared moments later with members of his family and a leather guest ledger he asked everyone to sign.

Not many names had been entered over the years and the most recent ones seemed to be of soldiers stationed at Post Freedom. As Le An flipped through the pages, she noticed the names of a few academics, including a familiar name in 1988—Doctor Jeremy Hilson. She motioned to Barry to shoot the page.

Jeremy translated as the caretaker pointed to a nearby house and explained it had once been the home of the rabbi who cared for the synagogue and tomb. He said the chief rabbi from

Baghdad used to stay there when he visited.

As more townspeople came to see the caretaker's long lost friend, Le An had a feeling the man's family would soon be inviting them in for tea, subjecting them to the dreaded, possibly-bacteria-infested water. She asked Khaled to go back to the Humvees to grab one of the three cases of bottled water they'd brought with them. One case was already gone, but if they presented the third as a gift to the tomb's caretaker, maybe when he made tea, he'd use their water.

"Who was Nahum?" Skylar asked Jeremy as he began his interview.

"An Israelite prophet, most probably born in captivity, more than 100 years on from the Assyrians taking his ancestors captive. Nahum prophesied against Nineveh—as the prophet Jonah had. However, Jonah said Assyrians had a chance to repent of their evil ways and not be destroyed. Nahum said their time was up and they were already marked for destruction. Nineveh fell during a flood in 612 BC, approximately ten to twenty years on from when Nahum said it would be conquered in a flood."

As more townspeople appeared to stare at the soldiers and journalists, Le An was glad to see the elders shushing the noisy, chattering children so they wouldn't interfere with the taping.

"Are you saying this tomb is more than 2,500 years old?" asked Skylar pointing to the green-covered object in the building.

"Well, obviously, we have no real way of knowing," he said, "but in Nahum's book in scripture, he refers to himself as Nahum the Elkoshite—and this is the town of Al-Kosh."

"Sounds the same," said Skylar.

"Similar in spelling, also. Most experts believe it's the same. And with the strong traditions associated with this location, most believe this was his burial site. However, two places in Israel also claim that honor. I favor this location as being more authentic, but we have no real way of knowing."

He spotted the Hebrew plaque on the wall and cocked his head to the side, then more to the side, and even more as if he were trying to read it upside down. All around him people cocked their heads to the side the same way and tried to look at what he was seeing.

Jeremy stood up, a slight smile on his face.

"What is it?" asked Skylar.

"My friend said the plaque fell off and he reattached it... a lovely gesture." He pursed his lips to try and control the smile, then whispered, "It's upside down."

Some Hebrew lettering remained on the walls, but Jeremy explained under Saddam most had been plastered over—a systematic way of ridding the country of Jews and anything associated with them. The last Jews had fled Al-Kosh after Muslims began murdering and purging Iraq of 'the infidels.' The rabbi and his family had left for Israel, entrusting his Christian friend with the synagogue's iron keys and leather guest book, asking him to care for the tomb. His friend had loyally maintained it ever since, keeping his promise as best he could.

"The last Jews in Al-Kosh left in 1948," said Jeremy. "The Muslims drove them out or killed them. I fear they may do the same to these Christians."

Le An glanced over at Khaled and noticed he looked angry at what the professor was saying.

"In 1990, Saddam Hussein's secret police took away Assyrian Christians in a pogrom and purging similar to the one they used on Iraq's Jewish population," continued Jeremy. "Some are still searching for missing family members."

With Skylar questioning and Jeremy translating, Christians in Al-Kosh expressed fears they might suffer the same fate as their Jewish brothers.

"It's not just Assyrian Christians," said Frank. "It's the Kurds, too. Saddam killed almost 182,000 Kurds here in the north within a few years during the late 1980s—mass executions called the al-Anfal Campaign. He wiped out about 4,000 villages. Used chemical weapons like mustard gas, Sarin and the nerve agent GB on 250 towns. Between that and the war with Iran, some say he killed more Arabs than anyone in history."

"He should not be called Saddam, but Haddam," said an angry villager.

Jeremy nodded and gently placed a hand on the man's shoulder, then said, "'*Saddam*' in Arabic means 'crasher,' '*haddam*' means 'destroyer.'"

"Does Iraq have weapons of mass destruction?" asked Skylar.

Many of the villagers voiced a loud "Yes!" punctuating it with animated hand motions, everyone talking at once. Many of them pointed to a middle-aged man, pushing him forward in the crowd. Frank and many of the US soldiers seemed to know him.

"He was an Iraqi fighter pilot under Saddam," said Frank, "but he refused to join the Ba'ath party."

The man said in November 1990, during the first Gulf War, Saddam was days away from sending ninety-eight of Iraq's Russian MiGs, Sukois and French Mirages to invade Jordan's and Syria's airspace in order to bomb Israel.

"With Sarin 1, Sarin 2 and the nerve gas Tabun," said the man, as Jeremy translated. "We had them all."

"What stopped him?" asked Skylar.

"Thankfully, praise be to God, someone, at risk of death, courageously and wisely explained to Saddam Israel's technology was far more advanced than Iraq's," said the man. "The Israelis would have shot down all our planes before we ever reached them."

26

Nimrud, Iraq
Thursday, 4 September 2003

From Al-Kosh, the convoy traveled back toward Mosul, driving five miles southeast of the city to the ancient town of Nimrud, on the eastern bank of the Tigris River. In the days of the Assyrian empire, the city had been called Kalhu—Calah in scripture—and had briefly served as one of the nation's capitals. Nimrud's name came from its founder Nimrod, Noah's great-grandson who had also built Nineveh and Babel—the forerunner of Babylon.

"According to Babylonian traditions, Nimrod married his mother Semiramis," he said.

Skylar, startled, was speechless.

"After his death," continued Jeremy, "his wife-mother claimed a dead tree stump overnight blossomed into an evergreen tree and on Nimrod's birthday, December twenty-fifth, she said he'd visit the tree and leave gifts. That was approximately 2,000 years prior to the birth of Jesus."

"Christianity's holiest days Christmas and Easter both started here in Mesopotamia?" asked Skylar.

"Yes," said Jeremy.

Ho, boy. Here we go again, thought Le An, as she sneaked a look at Barry.

He looked beyond annoyed, but at least his camera was still on.

Jeremy told how Sir Austen Henry Layard had first excavated Kalhu, but wrongly identified it as Nineveh. Layard may have been wrong about the city for a time, but his archaeological excavations, which included the palace of King Ashurnasirpal, were noteworthy.

"There are only two preserved Assyrian palaces in the world," he said. "We just saw the other one in Nineveh—Sennacherib's palace—and now this one. As you observe, the climate and lack of security are taking a toll on both."

Sand storms and seasonal torrential rains had eroded the great stone reliefs, carved 3,000 years before. There was no telling what looters had walked off with.

Jeremy continued, "After Iraq invaded Kuwait in 1991, the UN imposed sanctions preventing Iraqi archaeologists from importing even basic materials to help conserve sites."

"You didn't agree with the UN sanctions?" asked Skylar.

"Did they accomplish anything?" he asked, then repeated what he'd said before. "Saddam found millions to build his many palaces, but he couldn't find money to preserve Iraq's archaeological sites."

Two colossal eight-foot-high limestone and alabaster lamassu—each with the body of a lion, the face of a man and the wings of an eagle—guarded the entrance to what was left of the Northwest Palace of King Ashurnasirpal the Second.

Jeremy pointed to the north. "Over there was the goddess Ishtar's temple."

"The one we talked about at Nineveh?" asked Skylar.

"The same. Layard discovered a giant magnesite statue of Ashurnasirpal in the temple, placed there to remind the goddess how pious he was."

"The goddess didn't know that?" joked Skylar. "Where's the statue?"

Jeremy smiled because he'd said it so frequently throughout the day, "The British Museum in London."

As they walked around the site, he explained how the palace walls had been adorned with painted and glazed stone bas reliefs of Ashurnasirpal's victories, with inscriptions mentioning not only the king's genealogy, but also descriptions of the palace's architecture and furnishings.

"We know from inscriptions the palace was constructed of aromatic woods, such as cedar and cyprus. The Assyrian kings wanted grand looking palaces which smelled good, though they wouldn't have been the first. The palaces of Israel's kings David and Solomon, as well as the temple in Jerusalem, which predated Ashurnasirpal by more than 100 years—were all built with cedar from Lebanon—the same source for the Assyrians' cedar."

He said Layard had discovered thousands of delicately carved ivory plaques which had decorated walls and furniture, including a carving of a young man with tightly curled hair leaning back as a lioness ripped out his throat.

"Ivory had been used in abundance for royal residences about this time," he said. "Shortly after the completion of Kalhu, scripture records Israel's King Ahab also had a palace of ivory, no doubt wood covered with ivory panels."

Skylar looked stunned. He may have been dense about many aspects of journalism, but he did occasionally remember what he'd reported on. A year before, he and a USN crew had covered ivory poachers in Africa killing elephants for their valuable tusks.

"How many elephant tusks were needed to build an entire palace of ivory?" he asked.

"Rather a lot," said Jeremy. "At least one species of elephants became extinct before 200 BC and that may be due to the overuse of ivory, but it could also be because elephants were often used in wars, as tanks are today. Walruses and hippopotamuses were also a source of ivory."

Leading the group to a square, mud-brick opening in the floor of what had once been the Northwest Palace, Jeremy pointed down.

"That's the queen's tomb where the Treasure of Nimrud was discovered," he said as Barry turned on his camera's light to illuminate it.

At the bottom of the brick-lined pit, they could see a door opening leading to another subterranean room.

"Iraqi archaeologists discovered the Treasure of Nimrud in four burial sites in 1988," continued Jeremy. "More than 600 pieces of gold jewelry and precious stones, almost 3,000 years old. Some of the pieces were still on the skeletons of the people who'd been buried wearing them. The jewelry was put on display at the National Museum in Baghdad in 1990, but when Saddam invaded Kuwait, it was hidden. The jewelry hadn't been seen until American soldiers and museum staff found it in a Baghdad bank vault in June. You've heard of the mystery writer Agatha Christie?"

"Sure," said Skylar, looking confused.

"Sir Max Mallowan, her second husband, was a British archaeologist and excavated this palace in 1950," he said, then smiled a little mischievously. "As Agatha famously said, 'An archaeologist is the best husband any woman can have: the older she gets, the more interested he is in her.'"

Skylar burst out laughing.

"When Sir Mallowan cleared the floor," continued Jeremy, "he didn't notice some of the tiles were uneven and a different pattern. Thirty-eight years on, Iraqi archaeologists did notice and discovered this first burial vault with the jewelry straightaway under the tiles. It pays to be observant," he said with a twinkle in his eye.

"I guess so," said Skylar.

"The Assyrians liked beautiful things," said Jeremy, "but for all the beauty depicted in Assyria's jewelry and architecture, they were rather brutal warriors. The carved panels depicting their victories over neighboring nations describe how they cut off their victims' ears, noses, fingers, hands and feet. They would behead them, gouge out their eyes, burn men, women and children alive, flay them and spread out their skins. You didn't want to be on the bad side of Assyrians."

"Did archaeologists find any reference to Israel here? Or the House of Omri?" asked Skylar.

Le An was glad to see he'd read his notes enough to prompt Jeremy about one of the discoveries there in Kalhu.

"In the mid-1800s, Layard discovered a large, black limestone obelisk at this site, fittingly called the 'Black Obelisk.' It recorded the victories of the Assyrian king Shalmaneser and includes a description and illustration of Israel's king Jehu, described as being of the 'House of Omri.' Other inscriptions found here mention three more Israelite kings and one Jewish one."

After wrapping up the shoot and interviews, the convoy returned to Post Freedom and, as promised, Dark Knight drivers were waiting with three black, new-but-covered-in-dust, up-armored SUVs.

Le An had debated whether they should stay overnight at the 101, but they were due at the Iraq National Museum in Baghdad the next day. Since sunset was before 7:30, Le An hoped it would be dark by the time they drove through the Sunni Triangle. They wouldn't be able to see IEDS hidden on the roads and they'd have to push it to be back at the villa by Baghdad's 11:00 curfew, but driving through the Triangle in daylight in new SUVs was more dangerous. She made the decision for them to drive back that night.

Unfortunately, for one convoy, the main highway south into Baghdad would prove to be deadly.

27

Baghdad, Iraq
Friday, 5 September 2003

Le An slipped into the garden room at USN's villa and softly closed the door behind her. It was 1:30 a.m., 5:30 p.m. the previous day in New York. Since *Night News* went live on the East coast at 6:30 p.m., she knew she'd have to start setting up her live shot with New York within forty-five minutes. The assassination attempt on their vehicles was one of the lead stories on the evening newscast.

USN had installed satellites on the roof which provided both the villa's internet as well as direct phone lines to network offices in New York. Phones, as well as two-way radio access to their security team, had been set up in each room of the villa.

She reached Paul in his office and whispered, "Do you have a minute?"

"What's wrong?" he asked, a concerned tone in his voice.

"I wanted to run something past you."

"Are you OK?" he asked. "I can barely hear you."

"I'm trying to keep my voice down," she said, keeping an eye on the door to make sure no one came in. "I guess you heard we were shot at on our way up to Mosul. Skylar's doing a live shot on it with vid for *Night News* within the hour and the morning show's booked us for the A block."

"I know. Mike called me," he said. "Are you all right?"

She filled him in quickly on what had happened, then said, "Paul, you may need to pull Barry out before the end of the assignment. Wen Darlington's in Baghdad stringing for some networks, so he might be available to finish out the shoots and maybe I can get another shooter and editor in London. We're going to have to get some museum shots there and then edit the segments, but I wanted to give you a heads up."

"What happened? Did Barry freak out over the attack?" he asked.

"Not at all," she said. "He flipped into breaking-news mode when it all happened, picked up his camera and started shooting. He seemed OK with everything, just another story in a war zone. But then he wigged out on me at Mosel and was squirrely the rest of the day. At one point, he didn't like the interview and just quit shooting. I told him I could send him back to the States and probably get Wen, but he insisted on finishing the assignment. I think he's just burned out. You may need to give him some time off and then ease him back in with some cushy shoots."

"What do you mean he didn't like the interview?"

"He didn't like what Doctor Hilson was saying and decided not to shoot him at one point, then kept arguing with me and him and being nasty about everything else he said."

"Is there something wrong with this guy? Did we book another kook?" asked Paul.

"No, actually, this one's pretty good. He's not afraid to break with tradition or conventional wisdom, that's for sure. He makes you look at facts differently in a thought-provoking kind of way. And he's calming. Even in the middle of chaos, he's solid as a rock and comforting. I like him. For once, I think we booked the right religion consultant."

"He's an archaeologist, not a religion consultant," said Paul.

"He's a biblical archaeologist, so the areas kinda overlap," she said. "But Barry all of sudden developed this Catholic *fatwah* against him because the professor challenged his traditional thinking."

"I like this guy already," said Paul. "Controversial? Will it light up the switchboards?"

"Definitely," she said.

"Excellent. How are you doing?"

Le An was silent for a minute, carefully choosing her words. "I'm fine, but getting burned out, too. Paul, I'm tired and I really think I'd like a little time off when this assignment's over. I need to catch my breath and recharge."

"Done," he said without hesitating.

"I'm sorry."

"Why are you apologizing?"

"I hate to let you down. I hate to be a quitter," she said.

"Nothing to apologize for. I've been pushing you hard for a while. Just finish this and I'll give you some time off. You've got vacation time you need to take anyway. Send Barry back if you feel it's best. That's your call. And if you think Wen would be a good replacement, go ahead and hire him. Let me know what his day rate is. I'd give you one of our shooters in Iraq now, but we're stretched pretty thin. I can't really spare anyone and I know *Night News* can't either."

"I know. That's why I suggested Wen."

"How's Coltrane working out?" Paul asked.

"Sky is Sky," she said. He'd exhausted her that day with his lack of focus and preparation, but everyone had bad days. She was going to give him the benefit of the doubt. "He's not the best, but I'm sure he'll get better."

"He's no Luke Conte?" Paul joked.

Le An laughed. "Wise guy. No, he's got to do a lot of growing before he's that seasoned."

"I'm sure you'll shape him up. That's why I put you two together for this. Train him right, teacher lady."

"Yeah, yeah."

"Any sign of Saddam? It would help our ratings," he said.

"That might have been him shooting at us today. It did happen outside Tikrit."

"What's next on your schedule? Can Barry handle it or do we need to hire someone right away to replace him?" asked Paul.

"I'll have to use him today because of our schedule. We're heading over to the Iraq National Museum in Baghdad later today, but we have to take Saturday off, so that'll give me time to see who's available."

"Taking off a day because museums are too stressful for you?" he asked.

"Wise guy. No, Doctor Hilson observes the Sabbath. He can't work Friday sunset to Saturday sunset."

"He's Jewish? Now I know I like this guy."

"He's not Jewish...I think just Christian...but he keeps the Sabbath. Your rabbi uncle would love him."

"Listen, Le, if the good professor doesn't want to work on *Shabbat*, so be it," said Paul. "I'm certainly not going to insist on it. He's a consultant, not an employee. Take the day off. It's my *mitzvah*. I'd say you earned it after that assassination attempt."

"Well, everyone's pretty fried from today with the heat, the attack and the long hours, especially our security team. I don't want us to be overly tired in a war zone. That's how people get hurt or killed. I was going to head for Babylon and Al Kifl on Saturday, but we'll just make the arrangements to postpone that until Sunday. Taking Saturday off will give everyone a chance to rest and I can start writing the script."

"You know our schedule. How you coordinate your time is up to you as long as you make slot. You know how important it is with Brad anchoring."

"Have I ever missed slot?" she asked.

She'd always made her air time. Sometimes she'd only had seconds to spare, but she'd never missed.

There was silence on Paul's end.

"Don't even act like you're thinking about it," she said. "You know I've never missed slot or a feed window."

He laughed. "I was just jerking your chain. I knew you'd have a little hissy fit. You want me to add more security?"

"No, we're good," she said. "Dark Knight's doing a good job and the guys are great to work with. They've saved my rear end twice already."

"Twice? There was a second attack?" he asked.

She suddenly realized Paul hadn't heard about the gun-toting Iraqis chasing her down the street her first night back in Baghdad. Word would filter down eventually about her stupid decision to walk alone, but she was too tired to discuss it at that moment.

"Ah, nothing, nothing. Goodnight, Paul!"

"Le An!"

She quickly hung up and smiled, "Oops, lost the connection."

Just then, loud, rapid gunfire erupted and people started shouting.

Right after that, the power went out and the generator didn't come on.

28

Baghdad, Iraq
Friday, 5 September 2003

The gunfire sounded close, too close—like on-their-property close.

Le An pulled a small flashlight from her pocket to help her find the door into the hallway. Throughout the house, people were shouting as arcs of light emitted from their flashlights, blinding those in their path.

Dark Knight guards wearing night vision goggles threw open the front door, barking into their headsets for support teams as they ran through the house. One guard ran up the stairs to the second floor, two more exited through the back doors into the yard, followed closely by George Broadmar, USN's satellite engineer, the three of them almost colliding with two journalists who came running out of the main living room where they'd been working.

Khaled came out of the downstairs library. Since they'd returned to the villa so close to curfew, everyone decided it was safer for him to stay overnight with them at the villa rather than be on the streets by himself.

"What's going on?" asked Le An.

"Somebody's shooting at the villa and our generator's down," yelled George.

"Great," she muttered.

Mike, groggy from only an hour of sleep, stood at the top of the stairs, barefoot, bare chested and in shorts he was still zipping up. He shined his flashlight at Le An and asked, "What happened?"

"George said someone's shooting at the villa," she said.

Mike let out a string of profanity and came running down the stairs. Still not fully awake, and not able to see clearly in the darkened house, he missed a step, stumbled, tried to jump two and grabbed the banister just as he started to pitch headfirst down the rest of the flight, sending his flashlight crashing over the railing to the floor below. His left foot twisted under him and, as he sat back on it, he let out a grunt.

Le An ran toward him as she heard him start to fall and got to him just after he'd caught himself.

"Awww! Oh, man, I think I twisted my ankle," he groaned as he tried to stand up.

"You didn't break it, did you? Let me look at it," she said. "Sit down."

He tried to protest, but still groggy and now in pain, slid back onto one of the steps. Le An pushed the palm of her hand against the bottom of his foot and slowly rotated it. She gently felt around his foot and ankle, noticing the places where he winched at her touch.

"Any pain?" she asked.

"A little sore," he grimaced. "I'm fine. I'm going downstairs."

"No you're not. You're going back upstairs. Your ankle's not hot, maybe a little warm," she said. "That's good. Hot means broken. I don't see any bones sticking up, but if you're in a lot of pain, it might be broken and you should probably go get an x-ray to make sure. Hopefully, you didn't tear a ligament. I'm going to get some cold packs and I want you to stay off it, keep it elevated."

"We've got some ace bandages around here to wrap it," he said.

"Nope, no constriction. No shoes, no socks, no wraps. Cold packs for the next twenty-four hours and we'll see if it swells or bruises. Come on. Back upstairs to bed. I'll bring the packs."

"No way, Le. I'm going downstairs to find out what's going on."

"Mike, don't be stubborn. We'll come up and give you a complete progress report. George and I can handle everything. Besides, you're exhausted. Come on. I'll help you up."

"I don't need help," he grumbled. "I can walk. Is everyone OK?"

"Everyone except you, I think," she said.

"Don't forget your live shot with Skylar for *Night News* at 2:30," he mumbled.

"I know. We've got it covered," she said.

Mike stood up and tried to put weight on his foot, but the sharp pain made him quickly jerk it up off the step.

She put an arm around his waist. "Come on, tough guy."

Between leaning on her and the stair banister, Mike hopped up the remaining steps, then made it to his bedroom.

"I'm fine," he grumbled. "Stop fussing over me."

"Yeah, whatever. Sit tight. I'll be back with something to put on that. Prop your foot up," she said as she grabbed an extra pillow and put it under his foot. "You don't want it to swell."

Mike was already asleep by the time she came back with the cold packs a few minutes later. She balanced them on top of his foot, lightly wrapping a towel around them to hold them in place. He mumbled a faint 'thank you' and fell back asleep.

Le An softly closed his door and headed downstairs to see if anyone had been shot.

29

Baghdad, Iraq
Friday, 5 September 2003

Barry managed to get the villa's generator working and once again the complex lit up. The gunshots at the front appeared to have been a diversion, luring the majority of the security team to that location—away from the back where a small oriental rug was found thrown over the concertina wire atop the stone wall.

The power outage had shut down Dark Knight's security cameras so there was no video of who'd been on the property or how they'd taken the generator offline. The journalists discovered computers, phones, video equipment and cash were missing. Someone had definitely breached security at the villa, but the problem was nobody had seen anyone. Fortunately, no one had been injured or killed.

Skylar did his report for *Night News* from their set-up on the villa's rooftop where most of the crews in the house did their live shots. Le An finally fell into bed shortly after that, at 3:00, but awoke four hours later, the enormity of *AmeriView*'s Iraq special and her long list of interviews and location shoots weighing heavily on her. She figured she could catch up on sleep Saturday since Jeremy insisted on taking off that day. Secretly, she was relieved and was looking forward to a free day with no interviews and no driving around the country.

With the script she had to write forming in her head, she quickly dressed, then grabbed her computer and notes, before heading downstairs.

She'd showered when they'd returned to the villa last night and if she didn't think she was being piggy with the hot water, would have indulged again to fully wake herself up. But with this many people in the house, they had to conserve.

The house was quiet. A few TV reporters and their crews were up doing reports for their countries' news programs. Le An passed by the feed room and glanced at the six large clocks on the wall, showing time zones around the world. It was 4:30 a.m. in London. She didn't see Hugh, but figured in another hour he'd need to be on the roof for his live shot. His network began their morning show coverage at 6:00, an hour earlier than USN and the other non-cable American networks.

The New York clock read 11:30 p.m. In another seven hours, Le An and her crew would have to check in with USN's *AM Startup* morning show producers. Skylar and the DK guards were scheduled to be interviewed about the assassination attempt on their convoy outside Tikrit. Le An knew there was an off chance they might want her to appear on camera, but she planned to object as much as possible. She preferred working behind the scenes, pulling the power strings. She was deliberately keeping Jeremy off air, not wanting to alert any other networks to the archaeology packages they were working on.

BTN's producers had already contacted her about doing an interview with them for air in the UK, probably with Hugh conducting the interview, but USN wouldn't allow it for another twenty-four hours until the exclusive video had run on their network first. She figured most other US networks wouldn't want to interview them. They wouldn't want to alert their viewers to the competition's coverage of Iraq and would probably only run the video in a passing mention.

She checked in with New York's overnight feed coordinator, then talked to a morning show producer to give background information and make the final arrangements. The half hour before her crew was to appear on air, they'd be receiving frantic calls from the control room since they were the lead story for the 'A' block at 7:00 Eastern, 3:00 p.m. Baghdad time. That was going to chop up her day. They were scheduled to arrive at the Iraq National Museum at 10:00 Baghdad time and would need to finish up in time to either make a dash back to the house by 2:30 to do their live shots or take a live truck with them and do their live shots there. Staying at the museum was her first choice. It would allow her to get all the interviews and b-roll she needed without having to rush or make two trips.

Peeking in the kitchen, she was surprised to find it dark and empty, with no sign of their Iraqi cook. She was usually there during the day to accommodate all the rotating shifts of journalists demanding food, and, the rest of the time, she was out buying food. Her husband and brother worked for USN buying fuel for their vehicles.

It was Friday, the Muslim holy day, but Le An didn't know if the cook was Muslim or Christian. Whatever she was, she hoped Mike had a back-up cook.

She found a lemon and squeezed it into a glass of distilled water, taking it with her to the living room. If she was lucky, she could work on her script for an hour before the rest of the house woke up and started bothering her.

Before she'd gone to bed, she'd downloaded Barry's video from their shoot the day before and now opened the Final Cut Pro program to review the interviews and b-roll. As she listened, she opened her script writing software and started typing. Getting an idea for the direction she wanted to go, she paused the interview and started roughing in the overall script, clicking over to her iPod selections for her own listening enjoyment.

She'd lost track of the time until Hugh sat down next to her and pointed to her earbuds.

"Work or pleasure?" he asked.

She looked up and pulled out the plug so he could hear. "Pleasure. I downloaded a song from this new album when I was back in New York. It's perfect for over here."

"Why?"

"It's about winter, snow coming down. Good way to mentally deal with 120-degree Iraqi heat."

"Forty-nine degrees," he corrected her.

"You Europeans with your crazy temperatures and measurements."

"You Yanks with your crazy temperatures and measurements."

"Again, Hugh, Southerner, not a Yankee," she said. "Close your eyes. Think of a small town in Vermont, big thick snowflakes coming down, piling up in snow drifts, kids making snowmen and skating on frozen ponds. Night's falling, you look up at the street lights and see the flakes illuminated against the dark sky."

"Very poetic." He leaned back and closed his eyes, then opened one and looked at her in a you're-kinda-crazy way.

"Correct me if I'm wrong, but isn't Vermont in your so-called New England? Isn't that Yankee-land?"

"Yes. Close your eyes," she repeated. "Think snow falling in Scotland. Is it working?"

"I feel cooler already. And I do like the tune." He opened his eyes and turned to face her. "Heard about your little incident near Tikrit yesterday. Are you all right?"

"I'm good. It was scary, but I have to admit I'm finally coming around to the merits of Dark Knight Security."

"I think you and trouble are having an intimate relationship. Must you be in near-death experiences every day? Sorry I couldn't be there to save you this time," he said and smiled slyly.

"You probably shouldn't be in the same room with me. Lightning will strike next. But you'll be glad to hear I was with my security detail this time."

"Noted."

"Who told you?" she asked.

"Piet and Kent."

"The South African guys staying here in the house?" she asked. "Aren't they your crew?"

"They're freelancing as my producer and videographer, but they're also working for a news organization in South Africa. Piet's a correspondent as well as producer. He's from South Africa. Kent's living there now, but he's originally from Zim."

"Yeah, if I lived in Zim, I'd want to move, too," she said.

"Did you know someone fired on an armed convoy heading south into Baghdad on the main motorway yesterday?"

"The road we were on?" she asked.

"I suppose. They killed an American contract worker and wounded a US soldier."

Le An was silent for a moment, wondering how close the USN convoy had been to the scene of that attack. Were they a few minutes ahead of it? Hours behind? It just as easily could have been them with the casualties.

"Dodged another bullet, did you?" he asked.

"Yeah, apparently twice in one day," she said softly, then changed the subject. "Did you hear the commotion early this morning?"

"Slept through it. I was utterly exhausted. Just heard that bit. Bloody shame."

"Wonder if it was an inside job," she said.

He gave her a puzzled look. "You mean one of us?"

"No, inside as in our Iraqi cook. Or cooks. Do we have more than one?"

He shrugged.

"Well, I've been waiting for *a* cook, whoever she is, to get here to fix breakfast, but she still hasn't shown up. I'm about to go in there and cook myself. Either she's in on the heist or something happened to her, which would be awful."

"Think the thief was someone she knows?" he asked.

"Don't know, but DK guards said someone knew this complex well enough to pull it off."

"What about your sound man? Didn't he stay here last night?" Hugh asked in a low voice.

"Khaled? Yeah, but…no, no way," she whispered and frowned as she thought about the possibility. "You mean he was the inside man working with someone? No way. He didn't even know he was going to stay here last night until we got back. It was so close to curfew, we just told him to stay."

Hugh looked at her and pursed his lips. "You sure?"

"No, I'm not sure of anything anymore," she sighed. "I don't want to believe he could, but most Iraqis are pretty desperate for money these days. Five months of war will do that. Of course, we're all using Iraqi interpreters slash fixers, and most of them, since they speak such good English, probably had connections to Saddam's government, so who knows."

"Did Khaled and the cook know each other?" he asked.

She stared at him, the possibility finally forming that they may have criminals in the midst of their news organization. "I have no idea. Wow, good investigative thinking. I'm surprised my mind didn't go there right away. I must really be tired because I'm usually suspicious of everyone."

"Might be good to check," he said. "Or it could be any of our Iraqi fixers or drivers. They're in and out of here throughout the day."

"While I process this possibility, I'm going to start breakfast," she said. "You in?"

"If you mean am I hungry, yes," he said. "Need help?"

"You're hired."

The two fixed breakfast for twenty, including coffee, warmed pita bread, eggs and a fried mixture Le An came up with by throwing together butter, leftover apples, onions, peppers, dates and cinnamon.

Mike hobbled downstairs on his own and sat at the head of the large gold dining room table, his ankle propped on a white plastic chair next to him.

"How's the patient this morning?" Le An asked as she put a large platter of scrambled eggs with feta cheese on the table. She lifted the cold pack on his foot and looked at it, pressing gently in places to see where he winched. "No swelling. That's good. But it looks like it's going to turn black and blue."

Mike grumbled something indistinguishable and plopped a giant spoonful of eggs on his plate.

"Breakfast is lovely," said Jeremy. "Thank you, Le An."

"And Hugh," she said. "He gets equal billing. Coffee and eggs are his."

"This is good," said George, commenting on Le An's apple concoction and everyone except Michelle agreed.

"Le An's special creation," said Hugh.

"What is it?" sniffed Michelle, the French wire service reporter, pointing to the apple mixture and wrinkling her noise in disgust.

"Food. Don't like it, don't eat it. More for me," said Mike, as he took a big helping of it and glared at her.

"Pain making you cranky, Mikey," Le An teased.

"Maybe," he growled. "Where's our cook?"

"Didn't show up this morning," she said. "Either she's devout and praying in a mosque, was kidnapped or her relatives were in on the heist this morning."

Everyone looked up surprised, then looked over at the Dark Knight guards.

"We don't know," said Leo. "All we said was it looked like an inside job because whoever it was knew the complex and how to get around us."

"Could have been family or friends of the owner," said Skylar.

"Possibly," said Leo.

"Mike, did you hire our cook? What's her name?" asked Le An.

"Fatima something. I've got it written down somewhere. No,

I didn't hire her," he said. "She came with the house. She's pretty quiet, keeps to herself, never takes off on Fridays, not that devout. I think she's Christian. I've got a cellphone number for her."

"I called. The number's not working," said George.

"I don't know where she lives," said Mike. "We pay her in cash."

"Anyone know how to get in touch with her?" asked Le An. Everyone shook their head 'no.'

"Khaled, do you know our cook?" she asked. "Do you know how to contact her or her family?"

Khaled's eyes darted around and he shifted uncomfortably. "I do not know her. Baghdad is very big, millions of people. I do not know them all."

She smiled at him. "Yes, I know. I just thought there might be a possibility you knew her. She may not have shown up because something terrible happened to her or her family. They could be injured or sick, even kidnapped. That's happening in some areas, isn't it?"

Uncomfortable with everyone's eyes on him, listening to his every word, Khaled shifted in his seat again. "It is happening to many people. Bad people are kidnapping to get much money."

"Yes, that's why we need to find out what happened to her," she said. "In the meantime, do you know anyone who might want to cook for us?"

"I will ask my sister," he said. "I will speak with her today."

"Thanks, Khaled," she said and smiled at him, but now that Hugh had planted a seed of doubt about him, she wasn't sure how far to trust him or anyone he recommended.

The talk turned to favorite food festivals around the world, from the *Maslyanitsa* butter festival in Russia, to the Circleville Pumpkin Show in Ohio and the Ghirardelli chocolate festival in San Francisco. Everyone sighed, thinking about *blini* pancakes swimming in honey and butter, giant pumpkin pies and chocolate brownies.

"White truffle festival," said Hugh. "I was on holiday near Milan, passing through Alba..."

"You get a vacation?" Le An teased.

"Loads. You should try it. You Americans work too hard," he said.

The USN people snickered. It was always painful working

with foreign press knowing they had so much more vacation time.

The conversation eventually turned to the war, whether the Coalition forces should have invaded Iraq and how the nation should be rebuilt.

"What do you think, Jeremy?" asked Mike.

The professor was silent for a few seconds, then said, "While I'm glad to have somewhat easier access to historical sites, I fear your president has taken on a rather large task. The Shi'a have built up 1,000 years of ill will toward the Sunnis. They've suffered terribly under them for centuries. If the Shi'a can forgive centuries of abuse, there may be a chance. On the other hand, the Sunnis, I'm quite sure, don't like losing power. Then you have the Kurds whom the Sunnis also abused. With the three groups fighting, British and American troops are given the job of trying to keep peace, which may not be successful."

"I am Sunni. I did not abuse anybody," said Khaled.

"We didn't mean you, Khaled. Sorry," said Le An.

"It's South Africa and tribal conflicts all over again, like trying to keep the Zulus and Xhosas from killing each other," mumbled Piet, Hugh's freelance producer from Johannesburg. "Your president should have studied South Africa first."

"He should have studied Islamic history first," said Mike. "You have to wonder if he and his advisors really knew what they were taking on."

"Coalition troops are already becoming apartheid police because there aren't really any Iraqi police," said Kent, Hugh's Zimbabwean cameraman. "There's no order and it's getting worse each month. I wonder how long we'll all be able to safely report this war. How long are we going to be able to move round amongst the people and get interviews?"

"Most of the people we've interviewed say they're glad Saddam's not in power," said Le An. "Right, Khaled?"

"Many feel good, some not," said Khaled. "Many are afraid Saddam and Fedayeen will come back and torture them. Some want to be in power again and do not like armies of other countries in Iraq. Maybe Saddam and Fedayeen attacked us yesterday."

"Maybe. It was near Tikrit," she said. "Saddam's probably behind a lot of the attacks."

"The Shi'a think Sunnis are behind all the IEDs and roadside attacks and are hiding Saddam—which they probably are," said Hugh.

"All Sunnis are not behind attacks. I am not," Khaled was quick to point out.

"No, we didn't mean all Sunnis," she said.

"I am not hiding Saddam," he continued. "If I find him, I tell Americans where he is, beat him with my shoe and collect big reward."

Everyone burst out laughing.

"Go get him, Khaled," said Barry.

"A lot of Iraqis still smile and wave when American convoys go by," said Skylar.

"Yeah, they wave, then turn around and curse us under their breath," muttered Barry.

"Iraqis need to get their government up and running so we can all get out of here," grumbled Mike as he adjusted the cold pack on his foot.

"The majority may want peace and to start rebuilding their country after decades of dictatorship," said Jeremy. "But there are always those who wish to be in control and stir up trouble amongst those who don't share their ideas. They need to be isolated."

"How can you do that?" asked Hugh.

"Coalition troops will have to turn into police and really clamp down," said Barry. "I don't know that they can do that without causing a lot of resentment."

"Perhaps the best thing is to let each group form their own government," Jeremy said softly.

There was momentary silence as a few people looked at each other with raised eyebrows.

"Apartheid?" Piet finally asked. "Divide the country into Shi'a, Sunni and Kurd? I don't think the world would stand for that. Are you saying there should be three new countries? And how would you divide oil resources?"

"Aren't the Americans taking all the oil?" asked Michelle.

"Shut up, Frenchie," snapped Barry. "What do you people know about anything?"

Le An and a few others looked up at him wide-eyed and speechless. Michelle started to escalate the battle, but Jeremy interrupted, trying to restore civility.

"The British divided the Middle East many years ago with the Mandate," he said. "Iraq as it is today is an unnatural divide. We forced the tribes to form a country. Perhaps the biblical model is best—go back to the way the tribes had divided themselves."

"What's the biblical model?" asked Le An.

"Each group with common ancestry and beliefs in their own separate areas," he said. "Sometimes peace only comes from commonality. Iraq is a tribal nation, much like South Africa. You deal with tribes differently than you deal with societies which are more naturally mixed—where tribal borders have broken down and people are more accepting of the differences amongst other groups."

"A lot of people in Iraq accept the differences," said Le An. "Look at the mixed marriages between Sunni, Shi'a and Kurds. Infighting would rip apart their families."

"Those mixed marriages are only in certain areas, such as Baghdad, not the rest of the country," said Hugh. "Remember Saddam married his cousin, as do many. They marry within their tribes and within their families."

"Unfortunately, I don't think the harmony of a few mixed marriages is going to be enough to overcome the hatred of those who wish to cause division here," said Jeremy.

"How do you start getting people to accept differences in other people and cultures unless you mix them?" asked Mike as he shifted his twisted ankle and winced. "How can you get them to accept others when they're separate?"

"Look at New York. We're a melting pot and we all get along," said Barry.

"Yes," Jeremy said slowly. "That must be why crime is so low in New York."

The room erupted in laughter.

"That's why I live in Jersey," said Barry, giving him a dirty look.

"You live near the blind sheik who planned the first bombing of the Twin Towers?" teased Mike.

"That was before I got there," said Barry. "I'd have kicked some serious sheik booty if I'd been livin' in his 'hood."

"Obviously, Jersey has its own problems," said Le An. "That's why we try to keep a river between us, but those Jersey folks keep using the bridges."

"Hey, hey, hey. There's nuttin' wrong with Jersey," piped up Barry in his best Brooklyn accent.

Jeremy continued, "There are many societies where the citizens accept others who are quite different from themselves, even when those people don't live near them. They've been educated that way. I don't know that you can achieve that level of education here in Iraq—at least not in a time frame British and American citizens will accept. After all, they're the ones funding this grand experiment. I just wonder whether it might be better for everyone to go to their own areas..."

"Keep calm and carry on?" joked Hugh.

"Yes, keep calm and carry on," Jeremy smiled. "Set up governments under their own tribal structure, let peace settle in, then accept the differences in tribes around them. The Shi'a and Kurds have been treated rather badly for many years. Sorry to say, Khaled, and it's no reflection on you, but it's going to take a lot to get them to trust the Sunnis enough to work with them in government. I fear there's going to be quite a lot of distrust, anger and resentment for many years. Working together to solve differences takes a high level of maturity and I don't know that you'll find enough of that to make this transition proceed smoothly. Not to mention the Shi'a tend to be religious zealots, which comes with its own problems."

"And I'm sure Al Qaeda's mixing it up among the Sunnis," mumbled George. "Don't forget Osama's boys."

"I am not mixing with Osama," protested Khaled. "He is crazy."

"We should probably stop offending, Khaled," said Le An, mindful of her soundman's discomfort at the conversation. "Probably best to clarify we mean militant Sunnis might be mixing it up with bin Laden, not your average peace-loving, Baghdad-living, soundman-for-USN Sunnis."

The tension eased slightly, but not much.

"Professionals thrive more in a secular state," continued Jeremy. "I fear for the doctors, engineers and solicitors in a religious Shi'a society—which Iraq will surely become."

"You are right," Khaled nodded in agreement.

"You make it sound as if Saddam was a good thing, Jeremy," said Le An.

"Oh my, no, not a good thing," he said. "I'm saying the secular emphasis was probably beneficial to Iraqis, even if their leader wasn't."

Again, Khaled nodded in agreement.

Le An glanced at her watch, "Skylar and Barry, remember the morning show is interviewing you live with the guards about our attack yesterday, though I'd prefer to have Barry manning the camera, not be on air."

"You being interviewed, too, Le?" asked Skylar.

"Not if I can help it, so don't encourage that with the producers," she said. "You're the lead in A block. We'll try to make it back here, but Plan B is to set up for the live shot at 2:30 from the museum and use a sat truck. By the way, Mike, remember we're taking a sat truck with us. Then if we have more to shoot there, we can finish up when our live shot's over. And by the way, we're leaving for the museum in a half hour. We have to be there at 10:00. Professor, Skylar, we'll meet in ten minutes in the library to go over some of the points I think we should cover. And, Jeremy, if you think we need to add anything, let me know."

"Where are we going tomorrow?" asked Barry as they got up from the table.

"Nowhere," she said. "Rest day for the crew."

"We're taking a day off? Why?"

"We just are. We need to rest a little. Isn't it bad enough we were targets for assassins yesterday? I'll probably be writing the script, so we can get started on some of the editing. That way, we'll see if we need to add shots or locations. Better to find out now than when we're in London."

"We're on deadline and we have a lot more locations to shoot," Barry said, continuing to push the issue. "Is this because Jeremy won't work on Saturdays? We're paying him and he won't work?"

"Back off, Barry," she said and, as he opened his mouth to say more, she added sternly, "The schedule's not for you to decide. That's my call. Paul already knows and he's approved it."

"That's because Paul's Jewish," he sneered.

"What's with the attitude? Enjoy what little rest you're going to get," she said. "Go swimming, work on your tan, sleep late, drink heavily, make duct tape animals, I don't care. What is it with you?"

"Nothing," he said, giving her a disgusted look before walking away.

She closed her eyes and sighed heavily. As she turned to head into the living room to retrieve her computer, she noticed Jeremy standing behind her.

"Is there a problem?" he asked.

"Yes," she said, "and his name is Barry."

30

Baghdad, Iraq
Friday, 5 September 2003

Though their country was a chaotic mess, overrun with foreign armies, the pride of the Iraqi people lay in their archaeological heritage, including the National Museum in Baghdad. Situated in the al-Karkh district behind Haifa Street and across from what remained of a bombed-out Republican Guard compound, were the dozen buildings and eleven acres which made up the museum complex.

A special US investigative task force had been barracked at the museum for five months, since shortly after the invasion. The unit, headed by a Marine with a degree in the classics, whose other day job was prosecuting the lowlifes of New York, also included a crack thirteen-member team from the Joint Interagency Coordination Group (JIACG)—which US Central Command had formed a month after 9/11.

JIACG's intelligence team consisted of agents from the Justice Department, Immigration and Customs Enforcement (ICE), the State Department, the CIA, FBI, Treasury and military special forces, whose purpose was to coordinate a rapid counterterrorist response within CENTCOM's area of operations. Their job was to link military and law enforcement with counterterrorism in order to locate terrorist cells' financing and illegal weapons.

In Afghanistan, US troops had found money, arms and antiquities in the same caves. It was a source of debate between the military and archaeologists as to what was behind the theft of antiquities—terrorism or poverty. The military felt the sale of looted artifacts may be funding terrorist cells. The archaeologists seemed to feel the looting stemmed from poverty—with those in desperate need of money finding financial opportunities at unguarded archaeological sites.

In the days following the invasion of Iraq, the US had taken a lot of heat from the rest of the world for not doing enough to protect Iraq's ancient heritage.

"The whole country's one big archaeological site," one Marine had grumbled to Le An months before. "How do they expect us to protect every single site when even Saddam didn't do that?"

His point was justifiable. As Jeremy explained, the looting had gone on when Saddam was in power—and Hussein and his family were some of the biggest offenders.

Saddam had thought so little of the antiquities, he'd ordered as many as 150 of his Republican Guards to set up their sniper positions at the National Museum—not to protect the artifacts, but to fire RPGs at American forces, knowing they would risk international wrath by returning fire on a site holding items of archaeological significance. For the most part, Saddam's plan had worked. Americans had avoided returning fire, not wanting to hit the museum.

On April 8, Iraqi Republican Guards had taken up positions they'd prepared weeks before throughout the National Museum compound. After that, the last of the employees had locked the doors to the museum and storage rooms, then exited through the back door, locking it also.

That day, US forces were less than a mile west of the museum, having been on the outskirts of Baghdad for three days. They came under heavy mortar fire as they moved toward the museum. A US tank company, instructed to keep an important nearby crossroads open, took position about a third-of-a-mile away. For the next two days, the tanks came under heavy Iraqi fire from snipers at the Children's Museum and three other buildings on the museum compound—fierce enough to keep US troops pinned in their tanks the entire time.

Residents in the area said they'd seen Iraqi soldiers taking boxes out the museum's back door on April 9—the day after the employees left—as other Iraqi troops continued to fire rocket propelled grenades at the US tank company. Their task force commander finally gave them the OK to fire one tank round to take out the snipers shooting RPGs at them.

It succeeded in its mission—and left a neat hole in the side of the Children's Museum. The tank company then pulled back to save US troops and the museum. But that one hole took on a life of its own, causing international outrage as the press beamed images of it around the world.

Heavy fighting between US and Iraqi forces had continued in the area for the next two days, but on April 10, many Iraqi soldiers in the museum shed their uniforms and took off, leaving the museum doors wide open. Hundreds of looters entered the building that night.

The museum staff returned April 12 and the looting stopped, but by then it had caused an international uproar, fanned in large part by one of the museum's directors who grossly inflated the damage and the number of lost items.

"I understand they've been able to track down many of the museum's lost artifacts, which is fortunate," said Jeremy as USN's convoy headed toward the museum. "And you are clear, aren't you, which museum this is? There are two museums in Baghdad which are sometimes confused. The *Times* obviously didn't know the difference."

Le An frowned and looked down at her notes, wondering if April had given her wrong information. "What did they say?"

"The *Times* claimed when your American troops first entered Baghdad in April, an Iraqi archaeologist named Muhammad had convinced soldiers to come to the Iraq National Museum, which is where we're going. As you probably know, it holds many ancient treasures. This Muhammad said the museum was located near the eastern bank of the Tigris. He said the soldiers drove out looters, then left and, within the hour, the looters were back. But, as you can see, the National Museum here in the al-Karkh district isn't near the eastern side of the Tigris. We're approximately 900 meters—sorry, one-half mile—from the *western* bank of the Tigris. The Baghdad Museum, which has twentieth-century artifacts, is on Mamoun Street in the al-Rusafa district. That's the museum near the eastern bank of the Tigris."

Skylar started laughing. "I love it. The *Times* screwed up."

"So are you saying the looters were at the other museum—the Baghdad Museum—and were taking items which weren't that valuable, but the reporter made it sound as if they were here looting ancient artifacts?" she asked.

"Precisely. Artifacts were stolen from here at the Iraq National Museum, that much we know, but I've heard it's not the large numbers the press keeps reporting. The *Times* and the BBC, amongst others, reported 170,000 items were stolen here. The man they quoted as a museum employee was instead a *former* employee who happened to live near the museum. He had no facts to support his numbers and the reporters didn't verify who he was. What I'm saying is: please don't report either the museum or the numbers incorrectly as other reporters have."

"We always try to report things accurately, as much as possible, but it's hard to fact-check in a war zone," said Le An looking down at her background information and suddenly remembering Paul's comment about how the incorrect numbers of looted items from the museum might be a good story. "I see a current employee of the museum is also quoted as giving the same high numbers of missing artifacts."

"Yes, he did give that number, then appeared to backtrack and said there were 170,000 items in the entire museum, not those missing," said Jeremy.

"Skylar, read this on camera and let's get Jeremy's response to it," she said pointing to an underlined part of their research material. "Professor, this is a quote from an American university specializing in Middle and Far Eastern research: 'The looting of the Iraq Museum is the most severe single blow to cultural heritage in modern history, comparable to the sack of Constantinople, the burning of the library at Alexandria, the Vandal and Mogul invasions, and the ravages of the conquistadors...'"

"Yes, rather melodramatic," he said dryly.

"The looting here doesn't upset you?" she asked.

"Any looting of artifacts upsets me," he said. "But, as I mentioned, Iraq's archaeological sites were being looted long before this war and Saddam Hussein was the biggest offender. I dare say I'd fancy seeing some of this international ire directed his way. What he's done to damage this country's archaeological integrity borders on the criminal."

"That's because he is a criminal," said Skylar.

As their convoy approached the entrance to the museum complex, the US military manning the perimeter began checking their paperwork and identification, verifying who they were. USN's appointment and interviews at the museum had been scheduled for weeks.

"Did you know Gertrude Bell created this museum about 100

years ago?" Jeremy asked Le An. "She was British."

"I'm familiar with her name, but I didn't know she'd started the museum," she said.

"She was a writer, an archaeologist, a diplomat and a spy, spoke fluent Persian and Arabic," he said. "She also started the British School of Archaeology here in Iraq. And she's the one who formed the country you see today. She wanted to unite the cities of Basra, Baghdad and Mosul, but, unfortunately, without considering the consequences ethnic and tribal differences would bring."

"So she created this mess," grumbled Barry.

Khaled listened intently, but didn't say anything.

"You said she was a spy?" asked Skylar.

"Yes, in the British war office in Cairo during the Great War—the first World War," he said. "At the end of the war and the collapse of the Ottoman Empire, Miss Bell and T. E. Lawrence—Lawrence of Arabia—worked to convince Great Britain to establish an independent Transjordan and Iraq, with King Faisal as the ruler of Iraq. She said it was better to establish a ruler who was an ally of Britain's. Churchill wanted to let the area remain independent tribes. He only wanted to fortify Basra and its oil fields. That was Britain's only interest in Iraq."

"Yes, it is always about our oil," said Khaled in a disgusted tone.

"Miss Bell insisted on including the non-Arab Kurds in the new state of Iraq to shore up the Sunni minority, but Churchill wanted to leave the Kurds autonomous. He was afraid an Arab ruler would one day oppress them as a minority."

"Boy, was he ever right," said Le An. "Winston Churchill was such a visionary."

"He had wisdom many didn't appreciate, rather ahead of his time in many areas," said Jeremy. "Miss Bell wanted the Sunnis to rule Iraq because she felt the Shi'a were religious zealots and would unite with the Persians to turn the country into a theocracy."

"Which Iran would love to do today," she said.

"Thank you Gertrude Bell for creating this hell-hole," repeated Barry.

"Yep. What was that woman thinking?" said Le An. "And sorry, Jeremy, but what were the British thinking for going along with her ideas?"

"What were Americans thinking?" said Barry. "Like we're any better trying to do nation-building here?"

"You're quite right, Barry," said Jeremy, a comment which Le An appreciated, if only to try and tamp down Barry's ever-growing religious feud with him. "If we Brits couldn't inspire a Western-style democracy here in Iraq, I'm quite sure your country won't be able to either. Your president failed to realize democracy had already failed in this region."

"And your prime minister," she reminded him. "I think I'm coming around to your idea of three separate countries."

"Me, too," said Skylar. "How about you, Khaled? What do you think? It's your country."

"I think the blood may stop flowing if there are three countries," he said quietly.

"Too late after Iraq was formed did Miss Bell realize the mix of tribes and ethnicities wouldn't work," continued Jeremy. "But she loved the Middle East and its people. She's buried here in Baghdad at the British cemetery in the Bab al-Sharji district. Committed suicide at the age of fifty-seven after taking an overdose of sleeping pills. She never married and was apparently rather lonely at the end."

"How long has it been since you've been in Iraq?" asked Le An.

"Many years," he said. "Saddam hosted a conference for international archaeologists in March 2001, but I wasn't permitted to attend. He banned those he felt were Jewish or sympathetic to the Jews. I suppose my former Iraqi minders had reported to him I observed the Sabbath."

Le An suddenly became worried about his safety. She knew Khaled had worked as a minder in Saddam's government and, though he appeared loyal to USN now, she wondered who he might tell about Jeremy.

"The archaeologists permitted to enter the country after Iraq invaded Kuwait had to turn a blind eye to what Saddam was doing," Jeremy continued. "They knew if they didn't publically praise him for protecting the archaeological sites of the country and tell the world what a great preservationist he was, they'd be denied entry into Iraq. So they lied."

"They sold out," she said.

"They did. Many archaeologists had known for years how Saddam abominably corrupted and destroyed the sites, but they concealed that. They blamed UN sanctions for the lack of money to maintain the security of the sites, but the truth is Saddam always found money for himself and his family, not for his people and certainly not for preserving the archaeological integrity of Iraq."

"It's like news organizations who hushed up Saddam's torture of journalists," she said, as Khaled looked uncomfortable. "They didn't make it public because if they had, their network would've been banned from reporting here."

"Yep," said Barry.

Because it was Friday, the Muslim holy day, most staff members were home with their families or worshipping in mosques. Besides the US military stationed at the museum, only a few Christian employees were working, including a woman who'd been selected to give the USN crew a tour of the complex. She spoke English fairly well and led them through the almost twenty galleries.

Thornton Cromstock, an American member of CENTCOM's JIACG task force, also walked with them to answer questions, clarify facts and point out inconsistencies. He turned out to be far more informative than the museum employee.

As the group approached the museum's Assyrian Hall, Jeremy pointed out two winged bulls and stone panels from Assyrian king Sargon's palace in Khorsabad they'd visited the day before. The objects had been too large for looters to cart away.

"The *Times* reported looters took 170,000 artifacts," said Skylar, repeating what he'd just heard Le An and Jeremy discussing in the car.

"That number's incorrect," said Thornton. "Nowhere near that many. Looters did have access to the museum for forty-eight hours from April 10 through 12, but many news agencies reported an incorrect number of items stolen. We're trying to correct the error."

"Why was that number mentioned?" asked Skylar.

"The problem was there was no electricity right after Baghdad fell and none of the employees could tell exactly what had been taken," said Thornton. "Plus, there was no computer database listing the items. Everything was logged by hand on file cards scattered all over the museum. And some of those cards burned up when looters dropped burning foam on them. Curators had been using the foam to wrap artifacts just prior to the invasion and the thieves used it to rig make-shift torches when the electricity went out. The museum's inventory system was about as ancient as the antiquities. In some cases, when we couldn't find the inventory file cards, we were able to check old catalogues to identify some of the missing items, but I'm telling you, it was archaic."

"So when one of the museum staff told reporters 170,000 items were missing, it was because they didn't even know their own inventory?" asked Skylar.

"Sounds unbelievable, doesn't it? But true," said Thornton. "Some employees only knew about items in one section of the museum. Then we discovered some staff members had hidden items or taken them for safekeeping. The antiquities were returned, but not everyone knew they'd been hidden. The staff had also moved some artifacts into secret locations and storage rooms, so they were safe. Again, not every staff member knew about that. But the press should have known when they saw almost all the display cases empty, but not smashed."

"Meaning they were empty because the staff had removed the items?" asked Skylar.

"Exactly. It should have been obvious those cases were empty to begin with. The staff secured those items before the war," he said. "And employees at another museum moved about 40,000 ancient books and manuscripts into a bomb shelter for safe keeping, so they weren't lost either."

"They discovered ancient Torahs, didn't they?" asked Jeremy.

"Yes, sir, they found Hebrew books and photos in the basement of a building Saddam's secret police used," said Thornton. "There was even a book from the 1500s. The basement had flooded with water and sewage and the books were all damaged, but they've been sent to the US for restoration."

"All items which had been confiscated from Jews," said Jeremy.

"Yes, sir."

"So if 170,000 items weren't stolen from this museum, how many were?" Skylar asked.

"Let's go with how many are still missing—because we've managed to recover a lot," said Thornton. "We've had many artifacts returned through the amnesty program we set up. Return things, no questions asked. Some Iraqis said they'd looted items to keep them safe, but we suspect they took them to keep them from Saddam. Then they were either hit with a guilty conscience or decided it was a safe bet he wasn't coming back and decided to do the right thing by returning them. To show you how well the amnesty program is working, when the colonel was home on leave this summer, someone came up to him in a New York coffee shop and handed him an envelope with a 4,000-year-old Akkadian piece inside. It's back here at the museum now."

"Some of the looted items have already been smuggled out of Iraq?" asked Skylar.

"Unfortunately, yes," he said. "Most of the artifacts we've located overseas have surfaced in the usual places: London, Paris, Tokyo and New York, but many of the smugglers initially took them out of Iraq by land—through Jordan, Lebanon, Syria, Kuwait and Saudi Arabia—where we found them in the international antiquities markets. US customs agents have recovered 800 items. French police seized another 500 at an airport. We've located about 700 artifacts in Jordan."

"I understand the Vase of Warka was returned," said Jeremy, then explained to Skylar and the USN camera crew, "The vase is a 5,000-year-old Sumerian artifact carved from alabaster."

"We were mighty happy to see that come back," said Thornton. "Four Iraqi men drove up to the museum June 12, popped the trunk of their car and returned ninety-five missing artifacts, plus the vase, but, unfortunately, it had broken into fourteen pieces. There was considerable damage to the top and bottom, but it can be restored."

He explained how the 600-pound vase had been mounted to a display pedestal, but looters had toppled the stand, snapping off the vase at its base—which had remained attached to the pedestal.

"That's a shame," said Skylar.

"When German archaeologists discovered the Vase of Warka in 1940," said Jeremy, "it was broken in fourteen pieces. It had been broken in those same fourteen places in antiquity and someone had repaired it with copper wire, then, at some point it broke again along the same lines. When looters took it this time, the vase broke along the same fourteen fracture lines. It's been repaired twice—once professionally—and I'm quite sure it can be repaired again."

"That's exactly what one of the curators told us," said Thornton. "The museum sent it to Florence, Italy about a month ago to be repaired."

Jeremy told how the alabaster carvings on the vase depicted animals and nude men carrying fruit and grain, making their way in a procession up to the chief goddess of Mesopotamia.

"She was called Inanna then, but later became known as Ishtar—the pagan goddess of fertility," said Jeremy. "The same Ishtar who was Nineveh's primary idol."

"The same Ishtar we'd talked about where we get the name Easter?" asked Skylar.

"The same," he said. "You'll find Ishtar is prominent in Mesopotamian art and architecture throughout millennia. And just to clarify, the term Mesopotamian encompasses Assyrian, Babylonian and Sumerian artifacts."

"You mean Easter like the day Christians observe?" asked Thornton. "The name comes from a Mesopotamian goddess of fertility?"

"Yes," smiled Jeremy.

"How'd that happen?" asked Thornton.

"People didn't want to abandon their Ishtar celebrations when they converted to Christianity," said Jeremy.

Le An saw Barry's jaw clench and knew at some point within the next few hours, he was again going to make an issue of it. She sighed and shook her head, not looking forward to that explosion. Just to be sure, she checked whether the light on his camera was still on. She didn't trust him now and wouldn't have been surprised to learn he'd turned off the camera in protest to block the interview.

"It seems odd to think of people back then worshipping painted and carved statues," said Skylar.

"People still do today," said Jeremy. "Buddhah, statues of saints in churches, there's even a giant idol in Nashville."

"Nashville?" said Skylar, frowning.

"Yes, the city has a full-scale replica of the Greek goddess Athena inside a full-scale replica of the Parthenon," said Jeremy. "Some in ancient Greece honestly believed praying to Athena would give them wisdom and victory in war. Perhaps some still believe that."

They walked down the hallway and Skylar asked Thornton,

"What objects are still missing from the museum?"

"There were three crime areas," he said. "We figure about thirty items are still missing from the main public gallery and about 400 from the storage rooms, but many of the looted items from there were fakes."

"The looters stole fake artifacts?" asked Skylar, while Jeremy tried to hide a smile.

"Yes, replicas," said Thornton. "They'd been confiscated from counterfeiters prior to the war and, rather than run the risk of having them recirculate in the international antiquities market, the museum kept them in storage and used them for educational purposes. Some of the looters got fakes, though they were very good fakes."

The woman museum employee accompanying them on the tour nodded her agreement.

Thornton explained how, due to UN sanctions and a lack of funds, many of the museum's rooms, even before the invasion, normally looked empty—as if they'd been looted.

"Rooms we initially thought had been ransacked had apparently looked that way for years," he said. "The majority of missing artifacts number about 9,000 and they were stolen from the basement, the third crime area."

"That's nowhere near 170,000," said Skylar.

"Correct. About five percent of that," said Thornton. "That's a huge difference and we wish the international press would realize that. Hopefully, more archaeologists are becoming aware of the true numbers and are speaking up."

"We are," said Jeremy.

"The 9,000 items still missing are extremely small in size—gold and silver coins, beads, small cylinder seals," said Thornton. "But, to put it in perspective, each bead was counted, so if it was with thirty-nine other beads on a string, we count that as forty items missing. We've recovered some of the cylinders being sold at vendors' stalls here in Baghdad. In June, New York customs confiscated three 4,000-year-old stone cylinder seals from an American writer who said he bought them in Baghdad for $200 and didn't know where to turn them in. Said he was taking them back to turn in to his friends at the Pentagon. All three seals had the museum's ID number on them."

Jeremy explained each cylinder seal was only a few inches long, usually carved out of lapis lazuli, carnelian or other stone, hollow in the middle, through which a piece of leather or string would be strung to allow a person to wear it around their neck. The cylinder was used as a person's signature—an imprint rolled in wet clay to authenticate their correspondence—and collectors craved them. Some dated to 3200 BC and were worth as much as $250,000 each.

"The international stolen antiquities market is a $3-billion-a-year business," said Thornton. "Most looters here will unload a stolen artifact, say at a jewelry store in Baghdad, get $50 for it and the jeweler will then turn around and sell the same item to smugglers for $5,000. Within a short time, that artifact will be selling on the black market in London or New York for anywhere from ten to 100 times that. Sometimes we catch them in customs. Sometimes we get lucky and artifacts are returned or we crack an international art theft ring."

It was almost one o'clock and the woman museum employee who had been following them said she had to leave. Because of the deteriorating security situation, most female employees had their male relatives pick them up from work early each day.

As Thornton watched her walk away, he said, "We strongly believe the looting of the coins and cylinder seals in the basement was an inside job."

"The museum staff?" asked Skylar.

"Yes, and not just during the invasion. Staff members had been stealing from the museum for years—we estimate as many as 60,000 items."

"The current staff had been stealing?" asked Skylar.

"Probably most who had are no longer here," said Thornton. "They probably went into hiding in April. But for a decade or two, Saddam and his sons, particularly Uday, as well as Saddam's cousin who'd been in charge of the museum, and some other top-level Ba'athists, helped themselves. They made millions trading antiquities on the international market. Who knows if any of the current staff have, too. We also think some of the staff lied about the looting to make American forces look bad."

"You mean they deliberately said the number of items looted was more than it was?" asked Skylar.

"Exactly. Some of the staff had hidden a lot of the items and they knew they were hidden, but told the world press they'd been looted. Many valuable items had been moved into vaults at the Central Bank during the Iran-Iraq war in the 1980s. At first we were afraid Uday Hussein may have taken the Treasure of Nimrud from the bank vault. Before going into hiding, we know he took bars of gold from there, but, fortunately, he didn't take the Treasure."

"Yesterday in Nimrud we saw where the Treasure had been," said Skylar.

Thornton said photos were available from the day they'd discovered the gold and jewels in the flooded bank vault and a film crew from *National Geographic* had been with them, suggesting they could possibly access that footage of the discovery.

Le An knew her network had video of the jewelry on display, but made a note to track down still photos of the day it was found in the bank vault which might show more details.

"The National Geographic team found three pumps and volunteered to drain the bank basement. It took three weeks to pump out more than 500,000 gallons of water," said Thornton. "We showed the jewelry here at the museum when we opened it to the press on July 3, along with other items such as the Vase of Warka. Did your network cover that?"

Le An said USN was there.

"How did they display the Vase of Warka? Wasn't it still in pieces?" asked Skylar.

"The vase was displayed lying on its side with the broken pieces around it in a box of sorts," said Thornton.

"Where's the Treasure of Nimrud now?" asked Skylar.

"Back in the bank vault, along with other jewelry," said Thornton. "When we first went to the bank, we found looters had tried to break into the vault by firing an RPG at it. The door to the vault remained intact. The looter died. We found his body and two others who fired on each other in the bank."

"They shot each other?" asked Skylar.

"No honor among thieves, I guess," said Thornton dryly. "Here at the museum, the looters accessed the basement storage room where there were thirty storage lockers, twenty-nine of them still locked. They'd managed to open the first locker filled with about 100 tackle boxes full of coins and cylinder seals and those were taken. But here's the thing: the keys to the storage lockers were on a string and they were stored in a drawer in another part of the museum—a location only a few employees knew about. During our initial investigation, we found the keys under some of the empty tackle boxes on the basement floor. Our guess is the looters dropped them and couldn't find them in the dark, which is probably why they didn't steal more items from the other twenty-nine lockers. They even left about 400 cylinder seals still in the plastic tackle boxes they did have access to. Since they were using packing foam as a torch, they might have been overcome by fumes. All they got were the contents of those 100 or so tackle boxes."

"You're saying it had to be an inside job?" asked Skylar.

"That's what our investigation revealed. There were cardboard boxes stacked on top of the lockers and none of them had been touched, other than the few which had been accidentally knocked off. We learned the boxes were all empty, but how did the thieves know that? We surmise they didn't touch them because they already knew the boxes were empty. And the only way to know that was if you were an insider."

"What else is missing?" asked Skylar.

Thornton named a few items, then ended with, "Also, the Mask of Warka dating from about 3100 BC and an ivory carving called Lioness Attacking a Nubian."

Skylar looked confused. "Is that the same ivory lioness you were describing when we were at Nimrud, Jeremy?"

"We know of two such ivory plaques from the eighth century BC still in existence," he said. "The one missing from the museum is inlaid with carnelian and lapis lazuli and overlaid with gold. The other one found at the bottom of the well in Nimrud, as I told you, is in the British Museum. The limestone Warka Mask is one of this museum's most prized and priceless artifacts, dating from about 3200 BC. The carved facial mask of a woman is believed to represent Inanna."

Jeremy paused and looked at Skylar for recognition of the name.

"Inanna, a.k.a. the sex goddess Ishtar, a.k.a. Easter," said Skylar.

"Precisely," said Jeremy. "The Sumerian goddess of sex, fertility and warfare—also known as the 'Lady of Warka,' 'the Mona Lisa of Mesopotamia' and the 'Lady of Uruk.'"

Le An looked over at Barry to see if steam was coming from his ears yet.

Within days, the eight-inch-tall Warka Mask would be found wrapped in rags and plastic, buried in an orchard a few miles north of Baghdad. An Iraqi informant's tip would lead a joint team of American soldiers and Iraqi police first to a boy, then to a smuggler and finally to the 5,000-year-old carving.

31

Baghdad, Iraq
Friday, 5 September 2003

Le An started setting up for Skylar's live shot on USN's morning show to talk about the attack on their convoy the day before. Stepping outside, she used her satellite phone to call USN's control room to let them know they'd be broadcasting from inside the museum, then stayed on the line getting the proper satellite coordinates from New York so the sat truck engineer could tune in and establish the shot.

Barry set his camera on a tripod and positioned Skylar, Leo and Ryan on chairs in front, with the other four Dark Knight security guards who'd been USN's protection detail the day before standing behind them. Since there were so many, Barry had Khaled used a boom mic and gave each of the ones appearing on camera IFBs—ear monitors—to be able to hear the questions from the anchor who'd be conducting the interview.

The morning show producers had the video Barry had shot of the attack on their convoy, as well as the bullet-riddled cars, and planned to air it during the interview. The segment was scheduled to go live at the top of the 7:00 hour—the 'A' block—3:00 p.m. Baghdad time.

After the interview concluded and they were packing away their equipment, Le An looked around for Jeremy. Not seeing him, she waited a few minutes, thinking he may be talking to members of the staff, then asked Thornton if he'd seen the professor.

"No, ma'am. The last time I saw him he was with you," he said.

Just to make sure, she asked if he'd accompany her on a quick trip through the museum to look for Jeremy.

He was nowhere to be found.

Ducking outside to see if he was there, she found an impatient, tired and hungry crew ready to leave. Glancing up, she spotted the satellite truck leaving through the front gate.

"Come on, Le An. I'm starved," said Barry. "We need food."

"Where's Jeremy?" she asked.

They all shrugged.

"Did he go with the sat truck?" she asked.

Again, they all shrugged.

She pulled out her sat phone and called the truck's engineer. Jeremy wasn't in the truck with him and the two DK guards assigned to protect him.

Growing more concerned, Le An asked the commanding officer if he could have his men do a complete search of the museum. In addition to those in the main compound, he also assigned two soldiers to search and question the employees who lived in back of the museum. One by one the soldiers radioed in with 'negative.'

There was no sign of Jeremy.

"I think I'm going to throw up," Le An mumbled.

She pulled aside Leo and Ryan and snapped, "Why don't you know where Jeremy is? It's your job to protect him."

"Protect him from getting shot or killed, yeah," said Leo. "But not protect him from wandering off by himself."

"We don't know that," she said. "You were supposed to guard us—all of us. There are six of you and five of us. Whether you're doing zone defense or man-to-man, how hard is it to keep track of one person?"

Ryan clenched his jaw angrily and walked off to question the three remaining Dark Knight guards.

"Le An, if Jeremy wandered off without telling us, that's on his head," said Leo. "We don't take away your free will."

"Tell me how a man can just disappear from a secure location, right out from under the noses of his six-man, very expensive, security team and the US military, not to mention ICE agents on the JIACG team? Tell me how that's possible," she demanded.

"Because we thought we were in a secure location, Le An," he said. "And I'm telling you, if Jeremy isn't here, it's because he doesn't want to be here and he walked away of his own free will. No one took him."

"We don't know that," she snapped. "You weren't guarding him. You weren't keeping an eye on him."

"Le An," said Leo, now sounding irritated, "may I remind you, he disappeared while we were doing interviews for you and your morning show. How could we be doing that and watching him at the same time? There's a compound full of US soldiers. I think it's safe to say we thought he'd be safe for the twenty minutes we were out of commission with your broadcast. You're the one who made the call to put your entire security detail on the air instead of letting them do their job of guarding you."

She closed her eyes, annoyed at her own stupidity. It hadn't been her decision to put them all on the air. She despised large group interviews because they usually left one or two people sitting there looking stupid when the anchor forgot to ask them a question. But the morning show producer in charge of the segment had insisted Skylar appear with all six guards for the interview. She shook her head, wondering why she hadn't put her foot down and told New York they could only have two guards max.

Even more annoying was the fact the interview had been great. With Barry's video and Skylar's and the guards' eye-witness accounts of the attack, USN hands down had the best A block of all the networks that day. The other networks carried their updates on Iraq, but the only other big stories were the Democratic debates gearing up for the 2004 election, forest fires in the Cascade Mountains and hearings on the August blackout and massive power outages in the Northeast.

Good one, Le An, she said to herself. *Great segment for USN, but, oh, yeah, you just happened to lose your VIP consultant in the middle of a war zone.*

"I told you that guy was nuts," said Barry. "Look at the trouble he's causing us. And again today he had to rant about Easter. Maybe he's in the basement stealing cylinder seals."

She turned on him in fury, as panic rose inside her that something had happened to a consultant in their care.

"Do you have to whine and gripe about everything, Barry?" she said through clenched teeth. "I'm fed up with your attitude. As if I don't have enough stress on this job, you have to add to it. And I sincerely doubt Jeremy is stealing any antiquities."

Before he could answer, she spun around and walked at a brisk pace across the compound. At the entrance gate, she held up her digital camera to show a couple of soldiers a picture of Jeremy and asked if they'd seen him. They squinted against the sun, trying to dodge the glare to get a clear image of him.

One of them nodded, then looked at the museum's visitor log. "Yes, ma'am, I recognize him. He checked out, had a pat-down and cleared security at 15:00."

"He left willingly? No one was pointing a gun at him? Was he kidnapped? Did he say he was going to get food? Did he say he was coming back?" she asked, the questions tumbling out.

"Sorry, ma'am, I don't know, but I did think it was strange he came with you, but left by himself. Oh, yeah, before he left, he put on one of those Arab-looking outfits."

She felt sick.

"Which way did he go?" she asked weakly.

"Sorry, ma'am, I don't know."

Frantically, Le An spun in a semi-circle, trying to spot the professor in the crowd of people and cars. It was as bad as she feared. He hadn't just wandered off to look at artifacts somewhere on the grounds.

The Honorable Doctor Jacob Jeremy Winston Spencer-Hilson had completely disappeared.

32

*Baghdad, Iraq
Friday, 5 September 2003*

Le An reluctantly decided to return to the villa after soldiers stationed at the museum told her they'd notify her if Jeremy returned. Fortunately, the next day was an off day for the USN crew, so his disappearance wouldn't put them behind schedule, but she had a growing uneasiness something was wrong.

Had Jeremy gone off with a friend? And even if he had, someone could harm him while he was gone. Why had he left without telling her? Without telling anyone?

Khaled parted company with them at the museum and went home. He wasn't scheduled to rejoin them until Sunday morning for the trip to Babylon.

Jeremy wasn't waiting for them back at the villa and there were no messages from him.

"That guy is beyond irritating," mumbled Barry as he dumped his video gear and made a beeline for the bar to fix a strong drink.

"Princess! You joining us for happy hour?" Mike called out.

"Not right now," she said, halfway up the enormous winding staircase. She wasn't in a mood to deal with Barry's bad attitude or people questioning her about why Jeremy had left their group. "Did our cook ever show up?"

"Nope," said Mike, as he hung on the stairs' bottom newel post to take the weight off his sore ankle. "But some relative of Khaled's sent us a message she'd start working for us tomorrow if we need her. We're on our own tonight. Care to pitch in?"

"Not really. Maybe our cook went to the mosque today," she said.

"She's Christian, remember?" said Mike just as Hugh, Piet and Kent came in the front door.

"Weird. Everybody's disappearing," she mumbled as she turned to walk up the rest of the stairs.

"Who else is missing? Wait, where's Jeremy?" asked Mike.

"Jeremy's missing?" asked Hugh.

She turned and gave them both a cold, exhausted stare. "I don't know where he is. He left the museum compound while we were doing our live shot for the morning show. He didn't tell anyone he was leaving. He didn't say where he was going. All I know is he observes the Sabbath, so I'm assuming wherever he is, he'll be back here in an hour or so before sunset. We don't shoot again until Sunday, I have a splitting headache and I want to lie down. No, make that *need* to lie down."

"Whoa, whoa, whoa, whoa," said Mike. "Back up there, Boone. You lost our consultant in the middle of a war zone? Come back down here. I can't hobble up to you and we need to discuss this."

She turned and slowly came back down, sitting on one of the bottom steps.

"I've told you everything I know, Mike," she said. "We searched the entire compound and it's like he disappeared into thin air. The soldiers have a record of him leaving the compound, but that's it. He didn't tell anyone he was leaving and he didn't say where he was going."

"What were the DK guards doing? Leo! Ryan! Get over here!" Mike yelled. "Why weren't they keeping an eye on him?"

"Because the A-block producer wanted them all on camera, too, to talk about our ambush yesterday," she said wearily.

"Great," said Mike. "All right, call Paul and tell him what's going on."

"Can't we wait and see if Jeremy comes back in an hour or two?" she asked.

"No. Call Paul," he said, then hobbled back to the feed room. "And let's hope this isn't a kidnapping or a murder."

Le An buried her head in her hands, too exhausted to stand up.

Hugh sat down next to her and, leaning toward her, nudged her shoulder with his.

"How are you getting on?" he asked gently.

She looked up and sighed heavily, then shook her head. "Not good. And you?"

"I'm utterly and completely knackered," he said. "But I'm leaving Sunday and you're still quite in the midst of mess."

"That's a good way of putting it," she said. "Lucky you that you get to leave."

"You still talking about that nightmare troublemaker Jeremy?" asked Barry as he and Skylar pushed past them on their way upstairs.

Le An didn't answer, just closed her eyes and leaned her head against the ornate wrought-iron-and-gold balustrade.

"Anything I can do to help?" asked Hugh.

"Thank you, that's sweet. I don't know what I'm going to do. I guess call my boss and get royally chewed out," she said as she stood up.

As expected, Paul wasn't pleased at the turn of events, but told her to keep him updated every few hours.

Exiting the library where she'd made the call, Le An slipped up a back staircase and, once in her bedroom, flopped on her bed, just as a pain shot through her chest, leaving her winded. Gasping, she grabbed her left arm and pulled it in close. After a few minutes, the pain subsided and shortly after she dropped off to sleep.

When she awoke three hours later, it was dark out and she was disoriented, unsure if it was day or night. After grabbing her laptop, she went downstairs.

"Boone! Where've you been for the last three hours? We got pizzas from Pizzeria Napoli, Barry's favorite. And no, they're not cold. We're keeping them warm in the oven," Mike called to her from the largest of the villa's three dining rooms. "Though we could probably just throw 'em on the pavement and they'd stay warm. You're about three drinks behind us."

"I fell asleep," she said as she grabbed a slice of pizza and plopped it on a plate. "Is business picking up at Napoli?"

"Not much. Poor guy," said Barry. "The only authentic pizza joint in Baghdad and he can't understand why Americans aren't keeping him busy and making him rich."

"Because he's outside the Green Zone," said Mike. "The khaki wonks won't venture out of their cocoon. The troops like it, though."

"It only seats four," said Hugh.

"Yeah, that wasn't good planning. He should have gotten a

larger place," said Le An. "I don't know why the guy doesn't drop from heat exhaustion in front of that wood-burning oven. If it's 120 degrees outside, it's got to be 140 in his kitchen. Did Jeremy come back?"

Everyone shifted uncomfortably and shook their heads 'no.'

She knew she had to check in with Paul, but before she did, she decided to check her email on the off chance Jeremy had contacted her. Taking her pizza to the library, she fired up her laptop.

There were no emails from Jeremy, but as Le An was about to log out, an email came through with the subject line PAY OR HE DIES.

33

Baghdad, Iraq
Friday, 5 September 2003

Le An instantly felt nauseated and started shaking.

"Mike!" she screamed as she read the email. "Mike, get in here!"

The tone of her voice caused the others to come running, pushing past a hobbling Mike. They all crowded around her computer trying to read the email. Mike, the last to arrive in the room, roughly pushed them all away and sat down next to Le An to read the message for himself.

"He's been kidnapped," he said, causing everyone to gasp, "and this says we have twenty hours to pay."

"How much?" asked Skylar.

"Fifteen million dinar," said Mike.

Le An looked at the email again and frowned. "Fifteen million dinar? That's what? Like $10,000?"

"What else does it say?" asked Barry.

"That's it," said Mike, then turned to the other journalists around him. "I'm begging you, guys. News blackout on this kidnapping for a few days."

Everyone reluctantly agreed.

"Forward the email to Paul," said Le An as she dialed his number, her hands shaking. "Skylar, contact your FBI friend over in the Green Zone and tell him what's happened. I don't know if they'll help because he's British, but he's working for an American company, so maybe they will."

"On it," said Skylar.

As Le An gave Paul the information about what had happened, Mike picked up the two-way radio in the room linked to their security guards and asked Leo to come in.

"Le, DK has their own private hostage negotiation and recovery team," he said. "I'm bringing them in on this. I don't think the FBI will get involved, but they'll probably be interested in any info we get, especially if it's linked to a terrorist cell."

After handing the phone to Mike so he could tell Paul, she told Tim, "See if you can contact our kidnapper's email provider and get a name on the account. It's probably bogus, and I bet he closed it right after sending it, but we might as well try. Here, I'm forwarding the email to you."

Tim grabbed a sheet of paper from the reporter's notebook next to her, leaning in to look at the laptop screen as he jotted down the email address.

She reread the email. There were no instructions where to deliver the money, no photo of Jeremy attached, no proof of life—just the amount of the ransom, that USN had to deliver it by five o'clock the next afternoon, and that the kidnappers would kill 'THE PROFESSOR DOCTOR' if they didn't receive their money.

Kidnapping in Iraq was escalating each day as a way to earn money. That's what happened when a nation and its economy suddenly collapsed.

"How did they know my company email?" asked Le An. "How did they know to send it to me?"

Mike looked at her and frowned. "Jeremy would have named you as his contact, I assume. Did he know your email address?"

"Maybe... I don't know. I don't think so. April initially emailed him, but I don't remember emailing him. Everything I've given him has been printed."

"They could've found it on the USN website, figured out the pattern of our first initial last name configuration. And, don't forget, you're listed on the website."

"Yeah, but you really have to search to find my email. Correspondents are listed, but not producers, you know that. And I don't think Jeremy would have willingly given up my name... unless..."

"Unless what?" asked Mike.

"Unless they tortured him," she said slowly, tears pooling in her eyes.

Mike put an arm around her. "Come on, Le, don't go there. Let's stay focused so we can help him."

She nodded and wiped her eyes. "OK, let's think this through. He disappeared from the museum, where our names and contact information have been on file for weeks, so..."

"Do you think a museum employee saw an opportunity?" asked Mike. "Told him they wanted him to see something off the museum grounds? Lured him away and then kidnapped him?"

"I don't know," she said. "The soldiers at the museum said he left alone. He doesn't strike me as being that gullible, but maybe... what if... what if they said they knew where a stolen artifact was and they wanted him to go with them to retrieve it?"

"OK, would that have happened?" asked Mike.

She thought a moment and shook her head. "They have a whole investigative team tasked with retrieving artifacts and it's an amnesty program. No one's being arrested if they turn in stolen antiquities."

"But maybe the person with the artifact doesn't want to give it up," he speculated. "And the thief would be arrested if the investigative team came to get it because he wasn't willingly returning it. He was still hanging onto it or trying to sell it. Maybe the thief's friend or family member was afraid he'd be arrested or the piece would be damaged, so Jeremy had to go act as intermediary and something went wrong and he ended up a hostage."

She looked at him a moment, then weakly said, "Maybe. But then why wouldn't the thief's friend just take the piece and turn it in under the amnesty program?"

"Good point, Sherlock." Mike thought a few seconds, then said, "Maybe the stolen artifact is too big or too heavy. Or maybe the thief knows Jeremy. Maybe his friend thought Jeremy could talk his old friend into giving up the piece without anyone getting hurt."

"Maybe," she said.

"Are all those museum archaeologists, curators, whatever... honest, good-as-gold citizens?" he asked.

She looked up at him. "No, the American investigator at the museum said part of the thefts were an inside job—that as many as 60,000 pieces had been smuggled out over the last ten or twenty years and a theft of thousands of valuable cylinder seals back in April was probably an inside job. What if someone, maybe an employee, knew Jeremy knew something about that and they had to silence him?"

"You just went from kidnapping for ransom to murder to cover up an international art theft," said Mike.

"If the kidnappers had valuable cylinder seals, why would they take Jeremy for $10,000 ransom?" she said. "The cylinders are worth at least twenty times that."

"Too hot to fence?" said Barry. "Or the good professor could be dirty."

"What? No!" she gasped.

"What if he stole something from the museum and was going to meet someone to sell it, but the art theft crime ring nabbed him and the things he was selling?" said Mike.

"The soldiers told me they patted him down," she said. "They said they always check to make sure antiquities aren't being removed. I need to call Thornton Cromstock at the museum to update him and see if he's heard anything. He and the investigative task force there are a bunch of guys from the alphabet agencies, so they could give us access to a lot of US government data bases. Plus, I'm sure someone would be interested if this involves a terrorist cell."

"Good point," said Mike. "Give them a call."

Just then Skylar stuck his head in the room. "I think you'll want to see this."

34

*Baghdad, Iraq
Friday, 5 September 2003*

Skylar led the way to the villa's main dining room—now the official command center—where the rest of the journalists in the house had started going through their contacts, forming lists of who would be influential enough to help in a backroom negotiation for Jeremy.

On one long walls, they'd hung pieces from ripped-apart cardboard shipping boxes on nails where expensive gold-framed paintings had been only minutes before. On top of the cardboard, they'd taped white copy paper, designating in black magic marker four categories: Shi'a, Sunni, Kurd and Christian. Under those, they'd listed all the main tribal leaders they knew, with stars indicating who might be more inclined to help.

For hours, most remained on their phones and laptops, calling or emailing their contacts to ask if anyone had heard of a terrorist group holding a tall, middle-aged British man. No one had any information about a Brit, but a few sources confirmed an American contractor had been kidnapped and was being held in the northern part of the country.

That was new information.

The journalists contacted the FBI in the Green Zone to work on that kidnapping, thinking there was always a chance the same people could be holding both the contractor and the archaeologist.

Le An called Thornton Cromstock and asked him to keep an eye out for Jeremy if he and CENTCOM's JIACG task force conducted any raids for antiquities. Within a few hours, Thornton and a few other members of his team arrived at the villa. Less than an hour later members of Dark Knight's hostage negotiation and recovery team showed up. The team was made up of former agents from special forces, the FBI and CIA. Because Jeremy was a British citizen, a few detectives from Scotland Yard also showed up.

"This is great. You people are amazing," mumbled Pete Kleinfield, a former FBI agent on the Dark Knight hostage negotiation team, when he spotted the wall of information in the dining room.

The journalists' contacts were far better than those of the hostage negotiation team—on a par with those of the JIACG task force. Still, no matter which contact anyone spoke to, no one could confirm any British man was being held hostage in the northern, central or southern part of Iraq—only the American contractor.

"Let's hope the Kurds or Shi'ites have Jeremy," said Mike. "If the Sunnis have him, he may not make it out alive, particularly if any Fedayeen or Republican Guards get hold of him."

Le An blanched, knowing how true that was.

Hugh shot her a sympathetic look. "Maybe he's told them he's an archaeologist here to protect their country's treasures."

"More likely they'd accuse him of trying to steal their national treasures," said Barry.

"Keep the coffee coming," said Pete.

A Scotland Yard detective named Nigel Harrington agreed to let the more experienced DK American negotiator Clay Roney handle any ransom calls for Jeremy, while he maintained general control of the operation.

"His name's Jacob Spencer-Hilson?" asked Nigel as he opened his laptop.

"He goes by Doctor Jeremy Hilson," said Le An. "But the kidnappers didn't use his name in the email. Just called him 'professor doctor.'"

"Have you checked the morgues?" asked Clay.

The journalists slowly shook their heads 'no,' the grim thought registering on their faces. They'd all been to the various freezer facilities around Baghdad where unidentified bodies were piling up, haphazardly thrown in, the sheer volume of dead overwhelming the available space. Frantic relatives had to turn over each body to search for their missing loved ones. With the power going out frequently, the refrigeration was non-existent for much of the day, causing the bodies to decompose rapidly. It was a gruesome scene.

"Did Jeremy have a computer?" asked Nigel.

"We can't find it. He must have his laptop with him," said Le An.

Just before 11:00 p.m., a call came in on Le An's Iraq cellphone. Clay took the call and a husky voice speaking broken English asked for a woman they assumed was meant to be Le An. Though the caller repeatedly asked for the woman, Clay politely stressed she wasn't available to talk. As the caller became more angry, Clay asked gently if they needed anything—any food or medicine—then politely asked the kidnappers to put Jeremy on the phone so they could have proof he was still alive. The caller refused and said if USN didn't deliver $15 million, the professor would be killed.

"Fifteen million *dollars?*" Clay calmly emphasized the last word as everyone's mouth dropped open. "I want to make sure we understand exactly what you're asking because your email said fifteen million dinar."

"No!" shouted the caller. "Not dinar! American dollar! Fifteen million dollars! By five tomorrow in the afternoon."

"I just want to make sure we understand exactly what you're asking," Clay repeated in a soothing voice.

"Dollar, not dinar! Give us money or the professor doctor dies!" shouted the caller and hung up.

"Fifteen million?" gasped Le An. "That's what the government paid for each of the Hussein brothers. Why would they think we could raise that?"

"These guys are amateurs," said Clay. "They can't even make up their minds which currency they want."

"Is that good they're amateurs?" she asked.

"Not necessarily. We don't know how volatile they are or what would set them off," said Pete. "And we don't know if they'll sell Doctor Hilson to another group, which might be worse."

"They obviously knew—from the email and what the man said to me—that you and Jeremy work for USN and you're somehow in charge of him," Clay said to her. "But how did they know to call your cellphone? How did they know they could reach you on that number?"

"I don't know," she said. "It's a USN cellphone and number. When I leave Iraq, I leave the phone here. We all have sat phones and cellphones with local numbers, but most people we deal with in Iraq use our local cellphones. Did they ask for me by name?"

"No, he kept asking for 'the woman in charge of the professor doctor,'" said Clay. "So it could be someone who knows you or who's seen you with Jeremy. Or maybe because they know women work here, they think it would be easier to deal with a woman. They may not know you at all."

"But a lot of people do know that cellphone number," said Mike. "A lot of USN people have used that phone."

"Let's start making a list of people who might know the number," said Pete.

"And somehow they knew my email, which is weird," she said.

"Yes, that's something to consider," said Pete.

All the journalists staying in the villa donated as much time as they could without sacrificing their own assignments, with many working late into the night to find Jeremy.

Le An grabbed a large pillow and sat down on the dining room's rug, leaning against one wall to support her aching back. She knew she needed to stay awake and focused, but the need to sleep for a few minutes finally won out. She slumped down and put her head on the pillow, curling up in a fetal position as she tried to think where Jeremy could be, who could possibly have him. Why hadn't any of their contacts heard about his abduction?

Suddenly, she sat up.

35

Baghdad, Iraq
Saturday, 6 September 2003

Pete saw Le An's sudden movement and her panicked look.

"What?" he asked, fighting back a yawn. A few members of his team were already asleep on the many couches scattered around the mansion. "What're you thinking?"

Clay looked up from his laptop where he was entering all the contact names the journalists had compiled.

"He's dead, isn't he?" she said, fighting back tears. "That's why no one's heard he's being held. That's why they haven't released a tape. Because they've already killed him."

"If they killed him, in all likelihood there would be a tape," said Nigel. "They like to broadcast those things. We'd hear about it on Al Hazeera."

"Not if they accidentally killed him," she said.

"Even if they accidentally killed him," said Nigel. "They'd show video of the body, possibly even stage it to appear he was alive first, even if he were dead. It's a good sign if there hasn't been a video on Al Hazeera."

"It's after four. We've got thirteen hours," said Clay. "Nigel, what do you say we get some sleep. You, too, Le An. All of us need to be clear-headed to deal with these people and we won't be if we're exhausted. Pete, wake up the B team and let's grab a few hours sleep."

Le An felt guilty going upstairs to sleep in a bed, so she dragged more pillows into the dining room and built as comfortable a bed on the rug as she could—considering under it was a very hard marble floor.

By 7:30 most were awake, back in the dining room and sucking down massive amounts of coffee as they continued working their contact lists.

Shortly after eight, one of the guards came in to tell them a woman they'd never seen before was at the front gate saying she was their cook.

"That must be Khaled's sister. I forgot she was starting today," said Mike as he struggled to get up from a chair, his ankle still sore. "I'll be right back. I'm sure people are hungry."

"I'm not. I couldn't eat a thing," said Le An. "Don't get up, Mike. I'll show her where the kitchen is."

"Wait a minute. Who is this person? Is she Iraqi?" asked Pete. "Has she ever been here?"

"No, this is her first day," she said. "Our other cook hasn't shown up the last few days and our fixer audio tech said his sister could cook for us."

"Tell her to start next week," Pete told the DK guard. "Not today. Your cook is missing, too? Why didn't you tell us?"

"I don't know," said Mike. "I guess we didn't think the two were related."

"They may be," said Nigel. "Tell us everything you know about her."

"Not much," said Mike as a few people headed for the kitchen to start cooking breakfast and put on a fresh pot of coffee, resigned to the fact they were still the de facto cooks. "We don't even know how to contact her. She didn't show up yesterday morning and we haven't heard from her since."

"She didn't show up for work the same day Jeremy disappeared?" asked Nigel.

Le An and Hugh looked at each other, recalling their conversation the morning before.

"We had a robbery, too," Le An suddenly remembered. "Early Thursday morning after midnight someone stole some equipment and cash. They cut our power and took out our generator. Leo thought it might have been someone with an inside knowledge of the villa because they were able to get past them. Do you think it could be connected?"

"Maybe," said Nigel.

A few minutes later, the guard came back to tell them Khaled was at the front door asking why they didn't want his sister to work for them and if Jeremy had returned.

"How does he know Jeremy's missing?" asked Clay suspiciously.

"Khaled was with us at the museum when Jeremy disappeared. He was our audio tech for the shoot there," said Le An.

"Did he see him leave?" asked Nigel.

"No, he was busy with the live shot, same as the rest of us," she said.

"I think we should talk to him," said Pete.

He turned to the guard and told him to escort Khaled to the small library so they could question him.

"Khaled's gonna freak," mumbled Barry. "Maybe we should go in there with him."

"No, let them do their job," said Le An wearily. "Khaled worked as a minder in Saddam's government, so I'm sure anything these guys throw at him, he's able to handle."

As Khaled stepped into the front foyer, Pete and Clay motioned for him to follow them.

"Who are these men?" Khaled whispered to Le An and Barry, visibly unnerved.

"They're from Scotland Yard and our hostage negotiation team," she said.

"Why do they want to talk to me?" he asked, panic rising in his voice.

"It's about that troublemaker Jeremy being missing," said Barry as Le An gave him a dirty look. "What? Le An, he is a troublemaker. Relax, Khaled, just answer their questions and you'll be fine."

Le An and Barry waited in the main hallway for Khaled to come out of his interview and, as he left, he told them both, "If you want me to help, I will help. I will take money to the kidnappers for you."

"Thanks, Khaled," said Barry as he patted him on his back.

"I am sure if you pay, they will return him," said Khaled. "When Iraqis are kidnapped, we do not have money to pay, so they kill our families. They kidnapped the son of my neighbors and they could not pay. Three days later, they find his body by the road, shot in the head. Sometimes they never find body. But you are able to pay, so it will be good for Jeremy."

"We can't pay $15 million," said Barry. "These crazy idiots have us confused with the US government. Besides, USN doesn't pay ransom."

"You must pay!" said Khaled looking upset. "These people are bad. They kill when you do not pay. You must pay."

Just then Pete came up, frowned and forcibly pushed Le An and Barry to move them away from Khaled.

"We need to get back to work. Thank you for your help, Khaled," he said.

"I don't think we're going to be shooting tomorrow," Le An said to him.

"We'll be in touch," said Pete, as he put each of his massive hands on Barry's and Le An's backs to give them another push.

Pete directed the two of them into the small library and after closing the doors behind them, angrily turned to face them.

"You don't talk to anyone about these negotiations," he snapped.

"He's part of our crew," protested Barry. "He was with us at the museum when Jeremy disappeared and for hours after that when we were looking for him."

"I don't care," said Pete. "You don't talk to anyone outside of this house."

"We're sorry," said Le An as Barry huffed out of the room. "Won't happen again. We're just tired."

At two, Le An's Iraq cellphone rang again and the husky voice asked for 'the woman in charge of the professor doctor' to give final directions for the money drop. Again, Clay informed him she wasn't available and again the man refused to let him talk to Jeremy. Clay asked him about their group's ideology, trying to build a relationship with him while determining where their loyalties and connections were, what ethnic group they were with, but the caller refused to answer. However, this time the ransom amount had dropped to $1 million and he ended with a threat that his group would sell the professor to Al Qaeda if USN didn't come through with the money.

After the man hung up, Clay repeated what he'd said to the group assembled in the dining room.

"Can you hear that, Paul?" asked Le An who was on the phone with New York.

"Yeah, I heard," he said. "We're not paying for Jeremy Hilson,

Le An. It'll just encourage kidnappers to take other journalists."

"He isn't a journalist," she said.

"USN won't let me pay," he repeated. "We've been in touch with his brother in England and he said his family was going to try and get money together, but they need time. I'm not officially in favor of paying, but if the family wants to, we can't stop them. All you can do is try to stall them and give us some time. Let me talk to the lead negotiator."

Le An handed the phone to Clay who, minutes later, motioned for Nigel to talk to Paul.

Barry was the first to see.

"What the hell?" he muttered. "Le An. Le!"

She turned, alarmed at the tone of his voice, following the direction his finger was pointing. The room slowly grew quiet as all eyes turned toward the dining room's massive double doors.

There stood Leo—with a very-much-alive Doctor Jacob Jeremy Winston Spencer-Hilson.

36

Baghdad, Iraq
Saturday, 6 September 2003

Everyone in the dining room stared at the Arab-looking archaeologist, his head covered in a red-and-white *keffiyeh*.

Le An was the first to run toward him.

"Jeremy, are you all right?" she gasped.

The videographers made a rush for their cameras and suddenly the room lit up, courtesy of the cameras' top-mounted lights.

"What's this?" asked Jeremy, blinking from the bright lights in his face.

Reporters grabbed microphones and tape recorders, firing questions at him, as Pete, Nigel and Clay blocked their access, directing Jeremy to the library down the hall where they could talk in private. Le An, Skylar, Mike and Barry insisted on coming in with them, as did the other journalists who were crowding behind them.

"Lockdown!" screamed Pete to his team. "I want radio silence from everyone!"

"All right, back off, people! Back to the dining room!" said Clay. "You'll all get to interview him, but, right now, we need to find out what's going on."

He shooed away everyone but Le An and Mike. The journalists grumbled their compliance with his requests as the hostage negotiators and Scotland Yard agents waved their arms to get them back into the dining room.

"It's like herding cats," Pete mumbled.

"We're just doing our jobs—in very difficult situations, I might add," said Le An, then called out to the journalists, "I promise, y'all will get your interviews!"

Closing the library door behind him, Nigel turned to Jeremy

and said, "Doctor Hilson...may I call you Jeremy?"

"Certainly," he said.

"Jeremy, where the devil have you been for twenty-three hours?" asked Nigel.

37

Baghdad, Iraq
Saturday, 6 September 2003

"Why I've been here in Baghdad," said a stunned Jeremy, looking around the room at the small group. "I'm dreadfully sorry, but who are you people?"

"They're with Dark Knight's hostage recovery and negotiation team and Scotland Yard," said Le An as she introduced Pete, Clay and Nigel. "And we've got some FBI agents and members of CENTCOM's JIACG investigative task force in the other room."

"You mean Thornton Cromstock's team from the museum?" he asked. "What's happened?"

The three agents snorted.

"We're working on a couple of kidnappings," said Pete.

"Oh, dear. Has someone from the museum been taken?" asked Jeremy.

"Are you kidding me?" asked Mike, slapping his cheek and rubbing his hand over his day-old beard. "Yeah, Jeremy, you."

"Me?" he gasped. "I haven't been kidnapped. Why would you think that?"

"Where have you been?" repeated Nigel.

Jeremy hesitated a moment. "I'd rather not say."

Pete gave him a forced smile, then leaned toward him and said, "Well, you'd better say. Were you trying to locate stolen antiquities?"

"No," he said, sounding confused.

"Jeremy, were you trying to buy them in hopes of returning them to the museum?" asked Clay, taking a less combative approach. "We would certainly understand if you were trying to be an intermediary to return looted artifacts to the museum."

"Well, yes, much as I'd like to, that's not what I was doing," he said.

"You haven't been dealing in stolen antiquities?" asked Nigel.

"Absolutely not!" he gasped. "Why would you think that?"

"Jeremy, an awful lot of people have worked very hard trying to find you," said Le An, starting to sound annoyed. "Your brother thinks you've been kidnapped and, as we speak, is trying to get together enough money to fulfill a ransom demand. We're all exhausted, so would you please just tell us where you've been?"

"My brother thinks I've been kidnapped? By whom?" he gasped.

"That's what we'd like to know, Jeremy," said Pete. "Until you walked in the door, we weren't sure whether you were dead or alive."

"Oh, dear. I'm dreadfully sorry for the fuss, but there's obviously been some misunderstanding. I haven't been kidnapped, as you can clearly see, and I don't know why anyone would think I had," he said, then sighed. "I'd hoped to conceal this to protect the people I met with. I'd ask that what I tell you remains in this room. It's vitally important this information goes no further."

They all looked at each other, wondering what dark secret he was concealing.

"Afraid we can't guarantee that until we know what it is," said Nigel. "Now where the devil have you been?"

38

Baghdad, Iraq
Saturday, 6 September 2003

"I've been with the last Jews of Baghdad," said Jeremy.

"What?" Nigel exploded, looking exasperated. "You've been meeting with a bunch of Jews?"

Jeremy looked offended at his comment.

"Professor, why didn't you tell me?" asked Le An. "That would've been a great segment. We could've sent a crew with you."

"That's exactly what they don't want," he said. "After the invasion, they received some press straightaway and things became rather dangerous for them. They don't want the attention. They're a small group and the last few months many have received death threats. Some want to make *aliyah* and a few of us are working to get those who wish to leave safely out of Iraq."

"They want to make what?" asked Clay.

"*Aliyah*. They want to immigrate to Israel," he said. "A few others wish to go to America or the UK. They fear for their lives."

"Yeah, so do most people in Iraq these days," said Pete.

"You don't understand," he said. "For more than seventy years, Jews have been persecuted in Iraq, but since the invasion, it's become even more dangerous for them."

"How many are there?" asked Le An.

"Thirteen," he said.

"Thirteen who want to leave?" asked Pete.

"No thirteen Jews left in all of Iraq, living here in Baghdad," he said. "The older ones don't want to leave their homeland. They're utterly terrified of leaving, afraid of the unknown, though many have family members waiting for them in Israel, England or America. They've lived in this country their entire lives.

They're proud Iraqis and they love their country, but they're equally terrified to remain in Baghdad, afraid to venture from their homes. The younger ones want to leave, yet feel a deep sense of loyalty to the older ones and don't want to abandon them. A few are single and know the only way they'll find a Jewish husband or wife is to leave. There hasn't been a Jewish marriage in Iraq since 1978."

"They're just growing old and dying," said Mike. "I've been wanting to do a story on the Jews here, but we've been too busy with other stories."

"Did you know seventy percent of Baghdad was Jewish in the eighth century?" said Jeremy. "Even in 1917 during World War One, when British forces entered Baghdad, there were 80,000 Jews here—a third of the city. In the 1920s, Jews made up forty percent of Baghdad's population and ninety-five percent of the merchants. On Sabbath, the bazaars and marketplaces were empty. No one shopped because no Jewish merchants were there. Baghdad for centuries was essentially a Jewish city."

The statement contrasted so sharply with the current reality of Baghdad, they were all stunned into silence.

Finally, Clay said, "I didn't know Jews were ever that dominant here."

"Oh, my, yes," he said. "They held high positions in government and in the medical and legal professions. A Jew was Iraq's first minister of finance. In the 1940s, a well-known Jewish economist was secretary general of Iraq's foreign ministry. Jews dominated Iraq's trade and finance."

"That's mind blowing," said Mike. "To look at Baghdad now..."

"It's really hard to imagine this is the same city," said Le An. "What happened? Why did they leave? Was this what you said in Al-Kosh at Nahum's tomb, that Jews were run out of Iraq?"

"Precisely. When the British Mandate ended in 1932, Iraq became independent. Four years on, Adolf Hitler's *Mein Kampf* was translated into Arabic and published in Baghdad, which caused a rise in anti-Jewish sentiments, as did diplomats posted to the German embassy here in Baghdad. Then, in April 1941, a Nazi supporter named Rashid Aali al-Gaylani gained power in a military coup. He lasted two months, but during that time, he made anti-Jewish radio broadcasts and brought Nazi sympathizers into his government with a plan to exterminate the entire Jewish population in Iraq."

"Are you kidding me?" asked Mike. "Hitler and the Nazis were behind the change in attitudes?"

"Jews and Muslims get along great for centuries, but five years of Hitler's hate upends the whole country?" asked Le An.

"Sad, isn't it?" said Jeremy. "Jews and Muslims in the Middle East had always enjoyed more favorable relationships with each other than the Jews encountered with so-called Christians in Europe, but the Nazis managed to bring their hatred here. British forces invaded Iraq and overthrew Aali, but the damage had been done. Before they took control, as many as 800 Jews were murdered and more than 2,000 wounded in a violent two-day pogrom called the *Farhud*. The official count was 180 Jews killed, but those were only the ones they could identify. Another 600 were buried in a mass grave before their relatives could see them. Many were tortured before being murdered, pregnant women were raped, Jewish houses and businesses looted and burned, swastikas painted everywhere."

"The British weren't able to stop the slaughter?" asked Le An.

"They chose not to, to our shame," said Jeremy, as Nigel hung his head and looked down at the floor. "There was a two-day power vacuum, but British troops could have restored order. They were a mere thirteen kilometers—eight miles—from Baghdad. Sir Winston Churchill had given a direct order for them to secure the city, but, in a severe act of insubordination, the British ambassador here in Baghdad countered that and ordered the troops to stand down. He had a lovely candlelight dinner and played bridge, whilst hate-filled mobs slaughtered 800 Jews in the streets of Baghdad."

"That's just horrible," whispered Le An. "Did any Muslims stand up for the Jews?"

"Oh, my, yes," said Jeremy. "There were many exceptionally brave Muslims who defended their Jewish friends, even risked their own lives to do so. Not all Muslims were anti-Jewish. Many helped their Jewish neighbors any way they could. The mayor of Baghdad was Muslim and he and some of the police force defended them. They imposed a curfew the second day of the pogrom, then drove Aali out of Baghdad."

"Was Aali Sunni or Shi'a?" asked Mike.

"Sunni," said Jeremy. "The day the new nation of Israel declared its independence in 1948, three Iraqi brigades were amongst the Arab troops attacking them. The Iraq government accused Jews here of being spies and Zionists and blamed them for the Arabs losing Palestine."

"The fifth column?" said Mike.

"Precisely, which was completely untrue," he said. "Iraqi Jews were utterly loyal to this country. They trace their roots back 2,600 years to Babylon when Nebuchadnezzar first brought them here in slavery. They felt a deep sense of belonging. Then the Muslims turned against them."

"Is that when they left Iraq and went to Israel?" asked Le An.

"After being murdered and driven out, yes," said Jeremy. "Iraqi Jews began their exodus over land through Syria and Lebanon. Eventually, 1,000 Jews a month were leaving. It caused quite an embarrassment to Iraq's government—and a large impact on the economy."

"I guess so, since the Jews owned and operated a big chunk of the businesses," said Mike.

"Did Iraqis regret driving them out?" asked Le An.

"They regretted the loss of business, but many were glad to see them go. In 1949, government officials even offered to swap 100,000 Jews living in Baghdad for an equal number of Arabs displaced from Palestine," he said. "They offered to send Iraqi Jews to Israel and, in exchange, give the Palestinians the Jews' middle-class or upper-class homes in Iraq."

"Unbelievable," mumbled Le An.

"Did that happen?" asked Mike.

"No, ultimately Iraq's government leaders decided it was easier and more profitable to murder and terrorize their Jews in order to drive them out," he said. "That way they could benefit from their properties and the financial assets they left behind, worth billions."

"Theft by terror," said Mike.

"Precisely," said Jeremy. "So the Jews left Iraq. Between 1951 and 1952, more than 100,000 Jews flew out of Baghdad in an airlift dubbed 'Operation Ezra and Nehemiah.' Another 20,000 were smuggled out through Iran."

"Ezra and Nehemiah?" asked Le An.

"Two men in scripture who led some of the Jews in Babylon back to Jerusalem in the days of Cyrus the Persian and Darius the Mede," said Jeremy.

"Did most Iraqi Jews go to Israel in the 1950s?" she asked.

"Most, but a good portion opted instead to move to America and England," he said. "There are rather large communities in London, New York and southern California—some in Montreal."

"So they ended up with a better life," said Pete.

"Not at first," said Jeremy. "The Jews left Iraq virtually penniless, allowed only to take what they were wearing, one suitcase and a small amount of money. The Iraqi government passed a law stating Jews who wished to emigrate had to renounce their Iraqi citizenship, which then meant they weren't able to sell their property. Instead, the government confiscated their homes, land and bank accounts. Those who went to London landed in a country trying to recover from World War Two, with everyone living on food coupons. Most who went to Israel ended up in tents in refugee camps. Israel was a new nation, utterly unprepared for such large numbers."

"The Iraqi Jews had been prosperous merchants, professionals with money, houses..." said Le An.

"...inheritances from their ancestors," added Jeremy.

"...and they ended up living in tents?" she said.

"And doing menial jobs," he added. "We hear a great deal about Palestinian refugees, but not Jewish refugees. In the last sixty years, Arab countries have driven out nearly one million Jews in order to confiscate their bank accounts and property."

"What happened to the Jews who didn't leave Iraq?" she asked.

"Conditions became unbearable for them after the Six Day War in 1967 when Israelis again defeated the Arab nations which attacked them. Random Jewish men, even teenagers, were arrested and tried as Israeli spies. Two years on, Iraqi officials declared a national holiday and told everyone to celebrate as they hung Jews in the public square. They encouraged everyone to dance around the bodies."

"That's sick," said Mike. "Man, I want to do this story, Le An."

"I know," she said and looked at Jeremy.

"I'd like to see some attention to this long-overlooked part of history," he said, "but I'm afraid you'll have to do it without the cooperation of the Jews in Baghdad. They're too afraid."

"This has long-form *AmeriView* all over it, Le," said Mike. "You should pitch this to Paul."

"We could do it without interviewing the Jews living here, if we have to," she said. "Though, of course, I'd prefer to hear from them, even if we shoot them in shadow and alter their voices. Maybe if we contact Iraqi Jews in Britain or America, they could convince their relatives here to talk to us. We could interview you, Jeremy. This is a great story people need to hear about."

"It's not just Iraq," he said. "Remember, since 1948 a million Jews have been run out of other Muslim countries, as well."

"And now only thirteen remain in all of Iraq," she said.

"Let's get back to your kidnapping," said Pete. "We still have a lot of unanswered questions."

"But I wasn't kidnapped," said Jeremy.

"But we received ransom demands, very large ransom demands," said Pete.

"After you left the museum, you were with Jews in Baghdad until you returned here?" asked Nigel.

"Yes, I was merely observing part of the Sabbath with them and trying to help some find a way to escape Iraq," he said. "I'm dreadfully sorry for the confusion."

"Then who's behind the ransom email and phone calls?" asked Le An.

"Do you think one of the Jews you met with is trying to get money?" asked Pete.

"Impossible," he said. "They wouldn't do that and they don't need money. They all receive a monthly stipend from a fund. As well, a few of them are quite wealthy."

"Did any of them try to prevent you from leaving?" asked Nigel.

"Not at all," he said.

"Any of them act suspicious?" asked Pete.

"No, I've known most of them for many years," said Jeremy, "as well as many of their family members living outside Iraq."

Le An had been sitting on a corner of the massive desk, but now flopped down in a large red velvet armchair and threw her hands over her head in exasperation.

"None of this makes sense," she said.

"Something's not kosher here," said Mike.

Clay stood up from behind the desk and started pacing, shaking his head before offering another angle. "Maybe one or more of the museum employees saw you leave and they're behind this."

Jeremy shrugged. "I'm quite sorry, but I have no idea. I didn't even know I was considered missing."

"Why did you leave the museum and disappear without telling me or anyone where you were going?" asked Le An.

Jeremy looked confused. "But I did tell someone."

39

Baghdad, Iraq
Saturday, 6 September 2003

"What?" they all said in unison.

"Jeremy, we searched that entire museum compound for more than an hour yesterday looking for you," said Le An. "The Army guards at the gate told us they saw you leave. You mean you told the soldiers you were leaving?"

"Yes, those at the gate knew as well, but I wouldn't leave without making sure someone would tell you, Le An. I'm afraid with all the taping and tour of the museum, I quite forgot to mention it to you and for that I'm deeply sorry. Yesterday morning, before we left for the museum, I received an email from my Jewish friend here in Baghdad giving me a prearranged time and location for us to meet. I was planning to tell you after our tour of the museum, but had quite forgotten about your live interview with New York. Our tour took longer than I'd anticipated and I was late meeting my friend. I knew he'd be nervous. He rarely comes out because it's so dangerous now and I'd already kept him waiting. I needed to leave, but you were all quite busy preparing for your morning chat show interview and I wasn't sure how much longer you'd be. When Khaled came near me to retrieve new batteries for the microphones, I told him."

"You told Khaled?" Le An said in a small voice, frozen as if she'd been sucker punched. "You told Khaled at the museum you were leaving?"

"Why, yes," said Jeremy.

"What exactly did you tell him?" asked Pete.

"I instructed him to tell Le An I was planning to stay with friends and would be back today before sunset," he said.

"And Khaled understands English enough to know what you

were saying?" asked Clay. "I mean, he didn't seem to have any trouble speaking or understanding English when we interviewed him, but I just want to make sure there was no misunderstanding."

"He understands English just fine," said Mike.

"I believe I'd fancy another talk with Khaled," said Nigel.

"Wouldn't we all," said Pete. "Le An, we need you to give him a call and tell him you've decided you do need his help. Ask him to come back here. And we need to make sure no one tells him Jeremy's back."

Mike used the two-way radio to the security team and asked Leo to come into the library.

"Make sure you keep Khaled outside until we give you the OK," Pete told him. "Nobody comes in this house or leaves until we tell you."

He headed for the hallway into the scrum of journalists. "All right, everybody back in the dining room. I've got to talk to you. No one can say anything about Jeremy being back, understand? And stay off your phones. This isn't over yet and I need all of you to maintain radio silence. Just bear with us a little longer."

Again, as the hostage team members and guards tried to wave the journalists back into the dining room, they were greeted with shouting and arguments at being kept from the person they wanted to interview.

"Jeremy, if you wouldn't tell me you were going to see your Jewish friends, then why would you tell Khaled?" asked Le An, hurt he hadn't confided in her.

"My dear, I didn't tell Khaled they were Jewish," he said. "I'm not stupid. I know how he feels about Jews. I merely told him I was going to stay with friends here in Baghdad."

"And you said you'd be back before sunset last night?" she asked.

"No, before sunset tonight. Did Khaled say I'd been kidnapped?"

"No," said Clay, "but he said you hadn't talked to him at all. And we received ransom demands for you by email and phone."

"I'm dreadfully sorry, but I know nothing about this ransom demand," he said.

"Could Khaled have misunderstood?" asked Le An.

"I don't believe so. He acknowledged what I'd told him," he

said. "I didn't think it would be a problem since I'd told you I wouldn't be available on Sabbath and we were planning to make it an off day. Oh, my. I'm so dreadfully sorry to have caused this fuss. I was merely trying to meet with my friends and help them. I'm ever so sorry."

They all looked at each other and Le An slumped back into the chair.

"I feel sick," she said. "Khaled's behind this, isn't he?"

"It certainly appears that way," said Nigel.

"The five o'clock deadline was probably because he knew the ransom had to be paid and picked up before Jeremy returned to the villa by sunset tonight, which is what? Around 7:30?" she said. "Khaled never actually knew where Jeremy was, just when he thought he'd return and the time frame to pull off the scam with his family or friends. But now Jeremy's returned a lot earlier than they expected. I wonder if they've been watching the villa and saw him come in."

"Even if they are watching, maybe they didn't recognize him in the head gear. Jeremy looked like a typical Arab when he came in," said Clay. "I wonder if the woman who was here earlier—Khaled's sister—is in on this, too. She may have been sent to spy on you from the inside. Perhaps Khaled and his friends were behind the disappearance of your original cook. The two events may be related. We can't rule that out."

Mike slowly shook his head in disbelief. "Khaled probably figured whether the ransom was paid or not, he'd play innocent and we'd never know he was behind it. Guess he thought either way, he'd still be getting money from USN."

"He and his friends also weren't counting on y'all," said Le An, pointing to the hostage team. "They aren't familiar with the way Britain or the US handles negotiations when one of our citizens is kidnapped. They didn't know y'all would show up."

"They didn't know they'd show up because they're amateurs," said Mike. "Khaled did seem unnerved by you guys being involved in negotiations."

"What's he going to say when Jeremy reminds him he'd told him he was leaving?" said Nigel.

"He'll probably claim he didn't really hear what he was saying or he misunderstood," said Le An. "When I asked Khaled at the museum about Jeremy, he said he didn't know where he was and he never told me he'd talked to him."

"He told us flat out he didn't talk to Jeremy," said Clay.

"I don't think anyone at the museum would have known your timeline, do you, Jeremy?" she asked.

"I didn't tell anyone on the museum's staff," he said. "I only told Khaled just prior to leaving."

"So the only ones who knew you'd be gone until this afternoon were Khaled and the Jews you were with," she said. "And based on what you've said, I think we can rule out the Jews. If they're too afraid to leave their homes and they don't need money because they have access to a monthly stipend, I can't see them risking something like this. It wouldn't make sense."

"I guarantee it wasn't any of them," said Jeremy.

"That leaves Khaled and his family or friends as the number one suspects," said Mike.

"Appears that way," said Clay.

"Well, he's not working for us anymore, that's for sure," said Mike. "Guilty or not, we can't take any chances. Le, we're going to have to find you another sound guy for tomorrow. We've got a few other Iraqi translators we can use if we can get hold of them. Your Babylon and Al Kifl shoots are back on."

"I speak Arabic," Jeremy reminded them.

"That's right," she said. "OK, we just need a sound guy. And a second shooter would be good, too."

"How much longer are you going to be in country?" Nigel asked Jeremy.

He shrugged as he looked at Le An and she answered for him, "Only a few more days."

"Whoever's behind this may have marked you and your team. If it's Khaled, unfortunately he and his friends now know the villa and your security setup. I'd advise making changes."

"I wonder if Khaled was behind our stuff being stolen the other night," she said.

"He was staying here that night," said Mike. "He could have passed it over the wall to friends or relatives. DK said it looked like an inside job."

"If so, then we were royally duped and doesn't that make us look stupid?" she said. "Guess Khaled learned a thing or two working for Saddam."

"Remember what I said? There's no way to fact check in Iraq," said Mike.

"We need to make certain Jeremy's out of sight when Khaled returns," said Nigel.

Le An quickly flipped into producer mode and said, "I'd like to be in on it and have Barry tape your interview. We'll share it with the other networks after we run our package. We have to give them something. These people have spent hours helping us."

"No taping," said Nigel.

"We're taping!" demanded Le An and Mike, who ultimately won out and brought in Barry to set up his camera and lights.

"Jeremy, if you don't mind, when the others interview you, would you mind just telling them you were with friends, not that you were meeting with Baghdad's Jewish community?" asked Le An. "I still want to do this story for USN and I don't want anyone poaching it."

"I wasn't going to mention it," he said. "I only told you because I was forced to."

Mike sent Jeremy upstairs to his bedroom with Ryan guarding him.

An hour later, from outside in the hallway, they could hear Leo shouting, "Come on, people! Move! Move!" followed by a knock on the door. When Pete opened the door, Leo, surrounded by all the journalists in the house, cameras blazing again, told them Khaled was at the front gate.

"You didn't tell him Jeremy's back, did you?" asked Pete.

"No, we contained him outside as instructed," he said, then spoke into his headset to his security crew, using DK's nickname for Jeremy and Khaled, "Maintain silence with Minder K about Bookman. Repeat, maintain silence. Has anyone violated? Over." A few seconds later, he said, "Copy that. QSL," and turned to Pete, "No one said anything."

Leo shooed the journalists back into the main dining room, as Le An begged for their patience a little while longer.

Nigel turned to the small group in the library. "Everyone ready? Leo, bring in Khaled."

40

Baghdad, Iraq
Saturday, 6 September 2003

Though Khaled had seen a fair amount of torture sessions while employed by Saddam Hussein, and, prior to the invasion, had frequently intimidated members of the foreign press he'd been assigned to 'mind' or monitor, he seemed a bit nervous as Barry helped mic him for the interview. Le An smiled, reassuring him it was for the package they were doing about Jeremy.

The hostage team thanked Khaled for returning and asked why he'd offered to help.

He told them he knew he could blend into the Baghdad crowds, especially if they needed him to deliver a ransom.

"We can't pay the ransom," said Nigel, "and we were wondering if you had any ideas."

Khaled said forcefully, "You must pay. They will kill him. I know. I have seen it with my neighbors."

"Khaled, we'd like to," said Clay, "but USN won't permit ransoms to be paid for their employees. I know you're seeing a lot of this with your friends and neighbors being kidnapped. Surely, not all of them can afford to pay ransoms. What would you suggest we do?"

Khaled's eyes grew wide, then he said, "You must get money from his family or from your president."

"Neither the American president nor the British prime minister are going to pay his ransom, Khaled," said Nigel.

"You must pay something or they will kill him," said Khaled. "If you cannot pay the one million, pay any. They will kill him."

"Maybe if we had more time," said Clay. "We're going to try to convince the kidnappers to give us a few days while Doctor Hilson's family gets some money together—if they have any.

From what you've seen, do you think the kidnappers will wait for us to try and get money for the ransom? Do you think they'll be patient?"

"No, kidnappers are not patient," he said. "You must pay them something by five. Pay less, whatever you have. I am sure they will take it and return him."

"So you think we can pay them anything and they'll be satisfied?" asked Clay.

"Yes," said Khaled.

"I mean, they asked for fifteen million dinar first, then fifteen million dollars," said Clay. "We don't have much money available here. I'm not sure they'll accept it since they asked for so much in the beginning."

"They will take it," insisted Khaled. "I will talk to them and convince them to take it and return him. I can convince them."

"I don't know, Khaled," he said. "It's too dangerous. They've already kidnapped one USN employee. What if they kidnap you, too? Then we'd have to negotiate for both of you. It's too dangerous. We can't risk your life. I just thought you might have some ideas."

"I will take my brothers and cousins with me," he said. "They will not kidnap us. We will tell the kidnappers they must take any money and return Jeremy. People in Baghdad need money. That is why they kidnap. They will take any. I will take money to them and get Jeremy."

Clay nodded his head, thought for a minute, then said, "Doctor Hilson didn't tell you he was leaving the museum yesterday?"

"No. We had live shots with New York. When we finish, he was not there," he said.

"But before the live shot, he didn't come up to you and say anything?" asked Clay.

"No, he did not speak to me," he said.

"He didn't tell you to give a message to Le An or anything?" asked Clay.

"No, and that was very bad of him. We search for him for very long time."

"Yes, so you've said. Maybe when you were getting batteries for the microphones, he said something to you?" asked Clay.

Khaled froze for a second. "I do not remember that."

"Of course, because you were concentrating on doing a good job for USN," he said.

"Yes, I always do very good job for USN," he said.

"Do they pay you well?" asked Clay.

"They pay very good," he said.

"You wouldn't do anything to hurt anyone from USN, would you?" asked Clay.

"No, they are friends," he said.

"All of them? Le An? Barry? Mike? Jeremy? They're all your friends?" asked Clay.

"I would not hurt them," said Khaled.

Clay slowly nodded his head and asked, "Do you have any friends who don't like you working for Americans?"

"I do not tell them. It is dangerous to tell," he said.

"Because you're Sunni? A lot of Sunnis are angry at the Americans for removing Saddam, aren't they? Are you angry about that? Is your family angry?"

Khaled shifted uncomfortably in his chair. "Some are angry. I am not. I am glad Saddam is gone."

"But you worked for him. Did you like working for him?" asked Clay.

"Very hard to work for Saddam," he said.

"You probably saw some really awful things, didn't you? Saddam could be cruel and brutal."

"Yes," said Khaled.

Clay stopped and again looked at the floor, then asked, "Khaled, how did you know we needed to pay one million by five o'clock?"

Khaled panicked for a moment. "Le An and Barry tell me."

Le An started to speak, but waited until Clay indicated she could.

"Le An, did you and Barry tell Khaled you needed to pay a ransom of one million by five?" asked Clay.

"No, we didn't," she said. "We told him fifteen million and we never told him the deadline for the ransom."

"Yes, you did!" Khaled raised his voice, anger flashing across his face. "You tell me! You are lying!"

He stood up as if he was about to leave.

"Sit down, Khaled," said Nigel as he pushed him back into the chair. "We didn't know the ransom had been reduced to one million until after you left this morning."

"I...I think Le An and Barry say one million this morning," stammered Khaled.

"We never told you our five o'clock ransom deadline, Khaled," said Le An.

"You are lying!" he shouted.

"We know Jeremy told you he was leaving the museum grounds," said Clay. "Why did you say he didn't?"

"He never tell me! You are lying!" shouted Khaled, as he frantically looked toward the door.

Leo stood guard in front of it, a steely look on his face, an automatic slung over his shoulder.

"Are you behind these ransom demands, Khaled?" asked Clay.

"No!" he shouted. "I am here to help and you lie to me? Why are you lying?"

"Why would you do this, Khaled?" asked Le An. "We've treated you well, paid you well. Why would you do this to us?"

"I do nothing!" he shouted. "I am innocent! You are lying!"

"Khaled, we know where Jeremy is," said Clay. "And we know he was never kidnapped. We know he told you he was leaving the museum grounds to spend the night in Baghdad with friends and we know you're behind the ransom demand."

"No! You are lying!" he shouted. "That Jew is lying! Why do you believe a dirty swine Jew?"

Le An froze, then said quietly, "He's not a Jew. And you no longer work for USN."

41

Baghdad, Iraq
Saturday, 6 September 2003

The FBI agents still trying to locate the kidnapped American contractor in northern Iraq took Khaled to the Green Zone for more questioning to find out if he and his friends were behind more abductions.

All the journalists in the villa covered that since, as a group, they'd broken that story, but most opted not to mention Jeremy's disappearance. Focusing on a rogue Iraqi freelance employee made everyone uncomfortable. All the news agencies used them, though some did reconsider whether they might do better to hire more Shi'a or Kurd translators, drivers and news gatherers instead of Sunnis.

They hoped the many Iraqis who were helping them gather news were honest and trustworthy, but without any real way of fact checking their backgrounds or knowing about their lives, it was a gamble.

"Am I doing sound, too, tomorrow?" Barry asked Le An, clearly annoyed. He nursed a strong drink in one hand, tilting it first to one side then the other as he watched the golden liquid swish around the sides of the glass. "And who's going to be our translator now?"

"Mike's trying to reach Wen Darlington to see if he can work for us," she said as she sat down next to Hugh on one of the living room's couches. "Jeremy speaks Arabic so we don't need a translator."

"Wentworth Darlington the Third," sneered Barry, then asked sarcastically, "Wasn't he supposed to be my replacement, Le? You've got a thing for that guy, don't you?"

She closed her eyes and exhaled a deep, frustrated sigh, not wanting to start another battle with him, but also not willing to leave his remark unanswered. "Wen and I have been friends a long time. He's also a very good photog."

Barry snorted and finished off his drink.

"I'm returning to London tomorrow," said Hugh. "My replacement's coming from Basra on Tuesday, so between now and then, Piet and Kent are available for hire if you need them. They periodically file for a South African network and Reuters, but I'm sure they're available for sound and a second camera."

"That's a good idea. Thank you. It might be easiest to hire them for a few days," she said.

"If it weren't for that nut-job Jeremy, we wouldn't have to deal with this," grumbled Barry.

"How can you say that?" Le An asked. "Don't you realize if Khaled hadn't tried this now, he'd have done the same kind of thing in the future? He's already shown he's capable of going to that level of ripping off USN for millions. He wouldn't have blinked an eye if he'd gotten away with it. I'm sure he and his friends or family would've either faked his own kidnapping or committed an actual kidnapping of one of our employees. It's lucky for us things turned out the way they did with no money paid and no one hurt or killed. I bet he and his friends are the ones who stole our stuff the other night. Probably stuffed everything in a duffel bag and threw it over the wall to them."

"Afraid I have to agree with Le An," said Hugh. "Khaled and his friends most surely had been discussing this, waiting for an opportune time—which, unfortunately for you, turned out to be Jeremy."

"What a waste of twenty-four hours," Barry grumbled.

"Apparently not to your FBI," said Hugh. "We may have helped in the rescue of the American contractor being held in the north."

"Good point," said Le An.

"I'm going to get some sleep," snarled Barry as he left the room.

"Is it my imagination or has Barry developed an even dodgier attitude?" asked Hugh.

"Not your imagination," she sighed. "He really doesn't seem to like Jeremy and it's becoming a problem."

42

Baghdad, Iraq
Sunday, 7 September 2003

Le An leaned back against one of the white marble counters in the kitchen, waiting for a slice of left-over pizza to finish warming in the microwave. Curfew in Baghdad had already ended, signaling the start of another day in the paradise of war-torn Iraq.

She'd tried to go to sleep early the night before, exhausted from the ordeal involving Jeremy, but the shock of Khaled being involved in the scam kept her awake long into the night. Hours after her Danish roommate Kerin had gone to sleep, she still restlessly tossed from one side of her bed to the other.

Much as she loved covering the unique challenge which was Iraq, she knew she was rapidly approaching a breaking point where she needed a vacation.

"Having an early start, are we?" Hugh asked, interrupting her thoughts as he came into the kitchen. He dropped his backpack, duffel bags and laptop case near the door, then sniffed the air. "Smells good."

"Leftover pizza. You can take this slice if you'd like. There are three more in the 'fridge," she said.

"That would be lovely."

"Coffee?" she asked, pointing to the large commercial brewer. "I made a fresh tank. Tea? Fruit?"

"Fruit, thanks," he said, picking up two apples from a bowl on the counter and stuffing them into his backpack. "Did you decide about Piet and Kent?"

"Mike and I hired them for today and tomorrow. We debated whether to drive south from Babylon and Al Kifl, but I think we're coming back here tonight and attempting to fly out to Kuwait or Basra tomorrow—hopefully, Basra. We hope to embed with Brit soldiers for the southern sites we need. Piet and Kent said they're going to meet up with your replacement in Basra after that."

She'd debated whether to hire only one of the African freelancers as an audio tech, but, because of Barry's erratic behavior lately, opted to hire both in order to have a second cameraman as backup. Paul wasn't pleased at having an extra person on his payroll, but understood her growing concerns about Barry.

"Sounds as if all worked out well," said Hugh. "So you opted not to drive to Basra?"

"We looked at the threat reports and decided dicey things are happening," she said as she put the hot pizza on a napkin and handed it to him.

"Thank you."

"Plus, there are about twenty Shi'a tribal chiefs along that highway down to Basra," she said as she put another slice of pizza in the microwave for herself. "The Shi'a are friendlier than the Sunnis up north, but it's risky to negotiate safe passage twenty different times."

"Nineteen may slap you on the back and say, 'Righto, mates, have a go at it,' and the twentieth may say, 'Die, Yankee!'?"

"Exactly. Security's on the cusp of changing for the worse," she said. "It's not like it was right after the invasion when you could hop in a car and drive to Fallujah for kabobs. We might not hesitate to risk the drive, but after everything with Jeremy, I decided not to chance it with him. Especially after all we learned pooling our resources this weekend. I think it was an eye-opener for everyone. Unorthodox, but an eye-opener. My guess is we're gearing up for a major Sunni-Shi'a civil war. Jeremy's idea of a divided Iraq is sounding better and better."

"Agreed. Not to mention Iraqis are starting to turn against the Coalition because, as it turns out, the West can't fix all their problems and give them a perfect life."

"Imagine that," she joked. "Who'd a thunk it?"

Mike stuck his head in, "Morning, you two. Hugh, security at the front gate just called and said DK guards are ready to take you to the aiport. Hey, Le, I'm busy with feeds right now and I've got a conference call in five. Would you be a sweetheart and bring me a cup of coffee and a slice of that pizza?"

He gave a goofy smile and batted his eyes at her.

"How could I say no to that face?" she smiled.

"Hugh, my man, good to work with you," said Mike, shaking his hand and slapping him on the back. "Sorry to see you leave. Wish it was me."

"I left a few bottles of whiskey back in your office," said Hugh.

"You're a gentleman and a scholar, my man," said Mike. "See, Le, this is why Scots are such class acts. By the way, you know yesterday insurgents fired two SAMs at a plane taking off from the airport."

"Well, isn't that splendid?" said Hugh dryly.

"Oh, good, Mike," said Le An. "I'm sure Hugh loves hearing missiles may take down his plane. As if Route Irish isn't bad enough."

"Email me so we know you got back in one piece," said Mike, as he did a backward wave on his way out of the room.

"Well, I suppose this is goodbye," said Hugh as he turned to her and held open his arms.

She stepped toward him and smiled as he gave her a long, hard hug.

"It was great seeing you again," she said, flushing slightly at their first really close contact. "Stay safe."

"And you. I'm not going to be here to rescue you," he said with a slight smile, still standing close to her.

"I'll try to be good and not give my security detail fits."

"Ring me if you're ever in London," he said, pulling a business card from his pocket and pressing it into her hand. "My mobile's on there."

She nodded and smiled. "I will. We're flying back to London later this week. We have to shoot at the British Museum, then edit our segments at the bureau."

"Splendid," he said. "You'll be there at least a week, I'd imagine."

"If not longer."

They stood there for a second smiling at each other.

"'Til we meet again," he whispered as he leaned toward her and, in European fashion, kissed both her cheeks.

Then he picked up his luggage and left.

43

Baghdad, Iraq
Sunday, 7 September 2003

USN's three-car convoy traveled south on Highway 8 as it made the fifty-five mile journey to Babylon. Instead of the traitorous Khaled, African freelancers Piet van Gruen and Kent Barkley were now part of the crew as soundman and back-up cameraman.

Le An, again wedged between Skylar and Jeremy in the second row of seats, found herself smiling and daydreaming about a quiet dinner with Hugh in London. Not wanting to have anyone interrupt her moment of mental escape, she popped in her earbuds and hit play on her iPod, leaning back with closed eyes to enjoy the music.

"What are you listening to?" asked Jeremy.

"*Caledonia*," she answered as she pulled out one earbud. "My Irish soundman gave me a CD of a Dublin group I'd heard when we went pub hopping. I love it."

Jeremy smiled slyly. "I'm not surprised."

"You know the song?" she asked.

"Oh, yes."

"Good times in Irish pubs," said Barry from the back seat. "Ollamh Fodhla!"

"Jeremy knows about Ollamh Fodhla," she said.

"Of course, he does," muttered Barry.

"He was a lawmaker, right, Jeremy?" she asked.

"Law*giver*. One of Ireland's finest," he said.

She popped her earbud back in and closed her eyes, unwilling to get involved in any conversation. It was too early in the morning to endure yet another 'Barry fight.'

Babylon had once been the wealthy capital of the powerful

Chaldean empire, a place many foreigners had come—some voluntarily to admire its beauty, others involuntarily in chains. Now it was a popular destination for camera-and-camcorder-toting foreign soldiers, with enough of a steady stream the US military had even appointed tour guides.

"Numerous archaeologists excavated here in the early 1800s," said Jeremy as he led them through the area. "Unfortunately, many artifacts were lost—some to massive looting and, in one case, a raft carrying forty crates of antiquities sank in the Tigris. Sadly, some excavating caused damage because archaeologists in those days dug too zealously. And why American and Coalition troops felt the need to establish a base here on such an important archaeological site is beyond me. As if Saddam hadn't caused enough damage, they have to add to it. Couldn't they have selected another area?"

Babylon was an archaeologist's nightmare. Saddam Hussein had wanted to reap the financial rewards of a tourist destination and had built over the ruins instead of preserving the history buried beneath the sand. He'd used new bricks to construct smaller versions of Nebuchadnezzar's palace, pagan temples and the walls of the Procession Way, even building a modern theater and yet another palace for himself.

"Each brick in ancient Babylon was inscribed 'Built by Nebuchadnezzar,'" said Jeremy. "Saddam mimicked that, creating bricks for the new Babylon stamped with the phrase 'Built by Saddam Hussein, son of Nebuchadnezzar.'"

"What an ego," said Skylar.

Jeremy pointed to a plaque and translated the Arabic, "'In the era of the victorious Saddam Hussein, the protector of greater Iraq and the restorer of its civilization, this city was rebuilt once again.' Nebuchadnezzar defeated Judah and Saddam wanted to replicate that—boasting to the Arab world he would conquer Israel and the Jews."

"Iraqi Jews, what's left of them, trace their ancestry to the time of Nebuchadnezzar, 2,500 years ago, don't they?" asked Skylar, drawing on the information he'd learned the day before.

"Yes, he brought them to Babylon in slavery in three separate invasions—the final one in 586 BC when Jerusalem was sacked and burned," he said.

He recounted how, as Nebuchadnezzar's army breached

Jerusalem's walls in the middle of the night, the last Jewish king Zedekiah, along with family and friends, had escaped through a secret tunnel, only to be captured near the city of Jericho in Judah. Nebuchadnezzar had slaughtered Zedekiah's sons in front of him, then blinded him and brought him to Babylon in chains.

"The Babylonians were quite literate and wrote copious amounts, which included records of Jewish kings in captivity," said Jeremy. "German archaeologist Robert Koldewey began excavating here in the late 1800s and discovered clay tablets which mentioned the Jewish king Jehoiachin and his family's food ration."

"What happened to Jehoiachin?" asked Skylar.

"He was in prison thirty-seven years, part of that time with Nebuchadnezzar's son Evil-Murodach. They became friends of a sort. When Nebuchadnezzar died, Evil-Murodach took the throne, released Jehoiachin and made sure he was taken care of the rest of his life."

"Nebuchadnezzar threw his own son in prison?" asked Skylar.

"Just like Saddam, he had a reputation for being cruel. Remember, he'd blinded Zedekiah after making him watch his sons be executed. Some accounts say the day Evil-Merodach took the throne, he dug up Nebuchadnezzar's body and dragged it through Babylon's streets. Another account says he cut his father's body into 300 pieces to feed to vultures to ensure Nebuchadnezzar couldn't torment him any more. It's possible he did both."

As they walked through the site, Jeremy continued, "Many believed Nebuchadnezzar had never existed since his name only appeared in scripture. However, Koldewey uncovered written proof of Nebuchadnezzar on inscriptions, cuneiform tablets and stelae. He also discovered the ruins of Nebuchadnezzar's palace here, as well as the pagan god Marduk's temple and the Ishtar Gate."

"Ishtar?" asked Skylar. "The same Easter goddess of fertility?"

Le An sighed, knowing Barry would be on another rampage. She looked over at his camera and it was on, but his jaw was clenched and his face angry. She was thankful the Africans were doing backup.

"Yes, the same Ishtar we've seen throughout Iraq," said Jeremy. "The Babylonians, as most Mesopotamians, revered her. One of the most striking features of Babylon had been the brilliant blue lapis-lazuli-brick Ishtar Gate on the city's north side. Through that gate ran the wide Processional Way, its walls decorated with bas-reliefs of snarling, striding lions. Remnants are in museums throughout the world." He pointed to the bright blue gate near the site's entrance. "That's not the original Ishtar Gate. Saddam had a smaller reproduction constructed here in front of the gift shop."

He told how Koldewey had shipped the original back to his native Germany and reconstructed its fifty-foot-high inner gate, along with part of the Processional Way, inside Berlin's Pergamon Museum.

"The gate's back portion is too large to reconstruct and is still in storage there," he said.

He explained how Nebuchadnezzar had designed Babylon as a square, each side fifteen miles wide, straddling both banks of the Euphrates River, a city within a city, with three outer walls and two inner. Entrance to outer Babylon was through 100 brass gates, the walls so wide on top four-horse chariots could pass each other. A tunnel under the river and a stone bridge over it united both sides of the inner city.

"The Chaldeans thought Babylon was impenetrable," he said. "But its vulnerability was where the Euphrates entered and exited the city. Even though underwater metal gates were designed to block enemies, the Medes and Persians were clever. They diverted the Euphrates into a lake upstream in order to lower the water level. When it was sufficiently shallow—up to a man's thigh—they entered Babylon through the river bed one night, killed its king Belshazzar and conquered the city. That was the end of the Babylonian Empire."

"Didn't they realize the river was getting lower?" asked Skylar.

"Apparently not," he said. "I imagine they were used to the Euphrates being different levels throughout the year. The invasion occurred at night, so it was probably too dark to see. A Jew named Daniel, who'd been taken in Nebuchadnezzar's first invasion of Judah, told Belshazzar, in front of witnesses, his time was up and his kingdom would fall to the Medes and Persians. Within hours, that came to pass."

"Daniel of the lions' den?" Skylar asked.

"Yes," he smiled. "When Nebuchadnezzar first conquered

Jerusalem, he took Daniel and other young members of the Jewish royal family back to Babylon and taught them the Chaldean language and literature. Daniel and his three friends, Shadrach, Meshach and Abed-Nego, eventually became governors, with Daniel ruling the entire provence of Babylon, as well as becoming chief administrator of all Nebuchadnezzar's counselors. The Jewish historian Josephus writes Cyrus' co-ruler Darius the Mede took a fancy to Daniel, who was probably in his eighties at the time Babylon fell. He assigned Daniel and two others to be in charge of 120 governors, called satraps, some of whom became jealous of his high position and tricked Darius into tossing him to the lions."

"They threw an old man to the lions?" asked Skylar.

"Yes, but the written accounts say Daniel survived the night without so much as a scratch and Darius, who liked and trusted him, was furious he'd been tricked. After Daniel was safely extracted, he ordered the satraps be thrown to the lions. The lions attacked them straightaway and killed them all."

"We've seen shrines to Jonah and Nahum. Is there one for Daniel?" asked Skylar.

"No, there's no solid information where he's buried," said Jeremy.

"If Daniel was here when Babylon fell, did that mean a lot of Jews were still here?" asked Skylar.

"Yes, and they were here when Alexander the Great conquered the Medes and Persians 200 years on from that," he said. "And they were here centuries on from that. Even 500 years on from their captivity, Josephus records there were still great numbers of Jews living in Babylon. They grew in numbers and prospered, exactly as Jewish prophets had predicted they would. They even regained their freedom. Nearly five decades on from Nebuchadnezzar conquering Jerusalem, Cyrus decreed they could return to Jerusalem to begin rebuilding their temple. He believed their God would bless him if he was in his original temple. He even returned the temple's silver and gold items Nebuchadnezzar's troops had taken."

"Cyrus freed the Jews?" asked Skylar.

"Yes and no. Conquered lands such as Judah remained part of the empire, but their people were relatively free. In the late 1800s, archaeologist Hormuzd Rassam discovered what's called the

'Cyrus Cylinder,' written in Akkadian cuneiform. It said Cyrus' policy was all displaced people should return to their homelands—and all their gods had to like him."

Skylar started laughing. "That's why he let the Jews rebuild their temple?"

"Precisely. However, with the Jews, there was more to it. The Jewish prophet Isaiah had written approximately 150 years prior to the Jews being conquered that a man named Cyrus would cause Jerusalem and the temple to be rebuilt. Josephus wrote when Cyrus read that scripture, he believed he was that man."

"Did all the Jews go back to Jerusalem?" Skylar asked.

"Not all, but more than 40,000 did."

"Some Jews stayed in Babylon?" asked Skylar.

"Quite a few. Babylon was rich and sophisticated, the New York, London or Paris of its day. Jerusalem was a pile of rubbish. There was nothing there. The Jews began as slaves, but ended up fully integrated into Babylonian society, some, like Daniel and his friends, even holding high positions within the government. And about fifty years on from Daniel's time, a Jewish girl named Hadassah, who at first hid her heritage by changing her name to Esther, even married the head of the Medo-Persian empire King Xerxes."

"When Assyria fell in the north, did the Israelites return to their land like the Jews returned to Jerusalem?" asked Skylar.

"No, approximately twenty-five years prior to Jerusalem's defeat, the Israelites united with Babylon to help defeat Assyria—the enemy who'd taken them captive more than 100 years prior. Eventually, they left the area, pushing north and eventually west, not south. People, tribes, nations all migrate, even today. Wars displace people, as do natural disasters such as drought or floods. The Israelites migrated to new areas."

"You said Alexander the Great was here?" asked Skylar.

"He conquered Babylon in 331 BC and died here in 323 BC," said Jeremy.

"Is he buried here?"

"No, Alexander apparently wanted his body tossed in the Euphrates where no one could find it, in order to perpetuate the myth he'd been whisked away to heaven to be with who he claimed was his father—the pagan god Ammon. Instead, his generals took his mummified body to Egypt where it was buried.

Someone dug up his body and reburied it in Alexandria, but no one knows precisely where. It appears Alexander got his wish of not having anyone find him."

As they were walking back to their vehicles after completing their tour and interviews, Le An spotted Michelle Melois, the French wire service reporter renting space at USN's villa.

Michelle was embedded with Italian soldiers and, as the USN crew walked over to her, she accusingly pointed to the bright blue structure near the gift shop, and sniped, "Your American soldiers have damaged the Ishtar Gate."

"This fake Ishtar Gate or the real one in Berlin?" asked Le An.

Michelle looked startled, then, without saying a word, spun around and stomped away to rejoin the Italians. Piet and Kent burst out laughing, causing her to turn and level an icy stare at them.

"I'm telling you, there's something wrong with that chick," said Barry.

"The one-quarter French in me refuses to acknowledge her," muttered Le An.

As they drove twenty miles south to Al Kifl, Le An asked Jeremy, "Remember during our dinner at the King David you said Nebuchadnezzar's soldiers captured a Jewish guy who kept telling the Jews to surrender? Did they bring him here to Babylon? What happened to him?"

"Jeremiah?" asked the professor.

"A Jew told his own people to surrender?" asked Skylar.

"Jeremiah told them they were going to lose the war, but if they surrendered, Nebuchadnezzar would treat them better," said Jeremy.

"Bet he wasn't too popular," said Skylar. "What happened to him?"

"Advisors to Zedekiah threw him in jail and had him tortured," he said.

"Ouch. Le An, where's the food? I'm starved," said Skylar.

"Chicken pitas are in the cooler in back," she said, turning to point to the SUV's back well where their equipment was. She noticed the lid was flipped up and Piet, Kent and Barry were already scarfing down food.

"We were hungry," Barry said as he started to bite into his pita again, then added in a snarky tone, "and bored."

Le An was annoyed Barry was becoming more open in his disdain of anything Jeremy had to say.

"I'm not bored," said Piet. "But I was hungry."

"Hopefully, Mike will hire a new cook today," she said. "Piet, thanks for bringing back chicken last night. I'd forgotten about our lunches today."

"And she forgets again," mumbled Barry. "You're slipping, MacDonald. But at least you remembered to make lunch. Guess we're lucky you didn't forget and leave the food back at the house this morning."

"Thanks, Barr," she said, trying hard not to be snarky in return.

Barry dug into the cooler and pitched a wrapped pita to Skylar, then smacked Le An in the side of her head with two pitas, then smacked her again with two more for the two Dark Knight guards, Jeremy and herself.

"Smack me again and you'll lose the use of that hand," she said to him without turning around. "And you know I can do it. We'll make you one-handed audio and Piet and Kent can do cameras."

"Did that Jeremiah guy die in prison?" Skylar asked Jeremy.

"No, he didn't. King Zedekiah allowed his advisors to imprison and torture Jeremiah, but not kill him. Jeremiah had been a loyal advisor to Zedekiah's father Josiah, but Zedekiah was a morally weak king and utterly afraid to oppose his own advisors. He wouldn't surrender because he feared Nebuchadnezzar would allow the Jews who'd already defected to torture him."

"He should have worried more about what Nebuchadnezzar would do," said Le An.

"Indeed," he said. "The records indicate Zedekiah and his advisors summoned Jeremiah countless times, asking for advice, demanding to know what he'd written, where he'd gone, what he'd said. They demanded he be quiet, commanded him to speak, told him to leave, ordered him to stay."

"A little schizophrenic," she said.

"A position of power can inflate the ego," said Jeremy.

"How old was Jeremiah? If he'd advised Zedekiah's father, he wasn't young," she said.

"Probably near sixty," he said.

"They tortured him?" asked Skylar.

"They did. Zedekiah's advisors lowered him into a muck-filled cistern in the prison, then left him to die. One of the servants discovered him and notified the king, who somewhat reluctantly allowed him to be rescued. But, because Zedekiah was still afraid of his advisors, he wouldn't release him."

"Where was he going to go? The Babylonians had Jerusalem surrounded," said Le An. "What happened to him?"

"Nebuchadnezzar freed him," he said. "The Babylonians treated him well, gave him food and gifts and allowed him to go wherever he wished."

"Being a traitor paid off, eh, Jeremy?" said Barry.

"Jeremiah wasn't a traitor," he said. "He cared deeply for his people and his country, but he knew Nebuchadnezzar would treat the Jews better if they surrendered."

"Where'd he go?" asked Skylar.

"Mizpah, not far from Jerusalem. Nebuchadnezzar allowed a few Jews to farm there and a Jew named Gedaliah was appointed governor over the area."

"Being free in your own land sounds better than being a slave in Babylon," said Le An.

"Jeremiah would've been treated rather well in Babylon, I suspect," he said. "But he chose to remain in Judah because he had an assignment to complete."

"What kind of assignment?" she asked.

"He had to protect the heir to the throne."

44

Iraq
Sunday, 7 September 2003

"Jeremiah had to protect the heir to the *Jewish* throne?" Le An asked as she flipped through her notes. "What throne? There was no country. Didn't Judah become part of the Chaldean empire? Didn't Nebuchadnezzar kill Zedekiah's children?"

"He killed all the king's *sons*," said Jeremy.

"Who was next in line to the throne?" she asked. "The king's brother?"

He softly smiled, "I never said it was a male heir."

"A female? Zedekiah had daughters?" she asked.

"Records indicate at least two of his daughters escaped and remained in Judah," he said.

"Did Nebuchadnezzar know?" she asked.

"Highly unlikely. If he'd discovered there were royal heirs, he would have killed them or taken them to Babylon. The eldest daughter, with the imprisonment of her father and death of her brothers, became heir to the throne."

"Judah allowed women to rule? That's more advanced than I thought," she said.

"Judah's and Israel's inheritance laws allowed a daughter to inherit her father's estate if there were no sons, quite a progressive concept in comparison to other nations at that time. It took millennia for some to come round to that."

"Britain's entail and primogeniture laws come to mind," she said and smiled.

"Quite right," he laughed. "However, Britain has accepted women as rulers, something America hasn't. We've had queens and a female prime minister, but America's never had a woman president. Even in ancient Israel, a woman named Deborah ruled the twelve tribes, led an army against the enemy and was a judge over Israelites' legal matters."

"Touché, though we do have women judges and military commanders," she smiled. "How'd the princesses escape?"

"There are no written accounts of how, but we do know they weren't with Zedekiah and his sons when they were captured," he said. "After Jerusalem fell, they were with the Jewish governor of Mizpah, Jeremiah and his assistant Baruch. The eldest couldn't have been more than sixteen."

"What was her name?" she asked.

"Some accounts say Tamar," he said. "She was said to be quite beautiful."

"A hot princess," said Skylar. "Did Jeremiah marry her?"

"No, he merely became her guardian and helped find her a suitable husband."

"Tamar became queen of... what?" asked Le An. "Judah was part of the Babylonian empire."

"She didn't rule in Judah, but she did rule over Israelites and Jews," he said.

"Israelites? Did she marry someone from the ten tribes?" she asked.

"She didn't have to marry an Israelite to rule over them," he said. "When Jacob blessed his twelve sons prior to his death, he told them the family's scepter—rulership—was to remain with Judah's descendants—which it did with King David and his descendants, including the princess. After Israel's civil war split the country, the throne remained with the Jews in Jerusalem, within David's dynasty, but it was still considered the throne of all Israel."

"Princess Tamar inherited the Jewish throne, aka the Israelite throne, and united all the tribes into one country again?" she asked.

"Not quite," said Jeremy. "The twelve tribes were never again one nation, though each tribe did grow large and become its own country. After Jerusalem fell, straightaway the princesses went to Mizpah with Jeremiah and the Jewish regional governor Gedaliah, a kind and good man. A month on, a Jewish military leader named Johanan, who'd been in hiding with other former soldiers, warned Gedaliah an evil Jewish royal named Ishmael was plotting to assassinate him."

"Call me Ishmael," said Barry.

"Quoting *Moby Dick*, Barr? Why would Ishmael want to kill Gedaliah?" asked Le An.

"Because he couldn't get Moby Dick?" smirked Barry.

Jeremy continued, "Accounts say Ishmael wanted to become ruler in place of Gedaliah. Johanan wanted to kill him to prevent Gedaliah's assassination, but Gedaliah refused to allow it. A month on, Ishmael and ten of his friends paid Gedaliah a visit."

45

Al Kifl, Iraq
Sunday, 7 September 2003

Jeremy interrupted the story to tell them they were approaching Al Kifl, a small town surrounded by date groves, along the eastern banks of the Euphrates. Rising high above the one-story mud-brick houses was an imposing conical-shaped beige dome resembling a large pineapple—Ezekiel's tomb.

"It's good we're here now," he said. "I fear Islamic zealots will soon erase all traces of the Jews, particularly here in the south where Shi'a are prominent."

"I thought you said Muslims respect Jewish and Christian prophets. Why would they desecrate Ezekiel's tomb?" she asked.

"They respect prophets, not Jews," he said. "They claim prophets for Islam while erasing a connection to Israel. Look what they did to Jonah's tomb in Nineveh."

"Built a mosque over it," she said.

"They're already using the synagogue here as a mosque," he said.

"Ezekiel was deported from Judah to Babylon?" she asked.

"Yes, with 10,000 other Jews during the second captivity, the one which took the majority of royals, aristocracy and educated," said Jeremy.

"I guess being a prophet didn't protect you all the time," she said.

"Not always," he said.

"Tough gig," said Skylar.

The US soldiers whom the USN crew had been scheduled to embed with the day before, fortunately, were there at Al Kifl when they arrived. Le An had planned to cancel the embed Friday afternoon, but had forgotten, instead preoccupied with all the commotion over Jeremy's supposed kidnapping and Khaled's embezzling scheme. She'd tried Saturday night after Jeremy's return to contact the Army Public Affairs officer Lieutenant Roger Morris to see if they could reschedule for Sunday, but hadn't been able to reach him.

"Well, that's a lucky break," she said, eliciting a knowing smile from Jeremy. "What? You look like you knew it would work out."

He softly smiled and nodded.

Lieutenant Morris, a West Point grad, was not only highly educated—holding a bachelors in political science from Duke and a masters in international relations from Georgetown—but also well versed on Al Kifl. Piet miked him, as well as Jeremy and Skylar, then kept a boom mic handy for man-on-the-street interviews, while Kent shot video using a second camera, something which clearly annoyed Barry.

"The Third ID encountered four days of heavy fighting here in Kifl during Iraqi Freedom while trying to secure this and another key bridge," said Lieutenant Morris as he turned and pointed to the town's damaged bridge, now bowing and closed to traffic. "We needed to keep this bridge open for troops and supply lines and to stop the Iraqis in Hillah from trying to move reinforcements south to Najaf to block our advance, but the Iraqis had wired the bridge with explosives."

"Iraqis blew it up, didn't they?" asked Skylar, remembering when he and the Third Infantry Division had come through during Iraqi Freedom.

"Affirmative. On March 25, two of our tanks had crossed and a third was in the middle when Iraqis first blew it and pancaked a section. Kinda freaked out that third tank driver, but he made it safely to the eastern bank. They were afraid they had another 'Black Hawk Down' scenario."

"What happened?" asked Skylar.

"The explosives only slightly dropped part of the road," he said. "Engineers determined vehicles could still make it across. Scouts went under the bridge to cut most of the wires to the explosives, but they were doing it under heavy fire. The colonel called for a quick-reaction force just before sunrise that first day and they were in the middle of executing their mission to take and hold the bridge."

"What happened?" asked Skylar.

"The lieutenant colonel didn't think the damage was that bad and ordered his own tank across," he said and started laughing. "He was standing in the middle of the bridge and thought his driver would stop to pick him up. The driver just kept going. He wasn't about to risk stopping on a blown bridge, even if it was to pick up the boss. The bridge sagged a little, but the tank made it over to the east bank, so they brought over another tank and some Bradleys. The lieutenant colonel secured the bridge, even engaged in hand-to-hand. Wrestled away one Iraqi's AK-47 and swung it like he was batting in a home run. Dropped the guy, then had his medics patch him up and haul him away. Near sunset that first day, an Iraqi mortar round landed near him and knocked him unconscious for almost an hour."

"Was he all right?" asked Skylar.

"He was fine. He came to and took control of the fight again," he said. "We found out later Qusay Hussein was nearby in Hillah commanding three brigades—two of them Fedayeen—so they were probably fighting here at Kifl. There'd be ten Iraqi soldiers in explosives-loaded pick-ups trying to crash into our Bradleys. When their trucks were in flames, they'd jump out and run toward our tanks. How crazy is that? More than 200 Iraqi soldiers died here."

"Any US casualties?"

"None," he said.

"What about air support?"

"No choppers because there was a sand storm and it started raining, which turned it into a mud storm that lasted three days. You couldn't wear glasses or night-vision goggles because the mud caked them up," said Lieutenant Morris.

"I remember," said Skylar. "It was hard to see anything."

"That was part of the reason the fighting was so close—neither side could see each other."

"Were a lot of townspeople killed or injured?" asked Skylar.

"About ten or eleven died, and a few injured," he said, "but that first day a lot of them managed to leave town."

"How'd the bridge end up like this?" asked Skylar.

"Third day of heavy fighting, the Iraqis blew the bridge again. Apparently, 10,000 pounds of plastic explosives were still under it on the eastern side. It dropped two more sections of the bridge on the one already down and trapped a platoon on the west bank."

"US forces couldn't use the bridge?" asked Skylar.

"The lieutenant colonel called in Jungle Cats...the engineering battalion. They sent the data back to the Op Center in Mississippi and they told them where to put additional supports under the bridge...enough for the Third to complete their mission."

"Is the US going to repair the bridge?" asked Skylar.

"We'll fix it," said Lieutenant Morris. "There's a lot to repair, but we've already done a great deal. It's a Shi'ite town, so the people were pretty happy to see us. They hate Saddam and were glad to see him go. Some Iraqis really helped US forces in the invasion. The Third ID had a Bradley get wire and cables tangled up in its track and Iraqi civilians driving down the highway jumped out of their cars to help. They started using machetes and crow bars to pry the stuff out of the track the whole time Iraqi soldiers were opening up on them and our troops. The people started pushing our soldiers away so they could work on getting the Bradley moving again. It was amazing."

"That and maybe they were thinking armed Americans might do better to shoot at the Iraqi army and protect them while they did the repairs," said Skylar.

"Probably."

"Any trouble here since?" asked Skylar.

"Marines and Iraqi police arrested two men in July. One was suspected of being a colonel in Saddam's security forces. They searched the guy's house and found explosives, blasting caps and fuses. I think all the Sunnis have cleared out of town. It's mainly Shi'a. The only trouble is a lot of complaining," he said, pointing to his soldiers who were patiently trying to calm down agitated, arm-waving townspeople, shouting their discontent. "They want more done. They thought we'd come in and instantly fix all their problems, even though Saddam never did. The US gave the town five million and they've used that to repair their courthouse, schools, a sports stadium and the sewage plant. Kifl's marketplace is back up and running. There's a brick-making business that's doing well. Our medic helps when we're here. There've been some outbreaks of cholera, typhoid and meningitis and the hospital's always running low on supplies."

"Is there a local government?" asked Skylar.

"Kifl has a mayor and five council members. The townspeople are very proud of the fact they were the first local government formed in Iraq after combat operations ended," he said. "The mayor's a lawyer, fortyish, from the main tribe of Bani Hassan. Nice guy. Saddam had executed his father, uncle and brother years ago and he had to hide out in Saudi Arabia for a while. The Shi'a tribal chiefs picked him."

"Any looting here after the invasion?" asked Skylar.

"Not really," he said. "It's a poor Shi'ite town. Not much to take. A guy who owns a barber shop said someone stole his poster of Manhattan and the Twin Towers. He said everybody loves New York. Probably the most valuable things stolen were three Hebrew plaques and a menorah mosaic pried off the walls at Ezekiel's tomb."

Jeremy winced at the news.

Lieutenant Morris excused himself for a moment to speak with some townspeople and Skylar began his interview with Jeremy.

"Who was Ezekiel?" he asked.

"He was a prophet and Levitical priest who explained to the Jews in exile in Babylon why they were being punished and why they'd lost their country Judah," said Jeremy.

"Why were the Jews punished?" asked Skylar.

"They were heavily into idolatry," he said. "They mixed Judah's religion with paganism—exactly what the ten tribes had done prior to their captivity, only the Jews were worse than Israel. The false prophets instructed them to sacrifice their children in fire to idols such as Molech."

"That's sick," said Skylar.

"They believed the gods would bless them for it. Religious leaders also instructed the Jews to abandon the seventh-day sabbath—Saturday—and worship the sun god on the first day of the week—Sunday. Ezekiel, and another prophet Jeremiah, who was still in Jerusalem, wrote many of the same things, at the same time, but were 600 miles away from each other. At times, Ezekiel wrote in what today we call 'real time.' He would write what was happening in Jerusalem at the moment it was happening, even though he was in Babylon and couldn't possibly have known."

"How long did it take to go from Jerusalem to Babylon in those days?" asked Skylar.

"Three months," said Jeremy.

"So Ezekiel predicted doom and gloom, even hundreds of

miles away?" asked Skylar.

"Not always. He also gave Jews hope for the future. He promised they'd rebuild their lives and their families here and, eventually, they or their descendants would return to Jerusalem—which they did, seventy years on from Nebuchadnezzar's first invasion. But he did tell the Jews to repent and pray from here, right where they were, which was significant."

"Why?" asked Skylar.

"Because the Jews had been praying at the temple in Jerusalem for 400 years. That temple no longer existed. Ezekiel told them they didn't need a temple or animal sacrifices to worship God, merely obedience and humble attitudes. That was a big change. It was the beginning of synagogues."

They walked into a large courtyard surrounded by rooms and separate mud-brick buildings, now partially collapsed as a result of the fighting six months before. Because the site had morphed from a Jewish synagogue into a Muslim place of worship, the USN crew removed their shoes before entering through the shrine's green door.

"There are Muslims worshipping here," said Skylar.

"Muslims say a prophet named Zul-Kifl mentioned in the Qur'an is Ezekiel and he's buried here, but they claim he was Muslim, not Jewish," said Jeremy. "Al Kifl used to have a large Jewish population. Jews from around Iraq and the Middle East would make pilgrimages here on high holy days. They'd sleep in tents in the fields or in these rooms off the courtyard."

"Like they did at Nahum's tomb in Al Kosh?" asked Skylar.

"Precisely," said Jeremy as he pointed to a line of Hebrew above a door opening and translated, "'The gravestone of our prophet Ezekiel.' As I mentioned in Babylon, Nebuchadnezzar imprisoned his own son Evil-Merodach, along with Judah's next-to-last king Jehoiachin. When Evil-Merodach assumed the throne, he freed Jehoiachin and treated him well. According to tradition and Jewish writings, the king even allowed him to build a tomb here over Ezekiel's grave, as well as a synagogue next to it, which was called 'the Synagogue of Ezekiel and Jehoiachin.' Every year on Yom Kippur, they'd read from a copy of the Torah—the first five books of scripture—which Ezekiel himself had copied."

They moved into another room which contained an enormous, shoulder-high, wooden tomb, its top adorned with a fringed cloth and fresh flowers. Scattered across the floor were small prayer rugs. The building's Muslim caretaker, who remembered Jeremy from years past, greeted him warmly with kisses on both cheeks, then smiled and motioned for them to approach the tomb as he opened a small hidden door, revealing an inner stone tomb.

"Members of his family have taken care of this tomb since Ottoman days," said Jeremy, then ran his finger over the Hebrew on one of two plaques attached to it. "This is the word 'Yehezkel.' Benjamin of Tudela wrote in the twelfth century about this tomb and the large Jewish library here, with scrolls dating to before the destruction of Jerusalem, at that time more than 1,700 years old."

Outside, the caretaker invited them, along with Lieutenant Morris and some of his men, to come to his house for tea. Everyone graciously accepted the man's hospitality, but Le An saw Barry wince. Again, she offered cases of bottled water as a gift, hoping their tea would be made with it.

After more interviews with townspeople, the USN convoy headed back to Baghdad. Jeremy again mentioned how some Muslims were plastering over Hebrew writings at old Jewish synagogues and shrines.

"Not all Muslims are anti-Jewish, but many of their leaders are, unfortunately, and they encourage hatred," he said. "I fear 2,600 years of Jewish history will soon be erased from Iraq."

"I never understood anti-Semitism," said Le An.

"As we discussed, it started with a rivalry between brothers 4,000 years ago," he said. "Abraham had two sons: Ishmael, who was illegitimate, born of a servant woman, and Isaac, born of Abraham's wife Sarah. Isaac, though fourteen years younger, was legal heir to all his father's wealth—and Abraham was exceedingly wealthy. The Arabs, descended from Ishmael, have retained a jealousy toward Isaac's descendants—the twelve tribes of Israel."

"Isn't 4,000 years a long time to carry a grudge?" she asked.

"Was Sarah mad Abraham had an affair with the servant?" asked Skylar.

"It wasn't quite like that," said Jeremy. "Sarah was unable to have children and had given her servant to her husband so he could produce an heir. But fourteen years on, she miraculously conceived Isaac in her old age."

"That still doesn't explain why some Christians and other non-Arabs hate Jews," said Le An.

"Because they killed Christ," said Barry, immediately causing a chorus of incredulity from many in the vehicle.

"Spirelli, you did not just say that!" Le An sputtered.

"Technically, it was the Romans who killed him, not the Jews," said Jeremy.

Le An burst out laughing. "And, Spirelli, you're Italian. So did your family kill Christ?"

She glanced back to see him leveling a cold stare at her.

The day was ending well.

"An interesting thing about Ezekiel," said Jeremy, changing the subject, "is he wrote prophecies directed at not only the Jews, but also the Israelites—even though it was 130 years on from when the ten tribes had gone into captivity."

"He knew where they were?" asked Le An.

"He did," said Jeremy.

"You never finished the story about the Jewish princess," said Le An. "You stopped when Johanan told the Jewish governor of Mizpah that the power-hungry guy Ishmael wanted to kill him and become ruler."

"Johanan had indeed been correct about Ishmael's intentions," said Jeremy. "One day Ishmael appeared in Mizpah with ten friends and dined with Governor Gedaliah. Then they assassinated him, his guests and nearly 100 other Jews traveling through the area, along with all Nebuchadnezzar's soldiers in Mizpah."

"How awful. Johanan was right," said Le An looking at her notes. "Gedaliah should have listened to him. Why is it guys named Ishmael have such bad attitudes?"

"Call me Ishmael," sneered Barry.

"You have been an Ishmael lately," she muttered.

"What happened next, Jeremy?" asked Skylar.

"Ishmael and his men rounded up the remaining Jews in Mizpah, including the princesses, Jeremiah and his secretary Baruch," he said, "then force-marched them south to hide from Babylonian troops who might discover what they'd done. They didn't get far. Johanan and his men caught up to them and rescued the people. Ishmael managed to escape."

"The mass murderer gets away," said Le An. "That's a shame, but Johanan was pretty smart and a hero, too."

"Yes, well, not quite," said Jeremy.

46

Iraq
Sunday, 7 September 2003

"What do you mean?" asked Le An.

"Johanan did rescue them, but he and the Jews were afraid Nebuchadnezzar would hold them responsible for the murders Ishmael had committed and punish them," said Jeremy. "Jeremiah believed they could explain events and request more troops for protection; however, Johanan refused to listen to him. Instead, he forced the Jews to leave Mizpah."

"Forced them? He pulled an Ishmael?" asked Le An.

"Precisely. They traveled to Bethlehem, but Johanan thought they'd only be safe in Egypt. Jeremiah told them to remain in Judah and warned if they went into Egypt, they'd die horrible deaths or be exiled to Babylon in slavery."

"What'd they do?" asked Skylar.

"I bet they listened to Johanan," said Le An. "Nobody ever listened to Jeremiah, poor thing."

"Precisely," said Jeremy. "They went to Egypt to join other Jews who'd fled there during the war—and forced Jeremiah, Baruch and the princesses to go with them. The Jews asked Jeremiah, who was a prophet and Levitical priest, to pray to their God for guidance and protection, then rejected his advice and returned to worshipping pagan gods—in particular Ishtar."

"That Easter fertility goddess we keep running into all over this country?" laughed Skylar.

"The same," he said. "For many years prior to that the Jews had been worshipping pagan gods along with the God of Israel, a religion light on God and heavy on idolatrous traditions—one reason prophets told them they'd gone into captivity."

"Did Nebuchadnezzar come after them in Egypt?" asked Le An.

"He did. And everything Jeremiah predicted happened," he said. "Some died and the rest went to Babylon as slaves."

"What happened to Jeremiah and the Jewish princess?" she asked.

"Egypt's Pharaoh Hophra gave the princess a palace," he said. "In the late 1800s, the British archaeologist Sir William Matthew Flinders Petrie dug at Tell Defenneh in Egypt, known in historical records as Tahpanhes, where he discovered *Qasr Bint el Yahudi*, the name local Arabs gave it, which translates 'palace of the Jew's daughter.'"

Le An's mouth dropped open. "Get out!"

"Yes, please," muttered Barry.

"Petrie unearthed a palace, each level having sixteen rooms, the limestone walls of the royal apartments sculpted and painted. It appeared to have been sacked and burnt in an assault, though he still found a wealth of artifacts, including: jars, cups, saucers and tablets in gold, silver and lapis lazuli. He also found Greek weapons and vases dating slightly before 550 BC."

"Greek?" she said.

"Tahpanhes contained a Greek trading colony. The Greeks were expert sailors, who gathered goods from round the world and established colonies in what's now France, Spain, Ireland and England, as well as Egypt. They had trading routes which stretched from the Black Sea, throughout the Mediterranean, into the Atlantic Ocean and beyond."

"So Tahpanhes was an Egyptian city which allowed Greeks to set up a trade colony?" she asked.

"Precisely," said Jeremy. "But Greeks provided more than commerce. They were skilled in foreign languages and, at Pharaoh's invitation, set up academies to teach Egyptians. They also aided Egyptian troops in wars and at the border, as well as providing security for Pharaoh."

"They were mercenaries, too? They were the DK guards of the ancient world," laughed Skylar, prompting Leo to level an unamused look at him.

"The Greek historian Herodotus wrote in the fifth century BC Pharaoh Psammetich had hired Greek soldiers known as

Milesians to act as mercenaries and their fort was at Tahpanhes in the eastern Nile Delta. Scripture says Jeremiah, the princesses and the Jewish refugees settled there."

"Were Greeks there when Jeremiah and the princesses were?" asked Le An.

"It appears they were," said Jeremy.

"If Greek weapons and pottery at the palace dated around 550 BC, wouldn't that mean the palace was burned around the time Jeremiah was there?" she asked, looking down at her notes. "Nebuchadnezzar could have burned that palace?"

"Highly possible," he said.

"Did he kill Jeremiah and the princess?" asked Skylar.

"Records indicate they escaped—sailed off with a Milesian prince who later married the princess."

"No way," laughed Skylar.

"Way," Jeremy deadpanned. "I suspect they slipped away before Nebuchadnezzar entered Egypt, probably under cover of darkness—the only way to escape both the Egyptians and the Jews. After all, Johanan had forced them against their will to come with him and he wasn't willing to let them escape. He no doubt considered them a lucky talisman of sorts, a protection from harm."

"His own little four-leaf clovers. But didn't the princess have to marry a Jew or an Israelite?" asked Le An.

"The Milesian prince was a Jew," said Jeremy.

47

Iraq
Sunday, 7 September 2003

"A Greek prince was a Jew?" gasped Le An. "How is that possible?"

"Some Jews migrated," said Jeremy. "The prince was descended from Judah's son Zerah, while the princess was from Zerah's twin brother Perez."

"That's some serious inbreeding," snorted Barry.

"Not really. It was 1,000 years on from Zerah's and Perez's births," said Jeremy. "They were rather distant cousins. At birth, Zerah stuck out his hand as firstborn and the midwife tied a red string round it. However, his brother Perez pushed past and arrived first. Who was firstborn? The one whose hand came out first or the one fully delivered first?"

"Tie. Equal inheritance," said Le An.

"Which is what happened when the prince, descended from Zerah of the red string, married the princess, descended from Perez, uniting the two lines," said Jeremy.

"How did Jews end up in Greece?" she asked.

"When the twelve tribes left Egypt with Moses approximately 1443 BC, some from Judah, Dan and Gad sailed to Greece," said Jeremy.

"Cruising the Greek isles beats dragging through a desert," she said.

"Those guys were smart," grinned Skylar.

"The Greek historian Hecataeus wrote during the fourth century BC that Egypt had been troubled by calamities, the ten plagues, and expelled aliens, the Israelites, to avert divine wrath," said Jeremy, "He wrote some alien leaders migrated to Greece, but the majority under Moses' leadership eventually settled in the region of the eastern Mediterranean. Homer called some of the Greeks Danaans, the Israelite tribe of Dan. Even after the twelve tribes settled in Israel, they had trouble keeping Danites on land. They were adventurous sailors."

"My brain's about to explode," mumbled Le An, furiously jotting down the information. "The Greeks were Israelites."

"Not all Greeks, but ancient historians say Jews built Athens and Troy," he said.

"Helen-of-Troy Troy?" she asked.

"Yes," Jeremy smiled. "Historians wrote Israelites sailed to Asia Minor, built an altar to God thanking him for deliverance from the Egyptians, then built Troy. The Roman historian Tacitus wrote the Mycenaeans in southern Greece were fugitive Jews from the isle of Crete. And a Sicilian historian from the first century BC said Israelites emigrated from Egypt and founded Athens. It's not difficult to understand. The Greek isles are straightaway across the Mediterranean from Egypt. It's also possible some sailed from Egypt approximately 1600 BC when they sensed the twelve tribes were about to be enslaved."

"Did Israelites know about their Greek relatives?" she asked.

"Oh my, yes. About 300 BC, the king of Sparta sent word to the high priest in Jerusalem saying he'd found written proof they were kinsmen. The high priest wrote back saying the Jews continuously prayed for the Spartans' preservation and victory because they knew sacred writings showed the two groups were brothers."

"And that was the sound of my brain exploding," she said. "When you said the Israelite Scythians along the Black Sea traded extensively with the Greeks, they may have been dealing with fellow Israelites?"

"Highly possible," said Jeremy. "Israelites were also known as Parthians, a strong empire for three centuries which dominated trade on the Silk Road to China. The Parthians conquered the Persians and were the arch nemeses of the Roman Empire. Gave the Romans quite a go of it."

"The Israelites were everywhere," said Le An. "They were colonizing Greek islands, sailing the Black Sea, Mediterranean and Atlantic, wandering around 4,000 miles of the Eurasian Steppes...they were everywhere."

"Growing in numbers, colonizing, always on the move," smiled Jeremy.

48

London, England
Thursday, 18 September 2003

After completing their shoots in southern Iraq, Le An, Barry and Jeremy flew from Kuwait to London where Barry shot some of the Mesopotamian antiquities at the British Museum and Le An finished writing her script.

For long hours each day, they sat in USN's London bureau editing their segments. At one in the morning, an hour before they were due to feed their segments to New York, twenty-five hours before the special was to air, Le An struggled to stay awake in the chair next to Barry.

"That looks good," she yawned. "New York'll finish the edits. They've got to drop in graphics, some file video and music anyway. Burn a copy for Andrea to feed."

"No, I need to fix a few more things," said Barry. "You're tired. Just go back to the hotel. I'll feed it."

"No, your flight to New York's in a few hours," she said. "You need sleep."

"*My* flight? You're not going?" he asked, frowning as he looked over at her.

"No, didn't you know? The flights were packed. Travel could only get one seat and gave it to you. Mine's tomorrow. Just burn the disc and I'll stay here to monitor the feed."

"Stop pressuring me!" he snapped. "I said I'm not finished. I'll feed it!"

"Stop biting my head off," she snapped right back. "You're getting on my last nerve."

She'd had weeks of his irrational outbursts. He'd exhausted her, arguing for days about the script and Jeremy's comments.

A few minutes later, when Barry got up to use the restroom

and call his wife, Le An quickly inserted a DVD and downloaded their edited segments, nervously keeping an eye out for him. She'd barely had time to eject the burned disc and slide it into a jewel case when he returned. Keeping the case hidden, she walked over to Andrea, the London bureau's gothic-dressing, ex-pat-American, overnight satellite and feed coordinator. Le An slid the case onto the counter, prepared to feed it if Barry didn't finish in time.

"Go back to the hotel, Le!" Barry snapped, glancing over at her as he popped in a DVD and burned it. "I said I'll feed it!"

"What's his problem?" whispered Andrea. "He's been a bear all week. I'll be glad to see him go."

Le An let out a long, exhausted sigh and shook her head. "He's worn me out."

"Will you just go!" Barry screamed at her again, causing others in the bureau to give him strange looks. He popped out the DVD. "If New York complains it's not finished, it's your fault!"

"They know it's not completely finished. They need to do final edits," said Le An, clenching her jaw and trying to control her anger.

With their feed window only ten minutes away and the disc safely burned, she was satisfied she could leave. Anything to get away from Barry.

Back at the hotel, Le An tried to decompress from the long work hours—and Barry. He was one of her best friends and she wasn't used to fighting with him. Usually they were totally in sync.

Setting her room and cellphone alarms for 7:00 a.m., she called the desk to arrange for a backup call. She wanted to sleep in, but Barry needed her help getting the luggage checked in at the airport. The last time she'd left him alone, thieves had snatched half their video equipment. April would be waiting for him at baggage claim in New York.

Picking up the TV remote, she flipped through channels, finally stopping when she heard the soulful violin from the opening scene of *Fiddler on the Roof*. She'd seen the movie countless times and suddenly it dawned on her how similar the plot was to what she was experiencing.

Tradition was what ruled the movie's small Jewish village in early-1900s Russia. Even though the Jews knew the czar hated them and the soldiers persecuted them, they refused to leave because change, even if it was for the better, was too hard. The people kept their balance, even when their lives were threatened, because of tradition.

Tradition.

It didn't matter how dangerous or even wrong something was. It could all be a lie, but it didn't matter. Tradition was all that mattered. That's what gave people security and peace. They needed traditions to get through the day, to get through life. But was that really the best way?

Barry said he needed tradition, even if it was warm and fuzzy lies. Tradition was his foundation, not truth.

Le An dozed off watching *Fiddler*, waking a few hours later to a Gene Kelley movie, two buzzing alarms and a ringing phone.

"Get up. We're leaving in fifteen minutes," Barry said coldly.

"How long have you been up?" she mumbled, not pleased to hear he was still in a bad mood. "I thought it would take a cannon to wake you."

"I haven't been to bed yet," he said.

"Why not? Did something happen with the feed?" she asked sitting straight up in bed, suddenly wide awake and panicking.

"Nothing wrong with the feed. I just figured I'd sleep on the plane," he said and abruptly hung up.

49

London, England
Thursday, 18 September 2003

"Jeremy's a nut job, Le An. You always say we get the weird ones to interview for religion pieces and you're right," said Barry as he checked in his luggage and equipment at the airline counter.

"I think he makes sense," she said. "He had some really good points."

"Oh, come on," he snapped as he handed over his passport and ticket to the desk agent. "Are you telling me you think all these churches are wrong?"

"I don't know... maybe."

"All these churches have been wrong all these years? You're saying my Pope has been wrong?" he asked.

She would have been amused at his use of a personal pronoun to describe the Pope if she wasn't so annoyed they were once again arguing about it.

"Barry, how do you know *your* Pope and all these other so-called Christian churches are right? Just because lots of people have been doing it for lots of years? What kind of journalist are you?"

"A sensible one. Strength in numbers, baby," he said.

"That's ridiculous," she said. "Truth isn't determined by numbers. Truth is determined by *facts*. That's what journalists do. We sift through all the garbage and lies and find facts to figure out what truth is."

"You're such a purist," he said. "Our greedy corporation and its fat-cat board and CEO don't care what's true. They only care if they make money. And sometimes they care whether they'll get sued, but that's why we've got well-paid legal departments."

"That's not who *we* are," she said. "Network may not care

about truth, but I do. If you're going to choose a religion, I'd think you'd want one which has the most truth."

"How can you judge which religion is really true?" he said sarcastically.

"How can you?"

"Exactly. How can anyone? That's why the Pope makes decisions about stuff like that. He's got the connection to God."

"Says you. He's a man," she said.

"No, he's not. He's the Pope," he said, causing the airline agent to fight back a smile.

"You make decisions about every other part of your life, but when it comes to religion, you let the Pope decide for you, even when you don't agree?" she said. "Because I know you don't agree with him 100 percent."

He glared at her and she glared right back, determined not to back down.

"Think about it," she said. "What if someone way back got it wrong—either deliberately or innocently—and the changes stuck."

"Impossible," he growled.

"Why is it impossible?" she started raising her voice. "Why is it not possible that someone got it wrong and the truth got lost along the way?"

"You're saying all these people through all these centuries are *wrong*?"

"Maybe they are," she said. "And if they got it wrong, what are you going to do?"

He looked at her in disgust and shook his head. "Nothing. I'm doing nothing."

"What if..." she racked her brain trying to think of an example. "OK, what if... someone switched a Rembrandt with a fake, only everybody thought it was the real thing. Centuries go by and no one knows the painting's a cheap fake. Then you find the real Rembrandt worth millions. Aren't you glad you finally have the original? For value alone, isn't it better to have the real thing?"

"That doesn't apply to religion," he said. "I don't care if my religious traditions are 100 percent true. The truth is most people just want the same traditions they grew up with, because you know something, Le? We're never going to find the truth. You have to stay with what the majority of people believe."

His comment left her too stunned to respond.

He started walking toward his gate, then stopped and turned to her one last time. "I may not be the best Catholic in the world, but I know what that nut-job Jeremy's saying can't be right."

"Why, Barry? Because you'd have to change your whole belief system and that would make you too uncomfortable? You wouldn't get that warm, fuzzy feeling anymore?"

"When did you turn into a religious fanatic?" he snapped.

"I'm not a religious fanatic. I'm trying to find out what's true. Why is that so hard for you to understand? It's what we do every day with our jobs."

"This stuff Jeremy's saying... it's not true. You won't find the truth with him." He walked a few steps, then shouted, "Go talk to a Catholic priest. Then you'll find some truth."

He turned and swiftly walked away before she could answer. She didn't move, merely watched him as the crowds of multi-languaged people swarmed around her, jostling and bumping her, rolling their airline-crew-inspired luggage behind them.

She wasn't sure what she was feeling: anger? emptiness? burn out? a renaissance? an awakening? She felt driven to keep looking for answers, but she didn't know why or where. Or did she? Half walking and half running, she hurried through the nearest exit and quickly flagged a taxi.

"Where to, miss?" the driver asked as he started the meter.

She rummaged through her backpack and found the address, then settled into the enormous backseat, still feeling a little numb after her fight with Barry. Forty minutes later she rang the bell at a London brownstone.

"Is... is Jeremy Hilson here?" she asked the elderly, balding gentleman who answered the door. "I'm Le An MacDonald, the news producer he was traveling with in Iraq."

"Ah, yes," he smiled and motioned for her to come in. "I'm Henry Harknert. Jeremy's been talking about you. Won't you come in? Are you traveling with him?"

"Traveling? He's leaving?"

"He's packing now. You're not here to accompany him to the train?"

"Ahh..." she stuttered. "Yes...yes, I am, but he doesn't know it. It's a surprise."

"Apparently to you, too," he said with a smile. "I'll tell him you're here."

He pointed to the front sitting room, then disappeared up the narrow, dark staircase. She sat down on a floral-print sofa which had seen better days and stared down at the worn carpet, trying to think what she could say that wouldn't make her sound like a lunatic. Henry had probably already told Jeremy she was giving dicey answers.

She jumped up when she heard two sets of heavy footsteps on the wooden stairs and by the time Jeremy and Henry had reached the foyer, she was standing next to the staircase.

"Le An?" Jeremy said as he put his luggage on the floor. "Why, my dear, what a lovely surprise. I hadn't expected to see you again."

"Yes, I... had more questions," she said. "I wondered if I could go with you to your train."

"Why, of course, I'd love nothing more," he smiled, then turned to his friend and shook his hand. "Henry, always a pleasure. Thank you for your hospitality. I promise to be in touch. Let me know what you find out."

"Jeremy, you old buzzard, it was jolly good having you. I'll let you know the minute I get some information. Give Doctor Stringfellow my regards. And keep an eye on that one," said Henry, his eyes twinkling as he pointed to Le An. "Ah, Jeremy, you dog, you get all the lovelies, don't you?"

Le An blushed and stammered, then tripped over a corner of the carpet as she headed for the door.

"Henry, you're incorrigible," Jeremy shook his finger at his friend, feigning a scowl. "I'll not have you bothering her. Come along, Le An. I can't miss my train."

"Should we grab a taxi?" she asked when they got to the street.

"The Tube entrance is only a short distance," he pointed ahead of them, rolling his bag behind him.

"Are you going to see your family?" she asked.

"No, I'm popping up to Oxford to see colleagues and find out if anyone's planning to organize a formal protest of the motorway construction near Tara. I fear the archaeological damage to the site. Do you know 140 kings are believed to be buried there? Think of the lost artifacts. It's tragic."

"That's terrible," she said. "How long will you be in Oxford? Are you coming back to London? Do you have a cellphone in case

I need to reach you?"

"I don't have a mobile as yet," he said. "I'll be in Oxford about a week. I was planning to stay with an old chum, but his daughter and grandchildren are visiting, so I'll be at the Regency Royale Bed and Breakfast for a few days until they leave. I may travel to Ireland after."

"Our program airs tonight in the US," she said. "We've worked really hard on it. I think you'll be pleased."

"I'm sure I will. What was it you wanted to ask me?"

"I don't know where to begin," she said. "Traditions in religion…how do you know if they're good or true?"

They were passing a small park and, after taking a quick glance at his watch, he motioned for her to follow him. On one of the three benches, a nanny was reading to her young charge, the family Cocker Spaniel on a leash tied to her wrist. A businessman sat on a second bench, gazing into space as he munched on a pastry, a copy of the pink *Financial Times* folded next to him. Jeremy motioned to the available third bench and they sat down.

"Most religions have traditions," he said. "But you need to consider what the basis is for a particular tradition. Trace it back to its origin and you may discover some unexpected practices."

She slowly nodded. "What if some traditions started out bad, but then someone changed them to represent something good? Are they OK then?"

"It depends whether the change is aligned with truth or whether it was a way to gain converts who refused to give up harmful or non-religious traditions. For instance, did a tradition begin as an orgy to an idol, then change to mean something else? Did someone hope to gain converts by pasting a new meaning over top of it? And, more importantly, does the religion forbid worship in the way the tradition purports?"

"Like taking Mesopotamia's religious traditions and trying to make them Christian?" she asked.

"Precisely. Israelites were told specifically not to adopt pagan traditions in their worship. Yet, they did anyway. You have to determine what your absolute is—what sets your standard for right and wrong."

"You mean an absolute like the Pope or Buddha or the Qur'an or the Old Testament or all scriptures?" she asked.

"Precisely," he said.

She was silent for a moment, then said, "Most people don't want to go against the majority."

"Ah, yes, pressure from peers," he said.

"They're afraid people will criticize them and make fun of them. They don't want to stand out and be different," she said quietly. "Trust me, I know what it is not to fit. I'm brown—an AmerAsian who grew up in the South. I had to ignore all the teasing, hateful comments from some of the kids I went to school with. They used to knock me down on the school ground, sit on me and call me 'chink eyes.' They'd steal my books or knock them out of my hands. They were jealous I got better grades than they did."

He smiled and patted her arm. "Look what sterling character those experiences created in you. Look how strong you are. You're willing to search for truth. That's more than most even attempt. The unknown can be quite frightening for people. They don't want to risk losing family or friends if they stand up for something they truly believe in. I imagine you'd go out there all alone if you believed something was right, wouldn't you?"

Overwhelmed he understood her so well, tears welled up in her eyes. "I'm sorry Barry gave you such a hard time," she sniffled. "You handled it with such grace."

"Barry sincerely believes his religious views are correct, as I do mine, as billions do theirs. You, my dear, are a work in progress."

She wiped away the tears and nodded. Her exhaustion had put her emotions close to the surface, on a hair-trigger release. Regaining her composure, she said, "I wanted to ask you: what finally happened to the ten tribes of Israel? They were in the Greek isles and Eurasian Steppes and by the Black Sea and fighting the Romans and sailing the oceans. Do they still exist today?"

He smiled. "They remained within their family tribes for thousands of years, though not always all together as one nation. The individual tribes remained cohesive units for many centuries, even after they were deported, mainly because each was an extension of family. The national name 'Israel' disappeared until the tribe of Judah resurrected it in the twentieth century, but the rest of the tribes still exist today and you'll find them under quite familiar names."

"Like what?" she asked.

"The tribe of Dan's rather easy to find," he said. "Danites

always named places in honor of their forefather Dan. But in ancient written Hebrew, only the consonants were recorded and vowel points typically disappeared, which meant Dan became D-N. Danites were great seafarers, traveling on rivers they named Danube, Dniester, Don and Dnieper. Many finally settled in Dan's Mark—Denmark."

Her mouth dropped open and she gasped, "They're Europeans? Danes are Israelites?"

"Danites also settled in Ireland thousands of years ago and were known as the Tuatha de Danann—tribe of Dan," he said.

She sat there speechless for a moment. "The Israelites still exist," she whispered.

"Most experts agree the majority of the tribe of Reuben ultimately settled in France," he continued.

"The French are Israelites?!" she gasped. "I'm part French! Does that mean I'm an Israelite?"

"More than you know, my dear," he softly smiled. "Remember I said they eventually migrated north and west. The majority ended up in Europe, though some tribes expanded throughout the world."

"Europeans?" she said. "But the languages are so different."

"Today they are somewhat, though you'll find similar words," he said. "Until approximately AD 400, the Israelites who migrated into Northwestern Europe had virtually the same language. It stemmed from the Germanic or Teutonic branch of Indo-European languages. Even today many of those root words are similar to Aramaic Hebrew. For instance, Saturday in Hebrew is *Shabbat*, in Spanish and Portuguese it's *Sabado*, in Italian *Sabato*, in Polish and Czech *Sobota*, in Greek *Savvato*."

She smiled at his chosen word. "Saturday Sabbath. Are you saying German's the base of the Israelites' language?"

"No, the language branch is referred to as Germanic, which isn't the same as the German language," he said.

"Are the Germans Israelites?" she asked.

"Most non-Jewish Germans are Assyrians."

"Interesting."

"Quite," he said and glanced at his watch. "Oh, my, look at the time. I'm dreadfully sorry, Le An, but I must be going or I'll miss my train. Are you walking with me?"

He stood up abruptly, grabbed the handle of his suitcase and started for the sidewalk, wheeling his bag behind him as Le An hurried to keep up. She could see the red circle with the blue slash through it, the logo of the Underground, indicating they were at the entrance to a Tube station. As the crowds swarmed around them, she had trouble keeping up with him. He looked at his watch again and hurried toward the stall, sliding his pre-purchased Travelcard ticket into the slot at the gate, then grabbing it as both it and he passed through to the other side.

Le An called after him, but he didn't hear. She fumbled through her pockets and backpack, looking for her own card and, not finding it, ran to the ticket window, still looking in the direction he'd disappeared. She could see his head disappearing down the escalator which led to the tracks as the woman in front of her slowly finished her transaction. Le An jiggled up and down on each leg, nervous she wouldn't be able to catch him in time.

"Oh, hurry, hurry," she muttered under her breath, then stopped as the woman turned to glare at her. "Sorry, I'm late," she apologized as the woman walked away. "Um... zone one. One way," she said, passing £2 through the tray and asking for the cheapest day ticket, anything to get her down to the trains so she could finish their conversation.

She nervously glanced toward the escalator. As the agent slid the ticket toward her, she snatched it and ran for the stall. Weaving through the crowds, she made her way to the escalator which deposited her at the underground tracks. Just as she spotted Jeremy on the left end of the platform, he raised his hand to catch her eye.

"I still have questions," she gasped, out of breath from her sprint through the station.

"I'm so sorry, my dear," he apologized. "I didn't realize you weren't behind me. I suppose I was moving at a brisk pace. I didn't want to miss my train."

"You didn't finish," she panted, hastily pulling out her small spiral-bound notebook and a pen. "If the Jews are Judah, Reuben's in France, and Dan's in Denmark and Ireland, where are the other tribes?"

"The Levite priests are scattered, usually found with the Jews," he said. "The tribes of Simeon, Zebulun, Issachar, Gad, Asher, Naphtali and Benjamin are throughout Europe, in: Switzerland, Luxembourg, Belgium, the Netherlands, Sweden, Finland,

Norway and Iceland."

The list of European countries stunned her and she looked up at him speechless as she finished writing. "Oh, my word," she finally said and looked at the list, repeating the countries he'd mentioned to make sure she had them all. "Did you mention Spain?"

"No, I didn't. There were Israelite colonies in Spain and Portugal as early as 900 BC," he said. "They even gave the area the name of their ancestor Eber, where we get the name Hebrew."

"Eber?"

"It's called the Iberian Penninsula," he reminded her.

"Oh, yeah," she said.

"But round about AD 500, Jews and Israelites there began to be persecuted. They were stoned to death, beheaded and burnt alive if they didn't convert to Catholicism. That stopped when the Moors conquered Spain. Muslims were more tolerant of the Jews."

"How ironic."

"Quite. During the Spanish Inquisition, Catholics again forced Jews to convert or die," he said. "Many Jews made a pretense of converting, then fled. They're known as Crypto Jews, or secret Jews. When Spain colonized the Americas, many Jews and Israelites fled with their families to the New World, including America's southwest, to escape the persecution."

"I've never heard that," she said, jotting down the information. "They went to New Mexico and Arizona?"

"And Texas and Colorado."

"Are their descendants still there?"

"Oh yes. The Crypto Jews from Spain and Portugal openly practiced their Judaism until the Inquisition came to the Americas. Then they once again professed to be Catholics in public, but practiced Judaism in private, continuing their traditions."

"What kind of traditions?" she asked.

"Oh, for instance, some have a menorah which has been been in the family for generations. They light candles on Friday night to signal the start of the Sabbath. Some say Jewish prayers or have certain food customs, such as draining blood from slaughtered animals or not eating pork. Some fast on Yom Kippur, eat unleavened tortillas for Passover or even carve Stars of David on their familial tombstones. Many today continue these family traditions and have no idea why."

"They don't know they're Israelites, but they retained the customs," she marveled.

"I spoke with a Portuguese man who was raised Catholic," he said. "Family members always spoke in whispers about a street in his village named after their ancestors, yet no one in his family had that name and no one would answer his questions about it. Then he watched the movie *Schindler's List* and saw that name amongst the scroll of Jewish names at the end and realized his family's big secret was they were Jewish. They'd been forced to convert to Catholicism."

"The family secrets creep out," she said.

"Precisely. Christopher Columbus left clues in his will and in letters to his son Diego that not only was he Jewish, but also searching for a place Jews could flee persecution," said Jeremy. "He sailed for America on the day which King Ferdinand and Queen Isabella had set as a deadline for all Jews to be expelled from Spain—at the close of Yom Kippur."

"You said he left clues in letters to his son?" asked Le An. "What kind of clues?"

"On each page Columbus would write the Hebrew alphabet characters *bet* and *he*, an abbreviated form of *Baruch Hashem*, which means 'God be praised,' or *B'ezrat Hashem*, which means 'with the help of God'—a blessing of sorts. Jews for centuries had always added that to their letters to family and close friends, but never to outsiders."

"Columbus hid his ancestry," she said in amazement.

"Many descendants of Crypto Jews don't realize why their families have preserved the traditions they do. They may not realize they're Jews or Israelites. DNA testing has revealed surprising results."

"I definitely want to produce this for an *AmeriView* segment," she said.

"There are similar stories found in locations where Israelites used to live in large numbers, such as Pakistan and Afghanistan," he said. "Even today, some Pashtun tribes near the Khyber Pass observe very 'Jewish' customs. Even Palestinians. They may be practicing Muslims, but actually be descendants of Israel."

"Whoa. Big shock for them. Great story idea," she said, jotting down more notes. "So Europeans are Israelites."

"The Greek historian Herodotus wrote in the fifth century BC that Persians referred to Scythians as 'Sacae,' a variation of Israel's father Isaac. By the second century, the Greek writer Ptolemy called them Saxones...Isaac's sons."

"Saxons? You mean like Anglo-Saxons?" she gasped.

"Yes, the Saxons and the Angles were Israelites, as were tribes such as the Celts, Gauls and Goths. As I said, familiar names. Remember I said the Scythians were in the region of the Caucasus Mountains? That's where we get the word Caucasian."

Le An's mouth dropped open. "I always wondered why they called whites Caucasians."

"Did you notice? There are two tribes I didn't mention: Ephraim and Manasseh, Joseph's sons."

"Joseph, whose brothers sold him into slavery in Egypt and who became prime minister there?" she asked.

"Precisely. In scripture, Ephraim and Manasseh were promised physical blessings, more than any other group of people. They were to have the choicest physical blessings, the best crops. They were to be stronger militarily than any who attacked them. They were to be blessed with rain, with never-ending water from springs, with many children. They were to be set in praise, fame and honor high above all the nations. Who fits that description? Which nations at their peak were the wealthiest in minerals, in crops, in military strength?"

She stared at him, too dumbfounded to give the answer she was thinking.

Just then the train pulled up, the cars' automatic doors opening to allow hoards of passengers to disembark.

Jeremy walked toward it, but turned to add, "Ephraim was to be a company of nations. The British Commonwealth. At her peak, she encompassed twenty-five percent of the world's land mass, more than any empire in the history of man, more than 450 million people, which, at that time, was twenty percent of the world's population. Her GDP was greater than £600 billion. Britannia ruled the seas and the sun never set on her because she spanned the globe. No empire in the history of the world has ever achieved that level of wealth or land mass."

"Scotland, too?" she asked, thinking of her own ancestry.

"Scotland, too," he smiled, stepping on the train. As the doors signaled they were closing, he added, "As for Manasseh: which country has been the recipient of enormous physical blessings with an abundance of minerals, water and rich farmland? Which rose to become the wealthiest, most powerful nation on earth today and, combined with Britain, controlled three-fourths of the world's minerals, wealth and industrial might—more than all other nations of the earth combined? Which country was the Commonwealth's first colony to break away?"

"The United States?" she gasped. "It's us?! We're Manasseh? We're Israelites?!"

As the subway train's doors closed, Jeremy nodded his approval, a smile slowly creeping across his lips. "Yes," he mouthed.

Seconds later, the train disappeared into the dark tunnel.

Le An stood on the empty train platform, staring into the darkness where Jeremy's train had been. America's founders weren't Gentiles, but Israelites as much as the Jews were—descendants of Joseph, recipients of long ago promised blessings.

She stood there, not moving, the impact of Jeremy's revelation, combined with the heat of the subway tunnel, seeming to give her a numb, out-of-body experience. Gradually, more people came onto the platform in anticipation of the next train. Whatever her face was registering, and because she was standing so near the tracks, one man appeared concerned and said something to her.

"Sorry?" she asked.

"Are you all right, miss?" he repeated.

"Yes, I'm fine," she smiled at him.

Wanting to be alone with her thoughts, she turned and headed for the escalator before he could ask any more questions. She took the nearest street exit, but became disoriented when she realized she'd come out a different way from where she and Jeremy had first entered.

She needed to be quiet, to sit somewhere and process the new information. Glancing across the street, she noticed a small park and, as she looked to her left to check for traffic, stepped into the street. Just then someone roughly grabbed the collar of her jacket and jerked her backward.

50

London, England
Thursday, 18 September 2003

Le An's Krav Maga and defense training kicked in and she fought to defend herself. But she was exhausted, still in a fog from the day's events, and helplessly felt herself being pulled backward. She tried to swing her arms and elbows at her attacker just as a large truck blasted its horn and swooshed past in the curb lane where she would have been. The nearness of the massive, speeding vehicle, combined with the sudden mugging, frightened her even more and she fell backward, helplessly flailing away at her attacker.

"Catch her, Richard!" a gruff male voice said. "She's falling! Hey, stop fighting us! We're trying to help you, miss."

Stunned, she looked up at a plump, middle-aged Londoner, vaguely aware someone else was holding her from behind under her arms. Her backpack slipped from her shoulder to her arm, barely missing the pavement. She went limp and the man behind her, unable to lift her, slowly lowered her to a sitting position on the sidewalk.

"Are you all right, miss?" the one named Richard asked as both men bent over to talk to her. "It's a wonder that big lorry didn't flatten you. Another second and we'd have been taking you to hospital. We're not trying to hurt you. We stopped you from stepping in front of that lorry."

"Oh," she answered weakly.

Suddenly, she started shaking, the aftereffect of the adrenaline rush leaving her weak and unnerved.

"Look at her, Arthur," Richard continued. "She's shaking she's so scared."

"I'm sorry, I thought you were attacking me," she said and suddenly started crying, the release of exhaustion and built-up emotions surprising her. "I'm sorry," she blubbered, this time apologizing more for crying than thinking they were muggers.

"Don't cry, miss," said Arthur. "You're all right. You just have to remember to look *right*."

"You're the second person we've had to save today. See..." said Richard as he pointed to a street sign which read 'Look Right.' "You're in England, love. Traffic comes from the *right*. Look *right*."

She stammered and tried to say something, finally squeaking out a faint, "I forgot. Thank you. I'm...I'm so sorry."

She was mortified as she noticed people beginning to stare.

"Not every day we can be gallant knights and save a beautiful damsel in distress, eh, Richard?" smiled Arthur.

"No, the last one was a big, hairy bloke," Richard winked at him. "You Yanks are the worst stepping in front of traffic and looking the wrong way. It's a wonder more of you don't end up in hospital."

"Thank you for being so nice," she sobbed.

Now that her tears had been released, she was finding it hard to stop them.

The two men helped her to her feet and made sure she was steady, then slowly walked off to the right, glancing back a few times to make sure she was OK.

Suddenly, the park across the street didn't seem so relaxing.

Still shaking, Le An decided to start walking, but she was too embarrassed to go the same direction as her two rescuers. Instead, she turned to the left and noticed a tea shop a few doors away. Remembering she hadn't eaten all day, she headed for the door.

Once inside the restaurant, she relaxed a little in the soothing atmosphere of soft classical music and sunny yellow walls, the elegant china and silver gleaming on white-clothed tables.

Three giggling women in their twenties stood next to a table, and as Le An walked past them, she saw a man seated there appear to do a double-take. The hostess seated her at the table next to him, near the large picture window.

Trying to calm herself and collect her thoughts, Le An stared out the window for several minutes until her waitress appeared.

"Sorry, I haven't had a chance to look at the menu," she mumbled. "Could you just bring me a pot of Earl Gray and check back in a few minutes?"

"Le An, you didn't ring me," said the man behind her.

She groaned, annoyed he obviously knew her. That meant she'd have to make conversation and that was the last thing she wanted.

"I'm delighted you survived Iraq," he continued as she slowly turned to look at him.

It was Hugh Rose.

"And you," she smiled, relieved as well as pleased.

"Still editing your special?" he asked.

"We just finished," she said, surprised he remembered their last conversation. "It's running tonight in the States."

"Excellent." He started to smile, then looked at her and frowned slightly. "Is everything quite all right?"

She suddenly realized her eyes and lashes were still wet from crying.

"I...I hate yellow in decorating," she said pointing to the walls. "It's been upsetting me ever since I walked in."

He looked startled, then burst out laughing.

"It's been a really lousy day," she said as her waitress brought her tea.

"Sorry. Care to join me or would that make your day worse?" he asked and motioned to the empty chair at his table.

"It would be the one bright spot in my day," she smiled. "Thanks."

He jumped up and moved her teapot to his table, then pulled out the empty chair for her as she grabbed her backpack and picked up her cup and saucer. She glanced across at the three news groupies who'd been hounding him for autographs and thought she saw pure envy cross their faces.

When the waitress brought his order—a silver, three-level stand full of sandwiches and pastries—Le An ordered the same. The British did know how to serve a decent tea.

"I have to go back to BTN and present my last package before I leave on holiday. Care to join me at the studio?"

"Love to," she said.

51

London, England
Thursday, 18 September 2003

BTN's studio had changed somewhat since Le An had last been there. She recognized a few people and enjoyed catching up with them, but once BTN producers realized she was with their sister network in the US and had just returned from Iraq, they tried to persuade her to appear on one of their live news programs. She begged off joining a panel of guests discussing the war, saying she needed approval from her boss before appearing on another network, even if the networks did share stories and video.

The truth was she was tired and had a feeling the discussion would quickly dissolve into an attack against America's invasion of Iraq. Even though the UK was a close ally and its soldiers were securing southern Iraq, the war wasn't popular with most Brits.

Her prediction was right—much of the hour-long program was an attack against the US and she breathed a sigh of relief she'd dodged that bullet. No need to survive Iraq only to be slaughtered on live TV in London. British print and television press could be brutal.

While she waited for Hugh to appear on BTN's main evening news program, she called Tony in New York to make sure he'd received the feed of her segments.

"Everything OK?" she asked.

"Yeah, I've got your email with the shot sheets of where everything drops in, but some of your edit points are off," he said.

"What? Impossible," she said.

"It's not a big deal. Everything's dropping in fine," he said. "April had already pulled all the file video you needed, plus graphics and Sue's picking the music."

After hanging up, she tried to think what could have been

wrong on her edit points, but dismissed it since Tony had said everything was OK.

She stayed at BTN while Hugh fronted his package live for the early news. As she watched on a nearby monitor, she thought the camera didn't do justice to how great he looked in real life. His now stylishly-cut, chestnut-and-gray hair replaced the scruffier look he'd sported his last days in Baghdad, but then six months in a war zone weren't exactly conducive to great hair. It didn't matter. Whether he was wearing a designer suit or a flak jacket and jeans, Hugh Rose looked good. She wondered why she hadn't thought him that handsome on 9/11 or when she'd first seen him in Baghdad. His looks had improved directly proportional to her awareness of his intelligence and personality.

After Hugh was off air, she went over to tell him goodbye and thank him for lunch, but he asked her to wait for him. Noticing a few women in the newsroom staring holes through her, and guessing they might have been women he'd dated and dumped, she said in a low voice, "I'll wait in the lobby," before saying goodbye to her friends.

A few minutes later, Hugh dumped a cardboard box on the chair next to her, then disappeared, only to reappear a minute later with two other boxes.

"Do you not want to be seen with me?" he stage-whispered.

She grimaced slightly. "Sorry, a few women appeared to be giving me the evil eye. I didn't know if they were old girlfriends or if they just hate Americans."

He smiled and didn't answer, but motioned to the box on the chair and asked if she'd carry it. As they loaded the boxes in his black Range Rover, he said, "Care to join me for dinner?"

She'd planned to go back to her hotel, order room service, climb into bed and watch television, but his offer was better.

"I need to go back to the bureau later before our Iraq special airs," she said. "So please don't think I'm rude if I dash out."

"Dash away. Mind if I pop home and change?" he asked as he started loosening his tie. "My friends own a restaurant near my flat. Fancy eating there?"

"Sounds great," she said.

Traffic was typical London—bumper to bumper—and it had started raining. Gradually the cityscape changed from headache-inducing gridlock to a less congested, factory-laden neighborhood. A few trendy eateries, bars, art galleries and bookstores dotted the area, seemingly out of place for what appeared to have had a first life as an industrial neighborhood. Le An expected to see more off-track-betting parlors and bookies than books, but it appeared the area was going upscale and gentrifying. Instead of shutting down after the sun went down, shop and restaurant owners now enjoyed a brisk business.

Hugh drove into the garage of an old brick warehouse and parked between a navy blue BMW and a dented black Morris Minor.

"A Morris Minor!" said Le An. "I love these. My brother Jud owned three, probably the only ones in the US. Wrecked them all and rebuilt them."

"Did he instruct you?" Hugh asked dryly.

"Ha! He taught me to drive very well, very fast, to use radar detectors to avoid speeding tickets and to cry and act innocent if a cop ever stopped me," she said.

"Good to know," he said. "The Morris and Beemer are mine. I'm a bit of an auto fiend."

"You and my brother would get along well," she said.

Hugh's flat was large, but inviting, the combined living and dining space sporting deep-toned, oxblood-red walls with crisp white trim. Track lighting, as well as a wall of windows, brightened the room, countering London's rainy-or-overcast gray. Bookcases were packed with books, videos, DVDs and CDs, along with an abundance of electronics. Hugh popped a CD into the stereo and a luscious soprano poured from the speakers.

"I've been listening to this CD," said Le An.

"She's brilliant," he said. "Tragic she didn't become well-known until after her death. Strange she became big here in the UK first, even though she was American. Took you Yanks a while to finally notice your own."

Le An tried to politely take in the room without appearing too nosy. A large, framed, blue-and-white Scottish flag hung over a navy corduroy couch, reminding guests that even though the flat was in England, the owner's heart was north.

Souvenirs of Hugh's travels around the world—African masks, Asian artifacts, Greek pottery—were everywhere. Photographs of family and heads of state hung in matching black frames in the dining area. Two enormous red-hued Oriental rugs rested on random plank hardwood floors.

"Are your rugs from Baghdad?" she asked.

"No, Kabul," he said. "Were you in Afghanistan?"

"Yes, but not during the initial invasion," she said, gazing out the windows at a twilight-coated London. "What an amazing view."

"Better than Baghdad," he said as he came to stand behind her. "The area used to be industrial, but when I moved here, most of the buildings had been abandoned and were crack houses or hideaways for gypsies and illegals. A few of us began investing in the area and renovating. A few years on, more people moved in. This used to be four small rooms. I came in from a ghastly assignment in Rwanda, picked up a hammer and started beating the walls."

"Seriously?"

"Aye. After I'd put holes in every wall, I called my best mate Simon, who's a carpenter, and invited him over for a few pints. He wrenched the hammer away from me and told me to stop banging until he could figure out which walls and beams were holding up the flat above. I decided to stop short of bringing the neighbors' loo down on my head."

"One way to meet your neighbors—as they fall through your ceiling," she said.

"It felt good to destroy something. Wonderful therapy after stepping on row after row of dead bodies. The ground was covered with them. There was no place to walk."

"I'd heard. Pretty gruesome," she said, then tried to recapture a lighter mood. "Your remodeling paid off. This place is great."

He smiled and glanced around the apartment. "Thanks. I think Simon and I did a decent job. Mind if I change?"

"Not at all."

He pulled out two bottles of wine and held them up for her approval. "Red or white? Foch French-hybrid or a Napa Chardonnay."

"Foch sounds interesting. For the quarter-French in me."

"What're the other three quarters?" he asked.

"Quarter Vietnamese and half Scottish-American."

"Ah, yes. I remember you saying your father was of Scottish

descent. I knew there was a reason I liked you," he said.

She blushed slightly and turned to scan his music collection. "You have some oldies."

"I'm old. Forty-five last month," he said. "Not old enough for a pipe and slippers club, but too old to keep dodging through war zones."

"There are older out there. You've preserved well."

"Flattery will take you far, lass," he said as he handed her a glass of wine.

She took a sip, nodding approvingly. "It's good. Remember Barry, my photog with the bad attitude? We got into an argument over Jeremy's interviews. He thinks what he says is garbage and gave me a hard time when we were editing."

"What didn't he like?"

"Jeremy at times counters traditional Christianity," she said. "But he seems to have more facts to back up his beliefs than most people. Barry's Catholic and he believes his church's traditions are more important than facts. Are you Catholic?"

He shook his head 'no.' "What do you think?"

She shrugged. "I think Jeremy's refreshing. I've never been into religion, but what he says is common sense and historically accurate. I've done a lot of fact checking on it the last few weeks. Barry says people need traditions, even if they're wrong, if they give you emotional security. He refuses to consider anything else. The crazy thing is he's not that religious. I thought as a journalist he'd be open to truth."

"Change is difficult," he said, "and religion's always a sensitive subject."

"I suppose. Is tradition more important than truth?"

"Certain traditions are important to cultures, but as a journalist, I suppose I have to go with truth," he said.

"Me, too," she said and pointed to his television. "Do y'all still have to have a license?"

"Aye. Unfortunately, they haven't done away with that ghastly law. The Television Licensing Authority still monitors whether UK citizens are legally entitled to watch the telly. You know, the Beeb administers the TVLA."

"I remember. Do they still send TV police if you buy a set but don't buy a license?"

"Aye. You can be fined £1,000 if you're caught without a license."

"That's almost $1,700!" she gasped.

"And they heave you in jail if you don't pay the fine. The license is about £120 a year. Just our part to help the Beeb," he said sarcastically.

"That's so unfair to the poor," she said, shaking her head. "Doesn't it prevent them from getting TV news? How can they afford a yearly fee?"

"Good point, though most European countries have the same. Australia and the Netherlands abolished their licenses, no doubt trying to model themselves after you Yanks with your free TV."

"Good on 'em," she said. "What if you have a TV, but never watch BBC? Do you still have to pay?"

"You'd have a tough time convincing them you never watch," he said. "If you say you don't have a telly, they get warrants and search your home."

"Gives new meaning to Big Brother."

"Welcome to the UK. Telly or music? I've renewed my license, so you needn't worry about Scotland Yard dragging you off."

"I'll risk jail and go with the telly. Occupational hazard of working in TV. You always crave it. When's *Laird of the Highlands* on?"

"Sunday evenings, I believe. A fan of *Laird*, are you?" he asked, somewhat amused.

"Of course. I'm sure it's about my own long-lost MacDonald clan," she joked. "Are you a Scottish laird?"

"Nae, not a laird, not Clan MacDonald and I don't live at Glenloch. Sorry to disappoint."

"Do you have one of those little plaid skirts?" she teased.

"If you mean a kilt, yes. And it's tartan, not plaid," he said, handing her the remote and giving her a brief tutorial before disappearing into his bedroom to change.

She was asleep within minutes, but awoke with a start to find Hugh sitting on the coffee table next to her, staring vacantly out the windows.

"Sorry. I hated to wake you," he said softly. "You looked so peaceful. And I have bad news to report."

52

London, England
Thursday, 18 September 2003

Le An's heart started pounding as she sat upright, panicking more than if she'd been fully conscious.

Anguish was written all over Hugh's face as he said, "Piet van Gruen and Kent Barkley."

"What's happened?" she asked, her mouth now dry and cottony.

"They're dead."

The news sucker-punched her and she started gasping, finding it hard to breathe.

"What happened?" she asked.

"They were traveling with your American Marines today," he said, sadly gazing into her face, his eyes red. "Their convoy hit an IED. Two Marines and an American freelance cameraman were killed, too."

She grabbed both his arms above his wrists in a tight grip, unable to accept what he'd said.

"No," she whispered as her eyes also filled with tears.

One of the best decisions she'd made was hiring Piet and Kent to replace Khaled as her crew in southern Iraq. She could still see them cracking jokes at breakfast, teasing her about her cooking, lounging around on the tacky gold furniture, doing cannon-balls into the pool.

"Piet and I became close in South Africa covering the end of apartheid and we've remained close," Hugh said in a flat, not-fully-there tone. "He spent a holiday with me and my family in Scotland. He married two years past. He and his wife Helen have a daughter. I need to ring Helen."

Piet and Kent were dead—and she and Hugh were alive. Why?

She wondered whether she knew either of the Marines killed with them. Suddenly the last part of what Hugh had said hit her.

"Did you say an American freelancer died?" she whispered.

He nodded.

"Who was it?" she asked, her heart pounding even more violently.

"I don't remember. It's in the email."

"Could you check?" she asked, starting to feel sick. "It might be my friend."

It was bad enough knowing Piet and Kent were dead, but she couldn't handle losing Wen Darlington, too.

Hugh nodded and, as he stood, pulled her up with him.

As he rechecked the email at his bedroom desk, Le An stood behind him, gripping his shoulders as she leaned in to see the message.

"Not Wen, not Wen, not Wen," she whispered. "Please, not Wen."

53

London, England
Thursday, 18 September 2003

"Armenian, not American," said Hugh as he reread the email. "Andranik Manasyan. Sorry. I misread it."

Le An exhaled and sat down on the end of his bed. "It's not Wen."

She looked at the pained, vacant look on Hugh's face and asked, "Do you want to cancel dinner? If so, I understand."

He shook his head. "Nae, I don't fancy being alone. You?"

"Same. I was hoping you wouldn't take me up on that."

They looked at and through each other for a few seconds, their eyes filling with tears, grieving the loss of their friends and trying not to think how lucky they both were to have dodged death themselves. They knew—and every journalist in Iraq knew—it could happen to them. They tried to minimize risks as they did their jobs, but, ultimately, fate determined if they lived or died.

"Shall we go?" Hugh asked quietly.

Outside, he threw a protective arm around her shoulders, guiding her across the street toward Earth and Sky, a restaurant at the end of the block. She slipped an arm around his waist, snuggling in for comfort against the pain of their mutual loss. At the restaurant, Hugh grabbed her hand and pulled her behind him, bypassing the customers queued at the door.

Husband-wife owners Rupert and Carole Meade greeted him warmly. Rupert had been Hugh's videographer in New York on 9/11 and a month later in Afghanistan during the invasion. He'd taken early retirement from BTN, fed up with war, terrorism and news, opting to open the restaurant with Carole, a graphic designer.

It was a risk and had drained much of their savings, but the neighborhood was starting to grow. The Meades provided an eclectic menu and stylish decor, complete with live music most evenings. Instead of running in the red for years and folding within five, like most new restaurants, Earth and Sky, in just eighteen short months, had become a hot new destination for diners.

"Do you remember Le An?" Hugh asked Rupert as he seated them at a prime table in the main dining room. "The USN producer who helped us on 9/11?"

"Why, of course! Welcome!" said Rupert. He bent down and kissed her on both cheeks, then pointed to Hugh. "What are you doing with this hooligan?"

"Ran into him in Iraq and couldn't shake him," she teased.

"You were in Iraq? That deserves something special," he said and disappeared.

He reappeared with a bottle of champagne in an ice-filled bucket and poured glasses for the three of them.

"To survival," Rupert toasted and took a sip.

"To Piet and Kent, may they rest in peace," said Hugh.

Rupert look startled. "Piet van Gruen and Kent Barkley? They're dead?"

Hugh and Le An nodded.

His face dropped. "Iraq?"

"IED today," said Hugh.

Rupert stood there downcast, then grumbled, "Stupid war. What a waste of good men." He once again held up his glass. "To Piet and Kent."

"To Piet and Kent," said Hugh and Le An.

"Sorry, Carole will have my head if I don't get back. We'll be by to chat later," he said.

As he dashed off, Hugh said, "Rupert was smart. He took an early buy-out eighteen months ago."

"Burned out?" she asked.

"Afghanistan was the final straw. He stuck it out for two months and couldn't handle more. Carole'd been trying to get him to retire for years."

Their hearty meal of garlic-cinnamon lamb chops, mashed potatoes and glazed carrots, together with the flickering candlelight, champagne and wine soothed them into a somewhat mellow stupor, a welcome numbness after the news about their colleagues. When the band started playing *Avalon*, Hugh motioned toward the dance floor.

"Care to dance?" he asked.

Le An was taken aback, remembering his refusal to dance at the party in Baghdad. She glanced up at five couples already on the small dance floor.

"I thought you didn't like to dance," she said. "You wouldn't dance in Iraq."

"Didn't fancy it that night," he said and motioned again toward the small dance floor. "Care to?"

"You don't think it's irreverent?"

"I don't think Piet and Kent would mind," he said as he led her to the dance floor.

It was always awkward dancing with someone new—too physically close—but the alcohol and relaxing atmosphere had given her a slight buzz which took the edge off any self-consciousness. Still feeling a little numb from the news of their colleagues' deaths, she snuggled in close to him.

"This was the title track off the album. Do you know it?" he asked.

"Afraid not," she said.

"It's a London group. The album cover was a knight in a helmet, holding a falcon, moving across water toward an island, evoking King Arthur sailing to Avalon."

"King Arthur like Knights of the Round Table and Camelot?" she asked.

"The same. Avalon was where Arthur's sword Excalibur was allegedly forged and where he went to recover from his battle wounds."

"Is Avalon a real place?" she asked.

"Probably near Wales. Joseph of Arimathea allegedly carried the Holy Grail to Avalon and was buried there—a wee bit of a clue."

"Holy Grail?" she asked.

"The cup used at the last supper."

"Oh, yeah...the cup," she said. "Who's Joseph?"

"Tradition says he was Mary's uncle," he said.

"Mary?"

"Jesus' mum," he said.

"I thought Joseph was his dad, not his great-uncle, but then I don't know too much about religion," she said.

"Same name, two different people. I don't believe Mary married her uncle," he said, trying to conceal a smile. "Joseph of Arimathea allegedly gave his grave for Jesus' burial."

"Why would people think Avalon is near Wales when Joseph was in Jerusalem?"

"I forget you Americans don't know British history," he said.

"Do you know ours?" she asked.

"Not much," he grinned. "Tradition says Jesus' great-uncle Joseph of Arimathea lived in Glastonbury."

"Which is near Wales?"

"Aye. That area has tin mines and, as the story goes, Joseph of Arimathea was a tin trader with the Romans, that rather large empire which controlled much of the civilized world, including part of Britain," he said.

"Duh. I remember the Romans were here," she said.

"Never sure how much world history you Yanks absorb," he smiled. "Historical records show Joseph was given land near Glastonbury Abbey in the first century. Monks centuries on found King Arthur's grave there, too, along with a lead cross identifying it as the Isle of Avalon. Glastonbury used to be surrounded by a marsh. Its ancient Welsh name translates 'Isle of Glass.'"

"Arthur was a real king?"

"Supposedly in the sixth century. Tradition says he fought the Saxons and French and defeated the Romans. Geoffrey of Monmouth mentioned him in his history of British kings," he said as the song ended and he led her back to their table.

"Go back to Joseph of Arimathea," she said. "He moved from Jerusalem to England in the first century?"

"Aye. Tradition says a decade or two prior to the crucifixion, Jesus was traveling with his great-uncle Joseph and they were both in Glastonbury."

"What?" she gasped. "A physical Jesus was here in England? You're kidding, right?"

"Nae. The tradition says his father Joseph died whilst Jesus was young and, since he was the eldest son, he became the family's provider. In order to earn money to support them, he allegedly traveled the world with his great-uncle Joseph of Arimathea whilst he conducted his tin trade."

"Eldest son? You mean Jesus had other brothers?" she asked.

"And sisters supposedly," he said.

"Are you kidding? I never learned that at church. Are you like some religious guru?"

He made a face. "It's history and tradition associated with Glastonbury. Have ye ne'er heard England's unofficial anthem *Jerusalem*? They sing it at rugby games."

She slowly shook her head 'no.'

Hugh walked over to the band as they finished their next number and said something. As the band started performing *Jerusalem*, the entire room began loudly singing with them, overflowing into the restaurant's other rooms where those patrons joined in. The response overwhelmed Le An, leaving her slightly shell-shocked.

"And did those feet in ancient time, Walk upon England's mountains green? And was the holy Lamb of God, On England's pleasant pastures seen?..."

As the song finished, the restaurant's customers and staff all erupted in loud cheers, whistles and clapping.

"I've been in and out of London for years and never knew about this," she said, slowly shaking her head. "This is unbelievable. Whether it's true or not, Brits believe it."

"Aye," he said. "Or they like the song."

Suddenly she looked at her watch and gasped. "I have to go! Our Iraq special's airing in the States in a few hours and I need to get to the bureau. I left my phones in my backpack at your place, so if there's any problem with my segments and they tried to call me, I'm in big trouble."

54

London, England
Friday, 19 September 2003

Fortunately, there were no messages on her phone, but Le An knew she was late and had to get back to USN's bureau quickly. She figured the Tube was the fastest, but decided it was too risky to be on a subway platform that late at night. She wasn't even sure if trains were still running at that hour. But before she could call a cab, Hugh solved her dilemma by insisting he not only drive her, but come up to the bureau to wait for her and drive her back to her hotel.

USN's Iraq special was airing live in the Eastern and Central time zones from two to four in the morning London time. By the time Hugh dropped her off in front of the bureau, it was almost one. He left to find parking and she ran into the lobby, showed the guard her ID, signed in Hugh as her guest, then dashed for the elevator. At the fifth floor, she exited before the door had fully opened and slammed her shoulder into it. Running down the hall, she burst into the bureau slightly out of breath.

"Wondered if you were planning to make an appearance," said Andrea.

"Death and exhaustion have spaced me," she panted as she rubbed her sore shoulder. "By the way, Hugh Rose from BTN is on his way up."

A few people raised their heads and eyebrows at the mention of his name.

"Something you want to tell us," smirked Andrea, as a few people softly tittered. "Is he the death or the exhaustion?"

"Neither. We had dinner," she said defensively, hoping Hugh wouldn't come in while they were discussing him. "We were in Iraq together and ran into each other today."

She punched in the number to USN's New York offices. Elena didn't pick up her office phone and it routed to the main desk. By the time she picked up, she was out of breath, no doubt racing to finish last minute details before they went on the air.

"Just checking to make sure everything's OK."

"You must be really tired," said Elena.

"Very," she said.

"I can tell. Your run times were off and they're never off."

"What?" The comment caught her off guard. "What're you talking about?"

"A lot of your outcues and run times were off. Paul was annoyed, but cut you some slack because he figured you were tired."

"Impossible. I checked and rechecked them," she insisted.

She thought back to the previous evening when she and Barry had finished editing their segments. She'd been tired, but had stayed until her eyes were crossing to make sure everything was right.

"Off by how much?" she asked.

"Some segments a lot. Overall you were a minute ten short. We had to scramble a little to fill, but Jill's one segment needed more, so we split the time between hers and Kerry's. You OK? Your outs and run times are never off. *Chica*, what's up with you?"

"I don't know," Le An said slowly as she rubbed her temple. What had gone wrong? "Elena, I know you're busy, but email me the script, OK? I want to see what happened."

Le An quickly logged into USN's network on the closest computer and pulled up the rundown for the special, as well as her in-house email.

"You know your second script arrived after the first had already gone to legal," said Elena. "Why'd you miss your feed window?"

Le An gasped, "What?"

55

London, England
Friday, 19 September 2003

"Le, you didn't have any kind of brain injury in an IED blast, did you?" asked Elena. "You know two South African guys renting space at our Baghdad house were killed today. Skylar and the whole bureau are pretty upset."

"Piet was South African, Kent was Zim," she corrected her. "And yes, I know. They did sound and camera for me in Iraq."

"Oh, that's right. Good thing it wasn't you."

"They were great guys. Elena, what do you mean I missed the feed? Our segments were finished and Barry sent me home a few minutes before we had to put them up on the bird. He told me he made the feed."

"No, we had to rebook your feed time and Paul wasn't happy. You know how he hates to pay for unused sat time."

Hugh had come in by that time and was sitting near her. Seeing her puzzled look, he silently mouthed, "What's wrong?"

She shook her head.

"Elena, I need you to email the latest script to me right now," she said. "It's really important."

"Paul wants to talk to you, but now may not be the best time. He was pretty ticked off at all the screw-ups. Seriously, Le, what happened? Are you all right?"

"I'll have to get back to you. I don't want to talk to Paul until I can look at the script. I need you to send it right now."

"Gotta go. Crazy busy. In the mail," said Elena and slammed down the phone.

Le An tried to process the new information.

"Everything all right?" asked Hugh.

"No, and I'm not sure why," she said, "though I have an awful feeling I know who's behind this. Andie, did Barry give you our packs to feed to New York last night?"

Andrea kept her eyes on the monitor above her. "Ah...yeah. Last night, yeah. But Barry missed your window. He had me rebook."

"How could he miss our window?" asked Le An. "I watched him finish burning the disc ten minutes before we were scheduled to feed."

"He had me give the last fifteen minutes of the original window to the Baghdad bureau so they could feed us something. We couldn't get another window for three hours, but he needed that time to finish editing anyway."

Le An nervously ran her fingers through her hair. "Finish editing? We were finished editing. You're saying Barry fed our segments to New York at five instead of two?"

"Yeah," Andrea shrugged and went back to monitoring the feeds.

Now Le An knew why Barry said he hadn't been to bed before going to the airport. He'd been at the bureau until at least six. She dialed Skylar's Baghdad cellphone, listening to it ring five times before a groggy voice answered.

"Le," mumbled Skylar. "Horrible day and I just got back from an Army night patrol. Did you get the new tracks?"

She closed her eyes, the sickening feeling growing. "What new tracks?"

There was silence for a few seconds, then he said, "The ones Barry said you needed."

And there it was—what she'd hoped wasn't true. Barry had changed her script and re-edited without telling her. She fought to control her anger at the betrayal.

"Barry told you to track a new script?" she asked.

There was silence again and she thought they might have been cut off.

"Le, why do you sound as if you don't know?" he finally asked.

"Because I didn't change the script, Sky."

Silence again.

"Barry said you were making last minute changes. I didn't think anything about it, but..." Skylar's voice trailed off.

"But what?" she asked.

"The grammar and scripts weren't as good as yours normally

are. And some of the facts weren't right. It was odd, now that I think about it, but I was really tired. Le, did I do something wrong?"

"No, Sky. I've got your back, buddy. Don't worry about it," she said.

"Barry changed the script on his own?" he asked.

"Apparently."

"He can't do that," he said.

"Apparently he did. I know you're tired, but this is really important. I need you to forward Barry's email to me with the script changes he sent you. And I need it right now."

"I'm up," he yawned. "Firing up my computer. You'll have it shortly."

"Thanks, Sky."

"We lost Kent and Piet today," he said softly. "They were killed in an IED blast. It's been a horrible day, Le. You won't believe what it's like around here."

"Yeah, I heard. I'm sorry," she said softly. "Stay safe, OK?"

"I'll try. Listen, I'm sorry I teased you so much. It's all in fun. You know that, right?"

"No problem. You're a good guy, Sky."

"If anything happens to me, I want you to know it was a privilege working with you, Le. You're the best."

"Don't be maudlin, Sky. Listen, I'm in a time crunch. Send me that email right now, OK?"

"You got it."

"And, Sky, you did a great job on this assignment."

She hung up the phone, fighting tears of exhaustion and rage.

"My photog changed my script," she told Hugh. "Everything was edited and ready to feed and he changed my script and re-edited our packs."

Hugh looked shocked, as did most in the bureau. That a videographer and editor would dare to change a senior producer's script was unheard of.

After Elena's and Skylar's emails came through, Le An printed out her final script and Barry's revised one, then rummaged through drawers for red pens.

"Can anybody help?" she called out.

Three staff members ran over, eager to see how much Barry had changed, knowing the special was due to air within the hour.

"I'll help," said Hugh.

"These guys are already on the clock. You're on holiday," she said.

"My brain hasn't totally flipped off," he said. "And I did just down two cappuccinos."

As the four gathered around the conference table in the center of the room, she said, "I need y'all to number each page, divide them between you, then compare my script to Barry's revised one. Outline in red his parts different from mine and my parts he deleted. Check the outs and run times. New York said they're off."

She started rooting through her backpack, trying to find the backup DVD she'd burned off Barry's computer the night before. Now she knew why he'd kept trying to get her to go home without burning it.

It wasn't in her backpack.

"Where is it?!" she wailed, eliciting stares.

She hadn't had a chance to burn it to her hard drive yet. That was her only copy. Had she lost it? Her mind raced back through her day. It could have dropped out at the airport, in the cab, on the street outside the Tube when she'd almost stepped in front of a truck. Had she left it at the hotel? Had it fallen out at Hugh's? If so, she was doomed. There wouldn't be time for it to make air.

She went into a corner of the room and, after pulling out a few of the heavier items, upended her entire backpack onto the floor to frantically search the contents.

No DVD.

Had Barry taken it?

She unzipped all the pockets and searched through them.

No DVD.

She suddenly realized that even if she did find it, she needed feed time.

"Andrea, can I get a window to put something up on the bird as soon as possible?" she called out.

"I'll have to call and see what's available," she said as she popped out a DVD. "No guarantees. How much time do you need? What are you feeding?"

"I need about thirty minutes to feed my backup," said Le An, searching again through her backpack, hoping the DVD would somehow miraculously show up. "But I can't find it."

"That's because you don't have it," said Andrea. "You walked out of here without it last night. You were zoning you were so tired. You left it on the counter and took off before I noticed you'd forgotten it."

"What did you say?" Le An gasped as she slowly stood up.

"Hey, if I'd had a clue what Barry was doing last night, I would've stopped him and fed your backup," she said.

"Tell me you still have it," said Le An.

Hugh and the three others comparing the scripts stopped and looked at Andrea.

"Now wouldn't you just like to know? Hey! Why are you people staring at me? Get back to work!" Andrea barked at them. "Well, Le An, I tell you, I was going to give it to Barry, but, lucky for you, I didn't. I was going to keep it until it aired in New York, just in case anything went wrong."

"Are you sure it's the one I burned and not Barry's?" she asked.

"It's yours," said Andrea. "I watched you slide it onto the counter."

She pulled out the DVD and everyone started hooting and clapping.

"Andie, I love you," Le An said as she grabbed the jewel case and gave her a bear hug.

"Yeah, yeah, everybody does," she said and mimicked, "'Andrea, get us feed time!' 'Andrea, be Superwoman!' 'Andrea, save us!'"

The DVD couldn't air the way it was. There were black holes in some parts where file video needed to be dropped in and it didn't have the graphics or music track, but it was her original script and track. Someone in New York would have to bust a gut editing it to get it ready.

It was forty minutes to air. She knew a few other segments were before hers, so that gave her an hour, maybe longer, before her first segment aired. It was tight, but doable. She'd done it before, even editing right up until ten seconds to air.

"Who has the first segment?" she yelled.

"I do," said Hugh. "It's dealing with Mosul and Nineveh. Barry apparently made quite a few changes."

She glanced at the pages he held up and felt sick at the amount of red ink she saw. Barry had made major changes toward the middle and end of the first segment.

"This isn't happening," she whispered. "OK, even if we don't make Eastern and Central, New York will still have time to change it before Mountain and West Coast."

She dialed Paul's office in New York.

"Barry sent you the wrong version. You can't air what he sent you," she said, then closed her eyes and braced for his reaction.

"What?!" he screamed. "We're live in less than an hour! Brad! Live!"

She could just imagine him reaching for his Maalox.

"Stop yelling," she said. "I know Brad's anchoring. That's why you have to air my version and not the one you've got. Barry rewrote my script and re-edited after I left last night. That's why we missed the feed. He was re-editing his version. He sent his script to Skylar to retrack last night. That's why the outs and run times were off. Some of his information isn't even right. You can't air it."

"Are you trying to give me a stroke?"

From across the room Andrea called out, "If Paul gives the OK, I can give you our network window in five minutes."

Le An held up her index finger to wait, then frantically waved the jewel case for her to take. Covering the phone's mouthpiece, she said, "See if you can extend the network feed by thirty minutes."

Paul was still ranting.

"Look, I have my backup DVD," said Le An. "It needs some file video, graphics and music, but we could get it up on the bird in five minutes on the regular network feed. Please, Paul."

"What's on that feed we'd be bumping?"

"I don't know. I'll check," she said, then called out, "Andrea! What's on that network feed?"

At the same time Paul bellowed, "Shelly! Get me a list of what's on the next network feed! Now!"

"Look, Tony edited it this afternoon and knows where all the file video goes," Le An nervously pleaded her case. "He can pop this out in no time. And maybe we can extend the network feed so everyone can feed a half-hour later."

She looked over at Andrea for an answer, jiggling nervously as she bit her thumb nail. Andrea started nodding her head, giving a high-in-the-air thumbs up.

"It's cutting it too close and it's bumping a network feed," snarled Paul. "Besides that, we're live in Eastern and Central. And legal will have a fit if they haven't vetted it."

"Legal's seen my script, but they may not have vetted Barry's version, another reason not to use his. Please, Paul. Andrea says they can extend the network feed, so everything on there will only be thirty minutes late, but it'll be there."

She heard him sigh deeply.

"I should've known this wasn't going to go smoothly," he mumbled. "All right, get it up on the bird, call Tony and coordinate this thing. But I make no promises. If it's not finished in time, I'm going with what we've got. Are you in the London bureau?"

"Yes. Right here, ready to feed." She gave the thumbs up to Andrea to feed the DVD and mouthed at her, "Go, go, go!"

Everyone stuck their hands in the air in a silent cheer.

Le An called out, "Somebody call Tony's edit suite in New York and have him hold for me."

"Stay at the bureau, Le An," barked Paul.

"I'm not leaving," she said.

"I'm calling you after this airs."

"Yes, sir."

"You were more than a minute short. That means other segments are running longer to fill your time. You realize we're now going to have to edit those, too? What a nightmare," he muttered, then screamed, "Shelly! Get me Elena! She's going to have to clean up this mess."

"I had no idea Barry was going to go rogue on me," she said. "I should have stayed while he was feeding. It's my fault for not being here. I knew he'd been acting strangely the last few weeks."

"We'll discuss this later," he said abruptly and hung up.

She felt winded, but shook it off and quickly punched in *AmeriView's* main number.

"Tony's on two!" someone called from across the room.

She quickly put her line on hold and punched the blinking red button. "Tony? It's Le An. Hold for me. It's urgent."

Without waiting for a reply, she put him on hold and came back to her original line just as she heard the operator say, "...*AmeriView*. Can I help you?"

"This is Le An. Quick! Connect me to Elena."

56

London, England
Friday, 19 September 2003

After the special, as Le An entered Barry's home number on the wall phone near Andrea, she pounded each button with such force, the phone's outer cover came half-way off. She gave one good punch with the palm of her hand, slamming it back into place.

"Hey! Don't take it out on my phone!" yelled Andrea. "Calm down, girl. We're on your side."

"Sorry, Andie," she muttered, then, as Kristen answered the phone, without even a pretense of being civil, demanded, "Let me talk to Barry. And I don't care how tired he is or if he's asleep. Wake him up."

She tried to remind herself not to let her anger get out of control.

"He said he's too tired to come to the phone, Le An," said Kristen. "He'll have to talk to you tomorrow."

"Put him on or I'll climb through the phone and choke both of you."

So much for anger control.

"Uh, oh," said someone on the other side of the room, causing a ripple of snickers.

Le An heard muffled voices as Kristen put her hand over the phone's mouthpiece. After a few seconds, Barry finally got on the line.

"You snake," Le An started the conversation in a low tone through clenched teeth, her body shaking with anger. "You underhanded, back-stabbing, slithering-in-the-grass snake. Did you honestly think you'd get away with this?"

As the words tumbled out, her body calmed while her voice

climbed the decibel chart. She started pacing back and forth, jerking the long phone cord, then flipping it up and over the head of a startled producer before she almost strangled him.

"How dare you change my script! How dare you re-edit my segments! Who do you think you are to rewrite a senior producer's script? How presumptuous are you? And you didn't even get the facts right. How dare you drag Skylar into this and miss a feed slot! Do you know what it cost us to rebook feed time last night and tonight? We had to bump a network feed tonight to get the correct version to New York. Not to mention all the people in New York who had to spend extra time re-editing the segments. You made them do twice as much work. I should have sent you home after Nineveh and hired Wen Darlington because, let me tell you, snake, you've been out of control for weeks."

"And a good evening to you, Princess," Barry answered sarcastically.

"Shut up, snake! Unless you're apologizing to me, don't talk," she snapped. "Consider yourself lucky if you still have a job tomorrow, because I guarantee you, I will make it my mission to get you fired after pulling a stunt like this."

"Your script needed to be changed, Le An," he shot back angrily. "I was saving your butt and your job. You should thank me."

She was so speechless she could only spit out, "What?!"

"That's right," he continued. "You were buying into everything that phony professor-archaeologist-doctor-whatever was saying to you. Jeremy's crazy and he was making you crazy. You're forgetting everything and you're so burned out, you couldn't even tell he was giving you wrong information. You said yourself you don't know anything about religion. Well, I do. And that guy's crazy. I was doing you a favor. I did it to save your job and your reputation."

Le An was so livid, she couldn't push words past her tongue. Suddenly, a stabbing pain shot through her chest and she found herself unable to take a full breath. She dropped the receiver, sending it crashing onto the ledge under the feed monitors before it bounced off and fell to the floor. Using her right hand, she grabbed the upper portion of her left arm, sharply pulling it in close to the side of her chest in an attempt to stop the pain.

She could hear a collective gasp from those in the newsroom as Andrea and Hugh ran toward her. Hugh reached her first, a concerned look on his face.

"What's happened?" he gasped.

"Get me over to the wall," she whispered. "Lean me up against it and slide me down to a sitting position on the floor."

"Ring 9-9-9!" he called out. "She's having a heart attack!"

57

London, England
Friday, 19 September 2003

"No!" Le An gasped and protested as the small overnight staff gathered around her. "I'm not... having a heart attack."

"I'm going to need a Valium before this shift is over," mumbled Nigel, a young satellite feed assistant. "This is drama on steroids."

"Shut up!" Andrea snapped at him. "Back away!"

"Should we give her aspirin?" asked the producer Le An had almost strangled with the phone cord moments before. "Don't they give aspirin to people having a heart attack? Or is that a stroke? Or both?"

"Not...a heart attack," Le An whispered. "I'm fine."

"You don't look fine," said Hugh.

She leaned back against the wall, the pain subsiding a little. Finally able to get a breath, she exhaled slowly and smiled up at them. "Really, I'm OK. Everybody go back to work."

"All right! You heard her! Back away, people!" barked Andrea, the junkyard dog of the newsroom. She waved her arms, shooing them away. "Nothing to see! I said go! Yeah, you! Stop looking at me! Nigel! Are you monitoring those feeds? Am I the only one with a brain around here?"

Le An kept a tight grip on her left arm, the pain in her chest still there, her breathing still strained, but slowly returning to normal.

Andrea bent down to peer into her face and said matter-of-factly, "You look terrible."

"Thanks, Andie," she whispered.

"Have you had these attacks before?" asked Hugh, who by then was squatting down next to her.

She closed her eyes for a moment and exhaled again. "It's not my heart."

"So you have had them before," he said. "What is it, if not your heart?"

She looked away, without answering him.

"I think you should go to hospital," he said.

"*The* hospital," she said. "What is it with you Brits dropping the definite article before 'hospital.' I'm not going to *the* hospital."

"Unbelievable. She's snarky and giving grammar lessons even when she's having a heart attack," Andrea mumbled as she stood up, then snapped at her assistant, "What, Nigel? What do you want?"

"It's Paul ringing from New York," he said timidly, afraid to further arouse her wrath. "He wants to speak with Le An."

"Well, he's not gonna. Like she needs one more stressful conversation," said Andrea and snatched the phone from him, taking the call off hold. "Paul, it's Andie. Le An can't come to the phone right now because she's having a heart attack. We'll call you after paramedics check her. They're here now."

Without waiting for his answer, she hung up as the medical crew made their way through the newsroom.

58

London, England
Friday, 19 September 2003

Le An begged paramedics to leave her on the floor, afraid if they moved her, the pain would intensify. Within minutes, her heartbeat and blood pressure had returned to normal, but, in spite of their stern warnings, she refused to go with them for a more extensive examination. Shaking their heads at her obstinance, they reluctantly left without her, but not before warning her how much danger she could be in.

"Do you want to die?" asked one exasperated paramedic.

"After the day I've had, frankly, yes," she said. "We all have to go sometime."

Hugh shook his head, upset with her decision. "You should have let them take you to hospital to have tests."

"I had tests done a few weeks ago and my heart got an A plus," she said. "I'm not lying."

"What if it's something else?" he asked. When she didn't answer, he said, "All right, then. You need rest. We should go."

"I have to call Paul first. What's the closest phone so I don't have to get up? Andie, can you get Paul on the line?" she asked, pointing to the wall phone she'd tried to punch out earlier.

The scare over her health had mellowed Paul's reaction to the chaos which had hit just before the special's airing.

"Why aren't you in the ER?" he asked. "How are you?"

"They call it A&E over here," she said. "I'm fine. Not a heart attack."

"Then what was it?"

She didn't want to tell him.

"What was it?" he repeated. "A stroke? Or is that what you're trying to give me?"

"Not a heart attack. Not a stroke."

"I want you to go to a hospital and get checked out," he said.

"I don't want to," she said. "Besides, I was checked out a few weeks ago."

"What aren't you telling me?" he asked.

"I'm fine, Paul."

"All right. You can sit out for a while."

She gasped incredulously. "I'm suspended?"

She suddenly noticed everyone staring at her.

"Think of it as a paid medical vacation," he said. "You're taking a few days off. It's not a request, it's an order."

"Am I being punished because of the special or because I won't tell you what's wrong with me?" she asked.

"You're not being punished and you're not being suspended," he sighed, his voice one part exhaustion, one part exasperation. "I'd prefer you not die on my watch. I've got enough Jewish guilt. Do you feel well enough to calmly tell me what happened with the royal screw-up on your segments?"

"If I tell you what caused the problem…"

"Which problem are we referring to?" he asked. "The one that almost crashed my show or the one that'll require you obtain a doctor's clean bill of health before you come back?"

"I went to the doctor a few weeks ago," she said. "You know I wouldn't be able to travel oversees if I hadn't."

"I don't give a tiny rat's ass," he snapped. "You obviously need a new doctor or you've got a new disease."

Exhausted, she felt the events of the last few weeks tumbling in on her like giant dominos. She lowered her voice so no one else in the newsroom could hear. "My doctor said I was fine. Tonight was just a stress attack, courtesy of Barry."

"Tell me why we were minutes short of having a network special crash," he said, appearing to change the subject.

She slowly exhaled, relieved her health no longer interest him.

"What'd you think of the segments? Better or worse than Barry's?" she asked.

"You know they were better. Certainly more provocative. The switchboard lit up with complaints and accolades. I'm going to have to see what Barry objected to enough to risk changing a senior producer's script. Of course, both your names are dirt here for making everyone work triple-time before it aired." He paused a moment, then casually added, "Brad loved it."

She smiled broadly. "Good."

"Yeah, that's good."

"Paul, why didn't someone call me earlier and tell me my run times were off, that my outs were wrong, my segments were short?" she asked. "I know y'all knew. Why didn't someone yell at me, question me, something?"

"I told them not to," he said.

"Why?" she asked annoyed.

"Because I knew you'd dealt with a lot on this assignment and you're burned out. I cut you some slack, OK?" he said.

"No, not OK," she said. "Sweet, but not OK."

"Don't let that sweet part get around. It'll kill my rep. Let's address that stress attack you just mentioned," he said, clearly not about to let it drop, even after a fifteen-hour day. "Have you been getting a lot of these 'stress attacks,' as you call them?"

She ignored directly answering the question, saying instead, "It hit as Barry was telling me he'd sabotaged my segments for my own good because he thought Doctor Hilson and I were crazy."

"Altruistic, huh? I guess that would explain why, when he dropped off the equipment today, he told us you were having a meltdown."

"What?!" A sudden stab of pain caused her to once again shift the phone receiver and use her right hand to pull her left arm up close to the side of her chest. "Now I'm really going to slap him senseless, not that he isn't already," she gasped out the words, trying to will the pain to subside.

"I know the complaints you've had about him during this assignment," he said, "and his 'Catholic fatwa,' as you call it. But I had no idea he'd do something this stupid. I guess he thinks I'm crazy, too, because I liked Hilson."

"Are you going to suspend Barry?" she asked.

"I don't know. I want to get his version and talk to Skylar and Andrea. But I guess I can't assign the two of you to the same crew anymore and that's a shame. You did some great work together. Maybe you both need to cool off. He's probably as burned out as you are. Listen to me and listen carefully, because I'm not messing around, Le. You're not coming back to New York. Go to a doctor over there and get a thorough examination. Now. Do you hear me? The last thing I want is for you to get on a long flight, have a heart attack somewhere over the Atlantic and be hours from a hospital. I don't want you off-loading in a body-bag. Got it?"

"I'm suspended *and* I can't come home?"

He sighed heavily. "For the last time, you're not suspended. You're on medical leave and forced vacation, but if you keep pressing me on this, I'm going to suspend you for insubordination, so I suggest you stop arguing and make your way to a doctor ASAP. The sooner you get a clean bill of health, the sooner I'll reassign you. Keep a phone with you. And may I suggest while you're protesting my decision and rebelling against seeing a doctor, as I know you will, which is why I'm going to call and harass you every day, may I suggest you do some sightseeing, go to a spa, get some sleep—and go to a doctor. That's an order."

"Doctors already poked at me."

"Have them poke in different places. For all you know, you picked up some strange disease in Iraq."

"It's just stress—the same thing that makes you swig Maalox."

"Smart guy. Go to a doctor and get some rest. And, Le, great job, as always."

With that he hung up.

Le An stayed on the floor, too exhausted to move, waving the receiver above her head so someone would hang it up.

"Are you suspended?" asked Andrea, as she took the phone.

"No, Paul ordered me to take medical leave slash paid vacation, to rest and enjoy myself. Like I really know how to do that. I'm not allowed to fly home because he's afraid I'll flatline over the Atlantic."

"That wouldn't be good for his ulcer," said Andie as she went back to work.

"On holiday, are you?" asked Hugh. "Shall we leave?"

"We shall," she said and stuck out her right hand for him to hoist her off the floor. "You must be exhausted. I know I am. Thanks for everything tonight. You shouldn't have stayed. I feel horrible I've kept you up so late and you're leaving on vacation in a few hours. Are you driving or flying?"

"Driving. Wouldn't have missed the evening's excitement. I rang my bosses and told them they should air parts of your program. Don't know if they were planning to, but if it hadn't made their radar, they should consider it."

"USN would like that."

Le An thanked everyone for their help and, as she and Hugh walked back to his car, he asked, "What are your plans?"

"Well, I thought I was going home later today, but now I guess I'm sleeping late, ordering room service and going to hospital," she said, deliberately dropping the definite article.

"*The* hospital," he corrected her. "All right, that's settled. You're coming to Scotland."

"I couldn't impose like that," she said, stunned at his offer. "You're going home to see your family. They don't want a complete stranger intruding."

"My sister Taryn and her husband own a B-and-B outside Edinburgh. Their business is having strangers intrude on them," he said. "Unless you think you won't fancy my family."

"I'm sure your family's lovely."

"They're a bit daft, but we have brilliant doctors and hospitals in Edinburgh. Unless you don't fancy Scotland," he said.

"I've never been."

"And you call yourself Clan MacDonald," he chided.

She quickly accepted his invitation, suddenly having a strong desire to get far away from London. She was tired of noise, crowds, news and war. Secretly, she was glad Paul was making her take the time off she'd requested in Iraq.

She was even more delighted to have such a pleasant diversion.

Back in her hotel room, Le An called her New York home number.

"Dahlin', what a wonderful program tonight," Kate said. "I was wondering if you'd call. I was so proud of you, with your name there on the screen for millions to see. Oh, I know it's there every week, but this was special. It was wonderful, punkin."

Hearing her mother's voice was like opening flood gates on a swollen river. Le An burst into tears, wishing she could be close to her.

"Dahlin'. Dearest dahlin'. What's the matter, precious? Why's my baby girl crying?" Her mother's soft Southern accent with one soft tap cracked the hard veneer Le An normally kept around her for protection.

"I miss you," she blubbered. "I want to hug you.'

"Oh, dahlin'. You're making me cry. What's the matter, precious? Tell me."

"One of my best friends stabbed me in the back," she sobbed. "Elena?"

"No, Barry, my photographer. He sabotaged my segments."

Le An recounted what he'd done and the frantic rush to get her original edit on the air.

"That old mean Hun. You want me to beat him up?" Kate joked.

"Could you?" She knew her feisty mother wouldn't hesitate for a minute to verbally rip into him. "Go get him, Ma!"

As they laughed and joked, Le An felt the tension leaving her body, the pain in her chest fading. She leaned against the bed pillows and closed her eyes, soaking in her mother's voice, letting it transport her to less grown-up, complicated times.

"Thanks for helping me unpack, Mom," she said. "I've been checking the pictures on the decorator's website and it looks great."

"We're almost finished. I don't know if you'll be able to stand not weaving through that maze of boxes. April's anxious to move in. She calls every day reminding us not to rent the basement studio to anyone else. What a little character. She's a sweet girl, but that dreadful New York accent of hers is like fingernails on a chalkboard. I don't know how you stand living in this city. But the sooner April moves in, the sooner you can start collecting rent to pay for all this. Elena's been wonderful. We've gone to dinner a few times and she got us tickets to *Avenue Q*'s Sunday matinee. It's getting great reviews. Are you coming home tomorrow? Maybe you can go with us."

"Paul's giving me a few days off, but he doesn't want me to fly home yet."

"Why not?"

Le An wasn't anxious to tell her, but didn't want her to hear it from April or Elena. "I had a little incident tonight. Barry got me so upset, I got a pain in my chest, but it's just stress. I'm OK. I'm going to see a doctor."

"Oh, dahlin'! I don't like the sound of that. How do you know it's just stress? It could be something more serious. I want you to see a cardiologist."

"I'm sure it's nothing to worry about," said Le An.

"Maybe you picked up something in that filthy Iraq."

"It's nothing. I just got a little too angry with Barry."

"I'll give him a piece of my mind for getting my girl upset. What's his number?"

"You're a riot, Ma," Le An smiled.

"I don't want you to be alone if you're sick, precious. Maybe I should come be with you."

"Well, actually, a journalist friend invited me to Scotland. His family owns a bed and breakfast outside Edinburgh, so I'm seeing a doctor up there."

"Your friend's a he?" Kate teased.

"Yes, he's a he," she laughed. "You'd like him. He's very sweet. Tall, handsome, Scottish. But he's an on-air and you know I'm trying to wean myself off pretty-boy talents."

"Oh, pooh. Enjoy your little eye candy, as you and Elena call them. What's his name?"

"Hugh Rose, but don't say anything to Elena or April."

"My lips are sealed," said Kate. "Take lots of pictures. And see what you can find out about Robert the Bruce and the MacDonald clan."

"I think the Scots call it Clan MacDonald, but I probably won't have much time for genealogy. Professor Hilson told me the Bruces came from France and were Normans."

"So I've read. Well, I hope this Hugh's better than that Luke character. He wasn't worthy of my girl. Now, punkin, it's late. Goodness, what time is it there?"

"A little after five."

"Oh, mercy. Get to bed, you crazy girl. We'll talk later."

As Le An hung up the phone, she felt an immense relief, not only from talking to her mother, but from revealing what she'd kept secret. The problem was she was still concealing something.

No one knew she'd been having chest pains for months—and they were becoming more frequent.

59

London, England
Friday, 19 September 2003

Elena answered on the third ring.

"Were you asleep?" asked Le An.

"Is this the woman who likes to make my life hell?"

"I'm so sorry, Elena. Thank you for helping to fix this mess. I owe you big time, girlfriend."

"Yeah, you do. And don't think I won't make you pay up."

"You do know it was Barry who caused this?" she asked.

"Yeah, we know. By the way, he's telling everyone you're crazy, you've got PTSD and you're menopausal, suicidal and homicidal."

"Homicidal is right. If we were on the same continent, I'd hunt him down and choke him," said Le An.

"You're up early. What time is it there? Almost five?"

"I haven't been to bed yet," she said. "Did I wake you? That's all I need after putting you through this tonight."

"Hell, no, I'm not asleep. I was doing *cortadito* shots with Tony all night. Plus, Paul bought the staff four huge boxes of those chocolate chip cookies from downstairs and they were still warm."

"Maggie K's? I love those. And that *cortadito* paint stripper you call coffee?"

"It was great. But I had to smack the interns away from the cookies or they would've eaten them all, the little vultures. So right now I'm totally wired. I'm working my way through a blender of frozen margaritas to bring me off the caffeine, sugar and adrenaline high. I'm calling in sick tomorrow."

"You'll be buzzing all night. Listen, thanks for being so nice to my mom. Dinners? Broadway shows? You're totally spoiling her."

Elena burst out laughing. "She's great. You'll have to fight me for her. Wish she was my mother instead of that *Cubana loca* I got stuck with. When are you coming back? You're not suspended, are you?"

"No, but I need to get a checkup."

She didn't really want to tell Elena what had happened, but she knew the way gossip flew she'd soon find out—along with most of the USN staff.

"A medical checkup? Why? Did something happen to you in Iraq?"

"You didn't hear? I kind of had an incident at the bureau in the middle of Barry telling me he sabotaged my segments for my own good."

"OK, there is something seriously wrong with that guy. I think he's the one with PTSD. What kind of incident?"

"I got a pain in my chest."

"You mean like a heart attack?" Elena gasped.

"I think it was just stress from what Barry had done. And I've got a twitch in my left eye," she said, then changed the subject. "Would you sabotage another producer's segment if you didn't agree with the religious views of someone being interviewed? Let's say it's someone higher up, like Brad. Would you sabotage his segment if you didn't agree?"

"Are you crazy? Do I have a death wish to sabotage my superior's segment? Put my job on the line for insubordination? The answer would be 'hell no.'"

"What if you really disagreed?"

"Again, hell no. I'm not putting my job on the line for some sound bite about religion."

"Why do you think Barry did?"

"He's *loco*. Maybe he's seen too much combat and needs a therapy session or a vacation. He could be fried. By the way, I still can't figure out why he got so bent out of shape. I thought your segments were really interesting, but then I'm agnostic."

"But you cross yourself."

"Habit from school. The nuns would smack your knuckles with a ruler if you didn't."

"You went to a Catholic school, but you're agnostic?"

"Yeah, what does that tell you?" Elena laughed. "My parents thought Catholic schools were better than public schools. And they thought the discipline was better. Had nothing to do with religion. I didn't grow up in a religious family. My parents are from Cuba. Fidel doesn't do religion, remember? Communist country? Hello! My parents are Catholic, but not that much, just enough to be respectable. And me? Not at all. I don't care what the Pope wants me to do, I'm not doing it. You know *Cubanos*—we've got an independent streak ninety miles wide from Havana to Key West. We'd rather swim with the sharks than live with Fidel telling us how to breathe."

"I just thought since you're Catholic, you might object to things Doctor Hilson said that are different from what you were taught."

"It didn't bother me, but there are Catholics and there are Catholics," she said.

"What do you mean?"

"With *Cubanos* you never know what you're going to get. There are two groups of religious Catholics who love the Pope: the ones who always go to Mass and those who never go. A lot of us are atheists or agnostics, because that's what you get when your non-religious family is from a non-religious country. Then there are Catholics who are Santeria. They sacrifice a few chickens at the courthouse..."

"What?" laughed Le An.

"Oh, yeah! Miami-Dade courthouse is probably the only one in the country where they have a dead chicken patrol. First thing in the morning they clean up all the chickens the Santeria have sacrificed on the courthouse steps the night before."

"Oh, my word. How did I not know that? Is that for good luck or something?" she laughed.

"Good luck or putting a curse on someone they're going to court against. My family's not Santeria, but I had an auntie who was. Not blood related. My father's brother's second divorced wife. She's crazy. My uncle's convinced she put a Santeria curse on him and our whole family when they got divorced, but I don't know if I believe that."

"I thought Catholics weren't supposed to get divorced," she said.

"They find a way, either ignore the Pope and have a justice of the peace marry them or convince a priest to annul their previous marriage—even if they had kids. It's crazy."

"What about Barry?" asked Le An.

"Barry's Italian Catholic. Some of them think they own the Pope. You know, *Roman* Catholic."

"But he's from New York," she said.

"Doesn't matter. I bet his mother goes to Mass every day."

"He was an altar boy."

"There, you see. And his mother probably wanted him to be a priest. Don't think Barry's the poster boy for all Catholics. A lot are non-practicing, except when they get married, die or want their kids baptized or confirmed. Sometimes they'll go to church for Good Friday, but skip Easter. Or they'll go to midnight Mass Christmas Eve, but skip Christmas."

"But those are traditions," said Le An. "You're saying Catholics may not be religious, but they still cling to religious traditions. You just said you're agnostic, but you keep Christmas."

"Who doesn't keep Christmas?" asked Elena.

"Muslims, Jews... well, no, some of them get Christmas trees, which I totally don't get. They have a week of Hanukkah and get presents every day. Why do they need a Christmas tree? Do you think truth is more important than tradition?"

"Me? I'm a journalist. For me, truth is a biggie," said Elena.

"You just said you're not sure if you believe in God, but you keep a day supposedly celebrating his birthday out of tradition, even though you say truth is important."

"You're giving me a bigger migraine than I already had," said Elena. "When did you get on a religious kick?"

"No kick, just polling people about their religious beliefs."

"Well, stop it. People will think you're getting weird," said Elena.

"What if someone told you Christmas started as a day to worship green aliens? Would you still celebrate it?"

"Is that why we have green Christmas trees—in honor of little green men? Yeah, I'd still celebrate. I love Christmas. It doesn't matter how it started. It's what it means now."

"What does it mean?" asked Le An.

"Peace, joy, love and all that crap."

"You don't celebrate it for religious reasons?"

"No, for food, family and presents. Haven't you been listening to me?" asked Elena in an irritated tone. "Is this for some segment you're working on?"

Le An paused before answering, surprised she hadn't thought of that. If another network could do a documentary about looking for Jesus, maybe she could pitch a show on Christian truth.

"Maybe," she finally said.

"You make it sound like it's some big secret," said Elena. "Nobody's going to steal your idea."

"I've had ideas stolen before and so have you."

"Yeah, you're right. When are you coming back? You aren't suspended, are you? Is Barry?"

"No, I'm not suspended. I don't know about Barry. Paul's dealing with him. I'm going to take a few days off before I fly back. I want to relax. I've got a ton of comp and vacation time I have to use up before the end of the year."

She stopped short of telling Elena about Hugh and Scotland. One friend had already stabbed her in the back. She wasn't about to trust anyone else at USN.

Besides, she knew the gossip about her having dinner with Hugh and bringing him to the bureau was probably already working its way from Britain to New York via phone and email.

60

England
Friday, 19 September 2003

"I don't think I can do this anymore, Hugh," said Le An an hour into their drive north on the M1 motorway.

He gave her a startled look.

"You mean I'm going to have to find a train back to London for you?" he asked.

"No, I meant news producing. I don't want the stress anymore. It's killing me. I'm so over it."

"Welcome to my world," he said.

"Do you know why I never want to take a vacation?" she asked. "Because I'm afraid my bosses will realize they can get along without me. How bad a control freak is that? I've been having stress attacks for months, but I'm afraid to tell anyone because then I won't get the good assignments. And if my boss doesn't accept the stress and thinks I have a bad heart, he won't give me *any* assignments, I'll never get to travel and I'll be stuck in New York all the time. Which might not be bad because I'm not even sure I want to travel anymore, but once I get taken off the good assignments, management will start thinking I'm worthless and the next time they have to make cuts, they'll look at me and say, 'Why are we keeping her and why are we paying her so much? Boot her out.' And you cannot tell anyone what I just said."

He glanced over at her, then back at the road. "It's all off the record."

"The problem is," she continued, "all that overtime, no breaks, no personal life, war zones, airplanes, strange hotels, more airplanes, back-stabbing co-workers, exhaustion and more airplanes have totally burned me out."

He nodded. "You Yanks really need to learn how to go on holiday. Increases productivity. I've never figured out why American companies abuse their employees by not giving them adequate time off."

"You are so right," she said. "Thanks for offering me the chance to get out of London."

"Delighted you could come. Shame you had to be forced to go on holiday."

"Pathetic, isn't it?" she said. "I'm starting to envy Rupert and Carole with their restaurant."

"Don't. They have their stresses, too," he said. "They weren't certain they'd last the year, but fortunately business increased."

As Hugh merged his BMW onto the M6 motorway heading north toward Birmingham, Le An's Britain-based cellphone rang.

"Bet I know who this is," she said.

"Have you seen a doctor?" asked Paul before she'd finished saying 'hello.'

"And a good day to you, too," she said. "I don't get a hello?"

"Hello. Have you seen a doctor?"

"I think one just drove by. You ordered me to take a relaxing vacation and that's what I'm doing. I'm driving up to Scotland with a friend and plan to see doctors in Edinburgh."

"They don't have doctors in London now?" he snapped.

"I had an invitation I couldn't turn down," she said. "And if you keep asking me if I've seen a doctor, it's going to get annoying."

"I don't give a tiny rat's ass. I'll tell you what's annoying: you having a heart attack in the middle of the London bureau is annoying. Now get to a doctor."

"It wasn't a heart attack. It was a stress attack courtesy of Barry."

"Go see a doctor. And enjoy your vacation," he said before abruptly hanging up.

"Doesn't anybody say goodbye anymore?" she mumbled, then asked Hugh, "How long is the drive?"

"Bit less than six hours. About 500 kilometers. Allowing for stops, we'll arrive after nine. Think you'll survive?"

"I'm enjoying the drive. Let me know if you're tired and want me to drive."

He gave her a horrified look.

"I've driven stick in England before and haven't had an accident," she said. "Of course, I always end up with a big bruise on the back of my right hand because I keep slamming it into the door handle reaching for the stick with it instead of my left. And you might have to keep reminding me to stay left and look right. Sometimes, I think this country's trying to kill me."

He gave her a dubious look and said, "I'll drive."

Conversation flowed easily as they shared humorous, annoying and frightening stories of their jobs, lives and families, noshing on fruit, gourmet sandwiches and brownies from Le An's hotel restaurant. As they passed the exit sign for Glasgow, Edinburgh and the A74, she lost the battle to stay awake.

Mellow music and singing seeped into her dream, floating her above a Scottish field of purple heather, majestic mountains rising before her, spears of warm sun shooting through the mist. As she slowly regained consciousness, she realized Hugh had thrown his leather jacket over her.

"I like that song," she murmured.

"Sorry to wake you. I needed music to wake myself."

"Sorry I fell asleep. I didn't mean to," she yawned and stretched as much as the front seat would allow. "Is that a Scottish folk song?"

"Aye. The poet Robbie Tannahill wrote *The Braes O' Balquidder*, but this is an Ulster Scot's version. He changed the tune and some of the words."

"What are braes and what's an Ulster Scot?" she asked.

"Braes are hills, Ulster Scots are Scots who moved to Northern Ireland."

"So they're Irish."

"A Scot's not Irish. A Scot's a Scot. He just changes location."

She pulled the jacket over her mouth to hide her smile.

"Where are we?" she asked, peering into the darkness.

"Scotland," he said, a faint smile crossing his lips. "You've been sleeping for nigh on two hours. Didn't even wake at the last petrol stop."

"How close are we?" she asked as they passed a sign which said 'Causewayend.'

"Less than an hour," he said.

"How does it feel to be this close to home?" she asked, shifting sideways to look at him.

"Lovely." He looked over at her and smiled. "I'm glad you're awake. It was getting quite lonely and I'm tired."

"It's my fault you're tired after that long night at the bureau. My job today was entertaining you so you'd stay awake and I've failed miserably, so I'll try to redeem myself the rest of the way. Can you play the song from the beginning?"

He programmed his CD player for a repeat loop, then asked, "Have you had the Scottish national sweet?"

"I'm not sure. Are we stopping to eat? We have a brownie left if you want it," she said, rummaging through the left-overs. "Sorry, we've eaten everything else."

"Nae, we're near my sister's. She'll have food."

She was amused his Scottish accent was becoming more pronounced the closer they got to his home—the same way hers did the closer she got to Charlotte.

"What's the Scottish national sweet?" she asked.

"Deep-fried Mars bars."

"So they really do exist?" she laughed. "I've heard rumors. Are they as bad as they sound?"

"Crunchy outside, soft chocolate inside, with a wee bit o' fish and chips taste."

"They fry them with the fish and chips?" she asked horrified.

"Aye," he said, arching his back and moving his head from side to side to loosen his neck.

"That's disgusting. Scots having more heart attacks, are they?"

"No more than American news producers," he said, trying to hide a smirk. "Dreamin' of *haggis,* are you?"

"What exactly *is* haggis?" she asked.

"A wee three-legged creature," he said, looking straight ahead as he fought a smile. "Furry."

"I don't think I've ever heard of a furry three-legged creature. Where are the legs? All on one side?"

"Now that's just daft. One on either side and one in front."

"And where do the haggis live?" she asked. "What's the plural of haggis? Haggi? Haggia?"

"Haggis. They live in the Highlands."

"Of course. A mountain animal," she said.

"Their legs are shorter on one side, so they stand upright when they run round the hills," Hugh circled his hand to demonstrate. "The best way to catch one is to make them run the other way so they'll fall over."

She burst out laughing. "How long are you going to keep up this nonsense?"

He grinned, pleased with his storytelling.

"What is haggis?" she repeated.

"Chopped sheep's heart, liver and lungs with onion and oatmeal, all boiled together in a sheep's stomach."

"Seriously, what is it?" she asked.

"I'm not lyin'. That's what it is. Haggis is why Scots are never defeated in battle," he said and puffed out his chest. "Scotland's national poet wrote a poem about it. Do ye know who that was?"

"Ahhh..." She tried to think back to her high school and college English lit classes. "Burns?" she finally guessed hesitantly.

"Aye!" he exclaimed, somewhat surprised she knew. "Must be the wee bit o' Scot in you bringing Robbie Burns to mind."

"Well, I know who Robert Burns is, but did not know he was your national poet," she said. "Total guess. I suppose you can recite haggis prose?"

"Aye, as could any good Scot. It's *Address to a Haggis*."

"Of course it is. Please, quote on, young Scot."

He cleared his throat. "*Fair fa' your honest, sonsie face, Great chieftain o' the puddin-race!*"

He stopped and looked over at her.

"What?" she laughed. "Did I hear pudding?"

"Aye. The haggis smiles at ye from the plate," he said.

"What's a sonie face? A sunny face?"

"Sonsie," he corrected her. "Happy, a happy face. *But mark the Rustic, haggis fed, The trembling earth resounds his tread. Clap in his walie nieve a blade, He'll mak it whissle; An' legs an' arms, an' heads will sned, Like taps o' thrissle.*"

"Translation?"

"A haggis-fed Scot makes the earth shake when he walks. And he holds a large knife in his fist so he can cut off legs, arms and heads."

"Lovely. Al Qaeda's got nothing on haggis-eating Scots."

"Aye, we're fierce," he said.

"And you're still single after being able to quote haggis poetry?"

"It's a mystery, isn't it?" he grinned.

She paused for a moment, then asked, "Are you religious?"

"Nae. You?"

"No, not at all. I went through the motions of church when I was a kid, but I stopped attending when I was about thirteen because no one in my family ever went to church."

He nodded. "Mine, too."

"What religion are you...or were you?" she asked.

"Kirk o Scotland."

"The what of Scotland?"

"Kirk. Church. Kirk o Scotland," he repeated.

"Church of Scotland. Church of England. People say the names of national churches over here as if it's so normal, but if I say Church of America, it sounds so bizarre."

"Is there a Church of America?" he asked.

"No, but we have a National Cathedral in Washington. It's Episcopalian." She started laughing. "Church of England! I never thought of that! The Church of England is the religion of America's National Cathedral. That's hysterical. Is the Kirk o Scotland Anglican like England's?"

"No," he said and made a face as if he'd tasted poison. "Presbyterian. Most Scots are Kirk o Scotland. They broke from Catholics centuries ago like the Anglicans."

"So Scots and English have a history of rejecting the Pope?"

"Aye and the UK won't let a Catholic on the throne," he said, "There's no animosity like Northern Ireland, but that's political, not religious."

"Why do you suppose religion leads to so many individual and national wars?" she asked.

Hugh looked at her, then turned back to the road. "I suppose I'll have to think about that. You?"

"I'm still trying to figure it out," she said. "I just thought you might have some brilliant insight."

"Afraid I'm a wee bit too tired for brilliant insights."

"More music then," she said.

A half hour later, they turned into a wide, dimly-lit driveway and wound their way up to the front door of High Tower Hall Bed and Breakfast.

61

Meeples, Scotland
Saturday, 20 September 2003

Le An's eyes flew open and she quickly sucked in her breath as she tried to fathom where she was. She looked around the room, her heart pounding in panic, trying to remember her current country and assignment. Was she in danger or safe? War zone or feature assignment in the States? Her wake-up amnesia usually happened when her inner defenses knew she was in a place she subconsciously felt safe—even her own home. Still, she always felt terrified those first few seconds when she couldn't remember where she was.

Glancing over at the nightstand, she spotted a High Tower Hall brochure and relaxed. She was in a remote part of Scotland with unlimited days of vacation stretching before her. Smiling, she saw it was 11:45. She'd slept more than thirteen hours.

Not hearing any sounds, and figuring most of the guests were up and gone, she climbed out of bed, shivering in the cool room. Hugh had started a cozy fire for her the night before, but the fireplace's gas timer had switched off hours ago and she wasn't sure how to start it again. Pulling back heavy curtains, she blinked in the brightness at the bucolic setting. Below her, grazing sheep dotted the green grass, the white fluffy animals so abundant in places, the rolling hills appeared to be covered in deep snow.

Out of habit she grabbed the remote and flipped between the news channels. The world was a mess—as usual—and suddenly she was sick of it. For at least a few days, she didn't want to know what was going on. Instead, after a leisurely hot shower, she dressed and headed downstairs to find something to eat, spying Hugh's sister Taryn near the kitchen.

"Good morning," Le An called out.

Taryn laughed, "You mean afternoon. We wondered if ye'd ever be waking up. Thoug' ye must be deid, for sure. Are ye hungry?"

"Famished. I guess y'all have finished serving breakfast?"

"Yeh, hours ago, but come in the kitchen and Andrew'll fix ye something."

Le An tried to protest, but Taryn shushed her and motioned for her to come into the kitchen.

"Is Hugh up yet?" Le An asked as she perched on a stool at the end of the large center island.

"Up and gone with meh family," said Taryn as she set a glass of juice in front of her. "I booked your appointment with a doctor. They had an opening on Tuesday."

Le An stopped mid-sip. "You made me a doctor's appointment? Hugh told you what happened?"

"Yeh. He rang me yesterday morning from London and told me to schedule it. Sorry to hear," said Taryn. "Hope it's not serious. Ye wanted an appointment, yeh?"

"I didn't want it, my boss did. He won't let me come back to work until I see a doctor. But, I realized the longer I put it off, the longer I can stay on vacation."

"Ah, well, I did my part," said Taryn. "The rest is on you."

Andrew MacGregor, High Tower Hall's chef, dropped a box of vegetables on the counter. Brushing a curly lock of black hair from his eyes, he looked at Le An and said, "Wha' have we got here?"

"Hugh's journalist friend Le An," Taryn introduced them. "She's staying a few days to recover from Iraq."

"Ah, newswoman," he said. "Gi'e's your crack."

Le An had heard that expression over the years from Scots she'd worked with, at first assuming it had something to do with actual crack cocaine since there were those in the industry who indulged, blindly thinking it wouldn't affect their work. They thought 'no one would notice' if they went on air or tried to produce while they were high, stumbling over their words and picking paranoia-fueled fights with their crews. They always—almost to a person—ended up getting fired. News was too high stress and fast paced to accommodate drugged-out or alcoholic journalists.

"That's such a great expression," said Le An. "First time I heard it, I thought it was a drug holdup. News is crack for adrenaline-junkie journos. But I have no news, gossip or crack. Too brain-dead."

"So that's the problem," he said.

"Are you Taryn's husband?" asked Le An, sending both Andrew and Taryn into hysterical laughter.

"Never!" said Taryn.

"Wouldn't have her," said Andrew.

"Nae, Andrew's our chef," said Taryn. "Meh husband Kyle works in banking in Edinburgh. One of us has to have a steady job."

"Sorry," muttered Le An, embarrassed.

"Don't be. I got meh laugh for the day. Andrew, could you cook for Le An?" asked Taryn. "She's been tryin' to make up lost sleep, snoozin' away half the day."

"A bowl of cereal is fine," Le An protested, not wanting to impose.

"It's nae a problem. Porridge, potato scone, eggs, links and fried bread?" asked Andrew as he pulled a pan off a hook.

She nodded yes and gave a thumbs up. "But no links."

"*Ceilidh* tonight," said Taryn.

"What's a kaylee?" she asked.

"A get-together for the clan," said Taryn. "Food, drink, music, dancing."

"A knees up?" she asked.

"Aye, it's like a knees up," said Taryn. "The family decided Hugh bein' home safe from Iraq is a good excuse for one."

After fixing Le An's breakfast, Andrew took baking sheets of pre-cooked shortbread in tartlet tins from one of the industrial-sized refrigerators. He quickly filled the pastries, moving his pastry bag up and down the rows, mesmerizing Le An as she watched him.

"Treacle tarts," he said, looking up at her and holding her gaze a second too long, a flirtatious action which caused her to involuntarily raise her eyebrows. Andrew obviously figured the way to seduce a woman was down the aphrodisiac highway of culinary arts.

"I've had them in London," she said, not realizing she was making a face.

Andrew scowled. "Bah! What do the English know about cooking? Nothing! You'll like mine, warm with a large scoop o' ice cream perched a' top their wee heads. Or some treacle pudding. I'm makin' ye eat them."

"Andrew's are the best in Scotland," Taryn nodded proudly. "Everything he makes is wonderful. He won Scottish Chef of the Year last year."

"I feel privileged to eat here," said Le An.

"Aye, you should," he said matter-of-factly. Treacle tarts may have been his specialty, but humble pie wasn't. He picked up a small spoon, dipped it into the large bowl of treacle filling and shoved it close to Le An's face. "Here, give it a bit o' welly."

"A bit of what?" she asked, pulling her head back from the sudden intrusion, then leaned forward and tried to take the spoon. Andrew refused to release it, insisting he feed her as if she were the household's new baby.

"Vewee good," she said, covering her still-full mouth with her hand.

Satisfied, Andrew went back to filling his tartlets, telling her his menu for the ceilidh: haggis; a salmon dish called Tweed Kettle; Cullen skink, a soup made with smoked haddock; and something he called Chicken Bonnie Prince Charlie.

"Chicken with Drambuie. We liquor up the birds and they climb in the oven themselves." He looked at Le An with a straight face, then burst out laughing. "Ahh! You Americans will believe anything."

She ignored the dig. Europeans were always taking potshots at Americans.

"Was the prince a cowardly chicken?" she asked.

"He was probably a bit 'fowl' after losing the battle and his army," he said. "The Bonnie Prince Charlie, he's running from his enemies the English and he escapes to the isle of Benbecula. So Flora MacDonald, she decides to help him escape."

"MacDonald? I'm a MacDonald," she said, pointing to herself.

"A wee bit of Scot, eh? Maybe yer not such a bad Yank after all, even if you are a MacDonald," he smirked. "Flora's supposed to marry another, but hides Charlie for a week and falls in love with him, then dresses him as her maid, calls him 'Betty Burke' and gets him safely to the Isle of Skye. Do ye know the story of Drambuie, Le An?"

"Noooo. It has a story?" she asked.

"Aye," said Andrew and Taryn.

"Clan MacKinnon keeps Charlie safe," said Andrew, "and he's so grateful, he gives them the secret recipe for Dram. The MacKinnons keep the recipe, carefully passing the list of special herbs through the generations. Round World War One a MacKinnon starts brewing it as a business. As thanks to the clan, every year they'd ship a keg of Dram to every MacKinnon family round the world."

"For free?" Le An gasped, trying to figure the shipping costs.

"Aye," said Taryn. "Would keep all the MacKinnons lit up for a year."

"Did Chicken Charlie stay on Skye and marry Flora?" she asked.

"He went back to Rome, married a princess and became a jakey," said Taryn.

"Back to Rome, *Italy*? He was an alcoholic *Italian*?" Le An burst out laughing and slapped the counter.

"He was a Scot!" bellowed Andrew. "His father King James was exiled in Rome, ye nattering Yank. Charlie was trying to recapture the Scottish throne."

"What happened to Flora?" she asked.

"She got a lock of Charlie's hair," said Taryn.

"That's it?" snorted Le An. "She risks her life to save him and all she gets is a lock of dirty hair? At least the MacKinnons got the recipe for Drambuie."

"Flora was arrested," said Andrew, "thrown in the Tower of London, but they let her go and she married a Scot. They moved to America and fought for the English in your war of independence. Stupid move. The Americans captured her husband. Served him right, fighting for the bloody English."

"Wait, what?" laughed Le An. "She risks her life to hide a man who's fighting *against* the English, she's punished *by* the English, then she gets married and joins forces *with* the English? Oh, she so deserved to be captured by the Americans."

"Aye," said Andrew and Taryn in unison.

Hugh's out-of-town relatives streamed into High Tower Hall throughout the day. Taryn had given her paying guests fair warning if they were looking for a quiet weekend in the country, this wasn't the place. When they heard the dining room would be closed for two days for the private gathering, a few cut short their stay and checked out, going in search of more peaceful lodgings.

That night, a large contingent of kilt-wearing, exuberant members of Clan Rose gathered in the dining room for the ceilidh. Le An had tried to beg off attending, feeling she was intruding on family time, but Hugh, Taryn, Kyle and Andrew all insisted she join them. Taryn even provided a kilt for her in the Clan Rose tartan to wear so she wouldn't feel like an outsider.

Le An was surprised to learn both she and Hugh's family shared Robert the Bruce as a common, though extremely distant, ancestor.

As the food, music and alcohol flowed freely, Hugh's Uncle Donald rose from his chair and lifted his glass.

"May the best ye've ever seen, be the warst ye'll ivver see. May a moose ne'er lea' yer girnal, wi' a tear drap in his e'e. May ye aye keep hale an' he'rty, till ye're auld eneuch tae dee. May ye aye be jist as happy, as a wuss ye aye tae be. *Sláinte mhaith!*"

"*Sláinte mhor!*" everyone screamed in unison before throwing back their whiskey.

As the musicians began the opening notes of *Caledonia*, the whole family began singing and, for once that evening, Le An was able to enthusiastically join them.

"The American knows *Caledonia*!" shouted Uncle Donald, as he lifted a glass with one hand and pointed at her with the other.

A roar of approval went up and Hugh beamed with delight as she laughed and lowered her face in embarrassment.

When the song ended amidst loud clapping and cheers, Le An leaned over and asked Hugh, "Your family sings Irish songs?"

"Not if they can help it," he said. "Though there are a few Celtic songs both Irish and Scots sing."

"Isn't *Caledonia* a song about Ireland?"

"What?!" he bellowed. "Are ye daft, woman?! Caledonia's about Scotland!"

"But the Irish sing it. My Irish soundman gave me a copy of a Dublin group singing it."

"Then the group's got good taste, even if they are Irish. It's about Scotland, love," he said. "Caledonia's the name the Romans gave Scotland, the area north of Hadrian's Wall. Dougie MacLean wrote the song. 'Tis the unofficial Scot national anthem."

"Is Doogie Irish?" she asked timidly, afraid she might say something else wrong.

"Are ye daft?!" he exploded, screaming to be heard over his

raucous relatives. "Dougie's from Perth! He's a Scot! Dougie MacLean!"

"To Dougie MacLean! *Sláinte!*" roared his family, all lifting their glasses in a toast.

"I'm sure Dougie's played the song in Ireland with Irish musicians," a slightly tipsy Hugh added in a softer tone as he wrapped one of his long arms around her shoulders. He leaned in close, laughing as he locked eyes with her. "Figures the Irish would claim a Scot song as their own. But if you're going to be a Scot, even an American one, you've got to learn not to call Sco'lan' Ireland—that is if ye be wantin' to make it out o' Sco'lan' alive."

She smiled and nodded, snuggling enjoyably in his bear hug, just as a statuesque woman with long, curly, strawberry-blond hair tried to sit between them on the banquette. She ended up half sitting on Le An, an obvious attempt to move her away from Hugh, who seemed startled by the woman's appearance. Le An slid down the banquette to put some distance between them.

"Fi! You're sittin' on her!" scolded Hugh. "Le, this is Fiona MacLaren, a neighbor of meh parents. Fi, Le An MacDonald."

"A MacDonald, are you?" Fiona asked coolly. "Which MacDonald?"

Le An wasn't sure how to answer that, unsure if Clan MacDonald had different divisions. "That would be the Carolina MacDonalds of America."

"An American?" she said accusingly. "And you're here on holiday to see Hugh? I didn't see you at his parents' today."

"I'm on holiday, but..." she said.

"We were in Iraq and Le needed a holiday," Hugh interrupted. "I suggested she join me."

"How lovely," Fiona said icily.

Feeling like a third wheel, Le An got up and headed for the kitchen to see if Taryn or Andrew needed help. As she burst through one of the swinging doors, she almost collided with Andrew who was carrying a large tray of food.

"Bloody American!" he yelled. "Ye come in here like a mad banshee, threatening my masterpieces? I'll have yer head if ye upset me or meh food."

"Sorry," she whispered. "Give me something to do so I don't have to go back out there. Fiona MacLaren's giving me dagger eyes."

"Fiona?" Andrew and Taryn said in unison, then rolled their eyes.

"Wha's she doin' here?" asked Taryn in a disgusted tone. "Still huntin' down meh brother? She's divorced, with two whiney brats, and wants Hugh to be husband number three. She didn't know there might be a little competition tonight."

She and Andrew laughed and winked at Le An.

"Hugh and I aren't dating," she protested, then added with a puzzled look, "I don't think. He just knew I needed a vacation. But I definitely don't want to be in the middle of his little lovers' quarrel."

Andrew and Taryn collapsed on the counters, laughing uproariously.

"Oh, stop!" screamed Andrew. "Yer killin' me!"

"What's so funny?" asked Hugh as he and Fiona came into the kitchen.

Le An turned her back to them and, eyes wide, faced Taryn and Andrew.

"It's the American!" roared Andrew. "She's got the best jokes."

Taryn nodded, trying to hold back her laughter, until both she and Andrew erupted again, this time convulsing Le An, too.

"Care to share?" asked Hugh suspiciously.

"No, but Andrew's a really good storyteller. Well, Taryn, if you're sure you don't need me, I'm going to get out of your way. Nice to meet you, Fiona. 'Night, Hugh," said Le An as she started for the door leading to the main hallway, then turned to Andrew and said, "Chicken Charlie was really a drunk Italian who stole recipes!"

"He was a Scot, ye nattering Yank!" Andrew screamed back, as he and Taryn collapsed into another round of laughter.

"Not a Yankee! Southerner!" Le An shouted back, then headed up the stairs to her room.

62

Melrose, Scotland
Wednesday, 24 September 2003

The rose-and-gold colored Gothic ruins of Melrose Abbey glistened in the soft rain as Le An and Hugh made their way down the path leading from the small gift shop and entrance building. Hugh crooked a finger and motioned for her to follow him as he made his way to the left side of the church ruins.

"The heart of our ancestor Robbie the Bruce," he pointed to a small round sandstone marker surrounded by dark gravel. On the stone a cross-shaped, flattened '8' intersected a thick outline of a heart. Arched around the top were the words, 'A NOBLE HART MAY HAVE NANE EASE' and across the bottom 'GIF FREEDOM FAILYE.'

Le An's eyes grew large. "Are you serious? Robert the Bruce is buried here?"

"His wee heart is," he said.

"What does that say? 'A noble heart may have no ease...'"

"'If freedom fail.'"

"Why did they only bury his heart and not his whole body?" she asked.

"His body's at Dunfermline Abbey, but the Bruce wanted his heart taken to the Holy Land."

"Yuk. Crusades?" she asked.

"Aye. Sir James Douglas was taking the Bruce's embalmed heart in a wee casket to Jerusalem, but the Moors killed him in Spain. Sir William Keith brought the heart back here to Melrose to be buried. The Bruce had paid for the Abbey to be rebuilt after the English sacked it. Archaeologists discovered his mummified heart in a pyramid-shaped stone container when they were digging here in 1921. They'd read about it, but never knew where it was. When they reburied it, they put the original container in a lead one, but again didn't mark where it was buried."

"Brilliant."

"Wasn't it? Archaeologists rediscovered it seven years ago."

"So they basically lost it for seventy-five years?" she laughed.

"And for 600 years before that. They kept his heart in an Edinburgh lab for eighteen months before Scots' yellin' and screamin' forced them to rebury it."

"Were they doing DNA testing on it?" she asked.

"They said they were making a new memorial stone."

"It takes Scots that long to carve a little stone?" she asked.

"Apparently those Scots."

"My ancestor's heart is here," she marveled as she bent down and gently fingered the stone's pattern and words. "I'm touching the tombstone of my ancestor's heart from 700 years ago. I've got to tell my mom. She won't believe this."

She pulled out her camera and took a picture of it, then shot some of the abbey's ruins.

"If it weren't raining, you could take a rubbing of the stone," said Hugh as the rain ran down their faces and dripped off the hoodies of their jackets. "But this is Scotland."

"I remember a Scotch whiskey ad from years ago," she said. "Something along the lines of: if you can see across the loch, it's about to rain and if you can't, it's already raining."

"You've got it," he smiled.

"I had no desire to visit Scotland because of that, but turns out, I don't mind the rain at all. Thank you for bringing me here."

"There's more," he said and motioned for her to follow him into the abbey ruins.

"Is that a Jewish Star of David?" she asked, pointing up to a carved six-sided star encased in a small circular window high above them on the abbey's north side. "It looks like it's six little Stars of David forming a giant Star of David."

"Aye," said Hugh. "There's a Star of David in York Minster Abbey, too. I was attending a performance of Handel's *Messiah* there three years ago and saw it in one of the stained-glass windows. I'm not sure why there are Jewish symbols in churches in Britain. Odd, especially in York, considering they massacred Jews there in the twelfth century."

"Was that when England threw out all the Jews?" she asked. "I remember that from *Ivanhoe*."

"England tossed Jews in the thirteenth century, but the York massacre was before that. It started when two men who owed Jews money riled up the mobs."

As they walked out into the old cemetery on the abbey's south side, Hugh turned and pointed up toward the roofline.

"See the gargoyle?" he asked.

"What is that?" she asked, squinting to identify it.

"A pig playing bagpipes."

"No! Monks put that on their abbey?" she laughed, shivering a little in the cold rain. "They had a wee sense of humor, eh?"

"Every church should have a musical flying pig. It's a water spout," he said. "This place is full of things like that. Are you chilled?"

"A little. I packed for 120-degree heat in Iraq. Didn't know I'd be coming this far north."

Under her black, hooded raincoat she was only wearing a shirt and cotton jacket. She glanced with envy at Hugh's pullover, lined raincoat and gloves. She shivered again and rammed her hands into her pockets trying to keep them warm.

"Come on, we'll dry out over there," he said pointing to a small house. "And there's a woolen shop straight across the way if you'd like to purchase something warm."

They crossed a narrow lane and entered the abbey's old Commendator's House, then wandered through its two floors of displays which told the story of the historic complex.

"Look at this," Le An said, pointing to a display. "I wonder if Jeremy knows this."

Hugh read aloud, "'In Scotland all the old celebrations of Christmas, Easter and saints days with their processions and plays were banned as being pagan...'"

"Protestants banned the days?" she asked as they both scanned the display. "When was that?"

"The late 1500s. The Scottish Reformation banned Christmas for about 400 years," he said.

"What?" she gasped. "Into the twentieth century?"

"Aye, until the 1950s," he said and glanced at his watch. "Come along. We'd best be off."

At the woolen shop across from Melrose Abbey, Le An found

numerous tartans for different family lines, an overwhelming collection of colors and combinations—and that was just for Clan MacDonald. Not knowing the specifics of her genealogy, Le An asked to see the tartan the actors wore on *Laird of the Highlands*. The salesgirl fought back a smile and nodded knowingly, then produced a soft, muted tartan in lavender, green, white and navy.

Hugh was fighting back a smile, too.

"What?" Le An asked, not pleased they were making fun of her. "It's a pretty tartan. And, obviously, by the way y'all are laughing, I'm not the first to ask for it."

"Nae, definitely not the first," laughed the salesgirl. "'Tis a big seller. That's why we stock it."

Le An purchased a few wool scarves in the tartan for her family and herself, along with a lavender wool pullover sweater and matching gloves—which she immediately put on.

An hour's drive later, she and Hugh arrived in Scotland's capital Edinburgh. It was easy to see where the ancient city had first been established. Rising high above the busy metropolis, on a black, craggy extinct volcano, stood the imposing fortified complex of Edinburgh Castle.

As they approached the castle's main gates, Hugh pointed to one of two large statues high above them—a man with a sword strapped to his side and a crown on his head.

"Robbie the Bruce," he said.

"He's everywhere, isn't he?" she asked. "What made him the one king the whole country idolizes?"

"He defeated the English at Bannockburn."

"So, you could say he was the George Washington of Scotland," she said.

"Did Washington defeat the English?"

"Not big on American history, are you?" she asked.

"Don't really see the point," he said. "But you don't know Scot history of your own ancestors."

"Good point, smart guy. Pop quiz: how many states do we have?"

"Ahh... fifty-two?" he asked and shrugged.

"Eaah! Wrong! Fifty. Guam and Puerto Rico aren't states. OK, listen and learn, Scot man. Yes, Washington defeated the English. Final battle was Yorktown. Only Washington completely defeated them—at least until they came back in 1812 and burned Washington, DC and we had to smack 'em down again."

"That's William Wallace," he said, pointing to the other statue at the entrance.

"Braveheart? What does it say over the entrance?" she asked, squinting as she pointed to the Latin phrase above the arch. "NEMO ME IMPUNE LACESSIT."

"'Poke me and I'll flatten you,'" he said.

"Really?"

"More or less. It means, 'No one provokes me and escapes punishment.' It's the Scottish Royal motto." He pointed to the red lion crest above it. "And that's the Royal Standard of Scotland."

After purchasing their tickets, Hugh glanced at his watch, grabbed her hand and started pulling her. "Come on. We have to hurry."

It took them twenty minutes to briskly hike up the castle's steep, winding cobblestone road, through the castle's various iron gates of defense. They finally stopped at the Argyle Battery, located at the castle's 'Middle Ward' near the top of the hill on the north side, one of the best places to see Edinburgh. Below them stretched the vast expanse of the city's Georgian-style, charcoal-colored stone buildings, as well as the Firth of Forth as it flowed into the North Sea.

"What a fantastic view," she said, slightly out of breath from Hugh's rapid pace up the steep 400-foot-high hill. "But the buildings all look like they need a good sandblasting. They're so gray and dingy."

"Centuries of coal and soot," he said.

The rain had stopped and Le An was slightly warmer than earlier, but still shivered as a cold wind blew off the firth, the damp, penetrating cold slicing through her black jeans. In Iraq she'd almost passed out from heat stroke with all the protective gear she'd had to wear in the scorching weather. Now she wished she was wearing some of it.

"Still chilled, are you?" asked Hugh. "Your new jumper's not keeping you warm?"

He wrapped his arms around her, pulling her close as he started to vigorously rub her one arm which faced away from him.

"The sweater's helping a little," she said. "I can't believe a few weeks ago we were in 120-degree weather in Iraq. My blood's still thinned out from spending most of the summer there."

"Aye, mine, too. Taryn's amused I nae can handle the cold." He glanced at his watch, a big smile coming on his face. "We made it in time."

"In time for what?" she asked.

A crowd had started to gather on nearby Mills Mount Battery as a castle guardsman wearing white gloves and a dark uniform with a red stripe down either leg stiffly marched over to a large cannon which faced the sea.

"Do they fire that thing?" asked Le An.

Boom!

She jumped as the cannon went off.

"I guess they do," she said.

"One o'clock," said Hugh.

"Are those real cannon balls?" she gasped. "My word, where do they land?"

"Cannon balls?" he burst out laughing. "You think the castle's at war with Edinburgh or ships in the firth? Nae, it's a timing blast, lass. That cannon's been fired most every day since 1861. You can set your watch by it. If you're on a ship, take away fifteen seconds for the sound to reach the harbor."

"That's why they do it?" asked Le An. "So people can set their clocks? Do they do it every hour?"

"Nae, just at one. That's why it's called the One O'Clock Gun. It's cheaper that way. Only one blast," he said.

"You do realize the world makes fun of Scots who are cheap?"

"Short arms, deep pockets? We're not cheap, just financially sensible. What do you call a Scotsman who's lost seventy-five percent of his intelligence?" he asked as a smile tugged at his lips.

"A three-legged haggis?" she guessed.

"An Englishman," he smirked.

"You know, being a Southerner is a lot like being a Scot. We rag the Yankees as much as you do the English. I think we're kindred spirits."

"Besides being children of the Bruce."

Edinburgh Castle was, like many ancient fortresses, a complex consisting of numerous buildings on various levels. Though a few structures dated to the twelfth century, most had been built within the last few centuries, some remodeled to provide modern conveniences for tourists, including cafes and gift shops.

   Hugh and Le An wound their way farther up the hill, bypassing many of the sights. He wasn't allowing for a complete tour, just highlights he wanted her to see. They stopped on the Upper Ward at Saint Margaret's Chapel, the oldest structure in Edinburgh, which at one time had been sacrilegiously used as an ammunition storage facility. The chapel was small and cozy, a warm place to escape the biting, cold wind.

   "Who was Saint Margaret?" asked Le An as she glanced around at the handful of simple benches lined up in front of the small, plain altar. "Was she related to Robert the Bruce?"

   "Aye, she was his…" Hugh counted in his head through the royal line, "…great-great-great-great gran. I think that's right. She was a Roman Catholic queen, pious, helped the poor, had planned on being a nun, but married King Malcolm whose father Duncan was killed by MacBeth."

   "*The* MacBeth, Shakespeare's MacBeth?" she gasped. "MacBeth murdered King Malcolm's father?"

   "Aye, though Shakespeare's play has MacBeth murdering Duncan in his sleep at the castle when he actually killed him on the battlefield. And he had Duncan as an old man, but the king was younger."

   "A real-life MacBeth murdered my real-life ancestor King Duncan?" she sputtered.

   "Aye," he said, a slight smile crossing his lips. "Used force to take the throne."

   "Unbelievable," she said. When she'd read *MacBeth* in her high school English class, she'd had no idea she was reading about her long-ago ancestor and his murderer. "Are Duncan and MacBeth buried near here? Did they separate their hearts from their bodies like the Bruce?"

   "They're buried on the Isle of Iona, along with most of our ancient kings," he said.

   "Where's Iona?"

   "The Hebrides, off the coast of western Scotland. Have ye ne'r heard of the sacred Isle of Iona?"

   She gave him a blank look.

   "Ye call yourself a Scot and Clan MacDonald and ye don't

know the Isle of Iona? The Duke of Argyll at Inveraray Castle, the chief of Clan MacDonald, used to own it, but the father of the current duke sold it to Scotland before he died," he said. "Saint Margaret's son was King David who built Melrose Abbey."

"And the circle's complete," she said. "So when Robert the Bruce's heart was buried at Melrose, he was buried at the abbey his ancestor had built."

"Aye, his great-great-great grandfather David. And David's sister Matilda married King Henry to become queen of England, uniting the Saxon and Norman lines."

"The Saxons and Normans are allegedly Israelites, you know," she said.

"Aye, so I've heard," he said.

"You knew?" she asked, surprised. "How did you know? I just found out."

"Again, could make a comment about clueless Americans, but I'll refrain," he smirked. "Some call it British Israelism."

"Why? The majority of Israelite tribes settled in Europe. It's not like Britain's got a lock on it."

He shrugged. "That's just what they call it. Have ye n'er heard of the Declaration of Arbroath, the Scottish Declaration of Independence?"

She shook her head 'no.'

"In 1320, the Pope wouldn't recognize Scotland as a separate country with its own king. Robbie the Bruce and Scottish Parliament wrote him and said the Scots came from Scythia across the Mediterranean to Spain, then landed in Scotland 1,200 years on from the Israelites crossing the Red Sea..."

Le An grasped his arms, his historical revelation leaving her speechless. "This is everything Jeremy told me."

"Yeh, well, it's not a big secret," he said. "Arbroath influenced your own Declaration of Independence. Now who doesn't know American history?"

"Tell me everything," she said, pulling him down onto one of the benches.

"Basically, Robbie's letter said more than 100 kings of only Scottish royal stock, no foreigners, had ruled here in an unbroken dynasty. The Pope finally acknowledged the Bruce as king."

"So, they came here to Scotland 1,200 years after their Israelite ancestors left Egypt, which Jeremy said was about 1440 BC," she said, doing the math in her head. "About 240 BC?"

"Again, not a revelation to us, but glad you could join us," he said.

She nodded, deep in thought as she looked around the tiny chapel. "Go back to MacBeth," she finally said. "Duncan's son Malcolm obviously regained the throne. You called him king and Margaret his wife queen."

"Malcolm took the throne—after he killed MacBeth. When MacBeth's stepson tried to rule, Malcolm killed him, too."

"Revenge at its finest. Makes our politics look peaceful," she said. "Did the royal family live here?"

"Margaret died here, but none of these buildings existed. Her son David built this chapel in her honor and it's the oldest building in Edinburgh. The royal family lived here about 500 years, but most preferred Holyrood at the other end of the Royal Mile, Queen Elizabeth's official residence when she's in Edinburgh. Scottish royals only stayed here if there was threat of an attack because the castle was easier to defend than Holyrood."

"This is unbelievable," she whispered, slowly shaking her head in disbelief.

She was walking around the grounds of a castle which her ancestors had lived in at one time, had defended against invaders, had ruled a people.

"The Pope made Margaret a saint after her death," he said. "She died after learning her husband and eldest son had been killed in battle."

"How sad."

"When Catholic shrines were being destroyed during the Reformation, an abbot in Dunfermline, where Margaret was buried, put her head in a jeweled case and sent it here to a pregnant Mary Queen of Scots for safe keeping."

"That's disgusting!" she said. "Was he trying to make her miscarry?"

He shrugged. "Skull of a saint for good luck, I suppose. Mary gave birth to King James the Sixth of Scotland who united the English and Scottish crowns and became King James the First of England."

"So, in a sense, Scotland did conquer England," she said. "A Scottish king was ruling. And wasn't Queen Elizabeth's mother Scottish? That means the queen's more than half Scottish, right?"

"Aye. Scotland and England together in one monarch, I suppose. Come on, there's more."

He once again grabbed her hand and pulled her out the door, leading her farther up the hill to the Royal Palace and the building housing the Scottish crown jewels. On the first floor they entered a large area where illustrations of Scotland's monarchs and the dates of their reigns were depicted in a large mural around the room.

"It's so strange to see an entire line of your ancestors painted on a public wall," said Le An, her head tipped back to see it all.

The room next to it had a large white-and-gold display of Robert the Bruce being crowned King of Scotland. Above it, large gold lettering read: ROBERT THE BRUCE CROWNED WITH A CIRCLET OF GOLD 1306.

"I know this guy," she said. "That dude is everywhere. You obviously get more than fifteen minutes of fame when you defeat the English."

Hugh took out a penny and handed it to her.

"Is this my tip for being a good Yank?" she asked.

"Not a Yank. Sou-thern-er," he said, mimicking her.

"He's learning."

"Put it in the machine," he said pointing to a press in the corner of the room.

The device heated the penny, melting and elongating it into a long oval as it imprinted on it EDINBURGH CASTLE THE ROYAL SCOTS surrounding Queen Elizabeth the Second's insignia and crown.

"So you'll always remember Edinburgh," he said as she put the commemorative coin in her pocket and lightly fingered the raised border.

A few minutes later they entered a small, darkened room. A large glass case in the center was illuminated, with two guards positioned in opposite corners of the room keeping careful watch. A dark blue velvet cloth filled the inside of the case, cascading over different levels, the highest holding a gold crown perched atop a red pillow with gold tassels. Surrounding it were the Scottish regalia—the royal sword and scepter, as well as other crown jewels. In front of the crown, on a lower level, was an enormous pink rock.

The crown was encrusted with gemstones and pearls, topped

with red velvet and a rim of white ermine. Le An kept trying to concentrate on the Honours of Scotland—the crown jewels and regalia—but her attention kept coming back to the rock. Why would a huge, pink, cracked rock with two rusting metal rings be on display next to a magnificent gold crown?

"The Honours of Scottish are the oldest in Europe," whispered Hugh. "The jewels came from the old Scottish crown. The gold and freshwater pearls are from Scotland."

He didn't say a word about the big pink elephant in the room—the cracked pink rock.

"I'll meet you out in the gift shop," he said, pointing to the exit.

Le An stayed a little longer admiring the display, still puzzled by the rock. She found Hugh in the gift shop and the two walked across the courtyard to the Queen Anne Cafe for something to eat. Hugh had bought a few things and as they sat down at their table, he slid over to her a dark blue bag with gold lettering spelling out the castle's gift shop 'The Crown Jewel Collection.'

"For you," he said.

"That's so sweet. Thank you," she said.

Hugh's gifts were books about Scottish history: two small booklets, *Clan Bruce* and *Clan MacDonald*, along with two larger ones titled *Scotland's Kings and Queens* and *The Stone of Destiny: Symbol of Nationhood*.

The cracked pink rock had its own book.

"What's up with the old rock in the glass case?" she asked holding up *The Stone of Destiny* book.

Hugh looked at her, an incredulous half smile on his lips. "You're joking, right? You really don't know what it is?"

"No, am I supposed to? It's a rock. What's so special about a rock?"

"Your ancestor Robbie the Bruce spent his entire reign trying to find that stone," he said.

"Why on earth would he do that?" she asked. "It's not like he couldn't go out and find another rock. From what I've seen, this country's about eighty percent rocks."

Hugh closed his eyes and sighed deeply, as if exasperated Le An didn't get the point. "Sorry, I forget you Americans are in the dark most times. It's the Coronation Stone."

She stared at him, trying to figure out what that meant. The stone had nothing glamourous or elegant about it, certainly nothing befitting royalty. "You mean coronation like when a king is crowned?"

"Is there another meaning for coronation?" he asked. "Scottish rulers were always coronated on it, but a Sassenach choried it before the Bruce was."

Le An ran his last sentence through her mind, trying to match sounds to actual words. "OK, I give up. What did you say? A what did what before the Bruce could be coronated?"

"A Sassenach. An Englishman. Choried it. Stole it. An English king stole the stone along with the crown jewels ten years before the Bruce was coronated. The legend says whoever is coronated on the stone has access to its power."

"The cracked pink rock has power?" she laughed. "You don't believe that do you?"

"This is no ordinary stone," said Hugh.

"It's not like it's the Hope Diamond," she said. "It's a *rock*."

"It's worth more than the Hope Diamond," he said. "And it's far more powerful."

63

Edinburgh, Scotland
Wednesday, 24 September 2003

"The rock in the glass case has powers?" Le An laughed. "Are they super-duper magical powers?"

"Are you mocking our stone?" asked Hugh, looking slightly offended.

"Nooo, I'd never mock a stone with powers," she said, trying to hide a smile as she looked at the book, reading the title out loud, "*The Stone of Destiny.*"

"Also the Stone of Scone and Lia Fail," he said.

"I've never heard any of those names or anything about this rock," she said. "Why have y'all kept it so quiet?"

"We haven't. You Yanks just weren't listening," he said.

"Always taking potshots at the Americans," she said. "It's not like you know so much about our history. You didn't even know how many states we have. Did it ever occur to you the reason we're in the dark about your rock is because Americans long ago chose not to go the whole royalty route? We have enough problems with politicians without adding royalty to the mix. And since we don't have a king to put his little *tuchus* on a rock in order to tell us what to do..."

"Scot kings didn't sit on the Stone of Scone," he corrected her. "They stood on it. When the English choried it in 1296, they built a chair with the stone on a shelf under the seat. Have you n'er seen the Coronation Chair in Westminster Abbey?"

"If I have, I don't remember."

Hugh opened the book and, flipping through the pages, pointed to the picture of the antique Gothic-styled chair, its high back rising to a center point. The chair was an odd mix of simple and elaborate, with the inside comprised of plain, wide oak planks. The outer sides were carved with intricate Gothic arches, but the inside appeared as if choir boys and tourists had carved their initials into it. The entire chair rested on a gold base, each of the four corners supported by a snarling, fierce-looking golden lion which served as feet. Wedged tightly between the simple plank seat and the elegant gold base rested the Coronation Stone.

"The chair looks a wee bit tatty, but it's 700 years old," said Hugh. "Didn't help when suffragettes put a bomb under it in the early 1900s."

"Women tried to blow up the Coronation Chair to get the vote?"

"Daft, wasn't it?" said Hugh.

"Is that why the rock has a big crack in it?"

"The bombing slightly damaged the throne and the stone, though they say there was a crack in it before that. Probably when they put in the iron rings to make transporting it a wee bit easier."

"Maybe it cracked when the English choried it," she said and smiled.

"Maybe. No doubt the bombing didn't help."

"Oh my word, they have haggis," she said, looking at the menu. "Along with rabbit, deer burgers and wild boar. Are we in Possum Trot, Tennessee?"

They opted to split an order of blue-cheese croquettes and castle-cut chips, along with bowls of hot Scotch broth and a pot of tea—with a wee dram of whiskey.

"On Christmas Day 1950," continued Hugh, "four students from Uni of Glasgow stole the stone and it broke in two when they dropped it on the abbey floor. Other accounts say it was already broken from a crack which had been there for centuries. Of course, the students were heroes here in Scotland. People hid them and the stone. The English couldn't find it for nigh on four months."

"And it's been here in the castle ever since?"

"Nae, the students left the stone wrapped in the Scottish flag on the altar at Arbroath Abbey, called the police, then stood next to it waiting to get arrested."

"Arbroath? The same as the Declaration of Arbroath where Robert the Bruce mentioned the Scythians?" she asked.

"The same. That's why the students selected that location. It was symbolic. Scotland is the oldest nation in Europe, as you said from 200 BC. But England absorbed our nation. The students wanted Scots to desire freedom again."

"Did the students do jail time for the theft?"

He shook his head 'no.' "They were charged, but never prosecuted. That would have caused a major ruckus. The English were afraid the Scots would rise up and demand independence. After all, it is our stone. The English stole it from us, we stole it back. What's to prosecute? The English put it back in Westminster Abbey."

"How do you know the students left the real stone? They could have switched it."

He nodded. "They could have. Though in interviews they've given since then, they claim it's the same stone. I don't think they ever meant to keep it. It was a symbolic move, to reclaim an important symbol of Scottish independence in order to encourage Scots to break away from England."

"They wanted to create a groundswell of support and national pride, a call to action of sorts?" she asked.

"Aye. They were hoping Scots would rally behind them so they wouldn't be jailed—and that's what happened."

"But the students are the ones who stole the stone out of loyalty to Scotland, so why would they ever admit it was a fake?" she asked. "True patriots would keep quiet about the real stone. Or, what if everybody's lying? What if the English had a fake stone and the students stole the fake and replaced it with another fake and the fake's on display right now. Maybe everybody faked out everybody."

Hugh burst out laughing. "Why would the students risk prison time stealing a fake stone? It could be the real stone was stolen once, stolen twice, finally returned. Scots for centuries asked the English to return the stone, including after the students left it at the abbey. If the real stone had n'er been stolen, why would they keep asking the English to return a fake?"

"Could be Scots messing with the English trying to make them believe they'd returned the real stone," she said.

"Aye, but remember James the First of England was a Scot. Would Scots have wanted their own king crowned on a fake stone? Much as some Scots may hate it, Scotland and England are one Commonwealth now. Whatever blessings or curses come on the English come on us, too. If there's a blessing attached to the ruler crowned on the stone, it's best to have it be the real stone."

"Good point," she said. "So let's say the students took the real stone, but left a fake at the abbey. That was just a few years before Queen Elizabeth was coronated, which means she would have sat on—or over—a fake stone. And that means the next British ruler will also be crowned on a fake stone. The Allies defeated Hitler in World War Two, but maybe that's where the blessings stopped."

"We won in the Falklands," he reminded her.

"True, but you've continued to lose countries in the Commonwealth. Your empire is getting smaller and your world influence is diminishing."

He bristled at the comment.

"Ah, there's the Brit in you coming out," she smiled.

"First a Scot, always a Scot," he said.

"But think about it," she continued. "A fake stone could be causing all of y'all to lose blessings—Scots, English, Northern Irish. Maybe your whole Commonwealth is missing out on blessings because your rulers are being coronated on a fake stone."

"That's possible." He paused for a moment, debating whether to tell her more. "They say in the early 1800s, after a heavy rain, two bairns..."

"Two what?"

"Bairns...children...lads...discovered a stone in a cave near MacBeth's Castle Dunsinnan, allegedly the Stone of Destiny which monks had hidden before Edward and the English got to Scone."

"Was it the stone?"

"Don't know. The bairns couldn't find it again," he said.

Le An started laughing. "Convenient. But answer me this: how would a couple of kids know what the stone looked like in the first place?"

"Good question," Hugh said, a smile tugging at the corners of his mouth.

"If that was the real stone, why didn't the monks bring it out after the English left with the fake?" she asked. "You said Robert the Bruce searched for the real stone so he could be crowned on it, but never found it. Why wouldn't Scottish monks bring out the real stone to crown their Scottish king?"

"Too dangerous to risk anyone knowing the real Stone of Destiny was still in Scotland," he said.

"The monks never told anyone where the stone was?" she asked.

"They died."

"People do that. But why wouldn't they have told younger monks? Surely, if you can't trust your fellow friars, whom can you trust?"

"An old Westminster Abbey guidebook said more than 1,000 years ago the stone was carved with a saying that Scots will rule where the stone is, but the stone here in the castle has no carvings."

"But if the stone on the abbey altar had no carving and the English knew it did before, they would've known it was a fake and they wouldn't have taken it. I think that story's a lot of Blarney."

"Don't bring the Irish into this," he said. "There were people who'd seen the stone before the English stole it who claimed the stone was the same."

"Ah ha!" she said and pointed her finger at him. "Wait, have you just convinced me the stone is real?"

He tried to hide a smile.

"You are so sneaky," she said. "That's really slick how you did that."

"You like that?" he smiled broadly. "Here's something else to consider: in 1296 the English also stole the Scottish crown and scepter and both of them would have been easier to hide than the stone."

"Another point toward the stone being authentic. Where'd it come from originally?" she asked.

"Supposedly the Middle East," he said.

"Someone hauled that rock from the Middle East? Again, look around. Lots of rocks in Scotland. Why import? Besides, how do they know where it came from?"

"Geologists have tested it. They say the red sandstone is the same as rocks near Perth and Scone, though other geologists say the same type stone is also found in the Middle East." He shrugged. "Who knows?"

"Do you think the stone in there is the real Stone of Destiny?"

"I like to believe it is," he said. "It would be a shame to waste all the centuries of drama on a fake one. The homecoming was certainly triumphant. The stone returned to Scotland the thirtieth of November 1996—precisely 700 years after it was stolen from us."

"You remember the exact date?"

"Every Scot remembers the date. It's Saint Andrew's day. They had a rather large ceremony here at the castle. Prince Andrew came. RAF did a fly past. Twenty-one gun salute at the castle."

"Prince Andrew has a special day?" she asked.

He looked horrified. "Are ye daft? I said *Saint* Andrew. Prince Andy's certainly no saint and he'd be the first to admit it. *Saint* Andrew, as in one of the disciples."

"What disciples?"

"Jesus' disciples."

"Why do you have a day in Britain to honor Saint Andrew?"

"In Scotland, not Britain. He's the patron saint of Scotland. You know that world famous golf course Saint Andrews?"

"Jesus' disciples played golf?" she teased. "Why is Andrew the patron saint of Scotland?"

"He's buried here," he said.

64

Edinburgh, Scotland
Wednesday, 24 September 2003

"One of Jesus' disciples was here in Scotland?" Le An asked. "Now that's just daft."

"Nae, he wasn't here, his bones are," said Hugh. "Well, some of them. They were in Saint Andrews, but now they're in Saint Mary Cathedral here in Edinburgh."

"Dividing up another dead body, are we?" she asked amused. "What is it with you Scots not being able to leave a dead body intact? Why were *some* of his bones brought here when the live version never was?"

"Scythians," he said, as he took a sip of tea.

"What about them?"

"They say Andrew preached to them when they were living round the Black Sea," he said.

"As in Scythians, a.k.a. Israelites, who migrated here to Scotland?" she asked.

He nodded as he polished off the last of the blue-cheese croquettes.

"So Scots knew their Israelite ancestors had met Andrew when they were in the Black Sea region and that's why they wanted him for their patron saint?" she asked.

He nodded again and reached for one of the last castle-cut chips.

"Black Sea...wait...Georgia!" she said.

"Sorry?" he asked.

"Georgia. Not US state of, the Republic of. When we were doing a story in Georgia, everyone there talked about the country's patron saint Andrew. There were monuments to him all over the country. Is that the same Andrew?"

"Aye. He was also said to be in Russia and Romania," he said.

"Georgia's on the eastern side of the Black Sea, Romania's on the western side and Russia's on the northern side," said Le An, using her finger to point in the air to a map of the region only she could see.

"See this?" Hugh pointed to a brochure on their table which featured the Scottish flag, a diagonal white cross on a blue field. "The Romans supposedly crucified Andrew on a diagonal cross. That's why it's called a Saint Andrew's cross. A saltire cross."

"Andrew's so important he's even on your flag," she said.

"Aye. Patron saint," he said. "That's what they called him in the Declaration of Arbroath."

Staring past Hugh, Le An propped her chin in her cupped hands to process all the information.

"Is the Stone of Destiny here permanently?" she asked. "What happens when Prince Charles or Prince William is crowned?"

"We'll loan it to London for the coronation, but after that, it's returned to it's rightful place here in Scotland. The next monarch will be crowned whilst on the Coronation Chair which holds the stone under the seat."

"I still don't get why it's so special," she said. "Because I gotta tell you, it doesn't look like much."

"It's believed to give national power when a monarch is crowned on it," he said. "The Coronation Stone verifies the true ruler."

"How does it do that?"

"It shouts," he said.

"What?" she burst out laughing. "The rock shouts?"

"Are you laughing at our national treasure?" he asked. "Because remember, it's your heritage, too."

"Sorry. What happens if the stone doesn't shout? Did it shout when Queen Elizabeth was coronated?"

"Don't know. The trumpets and choir were too loud," he said.

"How convenient," she said. "The stone obviously doesn't protect the monarch from dying or being killed. Does it protect the country? Hitler still bombed London and the stone didn't protect the city. How many thousands died in the Blitz?"

"More than 40,000, half of those in London," he said. "But Britain wasn't conquered. The UK did win the war, so maybe the stone helped."

"Britain only won because the US entered the war," she said.

"Maybe the stone convinced the Americans to join forces with the British," he said. "Maybe the stone protected the British and helped them escape the Nazis at Dunkirk. Maybe it helped them on D-Day."

"Weather played a big part in the evacuation of Dunkirk, didn't it?" she asked. "Does the stone control weather?"

"Weather played an enormous part," he said. "Low cloud cover and light rain during most of the nine days kept the Luftwaffe from bombing the ships evacuating Allied soldiers. And calm seas enabled the soldiers to wade out to board smaller boats which ferried them to the larger ships. They saved more than 300,000 British, French, Belgian and Dutch troops and an additional 200,000 Allied troops were rescued from other French ports at the same time."

Le An nodded. "I know. I'm a World War Two buff. My granddad fought in it. But did you know there was a boatlift on 9/11 which evacuated almost the same number of people from Manhattan in less than nine hours?"

"Aye, I covered that story, remember? Come to think of it, weather played a part in defeating the Spanish Armada whilst on its way to attack England," he said.

"So we've determined the stone uses weather to fight for Britain during wars," she said. "What else?"

Hugh shrugged and took another sip of tea. "I only know the traditions round it, that a ruler must be coronated on it to be truly authentic and receive God's blessing."

Le An raised her eyebrows. "A blessing. That's interesting, if not a little vague. If the stone is supposed to have powers, why didn't Queen Elizabeth or her father sit or stand on it directly? Do you get the full blessing if you aren't touching the stone?"

"The Scots stood on it. I don't know why the English do anything. I suppose when they choried it, they failed to take the stone's instruction manual. Probably don't get the full power with it on a shelf underneath." He leaned toward her and whispered, "It's the Scots' little secret."

"Ahh, you sly Scots," she said. "But even Scots sitting or standing on it couldn't prevent it from being stolen or their country being merged with England."

"True. Rather bad luck," he admitted.

"Though, again, we come back to Queen Elizabeth being at least half Scottish." She thought for a few seconds, then shook her head. "I still don't get why y'all think a rock from the Middle East has power. It must be a superstitious thing."

"They say it's Jacob's Pillow, another of its names."

"Who's Jacob?" she asked.

"Jacob in the Bible," he said pointing to *The Stone of Destiny* book. "He was supposedly using it as a pillow and had a dream God was wrestling with him..."

Le An blanched and suddenly held up her hand for him to stop. "Wait, what? Jacob, as in the one whose name was changed to Israel, who was the father of the twelve tribes of Israel, whose son Joseph was sold into slavery and got a double inheritance, so there were thirteen tribes and they all went down to Egypt and became slaves and Moses led them out and the Red Sea parted? That Jacob?"

Hugh momentarily looked shell-shocked by the verbal barrage. "That's the longest sentence I've ever heard, akin to something out of the *New York Times*. Yes, I suppose it's that Jacob." He looked around. "Fancy a sweet?"

Le An wasn't listening, instead rapidly pulling out of her mental files all the history she'd absorbed in the recent weeks, pushing all the fragments around in her mind to see which pieces snapped together. Slowly, the picture of the puzzle started to reveal itself.

"Le An, do you fancy a sweet?" Hugh repeated.

"Hmm? Sure. Thanks," she said. "The lemon cake sounds good. Extra whipped cream, if possible."

Hugh got up to look for their waitress and while he was gone, Le An opened *The Stone of Destiny* to read the history of the mysterious pink rock. Minutes later, she spotted something and gasped.

"She's bringing our sweets and more tea," said Hugh.

Le An kept staring at the page, her left hand covering her mouth.

"Something amiss?" he asked.

Looking up at him, she tapped her right index finger on the book and said, "This is it."

"What's it?"

"I'll be back," she said as she jumped up from her seat.

Hurrying across the courtyard, she headed back to the Royal Palace, fighting her way through the tourists, dodging around people lingering at the displays. Winding her way through the circuit of rooms, she once again found herself in the Crown Room, the two guards still standing watch over Scotland's treasures.

When the room cleared except for two other people, she moved closer to the glass case to get a better look at its contents: the 300-pound pink stone, with the indentations in the top and the black metal rings driven into it on either end; the gem-and-pearl-encrusted crown; the royal necklace; the sword; and finally the scepter topped with its large crystal.

"That's it," she whispered. "Hiding in plain sight."

65

Meeples, Scotland
Wednesday, 24 September 2003

Hugh and Le An returned to High Tower Hall to find Fiona waiting impatiently on a bench near the front door.

"Great," he mumbled. "What's she doing here?"

Fiona walked around to Hugh's side of the car and asked, "Where've you been all day?"

Le An didn't wait to hear his response, opting instead to beat a hasty retreat to her room. She thought about checking her email to see if there was any word from Paul about the situation with Barry, but reconsidered. Her day had been pleasant and she didn't want to ruin it. Hours later, her curiosity won out and she logged onto her email to find eighty-seven messages clogging her inbox.

Scrolling through the list to see if there were any worth reading, her heart started pounding at the sight of one email address. Angry and disgusted, she pushed her laptop over to the far side of the bed and processed what she'd just read, then pulled the Edinburgh Castle penny souvenir from her pocket. Rubbing it gently, she thought back on her day with Hugh, how pleasant it had been, how much she'd enjoyed spending time with him.

She pulled her laptop toward her and reread Luke Conte's email: *LE, WHERE ARE YOU??? CALL ME!*

She snorted softly in disgust. Who was he to ignore her for more than a month, then suddenly drop back into her life as if he'd just talked to her yesterday? He'd probably heard what had happened with Barry and the Iraq special. No telling what gossip about her was currently making the rounds through the USN staff. Maybe something linking her with Hugh.

She stared at the long-awaited email for a few minutes—then

hit the delete key.

Fat chance, jerk, she thought. *You lose.*

She continued to rub her thumb over the raised dots forming the border around the penny souvenir, thinking about how much she enjoyed being in Scotland, far from her routine.

That's what made her decision so much harder.

She wanted to stay there in her vacation bubble with Hugh as long as she could, but she knew ultimately she'd end up paying for it in misery dollars. She didn't want to overstay her welcome, and besides, there was no chance of a long-term relationship with him. He'd go back to London, she'd go back to New York, they'd travel on different assignments to different cities and countries and continents every week and maybe, if they were lucky, they'd run into each other every couple of years. She had a better chance with Luke—at least they worked for the same network and occasionally traveled together on assignments. Even with all that, Luke had managed to forget about her as soon as she was out of sight. She was still hurt from his total silence and snub after Iraq. And she was angry for allowing herself to think it was going to lead to something permanent. Elena was right. She was at the age where she wanted a serious relationship which had the potential to lead to something longer lasting.

She was always trying to pretend it didn't matter, but the truth was it did. She'd put her private life on hold for years and now she wanted someone to worry when she didn't come home at night or when gun-toting Iraqis were trying to assassinate her.

That's why she wasn't about to let anything get started with Hugh. Anything beyond friendship would be impossible to maintain and she didn't want any more short-term romances. That and the Fiona factor. She'd made it clear she wasn't happy Le An was spending time with Hugh. Better to leave Scotland now.

A soft knock interrupted her thoughts.

And there stood the object of her dilemma, an earnest, innocent smile on his tanned face.

"I'm glad you stopped by," she said. "I was hoping to talk to you before I went to bed."

"Fancy some company?" he asked. "You said you wanted to chat?"

"I did. Come in," she said and stepped aside.

He gave her a puzzled look as he spotted her packed suitcases.

"You're leaving?" he asked, a wounded tone in his voice. "Did my history tour bore you that much?"

"No! Are you kidding?" she said. "I loved today. I had a blast. You were a wonderful tour guide. As a matter of fact, you were so good, you inspired me to leave."

"Have you been called for assignment?" he said, the hurt expression still on his face.

"No, but I might turn this into a segment once I get a little more information," she said.

"Segment on what?" he asked.

"Too soon to say. I need to find Jeremy so I can put all the pieces together. I'm going to take the train to Oxford tomorrow to find him and maybe travel with him to Ireland. I tried to reach him this afternoon after we got back, but, apparently, he checked out of his bed and breakfast. I tried calling his friend Henry in London, but there's no answer. And, by the way, I don't get the whole British concept of colleges."

Hugh sat down in a large armchair next to the fireplace and propped his right ankle on his left thigh, jiggling his boot.

"You don't have colleges in America?" he asked amused.

"I mean Oxford University has about forty colleges and they all teach the same things. That's just inefficient."

"How do brilliant Americans do it?" he asked.

"We have different colleges on a university campus, the same as you, but each college is for a particular course of study, like archaeology in one college, architecture and design in another, separate ones for English, business, music, engineering, journalism. Oxford's got at least ten different colleges, like Exeter and Corpus Christi, teaching archaeology. It's just gross inefficiency to teach the same class in ten different schools on the same campus."

"You've n'er been to Oxford, have you? It's like Uni of Edinburgh. It doesn't have a cohesive campus like your American unis," he said. "The colleges are throughout the city."

"Great," she mumbled.

"Of course, Oxford Uni is 900 years old, quite a bit older than your country, so you'll forgive it if it sprawls a bit," he said dryly. "You're a wee bit annoyed you haven't been able to locate Jeremy?"

She gave him a disgusted look. "Yes. I thought I could just call

Oxford's archaeology department and find someone who knew where he was, but there's no central archaeology department," she said. "You have to call practically every college. By the time I found his old CV online to see which college at Oxford he used to be associated with, it was after hours and I couldn't get hold of anyone. And I can't reach April, my AP who has all his contact information, because she has the nerve to be on vacation. I suppose I could find out how to contact Jeremy's family, but I don't know if he's in touch with them and, with the kidnapping scare in Iraq, I don't think they'd give out his information even if they did know."

"Stalking Jeremy, are we?" he smiled. "So you're not on assignment, you merely don't know how to go on holiday."

"You may be on to something."

"You Americans really don't know how to relax, do you?" he asked.

"I'm relaxed. The last few days here have convinced me I need to reconsider the whole vacation concept," she said.

He smiled and shook his head. "Fancy some company?"

"You mean now?"

"Well, obviously you fancy my company now or you wouldn't have invited me in," he smiled as she raised her eyebrows. "I meant in Oxford. We could collaborate on whatever story's cooking in your wee brain."

"*Wee* brain?"

He grinned. "USN and BTN always share video and some assignments. I can be your correspondent, you can produce. Do you have a crew?"

"No, I'm still fact gathering. It may be too soon to bring in a crew and we'd both have to clear it with our bosses. Besides, you're on vacation. Why would you want to go back to work? I'm surprised you want to spend time traipsing around the countryside looking for a wayward archaeologist."

"Well, I have a wee ulterior motive. I have mates in the city."

Le An first reaction was a slight twinge of excitement she'd be able to spend more time with him, but she felt it might be better to beat a hasty retreat before her emotions kicked in more than they already had. It was her usual tug-of-war between heart and head, emotions and common sense.

"Ahh, you'd get to see old friends," she said, wondering if some of those friends were female. "And BTN could reimburse you vacation days for the days you work on this assignment?"

He nodded, laughed and sheepishly looked up at her through bangs which had fallen across his forehead.

"Well, I can't blame you," she said. "You deserve a cushy assignment after more than six months in Iraq. Actually, you might be the perfect on-air for this assignment. You already know some of the background."

"I'm intrigued. Care to fill in the correspondent on what he might be covering?" he asked.

"Not yet. But bring your passport."

"Where are we going?" he asked. "If it's Ireland, I don't need one. But I'll bring it anyway."

"It may be Ireland. I'm not sure."

"Ah, mystery assignment."

"I'll give you background info when I've locked it down," she said. "Won't your family be annoyed if I drag you away?"

"They're fairly over me now and I have three more weeks holiday," he said. "I'll come back."

"You Europeans are so spoiled," she said and shook her head in disbelief. "I've never taken a month vacation."

"That's because you Americans are overworked. Try going on holiday. You'll unclench."

"I'm not clenched. I'm downright relaxed."

He raised his eyebrows dubiously. "Aye, you're so relaxed, you've managed to come up with a way to go back to work."

"What about your friend?" she asked.

He looked confused. "Who?"

"Fiona. She didn't look too happy when she saw us together this afternoon. I don't think she's going to approve of you traveling with me."

"We're just mates. It's not like she's my bit o' stuff. Probably best I leave now," he said and dismissed the topic with a brush of his hand, then whispered, "I don't want her to get ideas."

"Yes, wouldn't want a woman to get ideas," Le An said as she made a face, then thought, *I plan to be long gone before you say that about me.*

"To make myself perfectly clear, that doesn't pertain to all women," he said, as if reading her mind. "I don't fancy Fiona getting ideas. Not my bit o' stuff. But you and I get on and have a giggle together. You enjoy my charm, my sense of humor and definitely my tour-guide skills…"

Le An burst out laughing.

"…Joining you in Oxford would give me an opportunity to bore you with more UK history. Perhaps even give you more story ideas," he said. "I'm an invaluable resource."

"Without a doubt," she laughed. "Especially since you're familiar with Oxford. I'd love to spend more time enjoying your excellent tour-guide skills—oh, and definitely your charm. But, as I said, I'm not sure it's at the point where I can bring in a crew. It's just an idea. I'm still doing research."

"We'll leave in the morning after breakfast," he smiled as he abruptly stood up and headed for the door, having decided for her. "Sleep well."

Yep, she thought, *he's going to cost me a lot of misery dollars.*

66

Meeples, Scotland
Thursday, 25 September 2003

Le An's calls to Oxford the next morning revealed Jeremy and some of his archaeology colleagues had flown to Ireland the day before in order to protest the planned construction at the Hill of Tara. When Le An explained she'd like to do a news segment on the story, a woman working in one of Oxford's archaeology departments promised to contact the group and have Jeremy get in touch with her.

Le An impatiently waited until noon, 7:00 a.m. New York time, to pitch the story to Paul as part of her *AmeriView* Ireland segment, proposing it as a joint BTN assignment with Hugh as the correspondent. A barely-awake Paul at first dismissed it.

"Why would Americans care about a highway in Ireland?" he grumbled. "You woke me up for this?"

"Because it ties in with the Celtic Tiger segment Barry and I shot in Ireland before Iraq," she said. "That's my story and my research. You haven't assigned anyone to write it yet, have you?"

"No," he mumbled.

"This segment on Tara will fit right in," she said. "Ireland's experiencing this out-of-control growth, which is financially good for the country, but, to ease traffic congestion, they're bulldozing their history. They want to dig up archaeological sites considered the spiritual heart of Ireland where their high kings lived. A few American archaeologists are part of the group protesting there now—and there are millions of Americans with Irish roots who'll love this story."

Paul sighed heavily and yawned, then said, "OK, you can shoot this segment to go with your Irish story, but only if your

Scottish doctor says you're cleared to travel."

"This is my segment, Paul," she fumed. "Don't even think about giving it to someone else. And don't mention it to BTN until you've cleared me as producer."

"How do you know you can get Hugh Rose as your correspondent at the last minute?" he asked.

She hesitated for a second, then said, "Because he's here. I'm staying at his sister's bed and breakfast."

Paul burst out laughing. "All right. If your Scottish doctor says you're OK, you can go."

"I called him this morning and the results aren't back yet," she said. "You can call him, but I need to jump on this story. All the archaeologists are there now, which means we don't have to pay their transportation or housing costs. Why don't you just call Doctor Levin in New York? He examined me six weeks ago and he cleared me for travel then. I doubt my heart went from healthy to bad in six weeks."

She had to wait two more hours for Doctor Levin's office to open so she could give him permission to tell Paul her heart had been fine when he'd run tests.

"You can tell him you thought my chest pains might be from excessive stress and lack of sleep," she told her doctor. "The guy swigs Maalox like water. How can he balk at the effects of stress?"

Based on Doctor Levin's report, and because Le An hadn't had any recurring attacks during her mini-vacation in Scotland, Paul, at least temporarily, lifted her flight and work ban.

After BTN cleared Hugh for the assignment, Le An contacted Sean O'Flannery in Dublin to see if he was available to work with them again. He readily agreed and offered to do camera, with his cousin handling audio and second camera, a relief because Le An always preferred a two-camera shoot.

When Jeremy called Le An that afternoon, he told her the last full day he and his colleagues would be in Ireland and available for interviews was Friday—the next day—because they were flying back to Heathrow Airport that afternoon. That sent her scrambling to book a flight from Edinburgh to Dublin that night for both Hugh and herself. She did her own background research and, before leaving High Tower Hall, printed it out to prep Hugh for the interviews.

The proposed Tara highway wasn't the story Le An really wanted to cover, but it gave her an opportunity to tape an interview with Jeremy about the one she did want.

67

Ireland
Friday, 26 September 2003

Le An watched the congested city of Dublin gradually morph into smaller towns and lush, kelly-green, rolling hills as Sean drove his SUV northwest along the N3.

She and Hugh had only been able to grab a few hours sleep after their late-night flight to Ireland, but they were both energized. And, as the luck of the Irish would have it, Sean and Hugh knew each other. Sean had been part of Hugh's crew in Iraq before Piet and Kent.

Fifteen miles outside Dublin, they pulled into the visitors' parking lot at the Hill of Tara. Jeremy was waiting for them, as were some of the other archaeologists scheduled to be interviewed.

Le An wanted a chance to talk to Jeremy in private and suggested the two of them walk while Sean and his cousin prepared their equipment and Hugh did a pre-interview with the other archaeologists. An ancient castle had once stood on the hill, but the only thing remaining now were circular outlines of the long-ago foundations and walls.

"We've found evidence of the stone, bronze and iron ages in this area," said Jeremy.

"Really?" Le An pretended to be interested in archaeology-speak, then dove into what she really wanted to discuss. "Hugh and I went to Edinburgh Castle a few days ago and saw the Stone of Destiny."

He smiled and nodded. "Yes. The Coronation Stone."

"A book we got at the castle says before the stone came to Scotland, it sailed to Spain, then Ireland, with an Egyptian princess, a daughter of Pharaoh, who married a Scythian nobleman," she said and paused to look at him. "But she wasn't an Egyptian princess, was she? She was a Jewish princess fleeing Egypt and Nebuchadnezzar's army, sailing away with her Milesian Jewish prince and Jeremiah, right? She was Princess Tamar, wasn't she?"

He looked pleasantly surprised she'd figured out the long-ago mystery. "You've become one of my best students."

"The book about the stone said one tradition is Jacob slept on it and dreamed angels were going up and down a ladder to heaven," she said.

"Yes, scripture says Jacob believed the place to be sacred and poured oil on the stone to anoint it, then set it up as a pillar for a marker in the area where the Israelite tribe of Ephraim eventually settled."

"Ephraim, whose father was Joseph, whose descendants are in Britain and the Commonwealth countries?" she said.

"Yes," he said, a slight smile on his face.

"Some think the stone in Edinburgh Castle is Jacob's stone."

He nodded. "Even when the stone was in Westminster Abbey, a sign identified it as 'Jacob's Pillow Stone.' Scripture says in the latter days it would be found residing with Joseph's descendants."

"Some say the stone came from Scotland, not Israel," she said.

"The stone in Edinburgh Castle is calcareous sandstone, similar to that found in Scotland, but the same sandstone is also found in Israel. According to scripture, during the coronation of Judah's King Josiah, he was anointed with oil as he stood on a stone pillar 'according to the custom,' so it appears all Davidic kings did so when crowned."

"Do you think it was the same stone?"

"We can't know for certain, but it appears to be," he said. "The stone had great significance, a connection to God. Britain's the only country which anoints her monarchs with oil at their coronations, sitting atop the Stone of Destiny."

"Was Queen Elizabeth anointed?"

"Yes, and her father before her and her grandfather and back through English and Scottish history."

"Was the stone with Jeremiah and Princess Tamar when Jerusalem fell to the Babylonians?" she asked. "She was the heir and the next one to be anointed on it."

"Historical accounts say the stone came into Jeremiah's possession."

They stopped walking and Le An thought about a conversation she'd had with Sean on the drive there that morning. For weeks she and Barry had joked about the strange name, but now she understood what Sean had first tried to tell them.

"Ollamh Fodhla, the one you and Sean say was one of Ireland's greatest lawgivers, the one whose bas-relief used to be in the Four Courts building in Dublin," she said. "He was Jeremiah, wasn't he? Sean said that's what a lot of Irish believe. Do you?"

"I do and many ancient written records say the same," he smiled.

She slowly nodded. "Is Jeremiah buried in Ireland?"

"Irish writings and traditions say he is," he said.

"People finally appreciated him here, didn't they?" she asked. "Ireland seems to revere him. He endured torture and criticism in Judah, people calling him a traitor, but he completed his mission. He made sure the princess married a member of the Jewish royal family and he kept her safe."

Jeremy smiled and nodded.

Le An suddenly remembered something and spun around to look for Sean who was nearby. "Sean! The harp on the Guinness label and the Irish flag...it was King David's harp!"

He gave her a puzzled look and nodded, then shouted back, "I told you that!"

"When you said the harp was here, you meant here in Ireland, didn't you?" she shouted.

He nodded and shrugged. "I told you that!"

She turned back to Jeremy. "Is King David's harp here in Ireland?"

"Irish tradition says Jeremiah and the princess brought it with them," he said.

"The Irish say Tamar wanted her castle to be built here at Tara. Do you believe that?" she asked.

"I do."

"Some call her Tamar, but other accounts refer to her as Scota, or Tea or Tea Tephi. The dates for her being in Ireland are all over the place. A few accounts say it was the time of the Israelites' exodus from Egypt, but some say 580 BC."

"Yes, but which Israelites and which exodus from Egypt?" he asked and smiled. "Moses and the twelve tribes fled Egypt, yes, but so did Israelites such as the princess and Jeremiah, perhaps four years on from Jerusalem falling, round about 582 BC. There's no real way of knowing...yet. Many archaeologists wish to conduct extensive digs in this area to learn more. There's much information yet to be discovered. Perhaps one day."

"You want digging, but not with bulldozers," she smiled.

"Precisely. I realize for some the commute into Dublin is long because the motorway isn't adequate, but this area is far too archaeologically important."

"Did Jeremiah take the Stone of Destiny to Egypt?"

"Possibly. Or he could have hidden it near Jerusalem," he said. "When he, the princess, his assistant Baruch and the prince sailed from Egypt with the Scythians, they may have first traveled to Judah to retrieve the stone, then sailed west to Spain and Ireland."

"The book about the stone says it was taken from Ireland to the Isle of Iona in Scotland."

"Yes, after more than 1,000 years in Ireland, round about AD 500. The Scoti, who were the ancient Irish, expanded their conquering into Scotland and when Fergus MacEre became king in Iona, he had the stone brought from Ireland for the coronation."

"They never took it back to Ireland?"

"No."

"Then the English choried it from the Scots," she said.

Jeremy looked surprised and chuckled.

"Sorry, that's from Hugh," she said sheepishly.

"Yes, the Scots are quite devoted to their stone," he smiled and glanced over at Hugh. "Ezekiel wrote Judah's throne would be overturned three times, perhaps indicating a change in location, yet the line of descent would remain fairly direct."

"Ezekiel, as in Ezekiel's tomb we saw in Al Kifl?" she asked.

"Yes. The first overturn was from Jerusalem to here at Tara, the second from Tara to the Isle of Iona in Scotland and the third from Scotland to England."

"If the line of descent is direct, does that mean Queen Elizabeth's descended from Scottish kings?" she asked.

"She's descended from Robert the Bruce, who was descended from Scoti kings, who were descended from Irish kings, who were descended from King David and his ancestor Judah."

"If that's true, then Queen Elizabeth is Jewish, or part Jewish," she said. "But she's head of the Anglican church."

"Scripture says the scepter, the sign of rulership over Israel, would remain with those of the tribe of Judah, but in the latter days it would be located amongst Israel's other tribes, in particular Joseph's descendants."

"British monarchs descended from King David and Princess Tamar," she said. "A Jew—a descendant of David's—sitting on a throne ruling over Israelites."

"Precisely. And something else to consider," he said, "many current European monarchs trace their lineage to the British throne."

"European monarchs are Jewish, too?" she asked.

"And they're ruling over Israelites," he said.

"Then I don't understand why there's so much anti-Semitism in the UK and Europe," she said. "So many hate the Jews—have for centuries—but biologically the majority of the population of Europe, Britain and Israel are all descended from Jacob. They're all Israelites. They're family."

"Families, even brothers, fight," he said.

Le An remembered her discussion with Hugh, the night they'd had dinner together in London. "Hugh said y'all in Britain believe Jesus' uncle moved to England."

"Great-uncle," he corrected her. "There are records Joseph of Arimathea, the uncle of Jesus' mother Mary, was given twelve plots of land in Glastonbury. The travels of Jesus' family and his twelve apostles reveal quite a bit about where the Israelites were migrating."

"Really?"

"Jesus' half-brother James wrote a letter to the twelve tribes and condemned them for waging war amongst themselves—a hint where they were. The Roman Empire was at peace. The only wars were in Britain and Parthia."

"And the Parthians were Israelites," she said.

"Precisely. Their empire extended from the Roman Empire's eastern boundary to China and lasted round about 500 years. Rome could never completely defeat them."

"And the Scots are Scythians, which is mentioned in their Declaration of Arbroath," she said, then laughed when he raised his eyebrows. "I got that from Hugh, too."

"It was common knowledge where the twelve tribes were then. It's only in later centuries Israelites lost their identity," he said. "Are you familiar with Peter and Paul?"

"And Mary? The singing group? I've heard of them."

"They were apostles," Jeremy smiled, not sure whether she was joking or not. "Peter was assigned to the Israelites, Paul to the Gentiles. Historical accounts show Paul traveling in the southern half of what's now Turkey, speaking to Gentiles, whilst Peter was in the northern half, along the southern coast of the Black Sea."

"Where Israelites had migrated, right?"

"Precisely. But, according to Greek historians, Peter then traveled to Britain and remained there quite a while."

"I thought Peter lived in Rome," she said. "I've had assignments in Rome and that's all you hear about: Peter and Paul."

"The myth is Peter was head of the church in Rome. However, the church was never based there. The Roman empire was, but not the church."

"That goes against everything the Vatican says."

"The church was headquartered first in Jerusalem, then in the mountains north of there in Pella, then Antioch in Asia Minor," said Jeremy. "It was never headquartered in Rome."

"The Pope and Catholics would disagree with you."

"Rome was a Gentile city, assigned to Paul, not Peter. In Paul's letter to the Roman church, he mentions members, but never Peter, though Peter would have been alive at that time. As prominent as Peter was, if he'd been in Rome, Paul would have mentioned him. In another letter, which Paul wrote when he was in Rome, he sends greetings from Silurian royals, but not Peter."

"What kind of royals?"

"Silurian. The Silures were an ancient Celtic tribe located in what's now southern Wales."

"Celtic? So they were Israelites?" she asked.

"Yes."

"What were Celtic royals from Wales doing in Rome?"

"The Roman emperor Claudius captured the Silurian King Caradoc. Claudius is said to have found Caradoc's daughter Gladys so utterly lovely, he adopted her and changed her name to Claudia. She, her brother Linus and husband Pudens, a Roman senator, were all members of the church in Rome. Some records indicate Linus and Claudia were related to Joseph of Arimathea, perhaps his grandchildren."

"There's Joseph of Arimathea again," she said. "A lot of clues point to him being in England."

"As was Paul after the Romans released him."

"I thought the Romans killed Paul," she said.

"The Romans arrested him twice. They released him the first time, killed him the second. Both he and Peter were executed in Rome, but later buried in Britain."

"What?" she gasped. "The Vatican says they're buried in Rome."

"They were."

"They were dug up and reburied?"

"Yes. In the seventh century, England's Saxon King Oswy asked for their bones," he said. "Pope Vitalian didn't want them, dug them up and sent them, along with a letter, to Canterbury Cathedral."

"Are they buried there?"

"Possibly, though some say they're in Saint Albans, north of London," he said.

Le An shook her head in amazement. "How did history get so messed up?"

"It's like any news story you work on," he said. "The correct accounts are there if you search for them, but inaccuracies do happen."

As they gazed out over the countryside, Jeremy said, "On a clear day, you can see six counties from here."

They weren't seeing that now. A fine gray mist blanketed the area, and within minutes, large clouds blew in from the sea, the rain drenching them. They hastily opened umbrellas, trying to protect the equipment and themselves, especially those who would be appearing on camera. Sean's cameras were already in their own little blue rain jackets.

The wind whipped and swirled around them, driving the rain almost sideways at times, but within a few minutes, as quickly as it had appeared, the storm passed, dark clouds giving way to fluffy ones across the now-blue sky. The sun peeked out, illuminating a rainbow and making the wet grass glisten as if strewn with tiny diamonds.

Le An carefully stepped around the sheep droppings and promptly slid ungracefully on the wet grass, landing in a partial botched cheerleader split before rolling onto her side. Jeremy and Hugh came over to help her up, but slid, too, and landed on either side of her.

As they all laughed and struggled to get back on their feet, Le An's satellite phone started ringing.

It was Paul.

"I want you to stay in London," he said.

"I'm in Ireland, not London," she said. "Did you forget I'm on a shoot? Are you getting enough sleep? FYI, your memory comes back when you catch up on sleep."

"That'll be the day. It would help if certain producers didn't call and wake me up to share urgent story ideas. I'm surprised I remember anything from my conversation with you yesterday morning."

"Sorry, but I knew today was the only day I could get this group of archaeologists together here at Tara," she said, then joked, "Besides, I figured you should have been up."

"Thanks for deciding when I'm allowed to sleep."

"Wait a minute, it's earlier than that now," she said, looking at her watch and deducting the five hour time difference.

"I couldn't sleep. Big meeting this morning," he said. "Is Hugh Rose your correspondent on this?"

"Yes. Why? We talked about this yesterday morning," she said, turning to look at Hugh who was clipping a wireless microphone to his jacket while Sean's cousin helped a few of the archaeologists attach theirs. "Please tell me you're not replacing him with someone from USN."

"I'm not replacing him," he said.

"Just wondering whether you're making changes smack in the middle of my shoot."

"I'm not changing anything. I talked to Ed Murray at BTN yesterday," he said. "And no, I didn't forget you were in Ireland. I meant, when you're finished, stay in London."

"We have to stay in Ireland a few more days to get interviews with planning officials and locals," she said. "And we're renting a chopper to get aerials of Tara."

"I'm telling you, when you get back to London, I want you to stay there."

"I can't finish my vacation? I only interrupted it to do this story," she said.

Paul sighed heavily. "My kids listen better than this. Finish your shoot in Ireland, feed it from the London bureau, then stay in London. And you aren't on vacation. You're on medical leave."

"You mean I can't come back to New York?" she asked.

"We're giving you a promotion, if you'd stop yapping long enough to let me finish talking," he said, his voice rising. "We're promoting you to London bureau chief."

The news stunned her into silence.

"Yeah, thought that would shut you up," he said.

"Is this a joke?" she asked.

"No, I'm serious."

"I...I don't know what to say."

"Do you want the job?" he asked.

"Ye...yes," she hesitated. "I think so. It's kind of out of the blue, but yes, I think so."

Being made USN London bureau chief wasn't just a promotion—it was a huge promotion.

"We'll say it's temporary, that you're helping us out by filling in for six months," he continued. "That way you can decide whether you want the job on a permanent basis or whether you miss field work too much. If you don't like it, you can come back to *AmeriView*."

"Are you saying it's temporary so you can get rid of me?" she asked. "Is it because you're afraid I can't travel because of my health? I'm traveling now and I'm fine. I feel great."

"We don't get rid of people by giving them promotions and more money, Le An. We fire them. And you're not fired. You're being offered a plum assignment and a huge raise. I don't know how else to say it."

"But you're booting me out of *AmeriView*," she said.

He sighed heavily. "This is coming from higher ups, Le. Brad's been watching you for a while. So has the VP of news. They like your work. They like you. They asked me what I thought of the promotion and I told them I thought you'd do a hell of a job. I'm having second thoughts now because you're sounding a little neurotic, but I gave you a good recommendation. Do you want the job? Do you need to think about it? They'd like an answer soon."

"I'm focused on this shoot right now," she said. "I'll call you in a few days when I get back to London, OK? When would I start?"

"As soon as possible. November sweeps start October 30 and

we'd like you in place before then."

"When's Thanksgiving?" she asked.

"The day after sweeps end, on November 27," he said. "I know you want to go back to Charlotte for Thanksgiving. And USN could give you a few weeks vacation on the back end."

"I need to pack things in New York and do something with my apartment."

A few days before, she'd been ready to hand in her resignation. Now she was being offered a promotion and a new life in another country. If she took it, she wouldn't be able to live in her newly organized and unpacked apartment for quite a while, if ever. She could always rent it, but she wasn't thrilled at the thought of having someone else live in it before she did.

"I'll call you from London," she said. "Thanks, Paul."

"I liked the other story idea you emailed me about the persecution Irish soldiers faced after World War Two," he said. "I'll talk to you later about it. We're going to miss you if you take the job, but you've earned it. I hate to see you go, but it's nice to see good things happen to my people. Congratulations," he said.

"Thanks, Paul. For everything."

She hung up and turned to Jeremy. "They're offering me a promotion in London."

"How wonderful, my dear," he smiled. "Congratulations."

She nodded, still processing the news. As she again gazed out over Ireland's beauty, she tried to imagine what it had been like for the young Jewish princess, thousands of miles and lifetimes from the world she'd known. Did Tara remind her of Jerusalem or Judah? Did it make her feel safe and at peace after years of war and pain? She'd lost her family and country—as Le An had years ago. They'd both started over in new lands and their lives were better for it.

If the princess was Robert the Bruce's ancestor and he was Le An's, then she was historically tied to this spot and descended from Jewish monarchy. So was Hugh. She turned to look at him and he gave her a big smile.

London might not be so bad after all.

"Ollamh Fodhla," she whispered. "Sometimes you have to surrender."

OKANAGAN REGIONAL LIBRARY
3 3132 03795 3793